ALSO BY ANGELINE FORTIN

A Laird for All Time
Nothing But Time
My Heart's in the Highlands
A Time & Place for Every Laird
Taken: A Laird for All Time Novel

The Questions for a Highlander Series
A Question of Love
A Question of Trust
A Question of Lust
A Perfect Question
A Question for Harry

Pride & Penitence

A Laird FOR ALL Time

ANGELINE FORTIN

Published by
MY PERSONAL
BUBBLE LLC

ISBN-13: 978-1492759249
ISBN-10: 1492759244

DEDICATION

For Lori & Thelma
who have been subjected to this weird writing habit longer than
anyone and still talk to me.

1

Duart Castle
The Isle of Mull, Scotland
October 2010

"There she is, lassie."

Emmy gripped the edge of the window and stared at the panoramic view of the distant castle the driver's finger pointed toward as the bus traveled the winding road along the eastern coastline of the Isle of Mull.

In the distance was the last destination on her ten-day UK vacation. Starting naturally in London, she had taken in the sights of Wales and Yorkshire, before traveling from there on to Edinburgh and Glasgow. The distant edifice was the last spectacle she had come so far to see: Duart Castle— the ancestral home of the clan MacLean for hundreds of years.

Her guidebook told her the name Duart meant "Black

Point" in Gaelic and, based on the view from the ferry as she had crossed the Sound of Mull that afternoon from mainland Scotland, she knew why it bore that name. The castle did indeed sit on black earth that contrasted with the waters of the sound and the overcast sky behind it.

When she had first spotted the castle from the ferry on her arrival, the clouds had hung so low that they almost clung to the land between the water and the castle, nearly obscuring her view of it. Now, as the bus approached Duart from the ferry terminus at Craignure, she could see its prominent outline jutting out from the crag against the skies beyond. Dipping below the layer of cloud, the late afternoon sun lit the West-facing side as she neared, showing the wear of centuries on the face of the building.

Her guidebook also told her the clan MacLean had lived on this land since the 14th century, and remained in that castle until they were forced to leave during the Jacobite rebellion, retreating to the Treshnish Isles. After several years of military occupation, the castle had been gutted by fire in 1756, and Duart remained a ruin until it was bought back by the family in the mid-1800s and restored.

Now the castle was a fine example of medieval architecture; glorious, wonderful…

And open to the public from April until October.

What a vacation this had been so far. After four years of brain-numbing undergraduate work, two years of medical school full of rotations through various medical specialties, and four more years of harrowing residency with forty-eight-hour shifts and zero personal life, it was long past time for Emmy to have a vacation.

If there was a person on earth who ever thought that doctors didn't earn every penny of their billings, then that person was dead wrong. As a resident, Emmy had hung by her fingertips on the lowest rung of the ladder. She was barely above those medical students rotating through the departments and just below the lab rats. She had been the gopher, grunt and dumping ground for every job no one else wanted to do.

It'd been that long since Emmy had even been on a date. Not a single date! She felt more sexless these days than one would think was humanly possible. She'd brought it on herself, though. She'd heard the tales, seen the proof and knew better than to encourage a relationship during her residency. With all the long hours, overnights and demands associated with a medical residency, the future MDs had one of the highest divorce rates by occupation in the US. They were only nudged from the top spot by naval submariners, who spent up to six months at a time under water and out of contact.

Like a submariner, she felt like she'd been underwater for a long while now. But, here and now, she made time for herself. Though several of the other residents invited her to join them on their vacations to the Virgin Islands or Hawaii, Emmy chose to take her vacation alone. Most of her friends couldn't fathom why she wanted to 'do' the UK in the chill of fall, but Emmy was determined to enjoy her alone time to the fullest extent before starting her new career.

A little 'me' time was her explanation; she'd always been comfortable in her own company.

The bus shuddered to a stop outside the outer gates of the ancient castle - the keep, she'd learned it was called, and she accepted the driver's hand as the old man assisted her from the bus.

"Wow, Donell." Emmy addressed the old man who had

thus far been chatty and informative on the short trip from Craignure. "It's just as amazing as you said."

She was the only passenger today, most likely because it was the final day of the season. The castle would be closed from tomorrow. The weather was turning colder and most tourists were long gone from the area. Donell had probably just been happy for someone to show up and wanted to make her feel welcome. He'd entertained her along the way with outrageous tales of the region's past conflicts that he had surely embellished to make them more exciting.

The brisk October breeze had her clutching her short velvet blazer closed as she turned to the old castle. The heavy cloud coverage did nothing to alleviate the somber façade of the castle. The walls were dark and starting to crumble. Showing its age, Emmy thought, but magnificent nonetheless, appearing to grow from the rocky cliffs to tower five stories high at its hipped roofline.

"She's a bonny lass, is Duart," the old Scot commented with a thick brogue she enjoyed. Between his gravelly voice and the appearance of the clichéd old-timer, she could easily to picture him at the local pub taking a pint or two. His haggard, weathered features fell into more folds than a Shar Pei. His dark eyes were so deeply recessed that Donell almost gave an impression of unfathomable age. An ancient Scotsman in his battered cap and coat. A bit clichéd but the perfect person for the tourists to sidle up to, to beg for a picture or two with him.

Swinging her large tote and smaller purse over her shoulder together, she glanced up at the castle. Too bad the weather wasn't cooperating, she mourned; a bit of sunshine would probably do wonders for the old place. Digging in her tote for her camera, she swung it up to take a picture.

Look at the old girl, so beaten down with age.

"I'll bet it was really something a hundred years ago when it was restored," she commented aloud.

"Restoration was completed 'bout 115 years ago," Donell offered, leaning back against the fender of the shuttle with his arms crossed over his chest. "Ye wouldnae ha' wanted to see it then."

"Why not?" Emmy asked absently as she took a few more shots.

"They were nae happy times, lassie. Tragic, the old laird and his family." The old man shook his head with a soft cluck of his tongue.

"Really?" She glanced back at the building with a sigh. "What happened?"

"Family troubles mostly, bad luck."

"Still, I would so love to have been there to see it at its shining moment. How wonderful it would be…" her voice was wistful.

"Ye think so?"

She nodded. "I know so."

"Should be careful, lassie, what ye wish for."

"Wishing for simpler times? Where's the harm in that?" she asked absentmindedly as she took several more shots of the castle.

"Ye think old days were simple times, lassie?"

"Of course they were."

"Hmm…" Donell scratched his stubbled chin and considered her thoughtfully. "Would ye care to take a wager on that then?"

"What do you mean?"

The sun came out from behind the clouds then and seemed to grow brighter, reflecting off the ancient stones and bringing dark spots to Emmy's eyes. She shut them tightly as a dizzying wave of déjà vu hit her, as if she had been here before. As she looked back at the castle, the sun washed across the stone embattlements as if awakening the castle from a long sleep. The years seemed to melt away from the building as the sun beamed across it, crumbling block smoothed, discolored stones became brighter.

Well, that was weird.

"Did you see that?" she turned back to ask Donell, only to discover the driver had already left. She hadn't even heard him pull away. She frowned, annoyed. When did he do that? She'd just been talking to him. She could only hope he would remember to come back and get her.

Studying the castle again, she realized a little sunshine did indeed do wonders for the castle. Perhaps she'd just imagined the aged appearance on her arrival as a reflection of the dreary weather. After all, it had been rebuilt around the middle of the nineteenth century. Right now, it looked almost new. Funny, she would have thought in the hundred and fifty years since its reconstruction began, the structure would've aged a bit more than this.

Tucking her camera away, she approached the outer wall and laid a hand against the stones, absorbing the cold dampness. Weird, she thought again as a rumble coming from the road drew her attention. Shading her eyes, she watched a rider on horseback approach from the west at a fast pace.

Though the setting sun at his back shadowed the face of the rider, her jaw sagged unconsciously at the dramatic image the man and horse made as they approached the castle. The complete vision was like something out of a romance novel, or maybe a surreal shampoo commercial. Dark hair rippled back from a strong, tanned face. The wind pulled at the open collar of his shirt, exposing a tanned chest and muscular pecs. A kilt, no less, flapped against the long legs gripping the horse's sides.

Such a pure physical rush of lust swept over Emmy that she swore right then and there that she would never again go so long without a date, much less five years of abstinence.

The horse came to a rearing halt not ten feet from her. Startled, she leaped back out of harm's way. As the hooves landed on the ground, the rider swung himself to the ground and strode toward her. Eyes blazing with heat and anger, he walked—no! actually *stomped* toward her, slapping off dust of his kilt as came.

Mel Gibson, Christopher Lambert, Adrian Paul – those movie highlanders had nothing on this man. He was just that. All man! He wore his kilt slung over an ivory shirt. His thighs were bare and heavily muscled. He was taller than her five foot-eight by nearly a head; broad shoulders, dark hair…the whole masculine package was devastating. A god descended from the heavens. Emmy knew she'd never seen such a vision in her life, and thought she was unlikely to again.

She stumbled back several steps as he stalked forward. He easily caught her by the shoulders nonetheless and glared down at her.

"*Altachadh-beatha.*" His deep brogue bit out the foreign words.

Partially terrified, largely enthralled, Emmy did the only thing that seemed appropriate.

She fainted.

2

Willing her eyes to open, Emmy found herself laying on a large comfortable bed, the dark night broken only by a antique oil lamp on the table next to her. Resting in the darkness, she cringed at the humiliation of fainting in front of such a gorgeous guy. *How impressive it must have looked!* she thought disparagingly. She would never go so long without a vacation again.

Maybe it had all been a hallucination. A hallucination brought on by fatigue, stress and anxiety. Yes, of course. It was all brilliantly clear in retrospect. She'd just finished a horrific six-week rotation in psychiatry, after all. Six long weeks at a mental hospital where God checked in daily, and Al Capone and Joan of Arc resided alive and well.

The experience taught her psychiatry wasn't her calling, but she'd learned enough to self-diagnose. This was just simple anxiety; stress brought on by nerves and lack of sleep. Perhaps she would prescribe herself some Paxil or Xanax…

Her internal conversation ended in a very verbal shriek

as she rolled over and saw a man... *the* man sitting quietly in a chair next to the bed.

"What the..." she sputtered as she literally jumped off the bed. "*Ohmigod*, I thought I was imagining you. Who are you? What are you doing in here?" The words tumbled one over the other incoherently. "Go! Leave before I call the Bobbies or whatever they are called up here. You just can't walk into my hotel room..." She stopped and looked around, registering her surroundings for the first time. "Wait. This isn't my hotel room. Where am I? Who are you?"

A large male finger reached out and nudged up her chin, effectively closing her mouth and stopping the rambling flow of words.

"Charming, my love. Is this the way we're going to play it then?" His accent was a thick and deep Sean Connery rumbling...and so very, very sexy that Emmy was utterly disarmed. For a moment, at least. A little shudder passed through her and she shook free of his spell.

She shoved his hand away from her chin roughly, a move that clearly surprised him.

"What are you talking about?"

"Amusing," he murmured. He leaned back in the chair and rubbed a forefinger absently across his full, appealing lower lip. "Did ye nae think I'd recognize ye, Heather love?"

"Look, obviously you've got the wrong girl. My name is Emmy."

"Could ye nae think of a more clever alias, my love? Not a terribly original variation of Emeline Heather."

Alias? His nonsensical questioning had Emmy rolling her eyes. "Okay. Whatever. Point remains you got the wrong girl. Go back to the mother ship."

Too bad that he was absolutely round the bend, she

thought. He honestly had to be the most incredibly appealing man she had ever laid eyes on. And that voice! The voice alone sent little vibrations of lust along every nerve ending.

She rounded the bed to the safety of the opposite side, attempting to create a barrier between them. Her blazer and scarf hung on the end of the bed. Snatching them up, she slipped them back on. "What time is it anyway?" Hurrying over to the door, she ran her hand over the wall next to it. "And where is the damn light switch?"

"The what?"

"The switch? Or do you call it something else? Oh, hell, just turn on the damn lights, for crying out loud." She crossed her arms over her chest and glared at him.

"Ye've developed a most foul mouth while ye've been gone, my love."

Emmy threw her hands over her head in frustration. "I am not your love *or* your Heather."

"Did ye think I would forget ye even if it has been neigh ten years since ye left?"

That voice was doing things to her again. Despite her apprehension, she felt every word with a quiver deep in her chest. It was disconcerting to say the least since that warm melting feeling was completely at odds with her other reactions to him. She needed to get away from here before she did something stupid.

"Left? Read my lips. I-have-never-been-to-Scotland-before." She spoke slowly, enunciating each word while making a mouthing motion with her hand like a puppet. "Never. Comprende? You got the wrong girl. I am Emmy MacKenzie." She squared her shoulders. "*Dr.* Emily MacKenzie."

He stared at her in disbelief for a moment, then to her

surprise, burst out in laughter. A heartfelt, rich laughter that would have been incredibly attractive in a man not quite so insane.

Disgusted with him and herself, she wrenched the door open and left the room, determined to find the castle's caretaker—assuming she was even in the castle and he hadn't dragged her off somewhere—and get away from the madman.

Emmy stalked down the hall and down a massive stone staircase that led to the floor below, noting with relief, the central hall she'd seen on Duart's website. The thought crossed her mind, however, that it looked even more authentic than it had seemed in the brochure or on the website. She paused, uncertain. Where was the office? Surely the caretaker would have some sort of office or desk.

A heavy oak door opened to her left and a tall, lean man in a dark suit entered the hall. "Can I help ye, lassie?" he asked in a heavy burr.

"Thank goodness." She rushed toward him. "Are you the manager? There is a strange man upstairs who was harassing me and I'd like to report him."

"A strange man, ye say?" The man looked utterly befuddled by her statement. "Only the laird and his family are here in the castle, lassie. Are ye sure ye're no' mistaken?"

"No! There really is someone up there," she insisted and hissed, "He keeps insisting that I'm his wife!"

The man's eyes crinkled in amusement as they shifted up to the stairs behind her. "It seems the lass is having a hard time remembering ye, Connor."

Emmy spun around to face the man from her room above her on the landing, watching with an amused grin on his lips.

"It does seem to be the case, Ian. Perhaps ye should reintroduce us."

"Lassie, may I introduce Lord Connor James Lachlan MacLean the Second, Earl of Strathclyde, Laird of the Clan MacLean, Lord of Duart Castle and ye'll be remembering, yer husband."

"I am not his wife!"

"Aye, ye are," both men replied in unison.

✗✗✗✗

Connor MacLean stared down at his long-lost wife, momentarily enthralled by the woman before him, her beauty heightened by the high temper she was in. Her hair was lighter than he remembered and her figure fuller in all the best places, but it was definitely she.

Nor was she the frigid young thing he recalled from ten years past. Time had brought an assuredness to her manner, and clearly, enough self-confidence not to fear an argument or confrontation with him. She'd actually slapped his hand away. And her temper brought a high color to her cheeks that was unbelievably alluring.

He tamped down the beginnings of an arousal trying to recall his anger and the humiliation she'd dealt him all those years ago. It shouldn't matter that she had a fullness to her lips that begged him to forgive and forget and to take them with his own. He could not forget who she was.

She paced the hall with unconcealed agitation. Her stride manly in the shockingly tight trousers she wore. Strange that, for Heather had always been one for high fashion.

"Oh my God," she entreated again in a most sacrilegious way, "if you treat all your guests in this fashion, you'll be out of business in no time!"

XOXOXOX

Rubbing her hands over her face, Emmy tried to remember what she had learned about dealing with the mentally unstable. Damn, she never, ever wanted to go into that field, why would she retain any working knowledge on the subject? That *laird* had her totally frazzled.

"Connor, right? Okay, Connor, let's compromise here," she tried in a low soothing voice. "I'd be willing to concede that I must bear a striking resemblance to your wife, if you will just for one teeny tiny moment consider that I might just not be her."

"I might ha' considered that, if ye wisnae here, now, exactly ten years from the day ye left."

"Ten years later you think you'd know me? Her? Get real! I could not see my own mother for ten years and not recognize her. How can you be so sure?"

A female squeal sounded from a nearby doorway. As Emmy turned, a young woman who was her absolute double, but for her chalk-white pallor and stunned expression, whispered, "Gracious" and fainted promptly into the other man's arms.

Her shocked gaze met Connor's as he descended the stairs pointing at the other woman. "That's how."

With heavy feet, she followed the men into a nearby room as the one named Ian carried the woman over to a small sofa and laid her gently down.

Emmy stared in amazement. She'd always heard that everyone had a doppelgänger somewhere in the world. Here was hers. She could tell no physical difference between their two faces. She almost wanted to reach out and touch her to make sure she was real. A shudder passed through her that she couldn't identify... trepidation? Fascination? Fear?

14

The man called Ian took a small vial from a maid who scurried in after them, and waved it under the woman's nose until she started and began to revive.

When she opened her eyes, the other woman examined Emmy suspiciously for a long moment before summoning a small smile as she struggled to sit up. "Heather, we thought you'd never come back. Where have you been all this time?"

Emmy sighed, unsure of where to go next in this tangled mess. "Listen, uh... ma'am, I'm afraid we have a bit of a misunderstanding in the works here..."

"Come, Heather, ye're nae going to pretend that ye dinnae recognize yer own twin, are ye?" the laird taunted as he assisted the other woman into a sitting position.

"Twin?"

Her gaze locked with blue eyes that looked so much like her own and shivered. The light brown hair was identical to her original color... before she had it highlighted, of course. They could have been twins, that much was true, except the woman was obviously well along in her pregnancy, maybe the end of her second trimester.

When she remained stiff, the other woman's eyes narrowed slightly. "Oh, poor dear... you don't remember, do you? It's me, Dorcas, your sister."

Disarmed by the unusual name, Emmy snorted in surprise. "Really? You're kidding, right? Dorcas?" Unwitting amusement struck and she chuckled out loud, drawing puzzled stares from the room's occupants. "Listen, Dorc... Dorc... I'm sorry. It's just wrong. Is there something else I can call you?"

Dorcas and the men continued to look puzzled, but the woman finally sighed. "You may call me Dory, of course... as you always have," she added with a curious frown. "What is it about my name you seem to find so amusing now, if I may ask?"

Dropping into a nearby chair and tucking one leg beneath as was her habit, she slouched back in the seat and waved her hand. "You know? Dork?" She waited expectantly, but all three faces remained blank. "I guess it's an American thing. Let's move on, shall we, and get back to the issues here. This assumption that I am your sister." She jabbed a finger in the laird's direction. "And *his* wife."

The laird stepped forward, pointing a finger right back at her and opening his mouth to speak when Dorcas... no, Dory, held a calm palm out and urged him to sit as well. "Come, Ian and I were just going to pour some tea. Join us. We'll work through this."

Emmy glowered at the laird, Connor, who sat and stared back at her from beneath thick brows until, in short order, she found herself being handed a cup of hot tea. She frowned down into the cup. Hot tea. Of course, they drank tea in Great Britain, but like psychiatry, it just wasn't her thing. At least in the major cities, she'd managed to find a Starbucks or two. She set the cup and saucer down on the table in front of her.

"That's an interesting, um, *ensemble* you have on, Heather," Dory observed with just a bit of an edge as she poured tea for the men. Ian put his hand over his cup to stop her, and the men instead took glasses of some sort of liquor from an attending servant. "Is it the latest style in traveling apparel?" Dorcas poured her own cup and took a sip, analyzing Emmy over the rim.

Emmy looked down at the 'ensemble' she'd recently bought just for this trip. A nice pair of dark wash skinny jeans tucked into knee-high black suede boots for warmth and comfort in the cool fall of Scotland. Her white silk blouse was covered with a short, black velvet jacket and accessorized with a silver tasseled scarf. Maybe not as comfortable for travel as just jeans and a t-shirt, but that wasn't what she was going for. She hadn't wanted to give the impression of a sloppy American tourist for the locals to poke fun at.

"I think it was designed more for style than travel. Don't you like it?" she asked the room in general, only now noting the disconcerted and disapproving looks of the two men as they looked her over. Emmy had long been considered and treated as a fairly attractive woman. While she wasn't exceedingly vain about her looks, she certainly wasn't accustomed to men looking at her as these two were... as if she were distasteful in some way.

XOXOXOX

Connor studied her attire. He'd noticed as she slept upstairs that her clothes were more than unusual. Trousers! Positively indecent wear for a lady. The tight pants accentuated her long legs and the short little jacket accented her tiny waist. The blouse beneath was surprisingly sheer. It was also abundantly clear she wore little beneath it.

"Yer shirt seems to be a wee bit on the thin side," he offered at length, still staring at her chest.

"Ye can see her legs," Ian added with a hint of appreciation.

"You can't see my legs. I'm covered to the ankle!"

"Can see yer shape," he clarified as his eyes skimmed down her figure with appreciation, drawing an unpleasant cluck from Dorcas.

"Men have no appreciation for fashion," his wife scoffed and turned to Dory. "Don't you like it? I mean, it might be a bit trendy for conservative Britain, but a visit to the Queen wasn't on my itinerary."

Dory only pursed her lips in disapproval and changed the topic: "Maybe it would help us if we understood who you think you are."

Heather stared at Dory dumbly for a moment. Trying to summon another lie? How long was she thinking she could continue this denial of her identity? He wasn't sure whether he should be angered or amused by her tenacity.

※※※※※

"If you would simply check the visitor's list, my name is Emily Rose MacKenzie." The faces around her still looked skeptical, so she added, "Don't you have records of the guests you're expecting here? I'm the American who was crazy enough to come over in the fall rather than the summer? On the last day the castle is open to tourists? I was told the laird and his family usually lived in Edinburgh for the summer and that's why the house was open to visitors from May until October. I didn't know the owners would be here…" she stopped, suddenly aware that she was rambling while frowning confusion deepened on their faces.

"So ye came back now because ye wisnae expecting any of us to be here then?" Connor misinterpreted.

"No, I already told you I have never been here before," she insisted. The aggravating spiral of frustration that'd wound her up before tightened again. "I am a tourist… just visiting on vacation."

"Vacation?" the three repeated blankly.

"Yes, *vacation*." Emmy searched her memory. What did the Brits call it? "Holiday. I am here in the UK on holiday. For ten days."

"Ye returned here for a holiday?" Ian asked with bewildered frown. "Why would ye do that?"

A screech caught in her throat and the coil snapped. "Not returned! Listen, I'm just a tourist. I am staying in Oban across the sound; I have a room there. I just got in yesterday and came straight here on the ferry today because you close tomorrow for the winter!

"I am an American citizen. I live outside Baltimore. I'm originally from Richmond, Virginia." The brows grew even more puckered. "I did my undergraduate at UVA and attended John Hopkins. I graduated at the top of my class, I did my residency at Hopkins… I'm a doctor, dammit! I know who I am. Why don't you check my passport if you're unsure?"

"Passport?" The word echoed around the room from three mouths, as if it were foreign to them.

"Do you have another word for it maybe?" she asked, baffled by their confusion. "I can show it to you. It's in my large tote."

Again, three mouths silently formed the word "Tote."

"The brown leather bag." She spoke slowly, hoping to alleviate their bewilderment. Undeniably, something was being lost in the translation.

"I'll hae one of the servants fetch it for ye." Ian offered.

Emmy discreetly massaged her temples where a throbbing headache had begun to pound. This was all so unreal. Here were these strange people, dressed ultra-conservatively, having no sense of fashion, yet questioning hers and insisting that she was someone they knew. The woman who looked just like her was wearing a floor-length skirt and a blouse that buttoned up tightly to her chin. She looked horribly uncomfortable as she alternated between staring at Emmy as if she had seen a ghost and looking at her with deep suspicion.

Her head hurt, her eyes burned, and she wanted nothing so much as to take a handful of Excedrin and sleep until this was all over.

And that man! Unable to help herself she peeked up between her fingers at him. Oh, that man. The *laird*. He made her heart pound faster just looking at him. He'd changed from the kilt into a pair of tight charcoal pants and white shirt. The shirt had been left open at the neck and had only a short collar on it. Odd style. European probably. His hair wasn't actually black at all but rather a dark rich brown, nearly mahogany, in fact, with lighter variable streaks that could only be natural. Well over six foot, she guessed about two hundred-fifty or more pounds full of muscle, thick and heavy. He was built like a right tackle football player she'd known in college, but his were the kind of muscles built through heavy work, rather than reps in a gym.

He was rugged and beautiful. And angry. She couldn't help but wonder what he would look like if he were to smile.

His stare penetrated her as if he were trying to see right through her. As if he could see into her mind. If he were insane, it would be the greatest loss to womanhood she could imagine. He was otherwise the most compelling man she'd ever met.

"What did you say to me out front?" Emmy asked curiously.

Connor looked blankly back at her for a moment then shook his head as if remembering. "It was Gaelic. It meant welcome home."

"Didn't sound too welcoming," she muttered and his gaze returned intensely to her face.

The heat in his dark brown eyes was deep and turbulent, unsettling and thrilling to Emmy at the same time. He was the stuff of fantasies, she thought. All of her fantasies. Years of imaginings since she was a teen had always placed a man such as this at their center. She almost wanted in that moment to be who he thought she was.

"Who do you think I am, exactly?" her husky voice questioned before the thought even formed in her mind.

He let out a disbelieving snort.

"Humor me."

"Verra well. To humor ye, my love." His deep, intriguing brogue again brought Connery-esque fantasies to her mind. Fantasies, fantasies. "Ye are my wife, Emeline Heather Stuart MacLean, Countess of Strathclyde. Ye left here, ran away to be more accurate, ten years ago today and no one has seen ye since."

His wife. What woman would want to run away from him?

The thought of having all the benefits of marriage to him made her clench her knees together tightly. Remember, she reminded herself, he's insane… mental. It didn't matter; her knees quivered anyway.

"And what exactly happened ten years ago today that I supposedly ran away from?"

"Our wedding night." He turned his back on them and stared out the window, his arms crossed tightly over his chest.

It was a defensive posture Emmy recognized immediately. It was hurt. Pain of loss. Anger. All brushed away with harsh sarcasm. Unfortunately she wasn't in much of a mood to cater to his male pride.

"Must not have been an experience worth repeating," she muttered under her breath.

Unfortunately he heard.

He whipped back to face her. "Ye dare to mention such a thing?"

"Relax, big guy, I'm not here to bruise your tender male ego. If you have problems in the sack, not that I can imagine *that*," she rolled her eyes sarcastically, "it's none of my business."

"The sack, as ye so quaintly put it, was ne'er reached, as ye well remember. Ye left before that." His voice rose as he worked his temper back up.

She stood up to face him "It wasn't me," she yelled right back.

"I dinnae remember ye being so temperamental, my love."

"If you 'my love' me one more time, I swear I'm going to…"

"Ye're going to what?"

"Um, Connor?" Ian interrupted from the doorway.

"What?" they both snapped, turning towards him.

Ian held up her large tote in one hand, her purse in the other.

"Oh, thank God." Emmy huffed as she stalked over and snatched the bags from his hand. "Let's get this over with so I can get the hell out of this loony bin. Real shame, too," she muttered to herself as she rummaged through the larger bag. "Man, you finally meet a guy that curls your friggin' toes, and he ends up being some whacked out SOB who has nothing better to do than… Aha! Here you go, Laird MacLean. Read it and weep then call me a cab, and get me the hell out of here."

XOXOXOX

The grin that had been forming on Connor's lips faded at this last. He was sure that she had no idea she'd been talking out loud. It intrigued him that she said he 'curled her toes' though he had no idea what 'friggin' was.

Just as she had no idea that the words he'd spoken to her upon her arrival were 'welcome home, wife,' but did not feel the need to clarify given the insanity of her refusal to admit her identity.

She waved a dark little booklet at him, her lips pursed with annoyance. God in Heaven, he didn't remember her being so lovely even with Dory here as a daily reminder. The entire situation befuddled him and he struggled to maintain his anger toward her. It shouldn't matter if Heather had suddenly become the most tempting woman on the face of the earth. He loathed her.

Frowning, he took the booklet and stared down at its cover. There in shining gold letters was that word. Passport. Below it was some sort of emblem of an eagle and shield with 'United States of America' below.

It fell open to a colorful page of another eagle and flag. And there was her portrait as well. A *color* photograph? He'd never heard of such a thing. It was an excellent photograph, he thought. He'd never seen one that sharp, though there were lines all across it. To the right was printed her name, the one she'd provided. Her nationality listed as USA and her birthplace, incredibly, as Virginia, USA.

She'd gone to America? He'd been there years ago looking for her. It was only one of the hundreds of places it seemed he searched for her until they all assumed she was dead. But she'd been there, near Baltimore, she said. Then he saw her birth date. March 10, 1982.

"It seems that yer forger wisnae as good as ye maun hae thought." He tapped the booklet against his hand. "Yer birth year is listed here as 1982."

"Yes, I was born on March 10, 1982. What's the problem with that?"

"Because that would be impossible considering that it is only 1895."

"Get. Out. You think you can pull some prank like that on me?"

He shared a bemused look with Ian who nodded in agreement. "Aye, lassie. October 18, 1895."

His wife spun about, her mouth gaping like a landed fish as she looked around her.

Then she fainted...again, at his feet.

4

A horrible burning in her nose brought Emmy sharply back to awareness. "What? What happened?" she asked as she slapped away the smelling salts beneath her nose.

"Ye fainted... *again*," Ian remarked with some disgust.

"Well, my love, those travelling papers were an excellent forgery. Impressive yet imperfect." The laird had retreated and was now ensconced once more in his chair leisurely sipping his drink. "Are ye ready to ha' yer bluff called and explain to me why ye've decided to return after all this time?"

Emmy looked into his chocolaty eyes and knew that there was no way to explain this; she didn't have a clue herself. The Victorian furniture, their outdated clothing, the Gibson-girl hairdo Dory wore...It was beginning to make some sense. Illogical sense, but sense of sorts. But to explain it?

Sure, in her bag there was proof of where, and *when* she was from, but at this point they'd probably just think her mad. Maybe a witch or something equally unacceptable. She wondered what they did to witches in 1895. Oh, why hadn't she majored in history? She loved historic architecture, that was why she was here to begin with, but she'd never really studied history itself.

Maybe it was better for now to just play along. At least until she had a handle on what was going on. If she went along, faked her way through, she might work her way out.

"Yes," she lowered her eyes and tried to appear repentant. Ian helped her into a sitting position on the settee next to Dory, then took a seat himself. As one, the all waited expectantly.

But Emmy found she could do little more than stare at the man across from her. Slouching back against the cushioned back, she considered her choices, and him. What to say? What to do?

Play along, she reminded herself, *pretend to be his wife.*

But he hates his wife, a part of her mind argued.

She didn't want him looking at her with hatred. No, there were other emotions she wanted to see in his eyes. The realization startled her.

"Heather, please sit up. Your posture is absolutely atrocious," Dorcas chided, handing her another cup of tea. "Here, this will make you feel just the thing."

Again Emmy found herself staring down into another cup of tea with some disgust. "Could I get a large glass full of ice, please?" she asked Dorcas.

Though her eyes showed curiosity, the woman nodded to a footman standing near the door who left the room immediately to do her bidding. Emmy swirled the cup idly as she waited for him to return, staring down steadily into the liquid and making no move to look at, or speak, to any of the other three occupants of the room.

What to say? What to do?

Questions again raged through her mind, but no alternatives presented themselves. She was in another time. Unbelievable! Things like this just did not happen to normal people, to anyone for that matter, unless the government had come up with some portal through time and were covering it up? That had happened before. Well, not with time travel specifically, but it had happened in other scientific arenas. Wasn't there some fuss in the 1950s though about some ship that was in Philadelphia and disappeared, only to show up in Norfolk just moments later? Something like that? She couldn't remember. But there were always all kinds of stories about government cover-ups and conspiracies. That could be the answer.

If it was something of that nature, would they reverse it? Could they? How widespread was it? Were there others here like her? Others stuck in other times having this same discussion in their heads? Perhaps, but what to do until she knew for sure? She most emphatically did not want to be burned as a witch, or something equally repellent.

The footman's return roused Emmy from her reverie and she took the glass from the small tray he held out to her. Rather than the uniform cubes she was used to, this ice looked as if it had been chipped off a block. Still, ice was ice.

Nodding and whispering her thanks, she took the glass and carefully poured the hot tea into it, vaguely aware of the bewildered stares she was receiving. Even from the footman. She ignored them and took a few extra minutes to dig around her tote for some sweetener.

Connor watched, intrigued, as his wife slapped the little pink packets against her hand before tearing them open and shaking the powdered contents into her drink. He wondered what it was. Laudanum?

Her forefinger followed the powder into the glass where she stirred it for a moment before popping her finger in her mouth to suck off the excess liquid. That small action changed the course of his thoughts entirely. It was the most singularly erotic action he'd ever seen a woman perform. The images it provoked aroused him unexpectedly. Stifling the arousal without mercy, he embraced his anger and broke the silence.

"Well, Heather?" Connor prompted harshly, aware that she wasn't going to willingly begin on her own.

"Okay," Emmy looked up and met his dark gaze once more, feeling its pull like a whirlpool tugging her under the water. "Well, I returned here because I wanted to…"

She stared into his stormy eyes and felt the attraction between them, the chemistry, and knew that he had felt it, too. Strong and intense, unlike anything she had ever experienced before. A reaction like those you read about but are sure never actually happen in real life. So, the words, when they came, seemed to be the most truthful she had ever spoken in her life.

"I came here to be with you."

Duart Castle
The Isle of Mull, Scotland
October 1895

Emmy didn't even flinch as the door slammed shut behind Connor as he stormed out of the room. She was stunned as well by her answer. Yet it felt right. The minute she'd seen him—before she'd concluded he was simply mad, that is—her first thoughts had wished for a man like that to be hers. The feeling of romance novels and fairy tales...well, adult fairy tales. It wasn't real. It wasn't typical, normal or usual.

In one of her favorite romantic comedies, *French Kiss*, when Meg Ryan's Kate and Kevin Kline's Luc finally kiss at the end, there's this moment when his hands clench into fists on the back of her dress as if he couldn't hold her tight enough, close enough or long enough.

In Emmy's mind, that moment was probably one of the

most romantic, passionate kisses she had ever seen. Definitely top ten. She wanted to be *wanted* like that. She wanted to be in the arms of a man where an embrace wasn't enough, where he needed so much more from her. She wanted a man to hold her as if he wanted to become one with her. Be one with her. She'd always dreamed of being desired with that intensity.

Yet, if she were honest with herself, Emmy admitted she never expected to feel like that in her entire life. It certainly wasn't a feeling she imagined having within minutes of meeting a man.

Especially one she considered completely nuts.

But there it was. Lust that overwhelmed the senses and brought irrational thoughts and impulses to mind. She believed strong physical attraction was normally the result of getting to know a man. In her romantic experience, a good sense of humor was the most powerful attractor she'd ever come across.

With this laird, Connor, she wanted more than anything just to feel those strong arms wrapped around her, holding her tightly with all the desperation and desire she'd seen in his eyes. More than anything, she knew that one kiss with him would be the most memorable experience of her life.

"Oh!" she moaned, burying her head in her hands once again. "What I am doing? I am such a nitwit."

"I would agree on that point," Dorcas volunteered as she poured herself yet another cup of tea while Ian slipped out of the room after Connor. "You shouldn't have said that to him. Now he'll be a horrific boar for days and days. Not that he is ever in good humor, mind you. You've only made it worse. More tea?"

"You should really back off on that stuff. That much

caffeine isn't good for you." Emmy slumped back in her chair and sipped her own iced tea.

Not even realizing the other woman was repeating "caffeine?" while glowering at her posture, Emmy muttered to herself. "What am I supposed to do now? I'm sure I missed the ferry back to Oban by now."

"You should really sit up properly. Your posture is simply atrocious," Dorcas scolded as if she couldn't help herself, earning a glare in return from Emmy.

"You said that already," Emmy told her.

"Then you must accept it as fact." Dory pursed her lips and considered Emmy thoughtfully. "In truth, I am most curious how you arrived here today. There was no ferry from Oban today and Connor noted there was no carriage on the road when he arrived. Did you walk from Craignure then? It is a long distance."

"I didn't walk. I took the shuttle." Emmy said, though she knew the words would make no sense to Dorcas, as she rubbed her hand over her face as if she could massage this all away. "I'm not sure where it went either. Ugh, this is crazy. Like a bad dream."

"Well, it's late. Perhaps after a night's rest everything will be clearer. Don't worry, as long as Connor believes you are Heather, you will have a place to stay at least." Dory patted her hand.

That got Emmy's attention. "What do you mean 'as long as Connor believes'? Don't you believe think I'm this Heather person?"

Dorcas's eyes narrowed on Emmy and she questioned in return. "Don't you think I would know my own twin, no matter how long she'd been gone?"

"So you know I'm not her."

Dorcas nodded. "You are not."

"What makes you so sure? And why didn't you tell Connor that?"

"The Heather I knew would never come back to Duart. She disliked Connor on sight and had absolutely no intention of marrying him. She was unable to stop the wedding but ran away while he waited for her to ready herself for his bed. She would be a fool to come back after this time, and she was no fool." Dorcas sipped and regarded Emmy curiously. "And I did not tell him so, not only because he would not believe it no matter how vehemently I assured him it was so, but also because I am curious who you truly are. Moreover, what reason you have for coming here now, today of all days? Can you answer that?"

"I'm afraid I can't do that just yet," was Emmy's truthful confession.

"Well, Connor will be expecting you to stay until you can, so we might as well see you settled in." Dorcas heaved herself from the settee belly first and preceded her to the door, motioning for her to follow. "Since you had no other bags with you, I will lend you some more suitable clothing. But it is late and such things can be accomplished in the morning."

"Bags? I have bags. They are safe in my hotel room across the sound." Emmy made a little rowing motion with her hands. "Safely back in the twenty-first..." she clamped her mouth shut quickly. "Any clothes you can offer would be appreciated, I guess. At least I have my toothbrush."

✗✗✗✗

Dorcas led the way back up the stairs and through a labyrinth of hallways to the room where Emmy had been before. Reaching up inside the door, she twisted the knob on a large wall sconce and a small flame grew in the globe, lighting the room with a warm glow.

"Gaslights?" Emmy asked.

"Aye, all the main and family rooms are lit and a very nice convenience it is. Since the MacLean clan regained possession of the lands and castle, the laird has been doing much to restore the castle as his father, the first Connor MacLean had before him."

"The room is lovely."

It was, in fact. Probably a classic example of Victorian décor. The bed was a large four-post bed but the posts, headboard and footboard were all intricately carved in scrolling floral motifs. The bedding and curtains were a lovely lilac gray silk, though more frilly and lacy than she tended to like things. There was a dressing table and pair of delicate, upholstered chairs near the fire. Overall, it was aesthetically pleasing.

Dorcas, however, offered a short snort. "You should have seen this place ten years ago. It was a near ruin and almost uninhabitable. It truly is a transformation. Your dressing room is through there." Dorcas pointed out another door farther along the wall. "I will have my maid bring you a nightgown now and other clothing in the morning as well as a few gowns to choose from."

"Gowns?" Now Emmy was the one repeating words.

"Aye, we dress for dinner and you will be expected to join us tomorrow evening."

"If I'm still here," she murmured under her breath, then shrugged. "Well, I haven't worn a 'gown' since I went to the Sigma Chi Sweetheart Ball in college." Rueful humor prompted a chuckle. "It'll be just like prom night."

Dorcas again looked mystified by the foreign words, but simply shook her head. "The American way of speaking you've adopted is most strange. The bell pull is over there next to the bed. I will assign a maid to aid you. Breakfast is served until eleven in the morning. I would advise that you do not attempt to flee into the night. That would only serve to upset the laird more."

"I have nowhere else to go," Emmy answered honestly. Truly she was stuck here until she could find a way back to the ferry, to her hotel...

To her own time.

Once Dorcas had gone, Emmy noticed another door next to the dressing room door the woman had pointed out to her. It led to a large bathroom with a sink, commode and claw foot tub, all looking terribly Victorian and historic but, thankfully, familiar. At least she wasn't going to have to use an outhouse, chamber pot, or any other equally awkward or distasteful substitute.

Stripping down to her camisole and panties, she found her toothbrush in her tote and made use of the quaint bathroom. After trying the chain pull on the toilet several times, she washed her face, brushed out her long hair and put it in a ponytail.

A maid brought her a long, conservative nightgown, which she donned over her underclothes. She turned to see the maid watching her with curiosity. When the girl realized Emmy had caught her staring, she flushed and drew back the bedclothes for Emmy to get in.

Once she was settled, the maid left, turning down the light as she went. Emmy snuggled down in the deep feather mattress and warm comforters, thanked God for the warm flannel nightgown and tried to plot her departure. But thoughts of escape were not what came to her mind. Instead, visions of the laird filled her consciousness.

This man, this laird, Connor MacLean, was unlike any man she met before. He was raw masculinity, not just in his bulging muscles and rough handsomeness, but also in his demeanor. He was a ruler and not in a tidy corporate CEO kind of way. It was powerful and magnetic. She was fairly certain he didn't have a feminine side let alone one that he was in touch with, but just the same, his dominating persona was fascinating.

"Connor," she whispered, imagining him sweeping her into his arms. "Why would any woman want to leave you?"

If he engendered feelings such as these in most females, he'd be constantly surrounded by women. Of course, it was possible that he was a serious asshole or something. Possible? Likely? She wasn't sure.

Trying to focus on the negative, Emmy again found herself wondering about the other possibilities Connor represented.

"Ugh," she moaned, burying her head in the pillow. "I will never again go five years without sex if this is how the first hot guy I see affects me."

With that vow, she let herself be lulled into a fitful sleep by the sound of rain and thunder from outside, and a night of erotic dreams.

XXXXX

Connor leaned against the door that connected his chambers with the room where Heather now slept. The earl's suite. He wasn't sure why he brought her to those rooms earlier, the countess's chambers. What possessed him to open them up again other than the fact that she'd come back? But he had, and just knowing nothing more than a mere door separated them, drove him mad.

He could not remember wanting Heather this desperately before. When he'd first met her, she'd just arrived at Duart for their wedding. An arrange marriage, of course. The wish of his father and hers. Heather had seemed dismayed by him upon their introduction, though he had never known why.

Pretty, but shy and haughty, he'd felt no great desire for her either; only resolve to have the thing done. He spent a day with her, giving her a tour of the castle. It'd been a near ruin at that time; the restoration his father planned still in its early stages. She'd been distressed with her future home as well. Withdrawn, but her silence oozed criticism and disdain of everything at Duart, including him. The next day, he'd stood with her before the altar and said his vows, knowing it made her as miserable as it did himself.

And then she was gone.

Now she returned. It was if she had become a different person in the intervening years. Of course, she'd been just a girl then, not the woman she was now. Time had served her well. Her appeal, and the attraction he felt for her now, were strong—stronger than any he could recall experiencing in his entire life.

He desired her. No, he simply wanted her.

What she had said downstairs tore through him again. She had come back to be with him. Why? Why now? On this day? The questions stopped him. Held him. He could open this door now and demand his rights as the husband everyone thought him to be. Complete what had not been consummated before. Gain relief from the lust that held him in its thrall.

But he knew what held him back.

He needed to talk to her but he also needed to talk to his solicitor. Only his solicitor, Conrad Baines, was aware that Connor'd had this marriage annulled two years ago. Only Mr. Baines knew the woman next door was in fact, no longer his wife in truth or under law.

He didn't know why he had lied to her, other than pure rage at her appearance. Perhaps it had been curiosity over her arrival or... something else. He didn't know what it was but it served him, for now, to have her think of him as her husband.

Emmy woke early and stretched out muscles left tight from sleeping on the soft mattress. Bright sunshine poured through the tiny windows of the outer embattlements facing the east. Years of residency had trained her to get her sleep when she could and to function on very little of it. By habit and training, she was a light sleeper and early riser. She lay there for a moment, warm and cozy in the cocoon of the feather bed, although the nip on her cheeks suggested the air in the room was much colder.

Finally she rose and quickly dressed in her clothes from the previous day. Making quick use of the bathroom, she brushed her teeth, and washed her face with the bar of fragrant soap. She twisted her hair up in a claw clip and was soon slipping out the door.

None of the others were awake or perhaps it all been a dream, she hoped as she crept down the hall from her room without seeing another soul. Maybe the vision of Connor on horseback had been a hallucination from which she was only just now recovering and the rest merely a bizarre, stress-induced dream. It could now be 2010 as it should be and she was here at Duart on vacation…

A maid in a long gray, Victorian dress, white apron and cap on her Grecian knot crossed the hall carrying an armload of linens. Her appearance shattered Emmy's sudden hopes and she knew that the 'dream' was indeed reality.

What to do? The never-ending question again pounded in her mind like the beating of a drum. Duart, she thought. 1895. She still had no real idea how it had happened beyond her initial speculation that it had to be a government experiment gone wrong. Coping with her circumstances was top priority.

Logically, she knew she should pretend to be this Heather MacLean as long as she could get away with it. She was lost in time, and if she fought the battle and the laird accepted that she wasn't his wife, she'd be left without a place to stay or food to eat. That was something she couldn't afford to happen, especially with winter fast approaching. Of course, she also had no money to support herself in this time. The pounds and pence in her purse would only draw suspicion she wasn't prepared to defend against.

What she needed to do was figure out how to get back but she didn't have a clue where to start. Until she did, she'd do what she had to, even if it meant deceiving the entire castle. Better that than the nightmare of burning at the stake.

Emmy tiptoed toward the stairs before she shook her head for being such a ninny. Was she truly trying to sneak around this castle? It was so big her chances of meeting another person were pretty slim. Straightening, she strode more confidently, taking in the décor of the castle as she went.

The halls were paneled in intricately carved rosewood with lovely, fragile sconces lighting the hall at intervals. Plush carpet runners padded the wood floor and oil paintings in ornate frames hung on the walls. The staircase was another example of fine woodworking with its hand-carved spindles and elaborate newel posts. The hall below was lit by an enormous chandelier that bounced light off the polished marble floors.

It was all very extraordinary and indicated a wealth that boggled Emmy's mind. And, oddly, it all looked brand new as if it had just been completed. The MacLeans had only returned to Duart in the past twenty years from this historic date, having recovered the castle after centuries. Duart had been a near ruin on its recovery by the clan; she knew that much from her guidebook, but now she wondered to what extent it had been rebuilt. Perhaps she would find the courage to ask Connor.

Opening the massive front door, she slipped silently into the misty Scottish morning. The rising sun on the other side of the castle cast long shadows over the courtyard and outer walls. The castle itself was a thick U shape. The central section she exited from reached out with two deep wings on either side. On one side, the building was five stories high. The rear and opposite side were only three, and the top end of the U the wings created was closed by a tall defensible wall with only an ornamental iron gate leading to the entrance she'd arrived at the day before.

She hadn't seen this enclosed courtyard before. Connor must've been carried through it the previous day after she fainted outside the front gates. That open area might have been used in the past for the castle soldiers to train in or for work to be done. Today it consisted of a tidy network of pathways and low shrubbery with an impressive stone fountain at its center. Not complicated, but rather sparse overall. Compared with the lush gardens she had seen over the course of her vacation, Emmy appreciated its simple elegance.

The morning air chilled her and she clutched her blazer around her. The ground, damp after the storms of the previous evening, squished beneath her feet as she walked across the paths and through the heavy gate, the only exit from the entire castle she had found so far. She went down a series of stone steps to the drive where the bus had dropped her off the previous afternoon.

There she paused and turned to look up at the castle, the walls dark in the shadows of the early morning. It looked nothing like it had when she arrived yesterday. Pacing back and forth, she wondered if being in the right spot would whisk her back across the hundred and fifteen years into the future. Perhaps there was an invisible portal or something. She glanced toward the gates and back up at the keep, still shadowed by the castle.

Nothing.

She found another spot and looked around again.

Nothing.

"Well, hell," she muttered at her failure to be instantaneously whisked away back to her own time. Obviously it wasn't going to be that easy.

She pivoted around to face the rugged countryside sprawling out from the castle. To her right stood the stables in place of the dumpster that had been there the previous day. Flipping a mental coin, Emmy went left and rounded the northern corner of the building, coming quickly to an abrupt drop-off at the cliffs, which backed the castle. The castle jutted straight up from those rocky crags, overlooking the Sound of Mull and the mainland of Scotland beyond. Perfectly built for defense.

Only half interested in the architecture, she stared out over the white-tipped wavelets and considered her situation with a clear mind, not one clouded by the distraction that Connor MacLean presented the previous evening.

Surely something would get her home. Maybe a repeat of her movements at the same time and place would do the trick. It'd been nearing sunset when she arrived so maybe she should try again in the afternoon. There might be a wormhole that appeared regularly at that spot—assuming this was a random phenomenon and not a government accident of sorts.

There was something she remembered—maybe from *Star Trek*—that a time portal or wormhole might not appear in the same place twice. Being in the same spot may not work. Wasn't that how *Voyager* got stuck out in the Delta Quadrant? Maybe not. Emmy couldn't remember. She loved a good sci-fi movie but they tended to blur together after a while. Plus, she wasn't sure how the science translated into reality… if it did at all. That's why it was called science *fiction*.

As for reality, she could remember nothing about Einstein's theories on the whole mess. What if there was nothing she could do? She'd never been good at waiting for others to fix problems for her. She was more proactive than that.

Leaning over the edge of the drop-off, she stared down. It was not a cliff so much as an extremely steep hill with sharp, angular rocks jutting out from it now and then. And it ended not at the water but rather at a plain that angled out to the water. That beach of sorts was rocky and harsh. No plant life softened this landscape. Still, it was lovely.

She raised a hand to shade her eyes against the morning sun. The sun glistened and glinted off the rough waters left over from the night's storms as they splashed and hit the rocks far below. The roar of the waves was louder here filling her ears with their crash and growl. It was violent and terrific. Awe-inspiring, just as she had hoped it would be.

"It's phenomenal," she whispered in wonder.

XOXOXO

"Ye were once afraid to come out here," came that deep, delicious voice from behind her. Emmy jumped just a bit in surprise and Connor caught her arm to steady her. "Careful now, ye dinnae want to fall over the edge. Or were ye planning to jump? 'Tis nae far enough to kill, I think, but ye could do yerself some damage."

"I would think you'd be glad to see me go."

Memories of the previous night's dream-disturbed sleep assailed her once again as the heat of his hand seared through her jacket and warmed her arm. One touch, she couldn't believe it. One impersonal touch and she was quivering in her boots with desire. Emmy pulled her arm away and he let her go, crossing his arms across his broad chest. "How did you know I was out here?"

"My rooms overlook the courtyard and this side of the castle." He jerked his head back toward the keep. "I saw ye come out and decided to make sure ye wisnae tinking to kill yourself."

"You wish," she said, taking in his trousers and half buttoned shirt. "This whole situation isn't *that* bad yet." She wondered if he had dressed in a hurry to come save her from herself. "It'll take a lot more before I'm ready to off myself.

How 'bout you though? You look pretty rough," she couldn't resist adding as she cast a critical glance at him, noting the bags under his eyes and bloodshot eyes. "Nursing a hangover?"

"Hangover?" he raised an eyebrow.

"You know? Hit the bottle a bit hard last night and are regretting the result?"

"Dinnae gi' yerself the credit for any such condition. It'd been my plan for the evening long before ye arrived," he told her coldly with a curl of his lip at the reminder of his annual observance of his greatest humiliation. "I saw nae reason to change my plans simply because ye were here."

"Ouch," she said lightly.

So her arrival, or the arrival of his wife, as he thought she was, had not prompted a night in the cups. He had been planning on it anyway. Interesting yet sad that Connor seemed to have allowed the woman who had abandoned him all those years before to still hold such control over his life.

It softened her a bit toward him and, changing the subject, she offered pleasantly, "Actually, I just came out for the view. I've always loved stuff like this. Waves crashing, thunderstorms, lightning, that sort of thing. Nature at its most violent and beautiful."

"As I recall, ye once expressed a fright of those same things," he commented.

Emmy sighed and wondered if she could really do as Dory suggested and ride out this mistaken identity thing. Connor obviously thought of her as his missing wife and there was nothing she could say that was going to change his mind on that point. The laird was dug deeply into his beliefs and even Dory didn't even believe that her word was going to change his mind until it suited him to do so.

She forced herself to recall that she just needed to go with the flow as Dory had said. After all, she needed a place to stay until she figured out how to get back home. Surely somewhere someone was working on the fix for it. She shivered at the passing thought that perhaps no one knew what was going on.

"Come, ye're cold," he offered his arm gallantly to her. "Come inside and breakfast wi' me."

Emmy took the arm he held out to her but, when her hand touched the bare skin of his forearm, a delicious shudder rocketed through her and she withdrew with a start.

How was she to do this if his slightest touch had this effect on her? Connor jerked away as well, confirming her suspicion that it affected him equally. She shoved her hands as far as she could into her blazer's tiny pockets and stared up at the side of the looming castle, aware that he'd pocketed his hands as well.

They began to walk back to the gates side by side. Connor opened the heavy gate and bowed, indicating with a sweeping arm that she should precede him into the courtyard.

"I'll have to bring my camera out later when the sun is higher and take some pictures," she offered by way of light conversation as she walked through.

XXXXX

"Ye own yer own camera?" Connor asked incredulously, stopping to stare down at her upturned face, her eyes mirroring his own surprise. Why should *she* gaze at him with such confusion? He knew of no one save the photographer in Inverary across the sound who owned their own camera. It only served to rouse more questions about her when he already had so many. "Are ye a photographer then?"

"Only as a hobby."

"Ye must ha' done verra well for yerself in America to own such a thing." He pried for something, anything she might give him to answer his questions. "Did ye marry a rich man?"

"I'm not married."

"Are ye no'?" he questioned softly, the irony in the question apparent.

He paused and looked down at her. Tendrils of hair had escaped their loose knot and danced across cheeks bitten rosy by the brisk October winds. He fought the urge to cup her face in his hands to warm them.

Pray he was more successful in that than he'd been in stifling the urge to come out here in the first place. Connor had been dressing near the window when he saw her pass, her manly stride so visible in the tight trousers she wore. Her garb was mannish and inappropriate, but he acknowledged that she looked lovely this morning in spite of her unconventional attire.

"Are ye no'?" he asked again, hoping to rouse some anger to replace his budding arousal.

"Let's not go there today, okay? Can't we just have a nice breakfast without an argument?"

Connor shrugged, surprised by her request. He realized that he would like that with her. "Aye, I suppose. What are we to talk aboot then? What are yer plans?"

"My plans involved sightseeing, perhaps a boat ride around the sound, a bit of shopping and much relaxation," she told him. "But, somehow, I don't think I'm going to get any of those things now. Certainly not relaxation."

Her tone was sharp, and filled with a scorn and sarcasm Connor felt odd coming from such a lovely face. There were little crinkles in the corner of hers eyes and a slight natural tilt to her mouth that told him that she smiled and laughed often. He'd not yet seen her do so... at least from actual good humor.

"Ye seem verra angry, Heather, and bitter. Yet yer face tells a story of a happier life." He touched the corner of her eye lightly tracing the tiny lines there before even realizing he'd lifted his hand. Her skin was as soft as it looked. Dropping his arm, he looked away. "Did ye no' come here of yer own free will? I dinnae understand at all why ye insist on pretending ye dinnae remember what once occurred here." He pointed to a detailed metal and glass door set in the right wing of the castle. "The chapel where we wed."

XXXXX

She was trying to keep Dory's recommendation in mind, but she didn't like being the object of Connor's constant bitterness. She wanted him to like her. For what reasons, she chose not to examine too closely.

His handsome face had almost seemed filled with caring for a moment. His brown eyes were tender and warm. Yet, his face was not one that showed a life of laughter, she noted. There were lines, yes. A frown line between his brows. A mouth that turned down just a bit at the corners as if he hadn't smiled in a long while.

He was an angry man, she realized, bitter from the embarrassment this Heather once served him. Had he loved her so much then that he hadn't been able to live happily without her?

She reached up and rubbed the hard line between his brows away with the pad of her thumb. "I am sorry that you haven't been able to move on with your own life, Connor. It must have been pretty hard on you."

His gaze hardened and he pushed her hand away. "Spare me yer pity. Ye ken nothing of my life." He turned and headed for the castle door with strides as crisp as his tone. He spun back suddenly, stopping Emmy in her tracks as she moved to follow. "I looked for ye for years," he shouted angrily with a slash of his hand. "I went after ye."

"Out of love, Connor? Or pride?"

Connor snapped his mouth shut and turned away, disappearing into the castle without another word.

After filling plate of food from the breakfast buffet being laid out in the morning room as she passed, Emmy went straight up to her room, intent on avoiding the laird until his temper cooled. He ran hot and cold without warning, and she wasn't in much of a mood to tiptoe around him.

She shouldn't have pushed him though with that last volley, she scolded herself. She was used to getting the last word in and sometimes spoke without thinking. As Dory had warned, he would probably be a perfect boar because of her thoughtlessness.

Lost in thought, she entered her room through the wrong door and only then realized her room was actually a suite; a bedroom and sitting room with the large dressing room and bathroom attached. The door to the sitting room had been closed the previous evening but had been opened when the maids had straightened up this morning.

Where the bedroom was light and feminine with its light grays and lilac, the sitting room was more gender neutral, to use the modern phraseology. The antiques were, of course, not actually antiques in this time but new. Classically Victorian in styling but comfortable and upholstered in neutral grays, blues and whites that went well with the scrolled and flocked wallpaper that was typical of the era. Several landscapes and portraits added interest to the walls.

Two striped wingbacks faced a settee adjacent to a large fireplace with a mantel that was a work of art in its own right. The intricate scrolling woodwork facing that swept all the way to the ceiling. A large carpet kept the wooden floors from chilling the rooms, which were heated by radiators that Emmy assumed led to a boiler somewhere. The radiators heated the areas nearby nicely, but overall, did little more than cut the worst of the chill.

Thankfully, fires burned brightly both in this room and her bedroom. She ate her breakfast holding the plate in front of her while pacing in front of the fire. When she had finished, she chose a chaise near one of the few windows in the room.. The castle had been built for defense, she recalled. The windows to the outside were few and very small. These in her sitting room faced the side of the keep she'd visited this morning while her bedroom cornered the building to the same side and back of the castle overlooking the sound and its spectacular views

But they could only hold her attention for so long. To pass the time, Emmy tried to read one of the books she had picked up at the airport, but her mind kept wandering helplessly back to Connor again and again.

Should she apologize for deliberately goading him? Should she just let it go? Where was he? What did he do to keep busy all day?

Though she'd planned to spend the day in her rooms

avoiding Connor, curiosity drove Emmy to venture out from time to time. She'd inquired about his whereabouts as casually as she could manage. The butler, Chilton, told her the laird gone riding, gone into Craignure or anywhere elsewhere. *Rather than stay here and face his issues,* she thought.

Morning turned to afternoon. Margo, the maid Dory had assigned to her, offered to bring her a tray to her room for luncheon. Accepting, Emmy felt as she, too, were hiding out rather than facing the mysterious nineteenth century outside the doors. Gathering her courage, she finally asked Margo to give her a tour of the castle.

Bedroom suites occupied half of the second floor with more on the third floor and servants quarters and nurseries on the fourth. There was a small family parlor as well on each of these floors. The second floor also housed a large library. In all the rooms the outer windows were small, but in those rooms that faced the inner courtyard, they were larger, allowing more light into some of the main rooms.

On the main floor, Margo took her through the drawing rooms—both large and small—the parlor, a stunningly restored chapel, billiards room, dining room, morning room and kitchens. They passed a dark oak door the maid told her was the laird's office, but Margo's face expressed such shock when Emmy asked to see it, she dropped the subject. The kitchens, she was told, had once been housed in a separate building but the restoration of the castle had seen them moved inside to the first floor.

Like the main hall, all the rooms were large and luxurious, almost too formal in comparison to the medieval skin of the castle. Rich carpets covered the tile and wood floors. Inlaid patterns bordered the rooms. The furnishings were all beautifully carved or gilded and upholstered in lush velvets. The draperies were velvet as well, with ornate fringes along the edges. They were thick so they could block the cold air from seeping through the windows in the colder months. A logical idea, though Emmy had never seriously considered the practical applications of window treatments before. With the energy efficient windows of her time, who needed to?

It was overall an amazing example of Victorian architecture and décor. None of the museums she'd ever been to had shown the level of richness and opulence this period was clearly capable of. But for some reason, she just didn't feel that it suited Connor well. Of course, she'd only just met him, but still... it gave her something to think about.

Emmy thanked Margo for the tour and was grateful for her offer to build up the fire when they returned to her rooms. The afternoon had turned chilly, and rain slapped once again on the windows. An array of clothing had been laid out in her bedroom while she was gone. From Dorcas, Margo told her before leaving her alone.

Resuming her place on the chaise near the window, she tried once again to focus on her book, but as the warmth of the room rose and the previous day's travel set in, Emmy slipped into slumber.

XXXXX

It was with some surprise that Connor found Heather asleep on the chaise in the sitting room shared by the earl and countess's rooms. For some reason he expected her to be hiding out in her bedroom as she'd done the day they married, hesitant to face him after a long day in his company.

Lowering himself onto a small ottoman near the chaise, Connor studied his wife as she slept. Reclined in the chaise, with one bare foot tucked up under her other leg, she wore spectacles today. Framed in dark tortoiseshell, he believed. Narrow in height and wide across giving her a studious air even in slumber. He wondered if she needed them all the time or only wore them for reading.

Reaching over, he gently removed the glasses and rescued her fallen book, curiously noting the watercolor landscape printed in the front of the more intriguing paper cover. However, they weren't fascinating enough to hold his attention with their owner napping so soundly, so Connor placed them together on a nearby table. There, a glass held melting ice, which he assumed had previously been the odd libation of tea over ice she preferred. He wondered again what the little pink packets had held. Perhaps they were medication of some sort. Perhaps powders for headaches or illness. He knew almost nothing about her, he realized. Despite their new attraction, she was as much a stranger to him today as she'd been ten years before.

He brushed the shorter strands of hair that framed her face back across her cheek. Though the rest of her hair was still bound in some sort of clasp at the back of her head, some longer locks had escaped. He followed the tress with his fingers. How long it was. Laying it over her shoulder, he stroked the silky length then her cheek. So soft, as was the texture of her skin.

He'd heard that the Americas were a harsh place, where conditions outside the cities aged a person before his or her time. Clearly, Heather hadn't suffered in her time away. She'd left with little money or possessions. How had she supported herself? Disturbing images flew through his mind as he wondered if she had sold herself for monies.

No, surely not. Yet she insisted that she'd gone to university there, educated herself. One did not do that without money. And she also said she owned a camera of her own. It hadn't seemed an unusual thing to her so perhaps extravagance was a habit of hers.

Her long legs were still encased in those tight trousers that flaunted body and rear. Through her thin silk blouse, he could almost see the color of her skin. It was indecent yet alluring and, he had to wonder again, had she invented stories to cover years of degradation and humiliations? He wanted badly to know the answers but at the same time dreaded the response he might receive. Anger and a jealous rage tore through him and he wondered at that as well.

He hadn't loved Heather when they wed. It'd been his father's arrangement for him to wed the daughter of a friend he served with during the Crimean War. Connor hadn't even met her until she and her father arrived at Duart in the days before the wedding.

She'd been pretty enough then, nothing compared to the more mature beauty before him now. But here she was now, forthright and outgoing and, despite the harsh welcome she had received from him, rather pleasant and even humorous, if somewhat sarcastic.

She angered him. She intrigued him. In just a single day, she had enflamed him with both anger and lust until he didn't know what to do with her.

No, that wasn't entirely true. The physical attraction between them was powerful and explosive... he knew *what* he wanted to do with her, but could he take such a chance?

Connor traced her full lower lip with his thumb, relishing the tingling warmth that spread through him with that simple contact. She made a low moan in the back of her throat and raised a hand to brush away what disturbed her sleep. Unable to help himself, he leaned forward, lightly brushing his lips across hers and marveled at his boldness. Even so subtle a touch was as stimulating as their first contact earlier in the day. He pulled back as she opened her eyes.

She rubbed her lips and stared up at him in surprise. "What? Connor? What are you doing in here?"

"This room between yer bedchamber and mine." He indicated the doors to the right and left, hers standing open, and his closed. "'Yis part of our shared apartments."

Her mouth formed a silent O that sent his thoughts again toward kissing her but he shook them off and headed briskly toward his room, offering shortly as he went, "'Tis nearly time to dress for dinner. Yer maid should be attending ye shortly."

)O(O(O(

Emmy gaped at his bedroom door in confusion as it slammed behind him. He ran between hot and cold without warning. It was hard to keep up with his mood swings. When she had awoken to find him so close after avoiding her the length of the day, the look on his face had been almost... tender? His voice soft. It had set off a trembling response in her chest. Then it seemed as if he'd been angered by it, or by her? She wasn't sure.

What she did know was that he was as physically attracted to her as she was to him and he wasn't happy about it.

Of course, she wasn't pleased by their attraction either. Adrift from her own time and place, trapped in the past, she should be concentrating on finding a way out of this, regardless of the fact that she had no idea what to do about it. Her focus should be on home. The last thing that should be occupying her mind was a man. Even if he was the most amazing man she'd ever met. She longed to touch him, feel him. Her own response should have angered her. But it did not.

Emmy shook her head. They just didn't build them like that in her time. Connor was... marvelous. Physically he was beyond compare; way beyond the clichéd tall, dark and handsome. His broad muscular build belonged in a Calvin Klein underwear ad. Connor's ruggedly gorgeous face was dark and weathered from the sun and elements, not from a beach or, worse, tanning bed. All of it suggested hard labor showing a dedication to his work. Although she wasn't sure what that was, specifically, she admired commitment in people. Beneath all that angst there obviously lurked a dependable man.

A rarity.

Very intriguing.

Dorcas arrived then with Margo, drawing Emmy from her thoughts with a blush. When Dory inquired whether the dresses she had sent earlier fit, Emmy apologized and admitted that she hadn't tried them on. She followed the pair back to her bedchamber, firmly closing the door of the sitting room behind her. Laid out on the bed were the four dresses Margo brought earlier. She hadn't thought to look at them at all.

Now, her jaw dropped as one after another was held up and presented to her. Each one was a stunning piece of art.

"It's lovely," she whispered as she held one gown of heavily embroidered ivory satin against her, swinging it side to side as she looked in the full-length mirror. "I feel like it's speaking to me."

She bent her cheek toward the dress and whispered in singsong, "Put me on, put me on, we'll be gorgeous together." A giggle escaped her.

Even Dorcas, dour as she was, couldn't help but smile in the face of Emmy's childlike enthusiasm over the gowns while the servant laughed merrily. "Come, we'll help you put it on then."

"I can dress myself," Emmy objected.

"Nonsense, and I do mean nonsense," Dorcas injected sternly. "No woman can get in one of these by herself."

"Alright then."

Shrugging, Emmy peeled off her jacket. Jeans went next with a little work. The maid looked intrigued as she picked them up off the floor, but as Emmy's blouse fell open, both the maid and Dorcas gasped.

"What?" Emmy asked, puzzled.

Dorcas recovered first, shaking her head. "I apologize. I had assumed ye would be wearing the proper undergarments. We were not expecting you to be bare."

Knowing what her perfectly acceptable lace demi-bra covered, Emmy shook her head. "I am not bare."

"Bare enough," the other lady sniffed with scorn. "I will have Margo fetch you the proper foundations."

"The proper found… ?" Now it was Emmy's turn to gasp. "You don't mean a – a *corset*, do you?" She stuttered out the word in horror. At their synchronized nods, Emmy shook her head, clutching her shirt to her midsection and backing away. "Are you kidding me? I don't *think* so! I am not contorting my body for you or anyone!"

"It is what a proper lady wears," Dorcas argued, looking emphatically determined to have it done.

"Well, call me a peasant then, because I won't do it. I'll wear my own bra and it'll be just fine."

Emmy crossed her arms determinedly over her chest.

Really, time travel was one thing but a corset!

"I'm afraid the gown willnae fit ye wi'out the corset, milady," the maid, Margo, offered tentatively. "Yer waistline is trim, but yer bosom is too big." She held her hands out in front of her.

Again, Emmy found herself looking down and shrugged dismissively. "That's just a push-up bra. They don't do that all by themselves. Without it maybe we'll be okay."

Remaining solid in her stand that she would not wear the corset they offered, Emmy managed to get into the dress without it but soon found out there was no way it would fasten around her torso. So much for being slim.

After much cajoling from Margo, and a near lecture from Dorcas, Emmy reluctantly decided to try the corset. She stripped off her bra while Margo lowered a thin shirt, a chemise, over her head. The corset came next, again over her head as it was already partially laced. It was a beautiful creation of pale pink satin and lace and embroidered around the edges with tiny roses and cherubs.

Hiding the devil inside, Emmy thought.

"Are we talking whalebone or steel here?" she asked apprehensively, as Margo adjusted it.

"The supports are steel bands," came the answer and Emmy knew it was true as she felt its weight settle on her hips. The first pull of the strings brought a surprised grunt.

"This is so…not…good…for you," she gasped as the chuckling maid continued to pull and tighten the garment. It wasn't precisely painful, but it was uncomfortable to say the least.

Dorcas examined Emmy's discarded bra with interest. The ivory satin cups seemed to intrigue her as did the tag when she found it. "Victoria's Secret. What is the secret? And what does 3, 4, D, D mean?"

A flush grew on Emmy's cheeks despite her inability to take a deep breath. She'd always been large-breasted but well proportioned for her build. After all she was tall, and while narrow around her rib cage, had wide curving hips and broad enough shoulders to carry off her cup size nicely. Still, she'd been teased by the nickname 'Double D' since the 7th grade. Occasionally past boyfriends would toss out the old cliché that 'more than a handful was a waste', usually during an argument, but joke or not, it made her feel slightly self-conscious though she was otherwise proud of her body. "It's um, an item number, so you know which… um, color you like," she responded feebly.

"It is a very interesting garment."

"It seems that this thing does about the same job but with ten times the pain."

The corset was finally in place. Although it was tight, Emmy supposed that she had her natural thinness to thank for the little oxygen she was receiving. The corset pushed her up, out and held her firmly. When prompted, she stepped into a pile of fabric Margo laid out on the floor. It was all pulled up and tied about her waist. Petticoats, she realized. Then some sort of wire basket was tied on over her backside. What was that all about?

"So, Dory, what's the deal with Connor?" Emmy asked as the gown itself was finally lowered over her upraised arms.

"What do you mean?" Dorcas asked as she and the maid twitched and adjusted the gown until it hung as it was supposed to. Margo began the process of fastening the multitude of buttons up the back.

"Why is he… him?" was her reply. "I get the feeling he's like the boss or something. Is it the laird thing?"

The low neckline of the gown pushed her already up thrust breasts up even more until they felt as if they would spill out over the top of the dress. Well, that was a Saturday night in college not all that long ago. She could live with it.

"It is his life's work to provide for the earldom and his clan. It is all he does," Dorcas responded tartly.

"Ever?"

"It seems so." Dory pursed her lips. "The laird doesn't have much time or tolerance for anything else."

"What does that mean?" Emmy asked.

Dory only shook her head. "I should not have spoken so candidly. I will leave you now to prepare myself for dinner. Margo will help you finish."

"Candidly? You didn't tell me anything!" Emmy sighed at her departure but was quickly distracted when she turned to the mirror again.

The vision reflected back at her was stunning. The gown itself was amazing. The front panel of ivory satin was heavily embroidered with leaves and flowers. The rear gathered over the wire basket in the back made her butt look much bigger though, she thought. Tiny sleeves fell off her shoulders while the bodice nipped at the waist, flattering the outrageous hourglass figure they'd cinched her into, and despite her reservations, she felt ridiculously feminine in it. Feminine and beautiful.

"This gown is... unbelieveable. I feel like a princess, if you don't mind the cliché. But I have to ask... what is with the big butt thing? I feel like my butt is sticking out a mile behind me."

Margo giggled. "'Tis the *tournure*, milady.

"The torture what?"

"The big bottom... 'tis what it is supposed to do. 'Tis

the fashion."

Emmy released a snort of disbelief. "Well, I can tell you right now, I know tons of women who would cry 'hallelujah!' if a big ass were fashionable."

Margo gaped in shock over her language but Emmy ignored her and turned to the side again and back to the front, examining the outward thrust of her rear in the mirror. "How do you sit down with this thing on?

They practiced several times with the maid coaching her to the proper method of sitting to hit the edge of the seat with the *tournure* behind her but not under her. When she sat, the corset kept her erect but put more pressure on her stomach.

"I'm starving, but how am I going to be able to eat?"

"It'll work out in the end, milady. I dinnae hae to lace ye verra tightly to make the dress fit."

"This isn't laced tightly?"

Margo shook her head with a smile at Emmy's blatant disbelief. "No' a'tall, milady."

"Well, Lord help me then," Emmy muttered as Margo led her over to the dressing table.

"Now for yer hair," the maid announced.

"Oh, I got that covered."

Emmy pinched the claw clip that held her hair where she had twisted it. As her hair was released, it fell in a long shimmering mass to her waist. Her hair was her pride and joy. She cut it only to keep it healthy, highlighted it only to give it depth and texture. Only the long sweep of bangs she kept did not meet the rest at the lightly layered length.

"'Tis lovely, milady," Margo complimented, stroking it through her fingers. "Verra soft as well."

"Nothing better than a good conditioner and hot oil

treatment."

After a quick brushing, Emmy grabbed up the mass of hair and wrapped it around her fist. Pulling the ends through, she knotted it, then wrapped it around her hand and knotted it again. She wound the loose ends around the base of the double knot and secured the whole with the claw clip.

Although not a loose topknot the other women seemed to favor, the whole process took only fifteen seconds and looked elegant to her eye, with only her cheekbone length bangs remaining free and swept to the side. Digging in her tote, she pulled out her favorite tinted lip gloss and applied it. She had no other makeup with her and felt a pang of regret that she couldn't do her face up to match the elegance of the dress.

"Okay, I guess that's it then. Let's eat. Not sure how I'm going to manage it in this thing though."

8

It seemed that dinner in turn of the century Scotland was not just a sit down and eat affair, nor was it a formal extended restaurant affair. Dinner was indeed like the prom she'd joked about. First everyone got together to socialize before actually moving on to the dining room and eating. Ian and Dorcas met her at the top of the stairs and guided her to the large drawing room Emmy toured with Margo earlier.

Emmy was introduced around by 'her twin' to the few people already gathered as "Heather MacLean" as in "You remember Heather MacLean, don't you? Yes, the laird's wife." She was referred to as *countess*, *my lady* and *Lady MacLean* until she forgot who she was supposed to be and tried instead to concentrate on the other people present.

There was Ian, who she discovered was Dorcas's husband and Connor's younger brother. If she'd paid more attention the previous night she would've noticed the resemblance though Ian was slighter in build than Connor. Then there was a flock of aunts, uncles and cousins whose names all blended together. It took several moments for it to sink in that all of these people lived in the castle, but not much longer for her to realize that they all lived off the laird's good graces. Tidbits of conversation she overheard included comments about a person's allowance, how another was trying to move into a larger apartment in the south wing. Not once did she hear anyone mention a job of their own. In the end, it appeared there were seventeen people beyond the paid servants living in the castle... all supported by the laird.

To Emmy's astonishment, it seemed not one of them was required to ante anything, be it money or service, into the deal. If she had to provide for so many people, she might get a little cranky too, and wondered if that was Connor's problem.

When Connor finally entered the room, framed at the doorway, awe over the impossibly handsome picture he made swept over Emmy. Stunning in his formal evening clothes, his black jacket contrasted against his snowy white shirt, vest and even bow tie. She'd seen the movie *Age of Innocence* years ago. As far as clothing for men went, it was pretty much spot on there.

He oozed magnificent elegance, and she was immediately aware that he hated it. While he gave an outward appearance of nonchalance, Emmy could just see him on the inside, twitching and itching, and yanking at his collar.

As he crossed the room toward her, everyone present bowed or curtsied as he passed. He nodded in return but no one spoke to him at all, and he offered nothing either. But all eyes watched him as he approached her, and it seemed to Emmy that they were all either in awe of Connor or perhaps simply afraid of the man who held their relaxed lifestyles in the palm of his hand. Like he was their king or somewhat godly. Untouchable.

Yet, he did provide for them. *Hmm*, it made Emmy think.

His eyes captured hers as he neared. Emmy could easily see the desire and heat in them. It was astonishing to know that he felt the same unwilling attraction that she felt for him. It was powerful and undeniable… though she was sure they would both do their best to deny it anyway.

"Ye look verra bonny this evening, my love," Connor offered by way of greeting, taking her hand formally and raising it with a twist to press his lips to her palm.

"Thank you," Emmy responded curling her hand and surreptitiously scratching the tingling palm that had just been teased by his lips. "I feel lovely this evening," she confessed and rocked side to side to set her skirts swinging a bit. "You don't look so bad yourself."

A surprised half-grin jerked at the corner of his mouth and almost raised it into a full smile. "Thank ye, I think." A footman arrived with his drink and he held it up to her. "To yer return," he toasted softly.

Emmy held up her own wineglass and shook her head. "To my… something." She clinked her glass to his and took a quick sip. Responding to his raised brow, she said only "I'm not really sure I can call it a 'return'."

"Still trying to refute who ye are, my love?"

"I believe I have asked you not to call me that," she replied. "Besides why would I come here and try to deny it? It doesn't make any sense."

"There is much aboot ye that is a mystery, my…" the corner of his mouth jerked up again in an appealing lopsided grin. "My apologies, I shall strive to withhold my endearments as ye requested."

"Endearments?" Emmy laughed softly and took another sip of her wine. "You *do* know that you actually have to like someone to have it be called that, don't you?"

His grin took a devilish edge. "There are many levels of liking. In fact, I seem to ha' developed an entirely new *liking* for ye that I ne'er had before." The heat flared in his eyes and the soft brogue of his deep voice caused shivers to shoot down Emmy's spine. "Truly," he continued, running a finger down her bare arm, "I'd verra much like to…"

"My lord," Dorcas said sharply, interrupting his thought, "I can see you have not noticed that Chilton has called dinner. Perhaps you would care to lead dear Heather in?"

"As laird of my own home, I believe dinner maun hae waited another moment, Dorcas, until I finished my conversation wi' my wife," he responded in equal tones. He sighed and rubbed the back of his neck before offering an arm to Emmy. "My lady? May I?"

Emmy observed the exchange with interest. She took his arm silently and let him lead her toward the dining room, but she could not keep back the question for long. "Don't like each other much, do you?"

Connor sighed as much at the question as her unusual phrasing. "Honestly nae, we ha' ne'er been truly amiable to each other."

"A simple 'never have, never will' probably covers it, huh?"

A sharp, rusty laugh of surprise escaped him once again. "Indubitably."

She was unable to stop the question that followed. "Why don't you get along?"

"Perhaps because facing her every day has been a constant reminder of the humiliations ye once served me."

His voice was low and pleasant but the flash of anger in his eyes told another story.

As they entered the dining room, Connor bypassed the chair at the foot of the table and propelled Emmy forward to seat her at his right hand. Though Emmy saw no problem with this, displeasure showed clearly on Dorcas' face. Other places were taken around the table leaving the foot unoccupied before Emmy figured out why. "Shouldn't I be sitting down there if I am supposed to be your wife?"

"I cannae converse with ye way down there and I feel nae need to entertain anyone else." He signaled the waiting servants to begin their service. "And, alas, I feel that I maun *try* to speak with ye."

Emmy waited as a footman placed her napkin in her lap and stepped back before leaning toward him. "Well, don't put yourself out there if it hurts so much," she murmured drily.

Connor did not answer but looked around the table. She followed his gaze, watching his family chat with one another. None tried to address him directly. She wondered at that. Why would no one speak to him? Was he really such a bear that no one dared?

Shaking her head, she looked down at her elaborate place setting. She realized she only knew what to do with about fifty percent of the forks, maybe three-quarters of the spoons. Why did she need three glasses? She had been to plenty of formal dinners throughout medical school and during her interviewing process, but none of those up-scale restaurants had been as sophisticated as this.

She glanced around the table to get a clue about where to start. Giving up, she decided to work from the outside in and hope for the best.

Leaning toward Connor so her words wouldn't carry

down the table, she suggested, "How about we talk about why you are having this big formal dinner when it is crystal clear that you hate every moment of it?"

XXXXX

The question startled Connor. He turned to her to find her gorgeous face just inches away. The strong beauty of her features nearly took his breath away. Strangely again he didn't remember her being so lovely although Dorcas was there each day as a reminder.

That first sight of her when he'd entered the drawing room had almost had him tripping over his own feet. She was the bonniest thing he'd ever seen. The gown she wore heightened the natural bounty of her figure, accenting her tiny waist, full hips and pushing her glorious bosom to the edge of the square neckline of the bodice.

She was waiting expectantly for a response to her question, which in the face of her splendor he could not remember. "My apologies, what did ye say?"

Heather forked up a large piece of her first course and savored the buttery flavor of the fish. "You don't like the clothes and fancy dinner," she said around the mouthful. "It's painfully obvious. So why do you do it?"

The warmth that had filled him only moments before vanished into irritation. "My dear wife, ye more than anyone should ken why I do all this."

"Pretending *once again*, that I am not your Heather, why don't you humor me?" Her voice was hard and uncompromising.

Why did she insist on preserving this charade? Any fool could see that she was Heather. She was Dory's identical twin. What point was there in denying it?

Still, the temper flaring in her eyes was arousing beyond belief, but Connor was determined to crush any attraction he felt for this woman who betrayed him so long ago. "I believe one of yer greatest complaints aboot Duart was that we were a horde of uncultured heathens who couldnae even dine properly. Seemingly we wisnae refined enough for ye."

"You suffer through all of *this*... every night? Just to prove that you're not a heathen to someone who hasn't even been around to notice?" She stabbed her fork into her food and lifted it, waving it at him as a governess might wave a chiding finger. "Connor MacLean you have baggage, my friend. Serious baggage."

"Baggage?" His flash of anger faded at her curious statement.

"Deep, dark, serious, emotional baggage."

"Enlighten me. What is baggage?"

"You know, all those scarred, debilitating moments that you are carrying around with you and allow to rule your life." She waved the fork again. "Baggage. You need to let it go, honey."

"Let it go?" *Let it go?*

The words echoed in his mind while she slipped from her wine glass as she hadn't tilted his world on its axis. She wanted him, if he understood her implication well enough, to just forget what had happened between them? That day had been a defining moment in his life. The moment when he had gone from being a happy-go-lucky youth to the man he was today.

How was one to simply 'let it go'?

Instead of allowing himself to slide easily into the fury that such a blasé approach to his degradation would normally have caused, Connor reined himself in. He spent the next four courses silently pondering her statement, and her person as well.

Heather had changed these past ten years. Gone was the haughty girl he'd known and in her place was an introspective, if somewhat pedestrian, woman. She didn't even use the correct forks or pick at morsels like most women he knew. She actually ate and with gusto. Often, making comments with a full mouth. She was common and familiar in her speech and had lost all refinement in her accent, adopting that flat American intonation though there was also a trace of what he knew as the accent of their southern states.

And she pried into his private matters as if it was a normal event to speak of them.

And he found it all… charming, he thought with surprise.

From the expectant glances she occasionally sent him, she expected some sort of response to her advice, if it could be called that. In spite of her casual attitude to their shared past, she did not seem interested in raising his ire. Rather, she was merely curious about why he still 'carried' it with him.

Like baggage. Hmm, he thought. It was an interesting analogy.

"Heather?" he asked in a low voice meant to carry no farther than to her. "How does one 'let it go', as ye so delightfully put it?"

She didn't answer immediately or flippantly as he would have expected, but instead responded an almost scholarly way. "There are many schools of thought on this subject, Connor. Unfortunately, I am not a psychologist or psychiatrist… I did not enjoy that aspect of medicine a great deal, but I would have to say in most cases it all boils down to one simple truth. A key."

Dorcas motioned for the ladies to retire and Heather was forced to stand as the footman pulled back her chair. He rose and caught her arm before she could turn away. "And what is the key?"

"Forgiveness, Connor," she answered softly and left the room holding her skirts up a bit too far in front of her so she wouldn't trip on them.

Connor sat down hard in his chair and leaned back, stunned. Taking a long pull on the whisky that had been poured for him—he never liked brandy despite Dorcas's insistence that it be served to the gentlemen following dinner —he tried to ponder the idea.

Forgiveness. Could it truly be so simple?

Surely not.

9

The ladies chatted with one another in small groups while Emmy circled the perimeter of the room around them. The men hadn't returned to the parlor but were instead enjoying brandy and cigars after dinner, Dorcas explained when asked. Emmy didn't know Connor too well, but hoped he wasn't in there smoking. Just the thought almost made her nauseous. She shuddered. Lord, she hoped not.

Surveying the parlor, she noted the ladies had broken into several different groups, divided by age. Drinking yet more tea. One of the younger cousins was playing the grand piano in the corner while another accompanied with her on a nearby harp. The softly played music was a pleasant backdrop to the buzz of conversation.

Though Emmy was given many curious stares, no one tried to engage her in conversation as she passed by. Not surprising but, wondering what a Victorian gentlewoman talked about in her spare time, she drew closer to a group to listen. One of the older ladies, Connor's Aunt Millie, she thought, was relating a story of her youth and mentioned how her mother had died when Millie was just sixteen.

"It was difficult enough when she died but even more so entering into marriage with no mother to guide me."

"What did she die of, Millie?" Emmy asked with an academic curiosity as to what the causes of death were to young women in the nineteenth-century.

"I beg your pardon?" the older woman asked, twisting to face her.

"I'm sorry," Emmy apologized. "I wasn't trying to be rude. I was just curious about the cause of her death. I'm sure it must have been hard on you, losing your mom. I lost mine when I was nineteen. She had breast cancer."

The ladies' gossip all fluttered to a halt. As a flock, they turned to Emmy. "I know." She nodded feeling all their eyes on her. "It was terrible. She had a double mastectomy early on." Brows drew together on several ladies' faces. "She had both breasts removed," she explained quickly, drawing more gasps. "Years of chemo and radiation treatments, but in the end…"

"I'm sorry, dear, I must have misunderstood you. What did you say?" Aunt Millie asked, raising a hand to halt Emmy's detailing of her mother's cancer treatments.

"I said my mother had both breasts removed, but in the end still died of breast cancer," she repeated in a loud slow voice, wondering if the woman was hard-of-hearing.

A low murmur went around the room, the music stopped and Millie fanned herself frantically.

Puzzled, Emmy frowned at them. "What? Oh, I know breast cancer used to have this shameful taboo about it, not to be talked about, but we are all modern women, aren't we?" She waved her hand dismissively but remembered that as recently as the 1950's and 60's, breast cancer had been a subject rarely discussed. It'd once been considered ridiculously shameful or some such nonsense, she recalled now.

A hush settled on the room and the women's eyes turned to the doorway. Emmy turned as well to find Connor glowering at her from the doorway. He cocked his finger at her, signaling she should follow him out of the room. Still oddly intrigued by the upset among the ladies, she followed him out the door.

Connor took her by the elbow and ushered her farther down the hall until they were out of earshot. Leaning back against the wall, she watched with some amusement as he tried to figure out what to say.

"My love, I understand that ye ha' been away for some time, perhaps even away from polite society for that time, but surely ye hae no' forgotten how to make civil conversation?"

"It's a disease, Connor, nothing more shocking than that. I know it used to be kept a secret like there was some personal shame in being so afflicted but, really." she humored him.

"I dinnae believe it was yer reference to the disease in and of itself that has upset them," he rebuked her casual absurdity.

"What? Breast cancer... Breast? This isn't about some absurd Victorian sensibility about body parts, is it?" She joked, thinking such a thing could not seriously disturb him.

"This is nae laughing matter, Heather." He waved her off as she started to deny the name. "A lady converses upon the weather and social events. I cannae ha' ye speaking of such crudities in front of the ladies of this house."

"Crudities? How can you even say that? It isn't a crudity;

it is a body part, a breast!"

"Heather!"

Emmy cupped her breasts in her own hands and insisted, "Breasts, Connor. Body parts. Basic anatomy."

"Heather, I am warning ye…"

"I am not Heather! I am Emmy MacKenzie and I am a doctor, an OB for crying out loud! A breast is a breast is a breast and I'll be damned if I'm going to pussyfoot around basic anatomy to cater to the 'tender sensibilities' of a bunch of women who need to get out and get a life!" she snapped right back at him.

"Ye will cease this nonsense," he barked.

Emmy glared at him for a brief moment and then rolled her eyes. "Breast, breast, breast, breast…" she childishly chanted as she rocked her head back and forth with each syllable. She was being ridiculous but he'd driven her to this absurdity. "Breast, breast, breast…"

XXXXX

My God, she was exasperating, Connor thought. Difficult, a wee bit annoying, and utterly delicious in her indignation. When had she begun to be so outspoken? And to keep saying it over and over? Each reiteration of the word in question focused his attentions away from the offense to the ladies of his house and more entirely on the aforementioned body part still cupped in her hands. Her breasts cupped in her own hands. The word pounded through his head.

"Breast, breast…"

Her breasts were *marvelous*, he thought. Large, full and ripe.

What he wanted was those breasts in his own hands.

Without conscious thought, he reached for them.

She squawked to a halt as Connor's big hands cupped her breasts roughly. He pushed her up against the wall, pinning her there with his body as his rough fingers kneaded her flesh.

He must have stunned her into silence, for she spoke no more. Even so, she didn't protest. No, she heedlessly leaned into his hands. Staring down into her wide-eyed surprise, Connor was shocked by his own actions, but more so by her acceptance.

Her encouragement. Her eyes grew warm and her hands covered his as if to hold them there. He pressed against her more fully, reveling in the contact of their hips and thighs. Bending his head, he nuzzled her neck, savoring the intoxicating perfume she wore. Most women he knew wore the scent of a single extract, roses, lavender, but her scent was an exotic blend of citrus, floral and spice, light and heady. Complex, just as she was.

Connor leaned back and met her eyes once more, acknowledging her arousal and his own. She licked her lips as if to prepare for his kiss and suddenly he wanted nothing more.

"Heather, my love," he whispered huskily.

XXXXX

Harsh reality settled on Emmy as she realized what he said and where they were.

What was she thinking?

She couldn't believe she was allowing a near stranger to fondle her and in a hallway where anyone could see them as well! Granted, it'd been years since she'd been held in strong male arms, years she since felt real desire. With this man, she felt it in spades and wanted oh so badly to be wrapped in his strength, to feel his passion.

Madness! He thought her his wife, absent these past ten years. He didn't want her, he wanted his Heather.

Emmy drew in a shaky breath. Shifting away slightly, she wriggled out of his arms and then turned back to him. She found she couldn't meet his eyes as embarrassment washed over her.

"Well, that was… *um*…" Words couldn't describe. "Well then, we're agreed, I guess. I won't say words that disturb other people and you won't… do what you were doing." Her eyes drifted over the ceiling, walls, anywhere but him. "Agreed? *Um*… good. Good night then."

She backed away to the stairs before turning to flee up them.

She didn't look back until she reached the top. Pausing to glance over her shoulder, she saw him waiting at the bottom of the stairs, one foot on the lowest tread as if he were going to follow.

When their eyes met, Emmy was burned by the heated passion she read there. She hesitated. She could feel his want and desire even from the distance. Years of loneliness washed over her, and she knew she wanted him as well.

She could either open her arms to it and embrace it or run like the nervous chicken that quivered inside her.

She ran.

Once in her room, Emmy flung herself on the bed in a tangle of skirts and, closing her eyes, moved her hands to where his were moments ago. Her breasts felt swollen and tingling, her lust was high and aching. She knew that, for the first time in her life, she'd be willing to have sex with a man she'd just met.

This is where one-night stands came from, she thought. This kind of insanity.

But then, she couldn't imagine one mere night satisfying the yearning she felt. Emmy pressed the heels of her palms to her eyes and groaned.

"I am such a fool."

Connor didn't want her, Emmy, he wanted his wife. Oh, but she wanted him more than she had ever wanted a man, more than she could ever have *imagined* wanting a man. Right or wrong, she wasn't sure if she would be able to fight it.

XXXXX

Connor stood at the door that separated her bedchamber from their shared parlor, his hand raised, ready to knock.

This was madness.

He drew his hand back in a frustrated fist. He shouldn't want her so badly. Where was his anger? Where was the wrath that had burned within him these past ten years? He'd chased her across continents when she fled, not because he loved her but rather because he wanted to bring her back here and publicly divorce her. He'd wanted her humiliation in exchange for his. He wanted to watch her suffer as he once did.

Where was that vengeance now? Lost in the face of overwhelming lust?

When he'd seen Heather at his front gates yesterday, he would've thought that he'd gladly put her to a trial by fire for her sins of the past. Instead, he lifted her into his arms, stared down into her lovely face and felt almost sorry that he'd frightened her. He'd wanted insanely to protect her and had been more angered by himself than her in that moment.

Though Connor knew the mere sight of her should still

enrage him, he also conceded that he wanted to hold her and shelter her. He wanted to make love to her, passionately, tenderly.

Madness, he thought again.

"I hae lost my mind," he murmured aloud and raised his fist again to knock upon her door.

By all rights, he could go in and have her, knowing that she wanted him as well. She had responded to his touch. Had welcomed it, even. But as he started to reach for the door, he knew he couldn't do it. So much had changed. *She* had changed. He felt drawn to her in ways he had never imagined, much less experienced. Apart from her crazy insistence that she was not who everyone knew she was, Heather was a much deeper person today than she had been ten years ago.

Maybe that maturity and this attraction were worth exploring.

He pushed away from the door and headed to his room.

The sound of metal scraping against brick woke Emmy late the next morning. Margo stoked the fire into a roaring blaze but one arm out from beneath the covers told her the room was still cold and felt as damp as the cold October air outside probably did.

"Ugh," Emmy moaned, rolling over and snuggling deep beneath the covers.

She'd barely slept last night. Desire and unsatisfied lust had kept her awake for most of it. Other troubling thoughts had her tossing and turning for the rest.

How did she get here? How was she supposed to get back? What was she supposed to do about Connor? Here was a troubled guy who a little basic therapy could probably do a world of good for.

She had the feeling that underneath all that angst and anger was a romantic; a really great guy who just wanted someone to love, and be loved in return. She wondered what it would be like to be that lucky woman. What it would be like to have a man of such strong emotions direct love in your direction?

Probably the most fulfilling feeling in the world, she thought, and she found she envied the woman who might someday be the recipient of that devotion.

Emmy groaned again at her idiocy. What was she thinking? She'd only known the man for one day, for Pete's sake. It was just lust. She didn't want anything more than that. Her heart rebelled with a lurch and she felt an overwhelming urge to save Connor from himself. For herself.

"Margo, what time is it?"

"A bit after noon, milady," the maid answered. "Mrs. MacLean said I should let ye sleep since ye'd traveled and such. But luncheon is to be served soon and ye'll want to be up for that."

Remembering the never-ending parade of food that had comprised the five-course dinner the night before, Emmy stifled yet another moan. Too much food. She couldn't eat like that every meal of every day. She'd weigh as much as a horse in no time.

"I don't suppose it would be possible to just get a bowl of cereal around here?"

"Milady?"

"Nothing, nothing."

Emmy finger-combed her long hair as she climbed out of bed, allowing Margo to help her into a robe and shoving her feet into some slippers to keep them off the cold floor.

"Why do you keep calling me that, anyway?" she asked on her way to the bathroom.

"Milady?" Margo questioned. "'Tis only proper. Ye are the countess after all."

"*Ah*, that's right."

Emmy stared at herself in the mirror and wrinkled her nose. Her eyes were rimmed red with dark circles below. She looked as bad as she felt.

The countess. It had an ominous ring to it. Of course, in this time and place, the earl and countess didn't even share a bedroom. If she *were* the countess in truth...

She drew herself up short, rejecting the thought. That was not what she wanted. She had her new job waiting for her at a women's clinic in Baltimore, a job that she had worked hard and sacrificed much for. There was a new life as a practicing physician before her. She had plans.

"Mrs. MacLean and Susan will be arriving shortly wi' more gowns for ye to choose from. The laird sent for the seamstress to come later this week to fit ye wi' some clothes of yer own," Margo went on, unaware of Emmy's turbulent thoughts.

He did, huh?

A sharp rap at the door announced the arrival of Dorcas and her maid bearing an armload of clothes. Emmy moved to help as the young woman laid the pile on the bed, earning a surprised glance from both women.

"Thanks, Dorcas, I appreciate the loan of the clothes. I hope I'm not leaving you short in your own closet though."

"Not at all," she replied shortly. "These are just basic foundations, shirtwaists and skirts for day wear that I am currently unable to wear because of my delicate condition, so there is plenty for you to choose from."

"Delicate condition?" Emmy repeated and then frowned at the other woman. "Oh, you mean your pregnancy?"

Dorcas flushed hotly. "Yes, Mr. MacLean and I are expecting our first child."

Emmy eyed Dorcas's figure critically with the eye of an

OB. Well along but with a while to go. "When are you due then? In the spring?"

"I am not sure, of course, but I expect perhaps six weeks or so." Dorcas was still blushing and refusing to meet Emmy's gaze.

"You don't know? Haven't you seen a doctor?" Emmy's eyes widened. "Six weeks? Are you telling me that you are nearly eight months pregnant?"

"This isn't a topic for polite conversation."

Waving her off imperiously, she repeated, "Seriously? Eight months?"

"I believe so." Dory frowned at her incredulous tone.

"No way!"

To Emmy's mind, she didn't look more than six months pregnant or early in her seventh. There was no way she was heading into her ninth soon! A thought struck her. "Dory, are you wearing a corset?"

"Of course. The correct foundations are criti—"

"Dorcas MacLean," Emmy interrupted in her most superior doctor's voice. "You should not be wearing that when you are pregnant. The baby must have room to grow. And to not know how far along you are? To have not seen a doctor? Well." She flung her hands in outrage. "*I* will examine you then."

"What?"

"What?" the maids echoed.

She ignored them all and continued in a more professional tone now that the astonishment was fading. "Dory, I am a Johns-Hopkins trained doctor. I deliver babies and take care of expectant mothers for a living. It's what I do. You must let me check to make sure you are doing alright. Especially if you have been wearing that corset for what?

Almost eight months?"

Dorcas backed uneasily toward the door. "I don't think..."

Emmy grinned an evil little grin. She couldn't help it. There was something rather pleasing in jostling Dory out of her normal state of condemnation. "But surely you trust your own sister to help you, don't you?"

Dory fled, but Emmy was determined to win in the end. Imagine not having basic health care during pregnancy. And if there were no doctors nearby, it made her wonder what they did in cases of basic illness. Did they even have aspirin yet?

She peppered Margo and Susan with those questions as they dressed her in the daily wear similar to that she had seen Dory in that first day. A high-necked blouse which Emmy refused to button all the way up, a dark blue wool skirt under which she allowed only one petticoat. No corset. And her own boots rather than the torturous, skinny-toed little shoes they presented.

It would have to do. She was not in this for the long haul and refused to suffer the constraint of that corset any more than she had to. She'd had to call for help last night just to get ready for bed, for Christ's sake.

An hour later, she was finally able to go down for lunch only to learn that Connor rarely joined the others for any meal other than dinner. She wondered where and when he ate.

Picking her way through three formal courses, finding moderately healthy fish and vegetables t to eat among the heavy sauces, she did her best to eat a modest portion, remembering that an even larger meal would follow that night. She was thankful to have been seated near Dory where she could pester her freely.

"You really shouldn't keep that corset cinched up all the time," Emmy told her firmly. "It isn't good for that baby and I am telling you right now; it must stop."

"I've been having pains when I don't wear it," Dory confessed in a low voice, though clearly uncomfortable with the conversation. "They frighten me. It seemed easier this way."

She took the woman's hand compassionately. "Sure, it might be easier, but don't you want to have a healthy baby, Dory?"

"Of course I do." After an anxious glance around to make sure no one could overhear her, she added, "but Ian hasn't visited me since I found out. I don't want to appear even more unattractive to him."

"Visited you? Oh!." The realization struck Emmy as Dory flushed furiously scarlet. Really, Dory was a bit of a... well, prig, to use the British phrase. Stereotypical Victorian. She chewed thoughtfully on a bit of bread. "How long have you been married to Ian?" she asked, trying to backpedal from the topic that made Dory so uncomfortable.

"Almost nine years now," she replied, clearly thankful for the change of subject. "I came here shortly after Heather left; after my father died. Ian and I married almost immediately."

"So you've been married for nine years and this is your first pregnancy?"

Dory shook her head uncomfortably. "Well, no. I lost three babies before this one."

"Well, I would wager that Ian's reluctance to 'visit' you has less to do with your appearance and more to do with fear."

"Fear?"

"Naturally he's afraid that any intercourse between you might prompt another miscarriage." She shook her head. "Dory, I'll talk to Ian…"

"Oh, you mustn't!" she protested, glancing fearfully up the table at her husband.

"Oh, but I must," Emmy countered firmly. "I will help you take care of yourself and help him take care of you, too. Stressing out over this thing with Ian isn't going to help you carry this one to term."

"Oh, dear," Dory muttered, twisting her napkin in her lap.

"After nine years of marriage, Ian can surely accept that pregnancy will change your body if he loves you enough." With a pause, she considered that idea. This was another century after all. "Does he? Do you? I mean, did you marry for love or some misguided arranged thing?"

"I loved Ian the moment I saw him," Dory declared with obvious sincerity. "And I know he feels the same."

"Well, I'll talk to him then," Emmy assured her with a professionally compassionate pat on her hand. "In the meantime, I'll work on a diet and exercise schedule for you that will work with what's available here and, of course, I will have to examine you at some point. But, I'm serious. No more corsets."

"I must wear something, um, Heather." She looked uncomfortable for the first time addressing her as such.

"Leave that to me," Emmy assured her. "I think I have an idea that might do the trick."

After luncheon, she gathered Margo and Susan into her room. Taking one of Dory's older corsets, she had the maids first remove the steel boning. With a few quick sketches and a visual demonstration on her own bra, she showed them how they could convert the corset into a short bustier that was secured by a shorter series of lacing up the back. It extended only a few inches below the bust but gave Dory's bosom the support Dory would never go without under her white blouses. Combined with a heavier chemise, perhaps it would provide enough layers to allow Dory enough security to forgo the corset.

11

Leaving the women to their work, Emmy begged a coat from the butler and decided to take a walk down by the water. This time, she went around the right side of the castle and along the edge of the low wall that stretched perpendicular to the castle until it tapered away. Here the grade to the lower plain was still steep and rocky but traversable. Gathering all her skirts up in one hand, she used her other hand for balance as she picked her way down the slope. Inwardly laughing at the sight she presented, she was grateful to drop the skirts when she got to the bottom.

The plain area stretched about a hundred feet to the water's edge. Off to her right, just behind the castle, the terrain was rocky but to the left, where the shoreline curved in, there was a pebbled beach where the waters of the sound lapped gently against the rocks.

Emmy headed in that direction, marveling at the beauty of the October afternoon. The overcast skies of the previous day were gone, leaving blue skies with just a few high clouds.

The air was crisp and cool with a gentle breeze. The waters in the sound were fairly calm; the coastline of mainland Scotland was clear and seemed closer than the long ferry ride had suggested.

This is what she had come to Scotland to see, to feel. Rugged beauty. It seemed so untouched. The power lines that had looped their way along the shore on her arrival were absent, leaving her view of the Sound unobscured.

The wind was brisk and, as she drew in a deep breath, she found the chill of the air in her lungs to be energizing in contrast to the peaceful feeling the natural stillness around her inspired.

Drowsiness from the big lunch and lack of sleep faded away. Margo told her that most of the ladies of the castle took long naps in the afternoon, which she thought curious before, but now understood. Such a big meal did leave a person thinking about sleeping it off, but it was a bad habit.

A vigorous walk was a much healthier response, she thought, as she continued up the coastline in long strides.

The sounds of activity from the castle faded as she continued. There were no signs of other people, and she felt for a moment like the only person on earth. Her mind calmed; the mental churning of the past thirty-six hours receded against the call of the gulls and roar of the wind and water. No machinery, just nature. She wasn't sure she had ever heard such a complete absence of technology. No hum of airplanes or cars. No one talking on their cell phone. Emmy breathed in the fresh, clean air and closed her eyes. Just peace.

Of course, it wasn't meant to last. It was not long before the sound of hoof beats had Emmy looking north up the coast expectantly. Two riders approached. As they neared, she recognized Connor and Ian.

What magnificent men they were. Real men.

Oh, plenty of the male residents she had worked with had worked out at the gym regularly, but none of them had the natural manliness these brothers displayed. Despite the lack of convenience in the nineteenth century, perhaps there was something to be said for this time.

The men pulled up their horses next to her and dismounted. Their garb was more formal today. Jackets, vests, ties, and hats, as well. Though it all hung easily from Ian's relaxed frame, Emmy thought Connor seemed as uncomfortable in it as he had in his evening wear the night before.

Ian gave her a formal little bow. "My lady. How goes yer day? I am surprised that ye'd venture out into this cold when few ladies would do so."

Since it was probably near fifty degrees, Emmy wasn't sure how to respond to that so offered only, "It's a beautiful day. I did not sleep well last night at all." She slanted a look toward Connor. "I thought the cool breeze would be refreshing. What have you guys been up to today?"

Ian looked uncomfortable with the question. "We visited one of our neighbors this afternoon."

He glanced uncertainly at Connor, who showed no hesitation in responding. "I hae been courting the daughter of one of our neighbors and thought it fitting to gi' them the courtesy of a personal visit to inform them of yer return before they heard of it through the gossip mills."

Emmy stared at him as the word sunk in. "Courting? As in dating?"

"I dinnae know this word 'dating' ye use, but aye, courting." He gave her a hard look. "I was considering marrying again… until ye returned, of course."

She arched a brow. "Of course. I'm not much of a legal mind, but wouldn't that be considered bigamy?"

"It's been widely accepted for some time, my love," Connor clarified, "that ye met wi' some misfortune over the past ten years since no one had seen or heard from ye in all that time. None of the investigators we hired were able to find signs of ye. I myself traveled to the Americas twice in search of ye."

"I'm not…"

Connor waved his hand, cutting her denial short. "I dinnae wish to hear yer arguments and denials again today."

"Maybe I wish to voice them!" Emmy countered, hands on her hips, ready to do battle.

"Perhaps I should leave ye to yer argument," Ian turned away, leading his horse.

She glared at Connor but turned to Ian. "Actually Ian, I'd like to talk to you about something, if you have a moment."

"To me?"

"Yes, a little something has come up with Dory."

"She's well?" he asked anxiously. "Nothing has happened?"

"She's fine," she assured him quickly. The look of panic on his face said a great deal. Clearly he cared deeply for his wife, which would be useful since he would be more likely to sacrifice for her wellbeing. "Just something else, if you don't mind a quick walk together?"

"No' at all." He looked relieved and offered her his arm.

"Shoo, Mr. Cranky-Pants." Emmy waved off Connor with a frown as he scowled down at them. "We don't need any more of your negative vibes around right now."

"Cranky-Pants?" Connor echoed with a haughtily raised brow.

"Just go." She made little shooing motions with her hands. "Go!" He shrugged and remounted in a smooth motion that impressed her. Taking the reins for Ian's mount, he spurred them into motion back to the castle.

XXXXX

What just happened, Connor wondered as he rode away. He hadn't intended to fight with Heather today. The visit to the neighboring estate had been an uncomfortable one and he'd been awash with irritation over that unpleasant duty on the entire ride back to Duart.

And there had been Heather. Walking along the coast, looking lovely beyond belief in the afternoon sun with her cheeks and nose reddened by the cold winds. She looked so relaxed and comfortable... so cheerful in fact that she'd immediately rubbed him the wrong way.

Why should this be so easy for her when she was turning his life upside down? She didn't seem to care that she'd interrupted the course of his life with her return.

And then to deny her identity once again! It'd been the last straw.

Connor galloped back toward the castle, aware that Heather and Ian's eyes followed him along the way. He fumed silently once again.

And what were negative vibes?

12

"What are negative vibes?" Ian asked, clearly unable to contain his curiosity as they turned to stroll farther north.

"You know," Emmy said, waving her hand. "His nasty little habit of bringing everything down to a fight when others just want to go happily along their way."

"Ye hae developed an interesting way of speech in yer absence," he noted. "'Tis most curious."

"Let's not have you take up his fight right now, okay?"

"He likes ye, ye ken?" Ian said, allowing the subject to change.

Her heart raced like a schoolgirl's at the possibility, though her mind denied it. "What? That's ridiculous." Want her, yes. Like her, no. Nobody ever said the two had to go hand in hand. There was certainly little else about her that he seemed to care for. Indeed, all they'd done so far was fight. "Not that I believe you, but why do you say that?"

"Oh, wee comments he made today." Ian shrugged. "He seems to admire yer forthright commentary and new earthiness."

Emmy's eyes widened in surprise. It was hard to imagine Connor voicing admiration. She'd seen something like it in his eyes, but assumed it only masculine appreciation for her looks. Other than that, his dark eyes reflected either anger or desire every time she met his gaze, even just now. He was angry with his wife and it showed.

He wanted her. It showed in the deep turbulent heat of his brown eyes. And it angered him more. When he'd had her backed up to the wall the night before, the want and need in his eyes had been so compelling she had almost lost her self-control.

"He does?" She tried for a nonchalant tone.

"Aye, ye used to be much more like Dorcas. More serious-minded."

"*Hmm.*" She shook the lustful thoughts off and tucked that all away to think about later. "Well, Dory is what I wanted to talk to you about. But first, I am curious, how did you meet?"

"Dorcas arrived about ten months or so after ye left… verra well," Ian sighed at her arch look, "after Heather left. She'd no' been able to come for the wedding as their mother had been ill and then she stayed home afterward to nurse their father through the illness that ye… Heather's departure provoked. A sickness of the heart, I understand. When he died, the properties no' entailed came into Connor's possession as her sister's husband since Heather was the elder daughter and there were nae other heirs. Dory was his responsibility at that point so, naturally, she came here to live."

Another dependent here to live off the earl. There was she wished to say about relatives who came to Duart to sponge off Connor but kept her opinions to herself.

"So she came here, met you and you married," she summed it up.

"Aye, that's aboot it."

"What did Connor think of that?" she couldn't resist asking.

"He wisnae here when she arrived," Ian confessed, looking a bit regretful. "He'd gone to London searching for… regardless, he wisnae here. By the time he returned, I'd already asked Dorcas to be my wife." He stared pensively off over the waters, shoving his hands deep in his pockets. "Ye should hae seen him when he returned and first saw her here. He naturally thought her to be Heather and his rage was terrible. 'Twas years before he would… *could* address her directly. I confess they hae ne'er gotten along well as I am sure ye can tell, but Dorcas…" He trailed off with a little sigh.

"You love her," she confirmed with some amazement, for it seemed he loved her dearly despite her prickly manner.

"Verra much." He grinned sheepishly. "She is nae as stern on the inside as she portrays in public. She's softhearted, if somewhat proper and believes deeply in the rules of our society. She simply likes things to be as they should."

"We call that anal and neurotic where I come from," Emmy muttered to herself. "So you love her and she's pregnant now," she went on aloud, and then paused as Ian blushed. Obviously such talk wasn't only taboo among the women of Duart. "But it seems that Dory has been risking her health and that of your child in an attempt to keep herself from appearing unattractive to you."

"What?" he questioned in surprise. "I dinnae understand."

"You haven't had sex since she found out she was pregnant," Emmy said matter-of-factly, and had trouble hiding her amusement as Ian stammered and blushed.

"Bugger, Connor said ye were more forthright!" he choked in understatement, unable to meet her gaze directly.

"Yeah, well." She shrugged. "I've never really seen the point of beating around the bush." Plus it was sort of amusing to watch the shocked faces of those around her when she said something like that. "The point is, Dory feels that you don't find her attractive in her pregnancy. She thinks that she needs to camouflage it as much as possible by still wearing her corset. But she's not doing the baby any favors."

"That woman!" Ian shook his head ruefully. "I'd nae idea she felt that way. She's ne'er been one to... well, she's ne'er been as forthright as ye are. That maddening woman!" He ran a hand through his hair. "Naturally I feel the same attraction toward her as ever. But she's already lost three bairns..."

"I'm not saying that you're not justified in your fears, Ian," she went on as he trailed off, patting his arm. "Given her history, you do need to be careful. You are right to be cautious. Without having examined her, I cannot say to what extent. But I am pretty sure you're a creative enough man to realize there are a whole boatload of activities that can take place in a bedroom without involving actual intercourse."

She shot him a wink and dimpled her cheek in a suggestive smile. He blushed and blustered again in a way she had never seen on a grown man and she laughed out loud.

"Yer mouth, woman! 'Tis almost too much to contend wi'," he complained.

"Alright, alright." Emmy lifted her hands playfully to ward him off. "I'll try to lay off the shock factor with you. Seriously though, I think I can get her to lay off the corset but her stress over this whole situation between the two of you isn't good for her or the baby. I'm sure a little extra affection and a big 'O' will go a long way toward mellowing her out a bit."

She gave him a nudge towards the castle with an encouraging smile. "Go on, Ian. Git 'er done."

Ian got the gist of what she was saying and started back to the castle at a trot, shaking his head. About a hundred yards away though he suddenly stopped and stared back at her. "A big 'O'!" He let out a loud snort and laughed heartily. "*Och*, lass, that is prime good humor!" He waved a hand at her and continued home.

Emmy laughed as he finally caught on. How... *Victorian* they were when it came to discussing the human condition. No talk of body parts or sex out loud lest you make someone uncomfortable. Well, with sex mentioned on TV every twenty seconds or so, she supposed it was easy to become immune to what were once considered inappropriate topics. Between Dr. Phil and Oprah, there had been no topic left unexplored.

Mentally shrugging, she continued up the shoreline to a large rock where she took a seat and stared out over the water.

Farther northwest, a steamer was leaving the island and heading toward the mainland. It was nothing like the large ferry she'd taken packed with eighty cars and nearly a thousand people. It was much smaller and probably didn't carry many vehicles, if any at all.

She wagered it took much longer than the forty-five minutes her modern ferry had taken as well. No power lines, no big ferry and probably no big pier in Craignure to dock said big ferry at. She was definitely out of her own time. Out of her element. She couldn't even have a conversation without shocking someone. Pulling her legs up, she wrapped her arms around her knees and propped her chin on them.

What was she to do? Did she even have a choice? If she kept trying to convince Connor that she wasn't Heather and he finally believed her, what would happen to her? Would he kick her out of the castle? Where would she go? The questions mounted in her mind. It was terrifying, this uncertainty. If she were a weaker-willed person, it might bring her to tears.

As it was, a tear of self-pity escaped and she reached up to wipe it away.

"Finally feeling some guilt over yer behavior?" Connor asked as he seated himself next to her.

Despite the fact she hadn't heard his approach, Heather didn't jump at his approach. But she did have a ready scowl for him.

"Just don't, Connor. Or do you not remember how to have a conversation that doesn't involve picking fights with people? Really, who was the last person you had a normal conversation with? Other than your brother," she added, as he started to answer.

He exhaled the start of his reply in a huff. "My solicitor, then," he replied.

"Okay, someone who isn't employed by you or completely cowed by you," she amended.

Connor paused a moment then admitted a bit sheepishly, "Ye've made yer point. I'll admit I may hae made a habit of being an aggressor in conversation. Perhaps wi'out even realizing that it was so."

"It's a classic defense mechanism," she said. "Once bitten, twice shy. The first strike mentality. I don't know the medical side too well, but you seem pretty textbook to me."

"I do?"

Connor had no idea what she was talking about but loved the soft husky sound of her voice. It flowed over him but did not soothe. Rather her voice thrummed across his senses birthing an awareness that he had not felt in many years.

While she frustrated him a great deal, in the end she almost brought peace to his mind when he allowed it. He felt alive and good. He'd forgotten how that felt. Despite the anger and arguments they seemed to have, he couldn't stay away from her. And, when Ian had returned without her, he could not resist coming after her.

"Let it go. Remember?" she whispered softly, resting her cheek against her knees so her face was turned toward him. "You are fairly likable when you relax a bit and I bet you'd do pretty well as a happy man."

"A happy man?" he repeated, as if the words were foreign to him.

Now how would that feel?

Good, he supposed.

Connor took her hand and flattened it between his two open palms. His skin tingled and warmed next to hers. This is why he could not stay away from her. Indeed, why he wanted her so. He was wholly enthralled by her. Two sleepless nights had shown him that. He knew that he should stay away from her, knew it and eschewed it. He wanted to be near her.

The morning had been a long one without seeing her. But it wasn't just desire any longer, he admitted to himself. He simply liked her. Liked that she felt comfortable enough with him, with everyone, not to put on a polite façade to the world. She was what she was. And despite her endless sarcasm and occasional biting remarks, she didn't seem to have a mean bone in her body. She wanted to help him despite the animosity that should have existed between them.

And how soft and comfortable she seemed today! She had been perched on the rock as he approached, with her knees to her chest and arms wrapped around them. Face turned to the sun and cast in its brilliance. She had not risen or thought to rise and greet him formally. She was just like that.

The breeze teased a strand of her long hair from its clasp, and it rippled almost hypnotically in the light wind. He wanted to touch it again to see if it was as soft as he remembered.

When it strayed farther to tease her cheek and nose, he took the opportunity to tuck it back behind her ear. Her bright blue eyes met his, wide with awareness. At the open neck of her blouse, he could see her pulse beating rapidly, tempting his fingers to trail down her throat to feel the throbbing as it increased. A slight smile turned the corner of her lips and his heart in turn.

Just that tiny gesture and he was hers. No anger, no angst. He felt a corresponding gladness well within him. Suddenly, he knew that being with her, making love to her would be the most liberating of experiences. The driving passion, pounding of hearts and bodies would be a balm to his soul as well as a release of body and desire.

XOXOXOX

"Tell me about the woman you were going to marry," Emmy asked. The look on his face was unsettling and, although she wondered desperately what he was thinking, she wasn't so brave as to voice *that* question. She shook away her curiosity. A distraction was definitely required. "Had you asked her already?"

"Mary Guthrie," he told her, entwining her fingers with his. He cleared his throat. "Nay, I'd nae asked for her hand yet. Her father owns Duart House no' far from here."

"Really? I thought the MacLeans owned all the land around here?" She tried to remember that page of her guidebook. Emmy glanced down at their joined hands. Electricity flowed from the contact but at the same time it was comforting. She squeezed his hand in return.

"We had," Connor confirmed. "My family had been on this land for three hundred years before we lost Duart while Charles II was in power. Then during the Jacobite rebellion, the castle was burned and left in ruin. The land itself was sold and resold until part was bought and built on. A Colonel Campbell built Duart House twenty years ago but lost his fortune in investments as a result of yer War Between the States and sold it to Arbuthnot Guthrie who owns it now. It was then that my father was able to finally buy back the castle which was little more than a shell at the time." He twisted and looked back at the castle. "We hae worked hard to restore it and rebuild it to what it is today. Only the outer walls of the castle are original. The entire interior has been entirely rebuilt. Ye'll notice the interior courtyard is much more modern than the outer walls."

"You've done a wonderful job," she praised freely.

"I hae merely continued the work of my father," he shrugged but squeezed her hand again in appreciation of her words. "The first dozen years were spent just rebuilding the structure itself. The interior has only been worked on these past eight or nine years." He paused as if waiting for the same old anger to come, but to her surprise, it didn't. "I had thought recently to do more. Mary Guthrie is her father's only daughter. If I couldnae purchase the entire property back from them, I might at least gain a portion through her dowry."

"You would've married her for land then?" Emmy asked, amazed.

He nodded and added, "And for money. It has taken much of our fortune to carry out the restoration thus far. It willnae last forever."

"Unbelievable," she muttered, tugging her hand away from him. With a sigh, he let it go.

"Aye, well, I married ye because my father asked it of me. Apparently there is no' much I'd no' do for my family." She turned to scowl at him but found amusement dancing in his eyes instead.

"That was rude," she fussed. "Frankly, I think you do too much for your family. How can you let them live with you like a bunch of bloodsuckers and not ask them to contribute anything in return? Do they flock here for a free ride?"

Understanding her basic question, Connor waved it away. "They are ladies and gentlemen... and my family. They are no' expected to work and 'tis my responsibility as laird to provide for them as I do for all those of my clan."

"Bullshit!" Emmy countered with wide eyes, clearly shocking him with her speech. "You don't even seem to like any of them! How can you tell me you don't feel like they are a weight hanging around your neck... and wallet? What happens when you don't have the fortune to support them all? Will you continue to be the only one working while they live in the lap of luxury, waited on hand and foot?"

He shrugged, unconcerned.

She blinked once then let out an amazed breath. "Wow, you are a bigger man than I am," she admitted with incredulity, shaking her head.

"I should hope so," he said, appalled.

"Wait a minute. Isn't Duart House called Talully or something like that now?"

"Torosay," Connor corrected. "Aye, Guthrie has said the two properties now owned by different families should be named differently to avoid confusion. He's named it Torosay Castle. Yet most locals still think of it as Duart House."

"I had tickets to that," she whispered forlornly, staring out over the sound.

"Tickets?" he wondered aloud, curious at what she meant by that.

"For the house, gardens, gallery and tearoom. Open from ten-thirty to five p.m.," she sighed.

"Guthrie is selling tickets to view his house? And gardens? *Och,* they are nothing worth spending a ha'penny on." He stood in outrage.

"Six and a half pounds," she corrected, thinking that messing with him like that might be far more amusing if she weren't so depressed by her situation.

"Bluidy hell! That is highway robbery," he sputtered, his already heavy brogue thickening.

"I know," she nodded sadly, unable to stop herself. "Duart was only about five pounds."

"Someone is selling tickets to view my home?" His confusion overrode the anger. "Who is doing this? Someone in Craignure? Oban?"

Emmy rose and took his hand, pulling him to his feet.

"You can get them on the Net, Connor."

"What net?"

"Never mind, Connor." She turned and tugged on his hand, pulling him back toward the castle. "It was just a joke."

"Yer new humor is often befuddling, Heather."

)()()()(

Connor shook his head as he allowed himself to be led back home. She claimed to be joking but her voice was wistful, even sad. He wondered for a moment what reasons she could have to be upset. What she might have left behind in coming to Duart?

Why return at all? She'd hated Duart. He'd spent the last ten years restoring what he saw as the reason she'd fled. Bringing the castle up beyond the hovel Heather labeled it when they first met.

He wanted to ask her, to get an honest answer, but felt certain she'd only to continue to spout nonsense to befuddle him more.

"I often understand nothing yer saying to me, ye know."

"Well things are pretty different where I come from, you know?"

"It seems so," he grunted. "I traveled through Baltimore once while I was looking for ye but dinnae think to stop there. Did ye truly attend the university there?"

"Yes, I did."

"'Twas a bonny city."

"Best crab bisque on the east coast," she bragged, perking up at the mention of her home. "And there is this one restaurant at the Inner Harbor where you can get the best steamed mussels. Good eats, baby."

She prattled on about restaurants and the food to be had

in Maryland as they walked back down the coastline hand in hand. Connor listened with half an ear, wondering if she had in fact eaten all the different foods she spoke of. Apparently she loved seafood, not deep-fried though—whatever that was—wine and even beer; a confession he had never heard a lady make. She spoke of the tourist attractions of the area as well, of things called the National Aquarium, Baltimore World Trade Center and the Hard Rock Café.

Plainly the place which brought her the greatest bliss was an oddity called Ben and Jerry's where one could get a thing called 'Half-Baked'. He wondered where he might find some as he imagined watching her eat such a treat. It would be a most sensual experience based on the look of rapture she wore just speaking of it.

Her casual interspersion of profanities continued to astound him. There was a part of him that was appalled by her base language. He'd never heard a woman curse so often as she. Fortunately, that part of him was growing smaller with each moment he spent in her company.

There was another part of him that was delighted by her; by the instant familiarity she projected to everyone she met. It was if she knew no stranger, knew no bounds for those she met.

XOXOXOX

Emmy stopped abruptly at the gate to the castle. The sun lighted the front and a glance over her shoulder confirmed it - the sun was setting. This was it. She'd missed it the previous afternoon while she napped, but here it was. She turned back to the castle and stared hard, willing the newly restored façade to crumble away to what she had seen over a hundred years in the future.

Nothing.

Damn. A part of her soul cried out for mercy from this befuddling situation as the questions that had tormented her for the past twenty-four hours began calling for answers once more.

"Are ye well, Heather?" Connor asked, concerned with her motionless concentration. "Perhaps the walk has been too much for ye?"

She shook her head as his words registered. "Too much for me?" she snorted. "That little walk? Are you kidding me? I've done the Susan G. Koman 3-day... twice. Too much for me indeed. You have an absurdly low opinion of women, did you know that?"

"'Tis nae completely unjustified," he reasoned, gesturing toward the castle as if to indicate the women inside.

"Well, just try not to keep lumping me in with the pack, alright?" she asked as they continued through the courtyard to the main door. "I am not your garden-variety damsel in distress, you know."

"The evidence is truly in yer favor, my dear," he allowed, standing aside with a sweep of his arm to allow her to precede him into the main hall.

Emmy let Chilton take her coat and allowed Connor to take her arm as they went up the stairs and through the hallways to the right wing where the laird's rooms were. In silence, they entered their shared sitting room and turned to face each other in silence, aware that they had just spent the past hour in each other's company holding hands and in pleasant conversation.

There had been no recriminations, no accusations. Just simple companionship.

Afraid she might say something to spoil it all, Emmy

started to turn toward her room. Connor caught her arm and turned her back around. He stared down at her for a long moment, his dark eyes full of warmth, affection and questions.

"Connor?" she whispered. "What…?"

"*Shh.*" He raised his hands to cup her still chilly cheeks, warming them in his palms. His thumbs caressed the soft skin there and stretched farther out to rub lightly along her lips.

Unbidden, her hand rose to rub against the abrasive growth of his beard. Her eyes lit with amusement as she curled her fingers to scratch his cheek much as his beard scratched her. Expectation raced along her spine and nerves as she stared up into his dark eyes savoring the feel of his thumb against her lower lip, but still he did nothing.

"Are you going to kiss me or not?" she asked in a low whisper.

Connor exhaled a low laugh and rested his forehead against hers. "I'm no' certain."

"Well," Emmy teased breathlessly, "you *have* already fondled my breasts so I don't think… *mmmph!*"

Connor ducked his head and covered her lips in a deep kiss, catching her up in his arms and pulling her body firmly up against his. Up on her toes, Emmy stretched both arms up and caught him around his shoulders, threading her fingers into his hair as she went. Their lips met and melded together as heat flared from the contact of their lips down to her toes.

Literally to my toes, she thought as she sank into the embrace with a sigh of bliss. Connor's firm lips pulled against her lower lip, sucking on it lightly as his palms slid up her sides coming to rest just below her breasts. He moaned and pulled back slightly and she stared up at him with a shocked expression breathing as heavily as he.

"Wow," she said simply.

"Aye." He turned her slightly and caught her fully in his arms and kissed her again.

Dimly, she heard a bell being rung in the distance but dismissed it. Instead, she parted her lips slightly, inviting him to deepen the kiss more but felt Connor's retreat even as she did so. Kissing her lightly one last time, he heaved a sigh heavy with regret.

"Heath…"

"So, I guess it's that time when we dress ourselves up and do dinner, huh?" Emmy jumped in before he said something that might set off her temper. "Another night of good times and great conversation?" He laughed and she joined him. "I'll do my best to keep it civilized."

"See that ye do," he joked in return.

"I guess I'll see you on the other side?"

Emmy turned and went into her room aware that Connor stared at her bedroom door for a long while; unaware of the confusion that rolled through him.

The dress she wore that evening was even lovelier than the one she had worn the previous night, Connor thought as Emmy finally entered the drawing room more than an hour later. He'd heard her singing to herself as she bathed and had spent nearly a half an hour at her door listening to her muffled voice and imagining her there. Pictured her naked body immersed in the water with bubbles floating about her, caressing her.

Now the robin's egg blue velvet of her gown clung to her body, accenting all her lovely curves and bringing out the color of her eyes. His entire body tensed against the onset of arousal as the memory of their too brief kiss rushed into his mind. How would he make it through the evening without touching her, he didn't know.

"Good evening, Connor," Heather greeted him cheerfully as she crossed the room to his side.

With some self-mocking humor, she held out her hand to him and he took it in both of his, raising it to his lips for a lingering kiss. Her eyes flared but, aware that all eyes were on them once again, pulled her hand back with as much grace as she could muster. The stares were curious and avidly waiting, no doubt hoping for some sort of public confrontation to liven their evening as it had the night before. He was determined that it not be so. He just wanted a pleasant evening in the her company.

Ian and Dory entered together then. Ian was in an obviously good humor and Dory all roses and smiles by his side. "What's got into them?" Connor wondered aloud. "I dinnae think I've seen that woman smile in years."

Heather turned with two glasses of wine she had taken from the footman's tray and handed one to him. Examining the bright faces of the married couple, she gave a little laugh and clinked her glass against his before taking a sip.

"They are young and in love, Connor, what do you think has gotten into them?"

Confused, he looked at her and she raised her brow suggestively. "*Och*, surely no'!" he said in surprise, casting an assessing glance at his brother and sister-in-law. "In the middle of the day?"

She snorted indelicately. "Like you've never had sex in the middle of the day."

Connor opened his mouth and closed it again. Have you? The thought entered his mind and he shook his head in denial. The question that had bothered him so greatly the day before burned brightly through him again.

How had she earned her fortune and living while she was gone? She spoke most freely of sexual intercourse and referred with quite casual indifference to the subject most ladies refrained from even thinking of. Her kiss was not untutored. She had made love, he was sure of it. With whom?

When? The questions raged in him jealously.

Mistaking his silence as reproach, Heather apologized with sincerity. "I'm sorry; I promised you I would keep the conversation polite tonight, didn't I? I don't mean to upset you."

Wanting to drive the picture of her in bed with other men from his mind, Connor changed the subject, asking her instead about the education she received at university.

With open pleasure, she answered. "As I mentioned, though I am sure you weren't really listening at the time, I did my undergraduate work at UVA in Virginia, then did my medical school at Duke. From there was my residency at Johns Hopkins in Maryland. I was so pleased to be accepted there. It's one of the best hospitals in the country."

Connor didn't understand a couple of the things she said. He didn't know what a UVA was or of a school called Duke. "UVA?"

"University of Virginia," she clarified. "It was designed to a large degree by Thomas Jefferson, did you know that? He did a lot of the buildings and it's not far from Monticello. That's a beautiful place, too. Have you ever been?"

He shook his head. "I've seen illustrations in some books but I wisnae aware that his home was open to the public. So yer a doctor now?"

"Yes, OB/GYN," she answered. At his puzzled frown, she elaborated. "Obstetrics and gynecology. Basically I take care of pregnant women and help them deliver their babies."

With a sigh of relief, he nodded with understanding. "So yer a midwife."

His words must have offended her deeply for she nearly choked on her wine.

"A doctor, Connor, don't ever mistake the two, at least

when I am around."

Amusement at her outrage had him grinning broadly. "My apologies if I offended."

"You did, but apology accepted. But that was why I was talking to Ian today," she explained. "Dory's told me that she's miscarried several times already and Ian fears another."

"It does weigh heavily on him," he concurred, glancing again at his brother where he stood chatting with a couple of their uncles.

He was very fond of Ian. They had been close all their lives. Whatever feelings he might have had regarding his brother's choice of wife, Connor had truly mourned each of those losses with him.

"Well, worrying all the time won't help, I told them, and basically told him that they needed to get back in the sack and keep their marriage happy."

"Back in the…?"

She gestured to the couple and he noticed Ian's hand resting lightly on Dory's back… and absently creeping lower.

"*Ah*, I see," Connor said, and indeed he did. She had nosed in on another person's personal problem and tried to fix it.

Amazing that most of her solutions were such simple ones. Let it go, make love. The doctor seemed to give good advice. The Dory he knew would never allow herself to behave in such an unseemly manner in public. Yet there she was now cozying up to his brother while his hand practically fondled her rear end.

Astonishing. He said as much to Heather.

"Dory's not a bad sort, I think," she said eying the couple much as he was. "Just a bit retentive and OCD about things." Feeling his questioning gaze turn to her, she translated: "She's a control freak."

Connor laughed out loud freely, drawing the incredulous looks of his entire family. "That she is, that she is! Brilliant. *Och*, Heather lass, what a corker ye are."

"Thank you, I think." She accepted his praise and sipped her wine, studying him as he reined in his amusement. "Look at you, Connor," she whispered. "For a moment there you looked almost happy."

He reached out and caressed her cheek with his thumb. "Aye, for a moment there I almost was."

The butler called the assembly to dinner and the earl cocked his arm to her. She took it gladly as they moved into the dining room. "Felt good, didn't it?"

It did, he thought, looking forward to a meal for the first time in a decade. It did.

Connor couldn't remember the last time he enjoyed a meal more. Heather kept him amused with stories of her time in the Americas. It seemed she was a 'big fan' of baseball, a sport he knew nothing about. She related it to cricket and he was able to grasp some of the basic principles of the game. She enjoyed watching these games in person, she said but preferred football on the 'TV'.

She made Baltimore sound like the most wondrous place on earth, he thought, and considered that he might enjoy going there with her some time to see all the places she spoke of.

He lingered only briefly over his whisky, eager to join Heather in the parlor to continue their conversation. She amused him so completely with her stories and touched him with the depth of her caring for the women she treated.

She told him how she was joining a new medical practice when she returned from her holiday and Connor knew almost instantly that he didn't want her to leave again. He wanted her to stay in Duart permanently… with him. What did that mean?

Did he really want to try marriage again? Certainly not. How utterly appalling to even consider it!.

Yet as he entered the parlor and saw her seated at the piano, concentrating on the piece she was playing, he was not so sure.

He listened to her music for a moment before wandering over to the piano. He recognized the tune as 'Climbing over Rocky Mountain' from Gilbert and Sullivan's *The Pirates of Penzance*, which he'd seen in London several years before. She played the lively tune with spirit and a grin on her face. Clearly she was enjoying herself.

"Ye appear to be ha'ing a good time." He took a seat next to her on the bench.

XXXXX

Emmy watched him saunter over with a relaxed half-smile on his face where only moments before a nearly horrified expression took hold. She wondered what he had been thinking about, but didn't dare ask. Whatever it was, it wasn't pleasant.

"I am," she answered his question as she reached the end of the piece. "How did you like it?"

"Verra well done," he complimented sincerely. "Ye play with spirit and joy."

"Six years of lessons."

"I saw that opera when it opened at the Opera Comique in London."

"Did you? Lucky you." She tickled out a few notes, feeling slightly envious. "I just love musical theater and a good show tune. I've taken the train up to New York a few times to see some shows. Saw *Wicked* a few months ago. It was wonderful."

"Cannae say I ha' heard of that one."

"No," she sighed, her earlier depression slipping back over her at the reminder of where she was. "I don't imagine that you have."

Well, of course he hadn't!

She seemed so morose for a moment that Connor scooted closer to her and took her hand in his. "Are ye all right then?"

Emmy gave him a half-smile and shrugged. "Just a little homesick, I guess. Do you want me to play something else for you?"

Luckily he didn't argue and allowed her change of subject with a nod. She thought for a moment before launching into a slower melody.

"Ye're good, ye ken," he offered, hoping the flattery would revive her flagging spirits. "I dinnae even know ye played."

"*Mm-hmm*," she responded in time to the music. "And the guitar, too. Mom always insisted that music developed good math skills. She'd read some study on that years ago and thought better safe than sorry."

"I've ne'er heard of any such thing." He listened to her play for several minutes, watching her hands as they moved lightly over the keys. "Ye two maun hae been particularly close."

"I miss her every day," Emmy admitted. "It's hard not having any family left."

"Ye ha' Dory," he corrected.

Emmy glanced over at her 'twin' sister who was almost giggling as Ian whispered in her ear. She made a noncommittal '*humph*' and shrugged a shoulder. "You are fortunate, though, to have so much family around."

"Ian is a good friend and a good brother," Connor hedged.

"But the rest never even talk to you," she finished for him, giving him a sidelong glance as she continued to play. "It's because they're scared of you, you know?"

"Frightened? Of me?" he asked in surprise, looking about the room before meeting her amused eyes.

"Sure, big angry guy who holds their existence in the palm of his hand. Never smiles, never talks to them either," she continued. "They're all terrified that you are going to turn them out or cut off their allowance or something. It's all they ever talk about."

"Is that so?" he asked as he looked around the room. Everyone's eyes suddenly had somewhere else to look though he knew they had all been watching him a moment before.

Emmy noticed and smirked. "See?"

"Interesting."

"Isn't it?" She rolled into the chorus of the tune. "You could try talking to them every once in a while, you know. Just so they know that you are human and aren't going to drink their blood while they sleep," she teased and raised her elbow to point across the room. "Your aunt Millie, for instance, has a hip that nags her persistently. And your uncle, Robert, I think, has problems with his arthritis." When he gave a short snort, she laughed. "Well, it is what they talk about when they are not talking about you."

"I believe my estate manager keeps me sufficiently informed regarding everyone's status," he chuckled.

Emmy tilted her head, considering. "You're right. Your way might be best." She flowed from 'Once Upon a Dream' from *Sleeping Beauty* into 'The Music of the Night' from *Phantom of the Opera*.

"What is that?" he asked after listening for a moment to the dark music. "I thought myself well versed in opera, but I dinnae recognize it."

Emmy's fingers came down on the keys discordantly as she halted, startling the others in the room.

"Perhaps someone else would like a turn for a bit?" she said to the room in general. She pushed back from the piano and stood, as did Connor although she veered around him and headed for the door.

"Heather," he called, following her. "What's wrong?"

"Nothing, nothing!" she answered as she started up the stairs away from him. He followed, catching up with her easily at the top since he was unencumbered by heavy skirts. "I'm just tired, Connor, I just want to go to bed," she lied, avoiding his eyes.

"Nay, that's no' it, no' a'tall." Connor caught her arm and pulled her down the hall to the privacy of their sitting room before he turned her toward him. "Tell me what's bothering ye."

"This! All of this," she yelled, waving her hands around her. "You!"

"What aboot me?" he asked softly.

"You don't know the *Phantom of the Opera*, Connor!" she cried, unable to express herself more clearly.

"I certainly can see it, if ye like."

He was trying grasp the reason for her outburst, his voice calm and filled with worry instead of the anger she normally roused in him. His unexpected patience irrationally upset her more.

"No." She wrapped her hands around her skull and

127

groaned in frustration. "You can't, Connor. There is no chance in your entire lifetime that you'll see it." She turned and stared up at a painting over the fireplace. "This is ridiculous," she whispered more to herself than to him. "It's not real. Why am I here? I shouldn't be here. I should never have come here." She wrapped her arms around her waist and tried to swallow the hysterical sob that welled up in her. She failed and another sob soon followed the first, then another and another.

Connor turned her into his arms and held her tightly as she cried into his shoulder, clinging to him desperately. He had no idea why she was crying but still her comforted her.

The woman he thought wronged him.

"Tell me what ye want me to do, love, and I will try to do it."

She hiccuped a laugh. "Just like a guy. Always wanting to fix the problem. I don't think you can this time, though." She realized how close she was to him then, how warm, and stepped back, wiping her eyes. "I just shouldn't be here. I want to go home and I'm scared I'll never get there."

His narrowed his eyes irritably. "If ye dinnae want to be here, then why did ye come? Why did ye e'er come back?"

Caressing his cheek lightly, Emmy shook her head ruefully. "Don't get your back up, Connor. To use a horrible cliché, it isn't you, it's me. You just wouldn't understand."

Biting back his frustration, he covered his hand with his and looked down into her bright blue eyes. "Then tell me," he insisted, "and I'll try."

She stared up into his warm dark eyes and tried to pull together a reasonable thought. "I think I'm afraid, Connor."

"Afraid of what?" He cupped her cheeks in his hands and rested his forehead against hers.

Savoring the feel of his hands on her face and the heat of his nearness, she closed her eyes and swayed closer to him. "You."

"Me?" he whispered.

"I'm afraid of the way you make me feel."

When Connor had laughed, truly laughed earlier, the years had fallen away from him. Along with the angst. His dark eyes danced with light and humor and his lips tipped up at the corner showing his white teeth. The sight of him clenched her heart with emotion she'd never known.

He'd been happy for a moment.

And she...

"There was a moment down there that I was actually content with where I was. I'm afraid that if I stay here too long, I may never want to leave."

"And I'm afraid that ye'll want to leave," he responded. His thick brogue deepened seductively. "Ye're a completely different person now."

"You have no idea," she snorted but was unable to look away.

"Every moment I am wi' ye I want to touch ye." Connor stroked her cheek and continued down her neck. "I want to kiss ye."

Compelled by his words and the power of his voice with its alluring burr, Emmy leaned in and raised her lips as his mouth came down to meet hers. His lips brushed her top lip, then the bottom before they caught hers passionately. She gasped then returned the kiss fully. Her lips parted and caught his lower lip between hers and running her tongue across it.

Their mouths played ardently, desperately meeting time and again. She clung to him, digging her nails into his back as desire overwhelmed her. He backed her to the chaise and lowered her down without breaking the kiss.

Keeping their lips together, he shrugged off his jacket while, with heavy eyelids, Emmy worked his tie. He pushed her dress off her shoulder, moving his lips down her neck. He found a particularly sensitive spot that drew a deep moan from Emmy as he cupped her breasts, and then another just below her ear. She shuddered and clung to his shoulders, savoring the feel of his thick muscles below her hands.

"Oh, Lord," she moaned as his lips traveled lower.

Lowering her to the chaise, he pulled her bodice lower.

"I adore yer breasts," he whispered huskily. "So perfect. So bonny."

"People used to say," she panted, "that more than a handful was a waste."

His deep brogue rumbled near her ear, "I hae big hands."

His lips fastened over the nipple, nipping and licking before drawing it into his mouth. He lingered there, suckling deeply until she cried out.

"Oh, Connor!"

She pulled him down over her, reveling in his weight as his other hand traveled up her skirts, teasing along her ankle and calf and then the garter that held her stockings up. He stroked her bare thigh and moved higher, meeting her nearly bare bottom.

"What do ye hae on?" he murmured as he fingered the lace edge of her panties.

"What?" What was he talking about?

"I hae to see."

Kneeling between her legs, he pulled her skirts high. He ran a big hand up either thigh pushing the skirts and petticoats as he went. Her thighs were long and smooth and where there would have been pantalets and drawers on any other lady of his acquaintance he found only a scrap of ivory satin and lace. Intrigued, he ran his fingers under the edge.

"This is… fascinating," he whispered, leaning over to press a kiss just below the edge of the lace.

"Why?"

"They cover nothing," he whispered, pressing more kisses to her inner thigh. He groaned and ran his hands up inside the panties, cupping her bottom. "They bring all kinds of thoughts to my mind."

"Like what?" she whispered, propping herself up on her elbows.

"Like what ye'd look like wearing nothing but this."

His accent was so thick Emmy could barely understand him. She wondered, as similar scenarios flowed through her mind, if lust could make a man forget how to even speak.

"Help me take off the dress then," she offered breathlessly, "and you can see."

Connor drew back and his dark gaze penetrated hers full of need. Pushing back, he rose and offered her a hand, pulling her to her feet. Her mind was abuzz with want and she felt dizzy as she stood. She wavered for a moment before finding her balance.

"I want to see you, too, Connor. Take off your shirt."

Obligingly he loosened the top buttons and pulled it over his head, tossing it aside. Emmy ran both hands up his broad chest as he shuddered under her touch. She marveled over the heavy muscles that rippled and flexed under her hands. She ran her fingertips over the dark hairs that sprinkled his chest, feeling their rough texture. His skin was hot. "*Mmm*," she hummed in appreciation.

"Yer turn."

He turned her and worked the buttons on the dress quickly before pulling it down around her waist. He then set to work on the corset and ties for the petticoats she wore under the dinner dress. Just as the whole of it was about to fall to the ground, Emmy caught it to her chest and glanced over her shoulder through lowered lashes, her eyes meeting his in a look full of meaning, before allowing it to drop to the floor. Taking her hand, he pulled her toward him forcing her to turn and step out of the pile leaving her in nothing but her lace panties, stocking and garters and heeled ivory shoes.

XXXXX

She was so lovely, so perfect in her near nudity that Connor fell to his knees with a moan before her, running his hands up to her hips and pulling her to him. Pressing a heated kiss to her belly, a flash caught his attention and his focus shifted. "Is that a jewel?"

"What?" she murmured in confusion, her attention focused solely on the feel of his hot mouth against her skin. "Oh you mean my belly ring!" She looked down at it and up again at him with a frown. "Don't you like it?"

The delicate crescent of silver looped through the skin above her navel, ending in a large crystal. It was not a diamond or even a paste imitation, he noted, examining the larger one dangling from the lower end of the crescent. It drew attention to the center of her muscled abdomen and was erotic, aye, but *too* erotic, *too* provocative. It brought to his imagination many thoughts he didn't want to have.

"Nay, I dinnae," he answered gruffly.

"Really?" she asked in amazement. "Most..." She was going to say 'guys', but managed to stop the thought before it came out and she had to explain bikinis and midriffs to him.

Luckily he was too enthralled by the jewelry to notice.

"Why would ye do that to yerself?"

"I went through a rebellious phase after my mom died," she confessed. It was the truth. "Multiple piercings, belly, nose and five up the ear, tattoo, hung out with a bad crowd." She shrugged it off. "I was an angry kid, mad at the world for taking my mom from me."

"What about yer father?" he asked realizing she had not mentioned him.

"You want to talk about that now?" Emmy questioned incredulously. Her dad had left her mom when she was just a little girl. She didn't even remember him, but telling him that would only upset him and cause another argument, because he had known Heather's father and would try to point that out... again. She didn't want the same old fight. Not now. "Let's just say, I just had some issues, no biggie. Unlike your baggage, I learned to let mine go."

"I am learning," he murmured as he twirled his tongue past the jewel and over to nip her hipbone, lightly raking his teeth over the sensitive flesh there before moving further down. She moaned as her stomach muscles quivered in anticipation and he answered in turn with a moan of his own as if her excitement and arousal aroused him in turn.

Emmy rested her hands lightly on his hair, caressing it as she stared down at his dark head in wonder. Such an incredibly passionate man! She should have known that as fiercely as he could be brought to anger, his lust would be just as strong. And to have it directed at her! Emmy knew that this night would be one that she would never forget. "Connor," she whispered as he raised his head and looked up at her with his chin on her belly. "Make love to me," she urged. "Take me to bed and make love to me."

He stood and ran his hands up her body, catching her by the waist and lifting her into the air. Emmy gasped in surprise, grabbing him round the neck and wrapping her arms and legs around him as he kicked open his bedchamber door and carried her over to his bed. He captured her lips in a fierce kiss as they went. Not releasing her, he bent over the bed lowering them both down until he pressed her into the soft mattress. As she ran her hands down his back, his hands moved up, seizing her bare breasts and kneading them firmly. His lips found that sensitive spot below her ear once more and she shuddered in pleasure.

"Oh, Connor," she moaned, "this is incredible."

He had to agree as she spread her hands over his buttocks and pulled him closer to her heat. Her legs wrapped around him, anchoring him to her core. He pressed himself to her and they both moaned with pleasure. "*Och*, my love…" he moaned, "my darling Heather, I want ye so badly."

Emmy was so distracted by Connor's fingers slipping up her panties to find her wet heat that it took a long moment for his words to penetrate the spell that enveloped around them. Not again! She pulled her arms between them and pushed forcing him up so she could face him.

"Connor, I am not your wife," she insisted, determined to make her point this time.

"Now is no' the time for yer charade, my love," he whispered and tried to kiss her again.

Turning her head, she rolled out from under him and stood by the bed, crossing her arms over her chest. "I think now is the perfect time."

Connor rolled on to his back with a groan and stared up at her. His chest was heaving and already covered in a thin sheen of sweat. He looked so incredibly sexy that she nearly threw caution to the wind and jumped back into the bed. She closed her eyes against the sight of him sprawled against the pillows and took a deep breath, trying to control her emotions. Thank God he still had his pants on!

"Ye shouldnae have started something ye dinnae mean to finish."

"Oh, I meant to finish it," she replied, bringing a flaring heat to his eyes as he rose on his elbows in expectation. She held out a palm to him. "Whoa there, cowboy. I'm not done. I do want you, I do. God *knows* I do. I have never felt anything like this in my life and a huge part of me just wants to jump right back in there and get it going."

"Then come." He held out a hand in invitation.

"I can't," she told him, ignoring the hand and pulling a blanket from the bed to cover herself against the growing chill of the room. "Not until you understand that I am not your wife."

"Fine then," he tossed out casually. "Ye're nae my wife. In truth, I have nae wife at all."

Abruptly derailed, Emmy stared down at him in confusion. "You don't?"

He shrugged nonchalantly. "Nae one else knows of it, but I secured an annulment from ye two years ago."

Her brows shot up in surprise. "You did? Why didn't you say something before?" Actually she was glad to hear it. She knew people did it all the time but she hadn't been too hot over the idea of sleeping with a married man.

"It wisnae yer concern at the time."

"But now it is?" she asked. "Why now?"

"Ye dinnae want to admit to being my wife. Fine," he snapped his fingers. "Now ye're no' my wife. Isnae that what ye wanted?" The same old anger started to burn up in him. Now she wanted him. He knew she did. Even wanting him like this, knowing that as her husband it was perfectly acceptable to make love with him—without anyone looking askance at them, without scandal—and she still wouldn't admit it? What exactly did she want from him?

"Let me make it simple once again," sarcasm was heavy in her voice. "I am not Heather. Whether she is still your wife or not, I am not her. Not Heather!"

"Ye are!"

"I. Am. Not!" Each word was enunciated slowly. "Why, Connor? Why would I continue with this if it were not true? Why?"

"Most likely because ye're ashamed of how ye had to support yerself when ye ran," he accused, sitting up on the bed.

"What are you talking about?"

"Obviously ye've been wi' a man before. Ye ken what yer aboot." His brogue was so thick she could barely understand him. He gestured at her state of undress. "Nae pantalets! How many men did ye hae?"

Emmy blinked and stared down at him dumbfounded. "You… you think I was a prostitute?" she stuttered in disbelief.

"How else could a single woman earn enough of a living to go to a university and buy her own camera?" he asked. The jealousy was raging inside him now the question had been asked and he wanted, no! needed to hear the answer. "How many, Heather?"

"You think I was a *prostitute*?" she repeated, ending in a near screech. "Is that why you wanted to have sex with me? You think I'm that cheap?"

"Are ye saying yer a virgin still then?" he challenged insolently.

She opened her mouth and shut it with a snap. "No, I am not, Connor." She took a step forward and poked him in the chest with a finger. "I am not, but don't you ever, ever again make the mistake of thinking I have *ever* taken money for sex. Ever!" she hissed.

"How then? How did ye support yerself?"

"I earned my living the really old-fashioned way, Connor MacLean." She jabbed him again. "I worked for it. Worked real jobs. How dare you think otherwise?"

"So ye slept wi' men for fun then? How many?" he asked again, torn apart waiting for the answer.

"That is *so* none of your business." She threw up a hand in dismissal, gathered up the pile of discarded clothes and left the room, slamming the door behind her.

She managed to avoid Connor for most of the next day. In truth it wasn't too difficult, since it seemed he was avoiding her as well. He kept to his study and Emmy found safety in numbers with the other ladies of the house. She played the piano in the sitting room for nearly an hour while the other women talked over their embroidery. Emmy had little interest in sewing, or even learning how, and even less interest in conversation. Instead, she morosely mulled over her own thoughts as she played by rote for the six ladies who lived at Duart. Dory, Connor's aunts, Millie, Lizzie and Eleanor, and his cousins, Gladys and Nora.

But she couldn't help but think of Connor. She wondered where he was, what he was doing and thinking about. Was he thinking about her? About last night?

What a stubborn man, she thought darkly, throwing herself into the dark moody music of the Phantom. Thick-headed *man*! Did he really think there was no other way for a woman to earn a living? How did single women earn a living in this time? And what did he want from her anyway? Just a piece of ass? An admission? She'd bet he didn't even know. She'd been so incredibly angry with him for thinking that of her. and yet, looking back on it, he seemed almost desperate to know. How many, he asked over and over. Why was it so important? It made her wonder.

And then besides nearly having sex with a man she'd only known for three days, she'd blabbered on and on about how she felt about being here. How afraid she was that she'd never want to leave. Leave him.

Damn right she was afraid! On one hand she had a nearly perfect life on paper. A doctor joining a medical practice that would bring her a great living. She owned her own house and had an IRA that should allow her to retire early someday. She had friends – well more fellow residents than friends – but they were people she enjoyed going to dinner with, games with, or up to New York for an occasional weekend.

So she didn't have a boyfriend. So what? She was only twenty-eight for crying out loud! She was bound to meet someone in the next couple years and fall in love, so she could have marriage and babies and all the good stuff that went with it. A perfect life.

On the other hand, she was clearly stuck here in 1895 Scotland. How could that compete? No electricity, no movies, no baseball. Dozens of things bounced randomly through her mind from the minor faults to the major. Faucets that were either hot or cold but never just warm. No Internet. Uncomfortable clothes, uncomfortable shoes. She could go on and on about all the negatives of being stuck here. Why would she want to stay at all? What was life without her old friends Ben and Jerry?

And it was boring. She was the child of a multitasking generation. She was used to doing three things at once, always moving, always on the go. She had checked her cell phone that morning, just out of habit. No service. Well, of course there wasn't!

The music downshifted into a calming melody and her thoughts calmed as well.

But there was peace here, too. A beauty of nature that held its own appeal. There were brand-new—hundred year old—books in the library that she'd never read. They alone could keep her busy for years.

And there was Connor. She closed her eyes as she played and pictured him in her mind as he had been the previous night. So incredibly sexy. Appealing. Alluring. Laid back on his bed, hair mussed, eyes heavy, a nice six-pack of abs rippling and flexing in the candlelight...

Candlelight! Ugh, she thought, thrown back into the negative side of life. Candlelight wasn't for a romantic setting here. It was so you could see where you were going. Did she really want to cope with that for the rest of her life?

And the medical side of this time was appalling. People could die just from appendicitis at any time. From the flu! No antibiotics for infection. Chicken pox could kill. They still had smallpox, too. No hope for cancer at all. And what would childbirth be like here?

A morbid parade of disease with no treatment or cure danced through her mind as she lost herself in her personal horror show of disease, misery and death until a startled cry drew her attention.

Glancing around the room, she saw the other ladies flocking to Dory's side as she bent over, clearly in pain. Fresh from her recent apprehensive thoughts on childbearing,

Emmy rushed to her side pushing the other women out of the way. "Dory, what it is? Do you feel pain?" Emmy ran her hand knowledgeably down the woman's stomach and drew back in surprise. "Are you still wearing that thing? I thought I told you not to," she scolded.

"Please," Dory whispered as perspiration dotted her brow.

"Someone find a footman to carry Dory to her room," Emmy commanded, leaving the women to scatter as she turned her attention to the woman who looked so much like her. "Don't worry, Dory, it'll be fine."

"Are you sure?"

"Of course I'm sure," Emmy patted her hand as the footman arrived. "Take her carefully up to her room," she directed.

"Maybe we should call for a doctor or a midwife," someone commented - Cousin Gladys, Emmy thought.

"I'm a doctor," Emmy said firmly, "and I will take care of Dory." The women murmured among themselves at her pronouncement but she waved them away. "Someone should find Ian, though." *Just in case*, she added mentally but kept the thought to herself.

On the way up the stairs, she called for a maid to fetch her boiling water, the strongest soap they had, and some towels. What she wouldn't give for her small medical bag from the hotel. Or at least a pair of latex gloves. She was just getting Dory settled on the bed and shooing the ladies out of the room when a trio of maids arrived bringing what she needed. She was briefly surprised at how quickly they arrived, but of course Dory kept water handy at all times for her tea.

"Margo!" she called and snapped her fingers several times at Dory's personal maid. "I'm sorry, I don't remember your name."

"Susan, milady." Susan bobbed a curtsey.

"Susan, you and Margo get Dory into a nightgown, just the gown and nothing else." Dory blushed and started to protest, "Nothing else," she repeated firmly. "On top of the covers, not under."

Emmy went to the windows and flung the curtains wide open allowing as much natural light as possible to enter the room. Thankfully Dory's room faced the courtyard and thus had the larger windows. "You," she pointed to the third maid she didn't recognize. "Turn the gaslights up as far as they'll go and bring more lamps closer to the bed." As the maids scrambled to do her bidding, Emmy rolled up her sleeves and washed her hands thoroughly, hissing at the hot water. "Freakin' middle ages," she muttered under her breath. "Dark, no tools, no stethoscope. Could use one of those." Hmmm, they might have come up with that already... maybe. "Margo, does the local doctor, is there a local doctor? Does the doctor have a stethoscope?" When the girl looked puzzled Emmy explained, "Something that lets him listen to a heartbeat?"

Margo's expression brightened. "Aye, milady, I've seen him use it before on my Maw."

"Would it be possible to send someone to see if we can borrow it?" Emmy asked. "We don't need the whole doctor, just the stethoscope," she clarified to make sure they didn't bring some undereducated quack back with them.

"I'll send my brother to ask, milady." Margo bobbed a curtsey and left the room.

Emmy moved to the bed where Dory lay curled up against the pillows, still looking tense and scared. "Any blood?" She directed the question to Susan who'd helped

Dory change.

"Nay, milady."

"Good." She sat on the edge of the bed and looked down at the woman everyone thought to be her sister. "Relax, Dory. Breathe. You look wound tight enough to blow your cork."

Susan giggled and Dory offered a strained smile. "I'm scared, Emily."

She started at the use of her real name, but patted Dory's hand. "Just Emmy. And don't be scared, you'll be just fine."

"My baby," Dory moaned, stifling a sob.

"Well, let's just see, shall we?" She coaxed Dory on to her back, took her feet one by one and raised them up. Putting a hand on either side of her bulging stomach, Emmy pressed in. Intently, she waited for some sign of movement from within or, worse case, a contraction that would indicate a miscarriage or premature labor. Feeling nothing after a moment, she moved her hand to the top of her stomach and pushed down.

Wishing in vain for a fetal monitor, she changed the subject. "I thought we discussed that corset, Dory."

"I know, I'm sorry," she whispered. "I just thought I could still wear it."

Emmy tsked. "And after Ian was *sooo* nice to you yesterday, too."

Dory blushed then giggled just a bit. Her stomach jumped beneath Emmy's hands and Dory squealed in terror.

"*Shh*, Dory!" Emmy laughed. "It's just the baby kicking."

"Kicking?" Dory responded in confusion and squeaked again as the baby kicked more forcibly. Emmy put her hand over the spot and savored the feel of the baby's movement. It had always been her favorite thing about expectant mothers, the one thing she envied them for and longed for herself.

"Active little bugger," she said fondly. "See? Just kicking and a little gymnastics. Is that what you felt downstairs? Or is there actual pain?"

"No," Dory replied in wonder and put her own hands on her stomach as the baby continued to roll. "No pain now. But this is not what I felt before. That hurt. But this has been scaring me as well. I feel it all the time. Is it truly just the baby moving? I didn't realize what it was, and it doesn't happen as much when I wear the corset. Little nudges here and there but never that!"

"The corset probably inhibits the baby's movements. Leave it off and let the baby move, okay?"

"I've never carried a baby long enough before to feel this."

"Well, I'd wager you'll get to feel a lot more than that this time." Emmy shifted until she was sitting closer to the foot of the bed and put a hand on each of Dory's knees. "Susan, do you have a tape measure?" Not knowing how else to describe it, Emmy breathed a sigh of relief when the maid nodded and opened a box near the fireplace, withdrawing a length of string knotted at intervals. Well, it would have to do.

Dory stiffened and squealed again. "There it is. That's what scared me downstairs."

"Pain?"

"Yes," Dory nodded. "It was not like the movement before. It was..." she trailed off and shrugged helplessly.

"I am going to examine you now, whether you like it or not."

Dory clenched her knees together at the warning and stared at her. "Cannot we just..."

145

"No, we can't," Emmy interrupted. "This is no time for your Victorian sensibilities. I need to have a look. Don't you want to have a healthy baby?"

Dory's knees relaxed slightly and she glanced anxiously at her maid, the one person she'd probably ever been naked in front of besides her husband. Even if she bared herself completely for Ian. "Susan, please wait outside."

Uncertainly, the maid nodded and bobbed a curtsey before leaving the room and closing the door behind her. "Alright, Emmy," Dory said, lying back on the bed with all the martyrdom of a virgin sacrifice on her face. "Do what you must."

"Think of it this way," Emmy spoke quietly as she raised Dory's nightgown up above her knees and spread the woman's legs apart. "Better me than the doctor, right? He must be some old, gross guy if you haven't let him examine you before. Am I right?"

Dory was already red with mortification and had turned her head to the side to avoid Emmy's gaze but she nodded into the pillow. "I can't stand the thought of him touching me."

"Then he won't," Emmy assured her. "But I will have to touch you, you know."

Dory nodded miserably and Emmy got up on her knees so she was off to the side. Using her left hand to push down on the stomach, she used two fingers to examine the woman who had become her one ally in this place. She felt for a moment while her patient moaned in embarrassment. As quickly as possible, she finished her exam and moved back, allowing Dory to cover herself once more. She washed her hands again and came back with the tape measure.

"Just one more time, sweetie," she murmured as she

raised the gown again so Dory's whole belly was exposed. She was just taking the measurements she needed when the door burst open and Ian fell in, panting with exertion, and Emmy could tell he'd run to be at Dory's side as soon as he had heard.

Dory squealed once again and rolled over, pulling the full nightgown down over her feet. Ian fell to his knees at the edge of the bed and took her hands. "Are ye alright, lass?"

Dory looked to Emmy. "She's fine, Ian," Emmy assured them both. "The baby's movements startled Dory and gave her a scare, but the baby seems fine. There's no bleeding and the mucus plug is still intact. I think it's just Braxton Hicks."

"What?" they both asked.

"False labor," she told them. "It can be brought on from lack of exercise or dehydration. A warm bath will probably help right now, but you'll need to start going for some walks, Dory, and lay off the tea and just drink water," she added in her best physician voice. "But, rest assured that she is fine for now. But, seriously, Dory, no more corset."

"I won't," she said meekly.

"Promise?"

"I promise."

"Good."

Emmy stared down at the tape measure where she held the mark for the baby's fundal height, the measurement from her pubic bone to the top of the uterus. She did the mental math to equate the measurement to centimeters. *Well, that couldn't be right, could it?* She looked back down at Dory who was curled in a ball while Ian whispered softly to her as he stroked her hair back from her forehead.

"When did you say you thought you were due?"

"Six weeks, perhaps? Maybe more," Dory offered.

"Why?"

"Will you let me measure one more time?" Emmy asked rhetorically. She had every intention of double-checking her measurement.

"Must you?"

"I think we must," she replied with a little sarcasm. "*Ah, good!*" Margo entered the room carrying what looked like an ancient stethoscope with a large funnel on the end. "Thank you, Margo, you can go. Well, Dory? Does Ian stay or go?"

"I'm staying," he stated firmly before Dory had a chance to respond. "I'm staying," he repeated, looking down at his wife who finally nodded in consent. He took a seat next to her and held her hand as she turned back onto her back. Both looked at Emmy expectantly.

At this show of acceptance, she raised the gown again and took her time measuring. "How accurate is this tape measure?" she asked. "Each knot is an inch right?"

"It should be fairly accurate," Ian told her. "It measures the same as my tailor in Inverary."

Emmy nodded but didn't need the tape to confirm what her eyes knew. Without the corset, Dory was substantially larger than a woman of thirty-six weeks should be. She converted the measurement again and tried to refrain from shaking her head lest she worry them. Taking the stethoscope, she put the outdated piece on Dory's belly, muttering over how badly it worked. She listened for the baby's heartbeat. It was a fast and regular whoosh-whoosh as expected but as she listened closer she heard what she suspected. Moving the steth around the other side and lower, she listened again.

Pulling the instrument off, she set it aside and pressed here and there on Dory's abdomen. "What I wouldn't give for an ultrasound," she murmured to herself.

Finally, she stepped back and allowed her patient a moment to straighten her gown before answering the question in both their eyes. "Okay, so here's the thing," she prefaced. "It's twins."

"Twins?" they both echoed.

Emmy held up two fingers. "Twins. Two."

Ian grinned and whooped, turning to crush Dory in his embrace before apologizing and holding her more gently. He laid one hand down on her stomach and she covered his hand with hers as they stared at each other in amazement. He bent to kiss her tenderly, whispering in her ear. Feeling like an interloper, Emmy cleared her throat to remind them of her presence.

Ian hopped up and hugged her as well, and she returned the embrace with a smile. "Congratulations."

"I can't believe it," Dory said in awe, staring down at her stomach.

"Well, it's not surprising if you think about it," Emmy reasoned as she gathered up the tape and steth. "Twins are often genetic. They run in families," she clarified and they nodded. "We'll talk more about all that later. For now, I'll just give you a chance to celebrate." She excused herself from the room with a smile, but as soon as she got into the hall, she leaned against the wall and covered her face with her hands.

Worries cropped up in hrt mind as she pictured natural childbirth with multiples in this setting, with the antiquated medical advancements available. Twins were almost always done by C-Section in her time, just to avoid any complications that might crop up during a vaginal birth. Video from medical school replayed itself in her mind and she shuddered with dread.

She rubbed her hands over her face and pushed away from the wall only to see Connor standing just a few feet away. They stared at each other for a long moment. She was sure he was replaying the events of the night before in his mind, as she was. His version was probably different than hers though. Male recollection usually put a woman at fault when they were left with sexual frustrations. Well, she hadn't slept at all last night either.

"Connor," she nodded curtly. She moved to bypass him so she could return to her room and brood over medieval childbirth in private.

"Is Dory going to be all right?" he asked, catching her arm. "Did she lose the bairn?"

"Mother and babies are doing fine so far," she told him wearily.

"Babies?"

"She's going to have twins, Connor," she told him and enjoyed the surprised look on his face. "Shocking, isn't it?"

"Ian must be over the moon," he said with a smile, shaking his head.

"He is. They both are."

"But ye're nae. Why?"

No doubt her expression spoke volumes against her assurances. His curiosity must have outweighed his need to avoid her company. He turned and offered his arm to her. "Ye look like ye could use a drink. Shall we?"

"Why not?"

If he was willing to forget the previous night and move on, why shouldn't she? She took his arm as he escorted her down the stairs. He bypassed the parlor and instead led her toward his study where he ushered her in and shut the door behind them. It was a dark paneled room, scholarly and manly, like a condensed version of the Library of Congress. The walls were covered with bookshelves, filing cabinets and maps. A large desk in the center was heaped with piles of papers and ledgers. Obviously, he was not a neat freak, but it suited him. Thankfully the gas lighting shed enough light so the room wasn't cave-like. He sat her in a wingback chair near the fire as the October day was cold and went to pour her a drink. "Whisky or Claret?"

Emmy wrinkled her nose at the thought of whisky straight up. "Claret, I guess. Thanks."

He handed her a glass and sat with his own in the chair across from her. "I am curious, why are ye no' happy for them? Jealous?"

Emmy scowled at him as she took a sip from the glass. "Just love to think the worst of people, don't you?"

"People are often predictably self-absorbed."

"Sure they are, but a little optimism in the human condition wouldn't be amiss from time to time," she admonished. "Occasionally, they might even surprise you."

"And ye're an optimist?"

Surprised at the question, Emmy laughed in a self-deprecating way and shook her head. "No, I am and have always been a 'glass is half empty' kind of girl. If something can go wrong, it will. Murphy's law and all that. It's terrible really to always have worst-case scenarios running around in your mind. Seeing the worst in everyone, imagining the worst of every situation."

"Ye dinnae do that." He looked surprised that she said as much.

"Oh, but I do." She laughed at herself as she took another sip. She slipped off her shoes and relaxed into the chair tucking a foot up underneath her and allowing the other to swing freely. "When my friends are late meeting me somewhere, like a club or something, I always imagine that they've been in a horrific car wreck and are lying, bleeding and broken, on the side of the street. I sit at weddings contemplating how long it will last. When guys ask me out, it's never because they like me, it's just because they want a piece of ass. That kind of stuff."

He looked appalled at her words and she laughed again. "Oh, yeah, like you're Mr. Positive Thinker."

He finally offered a smile. "Ye dinnae seem that way... outwardly."

"I don't want to be. Things just pop into my head. Weird stuff. Stephen King-y kind of things," she told him, forgetting that he wouldn't know who the famous author was. "Worst case scenarios. But that's why I do obstetrics," she explained. "Babies are all light and possibilities. Innocence and new beginnings. Nothing is better or brighter than bringing a baby into the world."

"Yet ye aren't happy for Ian and Dory."

Swishing the wine around her glass, she hedged. "Oh, I am happy for them. I mean twins are a ton of work but two times the fun, you know?"

"But?"

"But, in this time and in this place, delivering twins could be..." she trailed off with a shudder of apprehension and shrugged. "I'm just afraid for a delivery under these conditions. It's like my personal nightmare."

"And yer Baltimore is safer?"

"Where I come from, it would be infinity safer," she clarified with complete honesty.

XXXXX

Connor imagined his brother's despair in the face of the loss of his wife or child. It would ruin him, he knew. Ian centered his entire world around Dory and had been devastated by the loss of the previous bairns in the past years. "It would help her if ye were here, though, would it no'? If ye ken more than our doctor or the midwives from the mainland, ye could help her hae a safe delivery, aye?"

"Experience always helps, but Connor, I'm just not sure about what could go wrong. There could be complications. There's just no way to know here," she vented in frustration.

"There's nae way to ken anywhere," he argued. "Ye just hae to take it as it comes and hope for the best."

"Next you'll be saying that whatever happens, it's the will of God," she laughed and took another long sip of the wine. "Believe me, Connor, there are ways to know."

Connor was momentarily affronted that she would mock the power of God's will, but did not venture from the topic. "Anything I can do to help ye, I will," he assured her. "Whatever ye need, I'll get it for ye."

"Well, a peek into a well-stocked medical bag would be useful," she admitted. "I'd like to see what's available to work with."

"Consider it done." He raised his glass and she saluted him in turn.

"There is one other thing that you could do for me," she said softly after a long period of companionable silence, running a finger pensively along the rim of her glass.

"What's that?" he asked, his voice full of dread.

"Believe me," was her simple request.

Connor studied her for a long while. She was slouched back in the chair, sitting on one foot while she swung the other idly back and forth. The way she leaned against the arm showed a complete lack of decorum, something Heather had prized. But still... "I cannae," he insisted.

"Why not?"

Because he wanted her to be Heather, he realized. He wanted her to be his long-lost wife, to belong to him, to have a life in Scotland and family worth staying here for, even if that family was her sister and future niece or nephew or both. He wanted to be able to her face lit up with pleasure when she spoke of her work. To witness again the glow that radiated from her in that moment, enhancing her beauty.

If she was just a doctor from Baltimore there was no reason for her to stay, nothing to keep her here. If he admitted to her or anyone else that he considered for even a moment that she was *not* Heather MacLean... Why then he might as well hold the door open himself as she left. He didn't want that to happen yet. There were possibilities here, something between them he meant to explore.

With her, he felt alive, not awash with the anger that had ruled his life for so long. She made him smile and even laugh out loud, something he felt like he hadn't done in years. This woman had brought that to him and he intended to keep her, even after the pain she had caused.

Yet, strangely, he didn't feel that anger in him any longer; that burning hatred and humiliation had dissipated. Had he forgiven her those trespasses? When did that happen? How had that happened? Had this new attraction between them, the affection he felt for her, allowed him to look beyond the past? Or even forgive? Connor shook his head and wondered.

XOXOXOX

While his silence reigned, Emmy admitted the terrible truth that had been plaguing her: "I wish I was your Heather, Connor. There was a moment last night when I wanted nothing more. But I am not."

"Ye are," he insisted.

Rising got to her feet, her fists clenched in frustration, she stuffed her feet back into her shoes. "You are the most stubborn ass of a man I have ever met."

"Wait." He rose as well as she left the room. "I was hoping we might ride together this afternoon."

Emmy flung her arms in the air. "*Argh*," she vented as she turned to flee, but Connor caught her arm, spinning her back to him.

Cupping her cheeks in his hands, he caught her gaze with his and held it. His thumbs caressed her cheeks as she glared up at him. "What?" she demanded.

"I'm trying to 'let it go' as ye suggested," he whispered gruffly. "I'm trying, but can ye no' gi' something in return?"

"I'm not your wife," she stated stubbornly.

"I ken. Hae I no' already conceded that I hae nae wife?" Connor leaned closer and nuzzled her cheek, cutting off her protest. "I've been thinking that we might try again, my love. Much has changed. We hae the chance to get to know each other this time. We hae both matured, hae we no'? Is there no' an attraction between us now that wisnae present before?"

Emmy couldn't stop her head from falling back to allow

him access to her neck. He began to kiss and suck lightly, bringing shivers of desire as she clutched his shoulders and pulled him closer. "Man, you're such an idiot," she whispered in a low tone that belied the harsh words.

"If wanting ye makes me one, than I submit to yer judgment." His lips traveled back up and caught hers in a searing kiss that had her knees giving way. He slid his arms around her and pulled her close as she wrapped hers around his neck.

Holy cow, this man can kiss, she thought fuzzily as his open mouth met hers again and again before settling over hers more forcibly. She could feel the frenzy building in him and felt the answering cry of her body in return. God, she wanted him. Would it be so wrong?

His big hands came up to cup her breasts just as a heavy rapping sounded on the door of the study. Jumping back, she caught herself on a nearby table as the door swung open, missing her by inches. Ian bounded into the room, beaming hugely.

"Connor! I ha' news," he announced enthusiastically before raising his eyebrows as he saw Emmy peeking from behind the door and his brother studiously rearranging papers from the front of his desk. "Or mayhap, ye hae already heard."

"Aye, Heather's just been telling me the good news. Congratulations." Connor returned his brother's smile and held out a hand for Ian's handshake.

"I'll just return to my room then," Emmy mumbled as she rounded the door, torn between embarrassment at nearly being caught in a compromising position and irritation that Connor again addressed her by that name.

"What aboot that ride?" he questioned as she left.

She continued on but her answer trailed sarcastically out behind her. "Not now, dear, I have a headache."

19

A footman delivered a medical bag to Emmy's room late that afternoon. She jumped when the knock sounded, thinking Connor had come to barrage her senses and sensibility once again. She told herself that she wasn't disappointed when it was only the delivery of the case.

In actuality, it was more of a small square suitcase, hard sided with two buckle closures. Curiosity overriding dissatisfaction, she opened it up and sorted the items on the bed. Most looked familiar, a fact she was thankful for, though she realized it was more of a surgical bag than one for everyday medical calls. There were various clamps and forceps as well as several scalpels. Though made of steel, all had brass fittings and wooden handles that were more decorative than utilitarian. There was also stethoscope, an orthopedic hammer, bandages with a spool of wire, some thread and two packets of needles. Lifting the tray underneath, she found a tourniquet, small auger and a hacksaw.

Emmy shuddered as she put the tray back in place. Amputations. Before modern medicine, infections often led to gangrene and eventually amputation. She certainly didn't want to wield the saw that performed the removal of a limb. It was part of the reason she hadn't chosen a general surgery. C-Section was one thing, taking a leg completely another.

Of course, while she considered the state of medicine at this time to be horrifying and outdated, the medical community probably thought themselves to be advanced. Perhaps they were when compared to the previous decade or two. But Emmy knew the future; knew what the next hundred years of medical science would bring. What they would be able to diagnose and treat without ever once cutting into a body. Here, she might as well be figuratively banging a wooden club over someone's head.

Her narrow spectrum of medical knowledge could save lives in this time, when a simple cold might lead to an early death. It bore consideration.

She was repacking the bag when Margo arrived carrying yet another gown. Thankful for the distraction, Emmy teased, "Time to put on the steel cage again, hmm Margo? What am I wearing tonight? Will it sing to me?"

The girl smiled at her playful attitude. "Aye, milady, it will. Actually Mr. MacLean sent it along with his thanks for helping out Mrs. MacLean this afternoon. 'Tis a new gown the lady ordered before she found out aboot the babe and they want ye to hae it."

"They didn't need to do that," she protested. "Dory sent enough clothes for me already."

"Mrs. MacLean said to tell that where the others were a loan, this one was to be a gift," the maid corrected her. She laid the gown across the bed.

"Oh, wow, it's amazing," she whispered in awe, reaching out to touch the froth of bead-encrusted lace that served as the sleeves. The label said Worth and even Emmy, a hundred years away from home, knew what The House of Worth meant. The aqua blue velvet bodice was heavily decorated with the embroidery of silver threads and crystals. The skirt, however, flowed freely unadorned until about a foot from the hem, where the crystal beading and embroidery resumed and did an intricate dance around the bottom of the full skirt. "I can't accept it. It is too much."

"Mrs. MacLean thought ye might say so and told me to tell ye she wouldnae follow yer instructions if ye dinnae take it." Margo bit her lip to hide a grin as she delivered this bit of information.

"Blackmail," Emmy accused, wagging a finger. "I see how she is. Fine, I'll wear it. It'll be a horrible burden, but I'll wear it."

The two women laughed together until Margo offered in all seriousness. "It might be a bit of a burden, milady. There may be nae *tournure* but I'll hae to lace ye up tighter to fit in it."

"Now you tell me!" Emmy complained and Margo boldly laughed again. She enjoyed the maid's merry company. Margo was about twenty and recently married to one of the castle's footmen. She'd had little education and knew only the work she did at the castle, but she was a happy sort, always cheerful. Her good moods were infectious. "How come you don't have to cinch yourself up all the time?" Emmy said, eying the maid's gray dress with its lace cap and apron.

"I do, milady," Margo countered. "Just no' as tightly as ye need to be to wear these gowns. Most of the ladies are laced tighter than the staff."

"There's one benefit of being a working girl, I guess," Emmy offered and Margo giggled with a nod. "It's just madness to be so concerned with this whole 'proper foundations' thing," she continued as the maid helped her out of her daily wear and turned her to lace her tighter. Emmy gripped the post of the bed and pictured Mammy lacing up Scarlett O'Hara as Scarlett held on to the bedpost in *Gone With the Wind.*

"At least I know why they made beds like this now," she grunted as she hung on tight while Margo pulled with all her might.

All the pain was worth it to see the expression in Connor's eyes as he watched her enter the drawing room before dinner. The heat lit and flared as his gaze swept her from top to bottom. She was glad she had let Margo do her hair tonight. The maid had twisted pieces this way and that, braiding others and weaving them all into an elaborate knot that covered the back of her head from crown to nape. Emmy had twisted between two mirrors to get a look at it and was impressed with the girl's work. With the sophisticated hairdo combined with some rouge from Dory, and this gown, she felt like an angel drenched in diamonds rather than mere crystals.

And he looked at her like she was one. The dark hungry gaze had her body heat rising. He'd had her a fired up, burning with fury just a couple of hours before, yet felt no ire now that she was once again in his company. No hard feelings. With a snap of his fingers, she was once again back to being putty in his presence. It was so unlike her.

As she made her way across the room, having eyes for no one but him, Emmy was surprised to be stopped by Connor's Aunt Eleanor. The old matron pounded the floor with her cane and waved Emmy over imperiously. "I heard what you did for Dory today, my lady."

"It was nothing," she returned in all honesty.

The old woman sniffed and pounded her cane down once again. "Nevertheless, well done of you. Well done. I was hoping you might be able to help with my maid."

"What's wrong with her?"

"She's reaching the end of her time and will probably deliver soon," the older woman told her as Emmy nodded in understanding. "I was hoping you might condescend to help her when her time comes. There hasn't been a good midwife around here for years."

"I'm not a midwife," Emmy ground out through gritted teeth. She forced herself to relax. "But of course, I'll look in on her if you like."

"Brilliant. I would most appreciate it." The woman tapped her cane again as if to mark the end of the conversation. With a nod, Emmy continued to Connor, scowling now where a moment before she had been smiling.

"What's wrong?" he asked when she reached him. "What did Eleanor say to ye? I heard the auld bag hisnae seen fit to speak wi' ye since ye've been here."

She realized that it was true. While she had listened in on many conversations these past several days, she'd only been included in those where Dory was present. Even then no one addressed her directly other than to greet her. She hadn't really noticed, having so many other things on her mind. "She called me a midwife," she confessed with a sniff.

"Ye dinnae care for that too much, do ye?" he grinned. "I'd get used to it if I were ye. That's what they call a woman who delivers babies here."

"I didn't endure a six-year residency to be called a

midwife," she protested emphatically. "Not that I have anything against the profession, but really."

"Well, as I said, get used to it."

She snorted. "Not likely."

He laughed out loud for the second time in as many days. again drawing the attention of his family to him. His aunts traded smiles with each other and looked on in approval, she thought, as if it pleased them to see Connor so amused.

Perhaps if they spoke to him every once in a while, he would've never come to be in the state he'd been when she arrived. Why had they never taken it on themselves to save him from himself? It boggled her mind that he was so untouchable to his own family. Of course, she had no family remaining of her own, so perhaps she was in no position to be critical of their family dynamic.

"Ye dinnae give me a chance to compliment ye on yer appearance tonight," he commented.

"But you did the moment I came in," she teased, turning her attention to him. "Words were not necessary. I could tell you liked the dress."

"It is no' just the dress but the woman inside," he murmured seductively raising her hand and placing a kiss on her palm, his lips lingering for a moment. "Ye're stunning."

She curled her fingers around the tingling he left behind. "Thank you."

"Ye've no' answered my question."

"Which question was that?"

"Whether ye would ride wi' me."

"Well, the afternoon is long gone, so I guess it's too late to matter," she responded evasively.

"Alas, there is always tomorrow."

Emmy sighed, knowing there was no way she was going to be able to gracefully decline. "Here's the thing, Connor, I don't know how to ride a horse."

"Nonsense, I ken verra well ye can." A puzzled frown wrinkled his brow. "Perhaps ye're merely out of practice?"

"I haven't been on a horse since Girl Scout camp in the fifth grade," she said honestly. "So, I'm just going to say, thanks, but no thanks."

Connor shrugged, wanting to ask for an explanation, but not wanting to rile her up again. "Verra well then, perhaps ye'd rather join me sailing on the sound. I believe ye mentioned ye'd planned to do so on yer holiday. Maryland does hae boats, I believe. Ye might be more familiar wi' them."

"You have a boat?" Emmy raised a brow in surprise as he nodded. "Where?"

"I keep it docked in Craignure," he told her. "The waters here are a wee bit shallow for a dock and the company there keeps it in good repair."

"How big is it?"

"She's a forty-foot schooner. Excellent for short trips to the mainland and comfortable enough for a lady to enjoy. I hae a small crew to navigate her so ye wouldnae hae to get yer hands dirty," he assured lest that be an issue for her. "What do ye say?"

Emmy narrowed her eyes. "How would we get to the boat?"

"We ride, of course." His eyes twinkled with his response.

"Hilarious," she muttered. The footman finally arrived with their wine and she gratefully took hers, thinking she might become an alcoholic if she stayed here too long. A glass of red wine a night was supposed to be good for the heart, but she'd kill for a simple bottle of Dasani or better still, God help her, a Diet Coke. Looking over the rim at Connor, she waited for a response, hoping that he was only joking. "Well?"

He sighed mockingly and took his own drink from the footman. "I ha' a comfortable carriage we can use to transport us to Craignure."

"Then I accept." She brightened and raised her glass with a smile.

"I'm sure ye'll find it most enjoyable."

"Well, I did want to get some sight-seeing in while I was here," she reminded him.

"Aye, sightseeing."

"I hae a question, if I might be so bold to ask it," he began hesitantly, wondering if he might be willfully destroying their truce by what he was about to say.

"Shoot."

There it was again. Connor frowned. Her terminology was unfamiliar but often self-explanatory, but again he was disturbed by the turns of speech and expressions she used when speaking. He didn't think it was merely the American vernacular either. Clearly she was comfortable with the cadence of her words, for she showed no hesitation in speaking or chagrin that her speech was low. There was no inkling of Scots left in her accent at all. It was most odd.

She took a sip of her wine but added when he didn't immediately continue. "That means go ahead. Ask away."

"That's just it. Yer speech patterns are most odd. I mean nae offense," he assured her quickly not wanting to prompt a fight between them.

"None taken." Her tone was dry. Sarcasm. "And? There

has to be an 'and' there."

"And, I was wondering if all Americans speak as ye do."

"What is wrong with the way I talk?" she inquired. "I realize that it isn't as melodic as your accent, but it is easily understandable whereas there are some people here who are barely intelligible."

"'Tis no' yer accent, in itself, that I'm asking aboot," Connor corrected, hedging a bit, but unable to drop the matter entirely. It was just one of the many questions he had that needed to be settled between them. The time had come for honesty in all things. Perhaps if he began spending time with her asking for answers to the matters that troubled him, he could find the truth somewhere within them.

"What is it then?"

"'Tis more the way ye phrase things, the euphemisms ye use." He tried to explain. "The way ye say things is most unusual and often confusing."

Her lips quirked. "That's American slang for you, honey," she drawled saucily in her best southern accent.

"Slang?"

✗✗✗✗

"Yes and I know you know what slang is even if you don't understand the word. Slang is a word or saying that's taken from pop... well, popular culture of the times to describe something else." The definition was easy but she searched her mind for an example from his time. She snapped her fingers a couple times as she racked her brain. *Aha*! "Like rack your brains." She smiled in triumph. "You know that one, I bet."

"I'm familiar wi' the phrase, aye."

"Well, you're not actually putting your brains on the

rack, literally, right?"

"Right," he agreed.

"That saying is like the slang of the medieval ages."

"Like 'drawing the line', for example." He nodded. "I see."

"So the way I talk is merely the result of the age and culture in which I live," she explained. "You see?"

"I do," he considered for a moment. "It is unusually colorful, yer slang. I hae wondered also aboot yer use of profanities. 'Tis most unusual for a lady to curse so often."

"I do not," she protested in surprise.

"Ye do." He looked amused by her shock. "Ye've said 'damn' and 'hell' on many occasions since arriving."

Emmy rolled her eyes dismissively. "Well, that doesn't count. I mean, everyone uses those words all the time without even thinking about it. Shit, too. People say that so much I don't think it even counts anymore. 'Oh, shit!' 'Holy shit!'" she exclaimed, not batting an eye as he stared at her, visibly torn between astonishment and amusement "People say that all the time without thinking twice. But I don't *really* swear, you know?"

"What do ye consider 'really swearing'?"

"Well, I don't take the Lord's name in vain if I can help it, and I try very hard not to use the f-word," she responded defensively.

"The f-word?"

"Oh, I know you know the f-word!" She flourished her finger at him. "*Everyone* for hundreds of years has known that word. Women generally dislike it as a descriptor for... well," she lowered her voice to a whisper, "sex."

"*Ah*, that word." Connor threw his head back and laughed. "Ye dinnae like that word and what it implies?"

"Tends to suck the romance right out of any situation." She sniffed and turned her head away from him in annoyance, feeling that he was making fun of her in some way.

Connor leaned in and whispered in her ear. "Does it now? Tell me, lass, would ye rather make love? When ye get hot and sweaty and come apart in my arms, will calling it 'making love' be enough to describe all we'll feel together?"

He traced a finger down the back of her neck, his husky words and touch sending a shaft of lust through her that left her quivering. Her hand began to shake and Connor took her glass from her before she dropped it, setting both their glasses on a nearby table. He turned them away from the others in the room and looked down at her, his eyes hot with an answering desire.

"When we come together," he continued in his low brogue. "Dinnae ye want me to fook ye, lass? Well and good?"

She gasped as he said the word, his accent nearly rhyming with 'book'. With that intonation, the word lost all offensiveness. Heat stroked at her belly instead. Her tongue darting out to lick her lips. His gaze dropped, his own lips parted as if he wanted to kiss her badly. Closing her eyes in denial of the word, Emmy shook her head despite the desire weakening her knees.

"Or," he continued, his breath tickling her ear, "do ye want me to make love to ye?" He drew out the last four words with his deepest brogue and her legs nearly collapsed under her.

Clutching his arm, she savored the images that flashed behind her closed eyes. She swallowed thickly and took a deep, shuddering breath. "Oh, Connor. My God," she whispered hoarsely. "What you do to me."

"If it's anything like what ye do to me, then we're in trouble," he guaranteed.

"I always thought that having 'weak knees' was just a euphemism," she admitted breathlessly, "but it's really true. Sometimes I can barely stand when I am around you."

His dark eyes grew molten at her confession. "And sometimes parts of me stand too much when I'm around ye." His voice was low and gruff, but Emmy understood his meaning all too well.

"Yup, we're in trouble." She took a step away from him and reclaimed her wine, taking a long drink and fanning herself with her hand. She noticed Dory and Ian approaching and smiled, thankful for the distraction. "Dory, you are looking so much better," she enthused, perhaps overmuch.

Dory blushed and smiled, running a hand over her large stomach now unfettered by the corset and covered with a much more suitable gown that was cut with several large pleats in the front to allow for her girth. Truthfully she now looked huge in comparison to her appearance just hours before. "I feel better," the woman confessed. "The babies have been carrying on all afternoon. I never imagined it could feel like this."

"Wonderful, isn't it?" Emmy grinned.

"Very much so now that I understand it," the woman said, her eyes bright with joy. "Truly I wish you'd come much sooner so I might have had a greater appreciation of what has been happening."

"I'll remind you that you said that when your ankles are so swollen you can barely walk and your back is killing you," Emmy teased.

"She already has been doing that," Ian said playfully,

earning a swat from his wife but he just kissed her cheek, causing a blush to rise in Dory's cheeks.

Emmy could feel Connor's amazement as he looked on. Who would have thought Dory could unwind enough in public to allow a kiss from Ian without scolding him roundly for it? It was astonishing.

"I want to thank ye as well, my lady," Ian continued, taking Emmy's hand earnestly, "for everything ye ha' done for us and for our babies."

"And I thank you for the beautiful gown, despite the blackmail that accompanied it, but truly, I've done nothing."

"Oh, but you have," Dory argued, taking her other hand. "We both feel like you've made such a difference for us since you've been here. I can't believe it's only been a few days. It's almost like truly having a sister again."

"Well, thank you," Emmy murmured, touched by the sentiment. "I'm just happy I can help."

"I do hope that ye'll be here to help wi' the delivery?" Ian asked. "We would nae ha' it any other way. Please say ye'll stay?'

"Please, say you will," Dory echoed.

Emmy looked up at Connor with a questioning glance, wondering at his opinion of their plea but he was staring at Dory, a frown again creasing his brow, tapping his lips with a considering finger. He looked puzzled and she wondered at the cause.

Didn't he want her to stay now? But perhaps this was the reason she was here! Maybe this was the whole point of this… this journey she had taken. In her past, maybe Dory did not survive the birth. Could that be it? Was that something like—heaven forbid—God's will that she come here to this time and place to save a woman's life? Oh, she wanted to run up to her room and flip through her guidebook immediately to see if there was any mention of this family in particular. Why hadn't she thought of that before? Perhaps it was all there.

"My lady?" Ian questioned, nudging her back to the moment. She started with a smile.

"I'd be delighted to help in any way I can when the time comes."

"Thank you!" Dory smiled again and even reached over to hug her briefly. Emmy was startled but returned her embrace.

"*Ah*, there is Chilton to call us for dinner at last," Dory announced. "I, for one, am famished. Shall we?"

)O(O(O(O(

What did Dory mean by that? Connor's head swam. *Almost* like having a sister? Again? Surely it was just a turn of phrase? Perhaps they hadn't been close before Heather left?

He looked between Heather and Dory, studying them. They were the same height, same build. Dory's current condition aside, Dory had always been as slim as his Heather. Their features were identical, same mouth, nose and bright blue eyes. The smile currently lingering on Dory's face made it almost impossible to tell them apart, whereas her habitual scowl had made the difference before. Heather's hair was a bit lighter with streaks of blond, and she had those long sweeping locks in the front, but other than that, they were the same. Absolutely the same. They had to be twins. There could be no other explanation.

But the way Dory said 'almost'. It ate at him. Why would she say that?

"Hello? Earth to Connor, are you there?"

Connor blinked and looked down at Heather who waved a hand before his eyes with a questioning expression. "I beg yer pardon?"

"You were lost in space there for a minute," she teased. "Welcome back. Did you have a nice trip?"

"What?" he questioned. His brother and Dory laughed lightly.

"Dinner, Connor," Ian reminded him, slapping him on the back.

"Aren't you going to escort me in?" Emmy asked, taking his arm. "It is, like, your job, you know."

"Of course," Connor put a hand over hers and led her from the room as the others trailed behind him. Clearly they had all been waiting for him to come to his senses.

"What were you thinking about?" she asked curiously. "Because you were completely zoned."

"Zoned?"

She whistled and fluttered her fingers away from the side of her head. "Gone."

Indeed, he had been gone for a moment, he conceded, distracted by the impossible confusion of his thoughts. "It was nothing, just business."

"*Ah*, the old 'just business' excuse," she teased as he sat her again to his right, leaving the seat on the end once again vacant. This time Dory didn't seem to mind as she seated herself next to Ian. "What kind of business?"

"*Uh*," he floundered.

"Ye know, laird." The old man sitting on her other side leaned in, sparing him. "I hae been meaning to ask how the market went this year."

"The market?" Heather questioned, looking back and forth between the two men.

"Aye," the old man continued in his gravelly tones. "The cattle market in Glasgow. How was it?"

Connor's astonishment carried over as he stared at his uncle, taken aback. He couldn't recall the last time he'd been addressed directly at the dinner table, much less asked a question that might have been intended to lead to actual conversation. Heather nudged him under the table and gave him an encouraging nod. "Go ahead," she mouthed.

"Well, Uncle Innes," he cleared his throat. "We took in almost four hundred head in this year."

"You raise cows?" she asked.

"Only the best beef cattle in all of Scotland, lassie," Innes corrected in blustering, gravelly tones that reminded Connor of the old days when his uncle would spin outrageous tales to him and Ian when they were lads. "Best there is. The laird here has more than tripled the herd these past five years. Sheep, too. In my day, we dinnae raise a third of what the laird does now."

"Really? Tell me more."

She had to nudge him once more before Connor could adequately collect his thoughts to form a response. But it wasn't long before he was actively engaged in conversation. Soon most of the men at their end of the table joined Innes in the discussion. The lively, multi-generational exchange soon had those seated at the other end of the table looking on in amazement as they watched the laird laugh with his kin.

※※※※

Emmy slouched back in her chair with an air of satisfaction. Even Dory didn't so much as raise a brow at such lively conversation disrupting her dinner table. Connor laughed and argued the finer points of livestock with his family. She could see his surprise when his young cousin, Nab, expressed an interest in taking a more active part in the work of the estate that was clearly much larger than Emmy had imagined. The home farm and range where the cattle and sheep were housed were over a mile away on a large acreage that covered most of the southern end of Mull. Interesting what one could learn when one had a chance to listen.

The women spent a while longer without the men in the parlor that night, but could hear the shouts and conversation of the men occasionally over their own chatter in the parlor. Instead of finding refuge at the piano once again, she was drawn into a conversation with the younger ladies, cousins of Connor's, and Dory on proper prenatal care. Gladys, who was married to Connor's cousin Gregor, admitted that she was also in a delicate condition—here Emmy had to roll her eyes—and wondered about how best to have an easy pregnancy. The youngest, Nora, who had just recently wed young Nab, listened wide-eyed with awe and trepidation.

By the time the men joined them, Emmy was more relaxed than she'd been in days. As she watched Connor saunter in her direction, she thought he was as well, perhaps more than he had been, not just in days, but months or even years. He turned to make a comment to Innes who slapped him on the back as he passed and Connor smiled. It was a full smile of happiness. No wryness or cynicism. Just happiness.

"Look at you," she commented lightly as he took a seat beside her. "You keep this up, people might think that you actually are a friendly, humorous man."

He took her hand and raised it to his lips. Placing a warm kiss to her palm, he looked into her eyes. "Thank ye," he said simply.

She shrugged and smiled. "Me? I didn't do anything. I

told you if you just lightened up a bit everyone wouldn't be so afraid of you. Of course, now you'll have to deal with everyone getting all up in your business all the time. Pestering you."

He closed his eyes and groaned. "Much thanks."

"That's more like it," she grinned and squeezed his fingers. "You've got a pretty decent family here, Connor."

He looked around the room and nodded. "They'll do."

"High praise." She released his hand and patted his knee. "Well, my work here is done I think."

He caught her hand as she stood. "Where are ye off to?"

"To bed, I think."

"'Tis early yet," he argued, trying to pull her back down beside him.

Emmy sighed and stared down at his handsome face. "Well, you see, I didn't sleep too well last night, or the night before for that matter. It's been a long day and I'm just tired. Will you forgive me for giving in so early?"

"I've no' been sleeping well, either," he admitted huskily. "I think we both ken the reason."

"I'm sure we do," she drawled with a little sarcasm and shook her head. "Before I start getting nasty, just let me go, okay?"

Giving in graciously, Connor kissed her hand again and rose. "At least allow me to escort ye to our room?"

"It might be better if you didn't do that," she said, knowing what might happen so easily if he did. "I really do want to sleep."

"Verra well," he conceded. "'Tis just as well. We hae an early morning ahead. Yer maid should wake ye at about dawn for us to start our sail." He kissed her hand once again, lingering until she pulled away from the heat and tingling his lips introduced. "Good night, Hea... good night, my lady," he corrected before she could do it herself.

"Good night, Connor," she whispered, offered her good nights to the room and left, thinking there was no way she was going to sleep well tonight either.

His kiss had seen to that and it was only on her hand! She scratched her palm to rid it of the lingering tingle and wondered how long she could hold out against him. Long enough for him to admit he was wrong? Suddenly she doubted it.

21

Surprisingly, she did indeed sleep well and was awake and looking forward to the day with Connor when Margo arrived the next morning with a light breakfast, and to help her dress. Wearing her own undergarments and again refusing the corset, Emmy accepted Margo's advice for dressing warmly against the cold winds likely to abound on the Sound of Mull. She allowed the long, woolen pantalets but wore them over her underwear, more like long johns, and wore two wool petticoats under her skirts. She also had a warm coat, gloves and scarf to help keep her warm, but rejected the huge, ridiculous hat as pointless against the cold.

She was thankful for it all when she met Connor at the carriage in front of the keep. The clouds were heavy and gray and, although the air was calm, it was chilly.

"Good morning, Connor," she offered with a cheery smile.

"Good morning, my lady," he returned, offering a hand up to help her into the carriage. "Did ye sleep well then?"

"Thankfully, yes. And you?"

"Well enough," he answered with a grin, settling himself next to her on the long bench. "So where shall we sail today? Any thoughts?"

"Why don't you just show me what you think I'd like best."

"I might miss something of import."

"It's universally accepted the locals always know the best stuff. I trust you."

"Let's be off then." He rapped on the roof of the carriage and it set off with a jerk, inciting a yelp from Emmy as she clutched Connor's arm.

"Not exactly a smooth ride is it?" she complained not a hundred yards down the drive.

"I hae one of the best carriages on the island," he argued, affronted. "Ye'll no' find a smoother ride nearby."

"This is a smooth ride?" She asked in amazement as the carriage swayed and jolted along the road. The crunch of the gravel under the wooden wheels was audible and reminded her of the sound of a rolling pin over graham crackers when she made a crust for a pie. The vibration grated against her nerves like nails on a chalkboard. She shuddered. "God bless the invention of multipoint suspension," she muttered as they bounced over a particularly big rut in the road. She hung on to him with one hand and a strap hanging on the side of the carriage with the other as they went along.

"Good God, lass," he scolded. "Ye act like ye've ne'er been in a carriage before. 'Tis no' that bad."

"I don't know, Connor," she denied with a slow shake of her head, gulping deeply as motion sickness started to overtake her, "if this is a smooth ride, I might have a problem." The closed carriage allowed for no airflow and no windows to view the passing landscapes.

With a look of disgust, he reached across her to pull down the window beside her. The cool breeze hit Emmy on the face and she turned to it gratefully, taking a deep breath of the fresh air. "Ye think this is bad, wait until we are out on the water."

"I've never had a problem with seasickness, not in my entire life."

"Well, I cannae wait until we get there then," he muttered with a measure of antipathy.

"Me neither."

The trip that had taken just ten minutes in the shuttle took almost an hour in the carriage. When they got to the dock, she was trembling and covered in a thin sheen of sweat. Shakily she accepted his offer of tea at a nearby inn while he made sure the boat was ready.

What a nightmare. Never had she been so sensitive to the motion of any vehicle she'd ridden in. Every little sway had her swallowing back the bile that rose in her throat. The only thing that she had to feel thankful for—besides the end of the trip, that is—was that she hadn't vomited in Connor's lap along the way.

Well, chalk up one more strike against this time, she thought as she patted her cheeks with some of the cold water the inn manager brought for her to aid her recovery. She nodded her thanks to the man and even drank the hot tea gratefully when it was placed before her.

"Will there be anything else, lass?" the jolly middle-aged man asked.

"No, thank you. I'm much better already." She pressed the damp towel to the back of her neck, refusing to even think of the return trip at this point. Indeed, for the duration of her stay, this might be her single expedition out of Duart. "I appreciate your help."

The man nodded and started to move off when a deep gravelly voice drew their attention. "Maybe ye should offer the lady some toast or something, Jimmy. She's looking a mite peaked."

Jimmy nodded and set off to do just that as Emmy stared in amazement at the owner of that distinctive voice. "Donell?" she questioned aloud but received no response. "Donell!" she commanded more firmly, and for her troubles got an eyebrow raised at her over the rim of a pewter mug, as the man sipped his drink.

It *was* Donell the shuttle driver without a doubt, but why not acknowledge it? Why was he looking at her as if he didn't know her? She grabbed her cup and moved over to his table without waiting to ask permission. Leaning forward, she whispered, "Did it get you, too, Donell?"

"Did what get me, lass?" he asked, wiping his mouth with the sleeve of his jacket. His bushy eyebrows rose in recognition that to her mind looked a bit contrived. "I ken who ye are, ye know?"

"I know you do."

"Ye're the Countess of Duart returned after all these years!" He raised his mug in a toast and drank deeply, though his eyes never left hers. "What do ye think of Duart these days? No' too simple a life, *eh*?"

Emmy slumped back in her chair and stared at him, flabbergasted. As thoughts and realizations raced through her mind, she gaped like a landed fish as she tried to formulate a response. "You? You did this to me? How? Why?" These last two words were vague and shot through with disbelief as he continued to drink and study her in turn.

"Ye seem to be doing pretty well fer yerself so far," he added, still looking at her. "*Are* ye enjoying your visit? Ye've come a long way after all."

Emmy's head began to nod automatically in response. "Yes."

"Ready to go home then?"

Hesitation, just a moment, and that was all it took for his wrinkled rugged face to crease into an expression of amusement. "No' yet then, eh?"

"Donell," she whispered, stunned by the realization that he presented. "How?" she repeated. "Why?"

"Tragic family, the MacLeans," he commented as if he never heard her questions. "What wi' the laird's wife leaving him like that and then the wife of the younger one…"

"Dory? It *is* about Dory, isn't it? I thought so. Am I here to save her? What of Connor?" Emmy reached out and squeezed the old man's hand in appeal. "They are good people, Donell. Tell me what I need to do."

The old man patted her hand between his in a kindly manner, and smiled as he continued on as if he hadn't heard her at all. He hadn't even admitted that he was behind what had brought her here. How had he done it? Laws of physics, and government conspiracies aside, Emmy wasn't one to believe in magic or sorcery. What other power could make this happen? She was believer enough to have just one answer jump to her mind, but taking Donell in with a shake of her head, denied *that* possibility.

Perhaps it wasn't happening at all but was instead some drug-induced delusion. More dream than reality but the old Scot didn't look evil enough to have been a part of such duplicity either. "What is going on, Donell? You must tell me."

"Everyone deserves a second chance at life, lassie. Even ye."

"Me?" Confused and frustrated, she frowned at him. "I don't need a second chance. I have a perfect life waiting for me."

"Do ye now?"

"It's what I've always wanted," she insisted stubbornly.

"Is it now?" he questioned again with a twinkle in his eye. "Ye came on yer holiday alone, lass. Nae friends wi' ye. Nae man. Perfect life? Do ye even ken what ye *really* want?"

"Of course, I do."

"Yet did ye no' envy these people their simple life?" he queried craftily. "*Ah*, but mayhap ye've begun to realize that it isnae so simple, eh? What say ye, lassie? Ye still thinking these people have a simple life?" He chuckled and shifted his eyes.

Hers followed the direction of his, and she saw Connor approaching the inn. Her long exhale spoke volumes. "A bit longer, I think." The old man rose and dropped a few coins on the table. "Ta-ra, Jimmy," he called as he shuffled to the door.

"Wait," Emmy called but Donell just raised his hand in farewell, and even held the door open with a slight bow to the laird as Connor entered the inn.

"Ye still look a wee bit peaked, my love," he commented with a hint of worry as he joined her at the table. "Are ye sure ye want to do this?"

"Connor," she asked instead, a touch of desperation in her voice, "do you know that man who just left?"

He looked over his shoulder and bit back a chuckle, "Auld Donell? Has he managed to wrap ye around his finger? Most of the ladies here would do just about anything he asked."

"Who is he?"

"He owns a small farm north of here on the coast. Been auld since I was just a wee lad, but ne'er seems to change." Enjoying the look of curiosity on her face, he leaned in and added in a confidential tone, "Rumor has it that he might be a wizard or such. His mother before him was said to be a powerful witch."

"Really," Emmy choked out. A wizard? Was it magic that had brought her here?

"Some others say he's a fallen angel."

"A what?"

"One of God's angels who has come down from Heaven to serve a penance of sorts," Connor's expression turned mischievous. "Dinnae look so serious, lass, 'tis all nonsense and superstition. 'Tis what happens when an auld man never seems to age and appears to hae a blessed touch aboot him."

"Blessed touch?"

"Some say he has a healing touch, but 'tis just coincidence more like." Connor paused, as if realizing that she was taking him seriously. "Ye need no' fear him, my love, he's just a harmless auld man wi' too much time on his hands who tends to poke around in other people's business ore than he aught."

Apparently, she thought sarcastically, *and now I'm his newest hobby.* What was she supposed to do now that her life—her future—was resting in the hands of an ancient bored wizard/angel? What did it all mean? And what did he mean when he asked did *she* know what she wanted? Rebellious youth aside, she'd always been career driven.

"Are ye ready to go?" he asked, interrupting her thoughts.

She stared at the empty door for a moment. "Yeah, I'm

ready."

22

"Are ye sure ye want to do this?" he asked again as they went down the wooden dock to his boat mooring. Connor had never seen anyone get sick from a carriage ride so quickly *and* she'd moaned and groaned the entire journey as if she were about to die. He'd thought her to be made of sterner stuff than that and was almost afraid to take her out on the open waters of the sound lest she take up her whining once more.

"Of course. I'm fine now, don't worry about it." She patted his hand reassuringly and put her troubles behind her. "Which one is yours?"

Connor pointed along the dock to a large sailing vessel moored about half way up. "There she is. *Buidhe Bean-Chèile.*"

Amazement flooded her expression. "Why, it's beautiful. That's no mere sailboat." Connor shrugged modestly. Indeed, his boat was more like a small yacht trimmed with brass fittings. "Very nice, Connor, very nice. What does the name mean?"

"A Good Wife," he answered, jumping down into the deck at the bow before turning to help her down. She stared down at him with bulging eyes.

"'Twas named for my mother," he explained with a low chuckle and she exhaled a doubtful laugh, taking the proffered hand, but jumping as he did to the deck before grinning up at him.

"Of course, it was. " She shook her head. "Wow, this is wonderful."

Her enthusiasm warmed him as she took it in. The deck here was edged in benches but currently also sported two leather sling chairs. "For us?"

"Aye, I had them brought up thinking ye might enjoy the view from here. It'll be windy, but I dinnae think too unpleasant."

"No, not at all!. Wow." she said again looking around her. "Pretty cool, Connor. Even Dr. Evans doesn't have one this fancy."

"Dr. Evans?" he queried curiously, feeling a stab of jealousy.

"One of the doctors at Hopkins," she told him. "He lives on his boat and keeps a berth out in Annapolis. He had some of the senior residents out on the Fourth of July to watch the fireworks on the bay. I thought his was nice, but he'd envy you, I think."

"He cannae afford a house?"

"Of course he can, silly. He lives on the boat because he wants to. I mean, no biggie, he's a single guy. Life's all about him at this point."

Connor wondered if this single 'guy' was one of the men she'd slept with, but didn't want to ruin their day, so he kept the question to himself. "What do ye think?"

"What? No tour?" she laughed.

"There's no' much to see," he demurred, but escorted her below to show her the main cabin. It had a small wood stove for heat and cooking, and folding doors that could be closed to section off an area for sleeping. Other than that, there was only a small water closet. It was small but the furnishings were elegant and she told him so.

He shrugged. "'Tis no' much but it does allow several people at once to travel to the mainland wi'out waiting for the ferry. Shall we?" He gestured to the short steps that would take them back on deck, signaling for her to precede him. As she started up however, her backside came right up to his eye level and Connor was hard-pressed not to help her up just to have an excuse to put his hands just there. Chuckling ruefully he shook his head, pocketing his hands in an effort to fight the temptation she presented.

She looked back over her shoulder suspiciously. "What's so funny?"

He shook his head in denial. "Nothing at all. Up ye go and I'll have the porter bring us some drinks on deck."

"It's a bit early for drinks isn't it?"

"I was thinking tea actually." But as she started to wrinkle her nose he held up a hand. "But since I ken ye dinnae care for it, I thought coffee perhaps? To warm us?"

The smile she offered was soft as she considered his thoughtfulness. "Coffee would be wonderful. Thank you."

※※※※

As they went on deck once more, preparations were already being made to make sail. The small crew of four was raising the sails and shouting to one another as Emmy took a seat in one of the chairs at the bow. A deckhand draped a blanket across her lap and she smiled her thanks. Connor had gone out of his way to make the trip about her and she was touched by his thoughtfulness.

Soon they were making their way into the sound and Emmy was cradling a porcelain cup of coffee in her hands. It had nothing on Starbucks, of course, but it was strong and hot, warming her in the chill of the late October morning. The winds off the sound bit at her cheeks and she raised her face to the wind in enjoyment, even as she turned her mind to Donell's cryptic words.

For his part, Connor held his cup but could do nothing more than watch the joy on her face as she raised hers, eyes closed to savor both the weather and the beverage. He wondered if he was being a complete fool to encourage this strange bond between them; to fantasize over the possibilities her return presented to him. If someone had told him a month ago he would be plotting ways to have her for himself, he would have laughed at them for a fool. Yet here he was with a woman who still denied her identity, though the duplicity continued to puzzle him.

It simply wasn't possible that another woman identical to Heather and Dory could exist and arrive at his home with the same timing she had. What then had motivated her return and denial? He had no answers and that in itself was frustrating.

But being in her company was not. He knew he should fight it, that he should hold tight to the anger and resentment, lest she play him for a fool once more. Perhaps she already was playing him for a fool, he thought. Perhaps this was some cruel game she had concocted to bring further misery to his life. Could it be? He shook his head. This Heather—his lady, he'd been thinking of her rather than calling her by that name to avoid arguments—was an open book. When she was happy, she laughed and teased. When she was angry, she made sure he knew it. Surely someone who so openly expressed every feeling could not be hiding sinister plots behind that façade?

She had to be Heather, yet some part of him recognized that, at least in manner, she was not the Heather he knew. This woman was playful, inappropriately casual and yet sharply intelligent and openly caring about other people. She worried for others; Dory, Ian and even himself. She'd mended in just a couple of days a family estrangement that had been in place for nearly a decade. He knew he owed her his thanks for that alone.

Beyond that, she was sensual, alluring and seductive without even trying. He closed his eyes and pictured the two of them together. The chemistry between them was profound. He wanted her with near desperation, yet wasn't sure it would be enough.

"Penny for your thoughts." Her low voice cut through his thoughts and he opened his eyes to find her studying him, much as he had been scrutinizing her moments before.

He shook his head in denial. "Naught of importance."

XOXOXOX

Emmy knew that was a lie. The expression on his face had been almost… well, longing, if she had to put a name to it. She wished she knew what prompted it. Was he thinking of her? Was it possible he might think as she did?

In the space of a few days, Emmy had experienced the most intense desire that she'd ever felt in her life. However, there was so much more between herself and Connor than just pure lust. At least on her part. She shuddered to think that everything else was just one-sided because Connor was rapidly becoming extremely important to her. She respected him, she knew. It was difficult not to. His devotion to his role as laird and head of his clan was remarkable. He took the responsibility so seriously, despite the lack of deeper personal relationships among those who depended on him. He was so caring, yet trying to mask it. His sense of humor was similar to hers. He was well read and liked music. And, as she suspected before, she was certain that he wanted badly to have someone to love.

And she wanted that love directed at her. The revelation shouldn't have been surprising but it was nonetheless. To be sheltered by Connor's love would be the most incredible thing. She knew it without a doubt. He was a bit gruff now, but thawing quickly and Emmy could easily imagine the role he would assume in a relationship.

He would be protector, provider and lover.

It went against her stalwart belief in the power of womanhood, of independence and self-worth to think that she might enjoy being taken care of. Being a wife in the sense it meant in this time did have a certain appeal to it. She inwardly recoiled at her internal confession. Did she really think she could give over her personal power into the hands of a man? *Be a housewife?* Figuratively speaking, of course, since, as a countess, she would have few duties. But that was the point. Countesses did not have careers. She met his dark eyes and they stared at each other for a long moment, each considering.

She could see it, Emmy acknowledged. She might even do it—for him. He wouldn't abuse his rights, she believed him capable of a giving, sharing relationship. She trusted him.

Holy shit! I think I am falling in love with him.

"And ye? A penny for yers?" he whispered.

Oh, hell no! she thought, shaking her head in denial.

✕✕✕✕

They were well into the sound by this point, heading on a southeasterly course closer to the coast than the ferry had traveled. As they moved along to the south, she caught a glimpse of a palatial manor tucked away among the hills and trees. She asked Connor what it was.

"Duart House. Home of the Guthries."

Surprised, she examined the beautiful building with a critical eye. It was so lovely, much bigger than she would have thought and as elegant as a French chateau. "Home of the exgirlfriend."

"Just so," he confirmed softly.

"Why didn't you just tell everyone the marriage had been annulled?" she asked, curiosity getting the best of her. "Why have you *still* not told anyone? You could still marry the woman, you know."

Connor rubbed his finger along his lower lip, in a gesture she was beginning to realize was a habit of his when he was thinking, and regarded the house solemnly. "I dinnae ken why I hidnae told anyone. I guess it dinnae matter much. Everyone thought, assumed, ye were dead anyway, but some part of me knew I had to make it legal. For my own peace of mind. As for Miss Guthrie, who knows? I might have that opportunity still."

That stung, but she hid the hurt. "Will you tell everyone

now?"

He turned his serious gaze to hers. "Do ye want me to?"

She shrugged nonchalantly. "Everyone thinks we're living as husband and wife and probably assume we're sleeping together. It would probably scandalize them if they knew we were living in sin. How long do you mean to go on then?"

"Until I decide what to do wi' ye, I suppose."

A seductive smile tilted a corner of Emmy's lips as she looked up at him through lowered lashes. "What do you want to do with me?"

His silence was broken by a harsh laugh and he grabbed up her hand to press a kiss to her fingers. "*Och*, lass, I think ye ken verra well what I want to do with ye."

She joined his laughter, caressing his chin with her thumb before patting his cheek. "Besides that?"

"Truthfully, other than that, I really have nae idea," he answered. "A part of me still wonders if ye have some ulterior motive in being here."

"And maybe the other half is inclined to believe me?"

He scowled and pulled back from her. "Nae, no' yet."

Emmy sighed and sat back in her chair crossing her arms over her chest. "Stubborn!" she huffed.

"Scots," he answered and she had to fight the twitch that threatened to bring a smile to her face.

She pouted in silence, ignoring the self-admitted stubborn Scot, and enjoyed the scenery as the waters widened to Loch Linnhe and Duart emerging in the distance. "How incredible the castle looks from here. Oh, it's beautiful," she said more to herself than to Connor. The castle rose up from the rocky cliff on its coastal side, showing off its great defenses. Clearly that was why it had been built just so. As they sailed past and the perspective rotated, she got the view from the southeast. The morning sun hit the side of the castle and the mountainous vista behind it was capped in the low clouds. The landscape around it seemed so barren.

She watched it until it was out of sight. Turning again, she noticed a small piece of rock barely large enough to call an island jutting from the water. If not for the small lighthouse that marked it, it might have passed unnoticed. "What is that?" she asked. "I didn't notice it on the way here."

"*Ah*, interesting story there." Connor leaned forward facing her, his tone filled with enthusiasm. An uncomfortable silence had begun to envelop them, perhaps he was as eager to change the topic as she. "'Tis the Lady's Rock."

"Lady's Rock," Emmy repeated. "Why does that sound familiar?"

"Hundreds of years ago my ancestor, Lachlan Cattenach, who was the laird at the time, stranded his wife Catherine on that wee island because she hidnae yet borne him an heir."

"Nice. Just like a man to blame the woman," she muttered with clear sarcasm. "Oh, I remember this from the guidebook for the ferry. The guy 'accidentally' left her on the island," She used air quotes around the word. "He expected her to get washed away by the tide because the rock would be underwater at high tide."

Connor nodded with amusement. "And when she had disappeared the next morning, my ancestor wrote distraughtly to her brother, the earl of Argyll, of her death."

She picked up the story, sitting forward with a smile. "And when the laird was invited to Inverary to meet the earl, there was Catherine sitting right next to her brother at the table, saved by a passing fisherman. I forgot, what happened to the laird? Did the earl kick his butt?"

Laughing aloud, Connor shook his head. "Nay, they let him go unharmed, though a couple of years later he was killed by another of Catherine's brothers, some say in revenge."

"Serves him right for trying to kill his wife for something she had no control over. I mean, they had other kids, right? A girl?"

"I believe so. Why do ye say she had nae control? If she gave him only lasses..." he dangled the question curiously.

"Gender determination is all on the father, Connor, surely you know that?"

✕✕✕✕✕

Her mind raced. When did they figure that out? Thinking back to her college courses, Emmy recalled that a woman—she felt a little smile lift her lips at the thought—named Nettie Stevens had discovered the chromosome pairings and their role in deciding the sex of a child. But that had been in 1905. Ten years from this time.

"What do ye mean, all on the father?" There was a bit of indignation there that amused her. Male pride never died.

"I'm saying the mother has nothing to do with the sex of a baby. The father is solely responsible for that." He snorted in disbelief and she leaned closer. "No, it's true. Okay, think of it this way," she held up a closed fist. "Here's the egg. In the woman," she clarified. "Let's call that egg, oh I don't know, X. No matter what, the egg will always be an X, with me so far?"

He nodded skeptically and waved her on.

With her other hand, Emmy wiggled her fingers with a flutter. "Over here are your little swimmers, the sperm." He flushed a bit but nodded again while she counted them off with her thumb. "Here's sperm X, this one's called Y, then another Y and another X, okay?" She poked her index finger X to her closed fist. "Mr. X sperm hits the egg and we have baby XX. Two X's together and you have a girl." She switched fingers and pressed her middle finger to her fist. "Mr. Y sperm gets to the egg first and you get baby XY, a boy. Got it?"

"I believe so."

Emmy waved her fingers back toward him. "X or Y it is all in the sperm. The woman has absolutely nothing to do with the sex of the baby."

"Nothing?" he echoed in amazement.

"Nada," she confirmed.

"How can ye know this?" Despite the question, there was no doubt he believed her. He looked astounded.

"Biology 101," she replied with a shrug. "It's pretty much the first thing you learn. This tendency y'all have of blaming a woman is barbaric."

24

"Did you go to college, Connor? I mean university?"

He sat back as she did, as they both sipped on their coffee. Her comment about his people being barbaric ruffled his feathers. Too many times in the past had people labeled the Scots thus. "Indeed I did. Cambridge."

"What did you study?"

"Business and land management, of course, as well as science, history and art," he answered, glad to prove he wasn't as barbarous as she assumed.

"So you consider yourself an educated man? A contemporary thinker?"

"I suppose I do," he replied, wary now, not knowing where she was going.

"What are your thoughts on women's rights? Suffrage. I'm sure they are up to that already... *um*, here, in Scotland," she added as if an afterthought.

"Oh, aye, the suffrage movement. Ye do hear a bit of it in Glasgow and London," he admitted. "So far, it hisnae gained much ground around here."

"Well, what do you think about it? About women having the right to vote? For it or against it?" She peered at him over the rim of her cup with a narrowed gaze that had him rethinking his impulsive response.

He wasn't about to tell her that he was against the idea. Not when she was looking at him like that, with daggers in her eyes. It would only serve to prove her point more readily, no doubt.

"There some women who…most women…" he hedged then scratched his chin and admitted, "*Och*, lass, I'm nae sure I hae an answer ye'll approve of on that subject. Most of the women I ken…well, I wouldnae trust them with a vote. Ye understand? They're no' aware of the issues and what is best for the country."

"Because they are women or because they aren't educated on the facts?"

He considered that clarification against the women he knew and conceded: "Mostly because they dinnae care to make themselves aware, I suppose."

"So education is key, then? What if I wanted to vote? Would that be all right?" Her gaze was so straightforward and assessing, so intelligent, that in that moment Connor felt he would trust her judgment, or at least consider it thoughtfully on almost any subject.

"Aye, I would trust yer vote to be well thought out. Ye're intelligent and dinnae seem the sort to make a decision based on emotion alone," he admitted truthfully and was pleased when she blessed him with a wide smile.

"Thank you, Connor, that means a lot to me."

"I've ne'er known a woman who has had as much education as ye ha'," he added. "It's unusual and rare. Most women . . ."

"Don't blow the moment, Connor," she said softly, patting his hand before settling back in her chair.

XOXOXOX

They sat in silence for a long while after that. Unlike their previous silence, this was companionable, not uncomfortable as long silences could be. They enjoyed the scenery as they came to the mouth of Loch Spelve, where they turned to the left towards the mainland of Scotland. Occasionally Connor would point out a landmark or point of interest, or she would offer comment or praise on the landscape or view. He took her hand in his at one point and simply held it for a long time and Emmy stared down at their joined hands wondering if life could ever truly be so contented.

Simple . . . *hmm*.

Soon they reached the southern point of Kerrera, a narrow island between Mull and the mainland and moved north up its sound to Oban. They docked in Oban for lunch. The restaurant Connor chose was ironically right across from where her hotel should have been, or would be someday. Emmy stared out the window at the building that occupied that spot now, a livery stable that was a far cry from the four-story hotel that would eventually be there.

Pondering her situation thoughtfully while she chewed, Emmy again questioned what she wanted from her life. Sometimes, it seemed she'd been here in this time for weeks instead of days. Other than the clothing and wondering what was happening on her favorite TV shows, she didn't truly miss anything from her time. Oh, that time would come; she was sure it would happen right about the same time that her

201

confidence in her DVR gave way to bigger issues. But for the moment she was strangely comfortable, content and not at all in a rush to return to her own time and place.

So what had Donell meant?

"Ye've been terribly quiet and thoughtful today," Connor commented at length, after watching her stare blankly out of the window for some time. "What's working in yer head?"

Thinking it might be a good time to bring it up, Emmy answered his question with one of her own. "Do you ever think about the future?"

"Of course, everyone does."

"No, I don't mean like next month or next year," she corrected. "I am talking about the far future, say a century from now. Don't you ever wonder what it will be like?"

Pointing his fork at her, he chuckled. "Ye've been reading Jules Verne, hae ye?"

"Jules Verne? Oh, like *20,000 Leagues Under the Sea*…or better *From the Earth to the Moon?*" she added with a snap of her fingers. "Okay, let's start there. Do you think that man will ever be able to fly to the moon?"

As if sensing she was serious in her question, he took a moment to consider the possibility. "I dinnae ken. Invention has changed much in just the last ten or fifteen years. There are inventions being developed every day that change the way we live. I undertand much of London and New York and other large cities are lit by electric lights now. Telephones are being put in many homes in Glasgow. We ne'er would hae dreamed of such a thing ten years ago. The automobile. Hae ye ever seen one? I saw a race in London last year. 'Twas fascinating."

"I might have seen one, once or twice." She twisted her

lips to stop a smile. "You're open-minded enough then to see the possibilities of the future?"

Connor looked offended. "I'm an educated man."

She held up a hand. "I know you are, don't get your back up. But let's go a little further. What if the technology of the telephone, for example, advanced so much in a century that everyone had one of their own? Not just a telephone in their homes, but one small enough to be held in your palm and be used without wires or cords of any kind? Could you see that happening?"

""'tis nearly unimaginable, but perhaps if science progressed so much," he allowed, enjoying that the lass challenged him with conversation beyond the weather or business of the earldom. Such an unusual woman she was!

"Let's go even further then." She thought for a moment. "How about H. G. Wells? Have you read *The Time Machine?*"

"Just a few months ago, as a matter of fact. 'Twas just published this year. I'm surprised ye've read it. It wisnae a genre of books any of the ladies of my acquaintance would ever dream of read... Aye, well, I suppose I've answered my own question wi' that, aye?"

"Ladies of your acquaintance mostly reading...?"

"Novels or fashion magazines." He paused. "I'm afraid most in my household rarely venture into the library in search of intellectually stimulating materials."

"I suppose I won't argue again about the reasons for your views on women's rights then," she murmured under her breath then turned back to the matter at hand. "So *The Time Machine*. What did you think of it?"

"I thought it was well written..."

"No, no," she corrected in exasperation. "Not the writing or even the story. What did you think of the premise of the book? About time travel itself?"

"Such an intense question. It's fiction, lass," he said, as if reminding her.

"This from a man who just moments ago conceded that travel to the moon might be possible someday?" She tutted lightly. "That was fiction, too, Mr. Educated Man. Look at this with those same eyes."

"But there is nae scientific basis for time travel," he argued, "whereas travel to space could be seen as the progression of current science."

"There is no scientific basis *yet*," she corrected firmly. "What if I were to tell you, right now, that I am from the future, have seen the future, and time travel will be possible someday, far beyond your lifetime, what would you do?"

"Lock ye up in Bedlam?" he responded with a laugh. She didn't join him.

"Surprisingly narrow-minded of you, Connor."

He reached across the table and took her hand, patting it. "*Och*, lass, be serious. There are just some things that are no' realistic even in the far future."

Emmy gritted her teeth at the patronizing pat and opened her mouth to retaliate but changed her mind, deciding now was not the time to argue the point. The laird hadn't even been able to accept that she wasn't Heather MacLean yet. How could she expect him to swallow the idea of time travel so quickly, when she wasn't entirely sure she believed in it herself, despite her current situation? Instead she applied herself to finishing her lunch, a nicely done roast beef with potatoes, or 'tatties' as Connor called them, and veggies. Comfort food for a cool fall day. She felt much better when she was finished.

When they were done, he tucked her hand into the crook

of his arm as they walked slowly back to the waterfront. "Yer fingers are getting cold."

"I left the gloves on the boat. I'll be fine when we get there."

However, the sound was choppy on the return trip and the temperature had dropped dramatically. Shivering, Emmy accepted Connor's urging to remain below, near the stove and out of the winds without argument. By the time they docked in Craignure, she would've wagered the temperature was near freezing and the clouds were definitely threatening rain.

The rain began in earnest during the sickening drive back to Duart. Emmy could see ice crystals in the drops as they splattered on the carriage windows.

The carriage swayed and jolted even more with the buffeting winds and icy rain pounding against the side. She was weak with motion sickness and drenched when they made it through the courtyard and into the castle. Exhausted, she leaned against the wall in the hall, stripping off the wet coat and gloves, and wishing she could drop the sodden, heavy skirts and petticoats right there as well.

"I'll call Margo to draw a hot bath for ye," Connor offered, not liking the pale color of her cheeks. "I dinnae want ye to take a chill."

"A bath sounds wonderful, but I can do it myself. Don't bother Margo," she begged. "I gave her the day off to spend with her mom; apparently she hasn't been feeling well."

"At least allow me to help ye to yer room."

"I'm not an invalid, Connor." She declined his offered

assistance and straightened determinedly. "I'm sure I can haul my cookies up one set of stairs."

"Cookies?" The word echoed behind her as wearily climbed the sweeping staircase.

Once in her bathroom, she started the water and stripped off her soaked clothing. Immediately she felt better just shedding the icy clothing. Stepping close to the tub, she toweled her arms and legs over the heat of the steaming water, warming herself at the same time.

Deciding to kill two birds with one stone, she filled up the sink as well, thinking to hand-wash her bra and underwear before she soaked in the tub. Her white silk blouse had gone to the laundress the previous day only to come back an interesting shade of yellowed ivory. Obtaining a more gentle soap from Margo, Emmy had taken it upon herself to preserve her only real bra and underwear. A day in pantalets the previous day had shown her that such a bulky feeling wasn't for her. So she washed her bra and panties at night in the little sink, leaving the delicate undergarments to hang dry overnight, although she couldn't expect them to last long under such abuse.

Poking through her tote bag while the water ran, Emmy pulled out her iPhone and earphones and pushed the little buds into her ears while scrolling for a playlist of relaxing music. She missed the music of her time. Usually she had those white cords coming out of her ears all day long. Music just made her happy.

Humming along, she propped the iPhone on the side of the sink as she swished soap into the warm water. Tim McGraw and Faith Hill's ballad 'Let's Make Love' was playing. Emmy undeniably felt the message in that song. Wriggling out of her camisole, she started to sing along.

XOXOXOX

Connor entered her room to check on her, despite her declaration that she could take care of herself. He heard her voice and paused outside the bathing room, thinking she was talking to someone. Nay, she was singing softly to herself again as she had the previous day. Sneaking a look around the corner, he was captivated by the sight of her. She was facing away from him as she pulled her short silk shift up, exposing the long line of her back. Over her head it went and into the sink.

She fiddled with something for a moment, her long hair unbound to her waist and swinging from side to side as she tossed her head first one way then the other. She turned slightly, giving him a glimpse of her tantalizing silhouette. Her full breasts were encased in a white lace contraption he was unfamiliar with, but stirred by. Again she wore that wee bit of lace that barely covered the luscious curve of her buttocks. The sight of it aroused him easily. Her legs were long and muscular, her stomach flat. Her long hair, swinging across her back and shoulders in a caress he felt as it were brushing him. He'd not seen it down before and the gleaming length captivated him.

As she reached up behind her to unclasp the lacy covering from her breasts, the well-toned muscles in her stomach and back flexed. She was a healthy lass, to be sure, and there was no denying the beauty and appeal of her body.

She dropped that garment into the sink before her hands next slid into the top of her lower piece of clothing. Emmy pushed it down. Her hair fell forward, exposing her back and a colorful scrolling of loops and spirals on her skin starting just at the top of her buttocks and twisting up her spine. A tattoo? Where would she have gotten a tattoo? Why? It was hypnotically entrancing, though. It made him want to kiss it or follow its trail with his tongue. Perhaps that was the point. He scowled as the wondering and jealousy roared to life within him again. Had other men thought that very same thing when seeing it?

The words *make love* drew his attention to her song as she kicked off the lower garment and scooped it up to toss it in the sink as well. "'Do you know what you do to me?'" she crooned softly, almost under her breath. "*'Everything inside of me is wanting you, needing you. I'm so in love with you.'*" She sang this last with such heartfelt feeling that it caused a gripping ache in his chest. "*'Look in my eyes, let's get lost tonight...in each other. Let's make love, all night long until all our strength is gone. Hold on tight, just let go. I want to feel you in my soul. Until the sun comes up...let's make love.'*"

Connor needed no further invitation beyond her softly sung appeal; the words and the way she voiced them incited undeniable lust in him. Approaching her from behind, he slid his hand around her ribcage and cupped her breasts from behind. Burying his face in her hair, his lips fastened on the side of her neck. She squealed in shock and surprise, leaping away from him. "Connor! What are you doing in here?"

XOXOXOX

Emmy nearly tripped on the cord of her ear buds as they were jerked out of her ears. The phone landed with a thud on the floor in her haste to back away as she scooped up a towel and held it against her breasts. The final tones of the country song dissolved with a tinny farewell before the headphone jack was pulled out of the phone.

"I wanted to make sure ye were feeling better. I knocked but ye dinnae answer." His brogue was thick and husky as he approached her in what could only be defined as a predatory manner.

"I didn't hear you."

"That was obvious." Connor followed her as she skirted the edge of the room. "Yer song was quite...stirring." He cornered her before she reached the door. "The words were most provocative. Was that yer intention? *Och* lass, give over, will ye? I want ye so verra, verra much." His big hand cupped her shoulder as he bent his head to softly nuzzle her lips before sliding down the curve of her back to cup her buttocks. "I maun hae ye."

With a moan, Emmy flung her arms around his shoulders and pressed her body fully against him. This was just no time to be prudish. She wanted him badly herself and his tender plea utterly did her in. "Oh, Connor! Okay, okay...you win," she sighed against his lips before capturing them in a hot kiss.

He groaned in triumph and defeat. Wrapping his arms around her waist he raised her up against him, devouring her mouth over and over. He pressed her up against the wall and her legs came up of their own accord to wrap around his waist.

Her surrender brought a shaky breath from Connor. "Bugger it, lassie, ye make me tremble like a schoolboy."

His arms *were* trembling, his breath shallow and uneven. Emmy marveled in his size and strength as he held her easily against the wall. She felt petite and desirable. She'd never felt so before. Already her breath was coming rapidly, her belly tightening with promise and he hadn't even touched her yet. His lips left hers to fasten again on her neck, sucking and biting lightly. She cried out as the passion overwhelmed her.

"Oh, Connor. Now. Now." She fumbled with the

buttons on his shirt, urging him to hurry.

XXXXX

Connor broke away slightly to look down into her face. Her eyes were unfocused, her cheeks flushed. Never had he imagined that she felt this overwhelming passion as deeply as he. "*Och*, my love. Ye precious lass."

Still carrying her, he walked into the bedchamber and placed her on the bed. Pulling his shirt over his head in a fluid motion and losing his trousers in equally short order, he lowered himself over her. His arms shook from the force of his want and lust. "I dinnae ken how long I can wait, lassie. I feel as if I hae wanted ye fore'er."

"Then don't wait." She wrapped her arms around him and pulled his weight down on her.

Still, he managed to find the strength to refrain from pouncing on her like a callow lad, Connor's lips instead found her breast and suckled deeply on her nipple, drawing a cry and a moan from her. She wound her long legs around his waist and urged him closer with her muscled thighs while her hands roamed his chest and shoulders, before skimming lower to massage his buttocks. Determined to prolong the moment, he drew back to make space for his fingers to travel down her belly and down farther still.

She gasped as he touched first the inside of her thigh before heading upwards. She was hot and damp already as his fingers circled the sensitive nub there, before dipping inside. With a moan, she thrust her hips up to meet his hand as he stroked her again and again. Her thighs shook with tension and she clutched his shoulders, moaning his name. Ending his control.

He caught her lips again in a probing kiss as he reared

back and drove into her in a single thrust. A deep throaty cry escaped her lips before she deepened their kiss and urged him onward. Praying for strength, he withdrew and plunged deeply again and again. Her hands ran down his back again as her legs climbed higher around his waist. She hung on tightly as he found a rhythm that pleased them both. Her inner muscles clenched around his length nearly driving him mad. She murmured over and over between kisses, "Oh God, oh God!"

He shifted position, hooking his arm under one thigh to change the angle of his thrusts, and her breathing changed.

)X(X(X(X

The tension was building in Emmy's center as she reveled in the power of Connor's lovemaking. He was so large and muscular. She loved the feel of his heavy arms around her, his weight bearing down on her. The hairs on his chest rubbed against her nipples, arousing tingles in the sensitive peaks. She never imagined sex could be so thrilling. Normally, it was almost a chore following foreplay, but she had wanted nothing more than to feel him inside her. Then he shifted, drawing her leg up higher and pulling his chest up to change the angle of his thrusts and, with that, a new feeling struck her core.

She drew in a short, shocked breath as a new ache built deep inside her. Not painful by any means, but a pleasurable cramp that reached out with its fingers across her abdomen and radiated down her inner thighs. Not unfamiliar by any means, but not a feeling she'd ever attained from this exact position. She grew tighter and tighter, until a feeling of near panic overtook her.

"Connor?" she panted, opening her eyes in surprise,

feeling a need to deny it. "No, no," she moaned.

Connor looked down at her and lowered his head to kiss her once more. "Just let it happen, my love, let it come," he urged.

Then it did; the ache built almost painfully and broke in waves of ecstasy that flooded hotly through her. Her muscles contracted rhythmically around his erection as he plunged once again to her core and cried out his own release. He gathered her against him and drove in one last time before holding her close. The spasms continued for a while, decreasing in intensity until Emmy relaxed against him and savored his weight above her.

She closed her eyes in wonder. She thought she had had orgasms before, usually during foreplay when in the company of a considerate lover but she had never felt one during intercourse. Oh, she generally enjoyed the act and found it pleasurable, but the mystery of the vaginal orgasm had eluded her to the point of being mythical.

Nothing in her experience compared with this...this moment of shared release and bliss. Emmy turned her head and kissed the side of his neck. "Thank you," she whispered.

Connor chuckled and rolled on to his back, pulling her with him until she was nestled against his side. "Nay, my lady, thank ye."

Playfully, she slapped his sweaty chest and tugged on the chest hairs there. He had a magnificent chest. Thick and muscular with deep, sinewy lines and definition. In fact, his whole body was like that. Large and...she giggled as she included another aspect of his anatomy in the description. She raised her head to look down before returning to the pillow of his chest. Yup, definitely large and...everything. His hand cupped the back of her head and stroked her hair in a comforting fashion.

After a long, languid silence, the wind and rain slapped against the windows, reminding Emmy where she was. Raising her head, she looked up to see him watching her. His dark eyes were warm but wary despite the coziness of their embrace.

"What?" she asked, although she had an idea what he was thinking. He didn't take long to prove her correct.

26

"Ye were nae virgin." It was not an accusation as much as an observation.

"I think we already discussed that," she said softly, so as not to provoke him.

"Did ye hae to sell yerself to survive?"

The question was voiced with such anguish that Emmy could not be angry with him this time. "I already told you that I've never taken money for sex. I hope you'll believe that."

He conceded with a nod. "So ye took lovers then?"

"I've had lovers, yes." He tensed but she kept her eyes locked with his. "So have you, I'd wager. Don't be a hypocrite, Connor. We're both adults here."

)(O)(O)(O(

The question tortured him. He didn't want to know, but he had to. "But how many?"

His lady rolled away from him with a groan and he regretted ruining the moment but not asking the question.

Rising to her feet, she padded naked to where her robe hung and slipped her arms into the sleeves before turning back to him.

The sight of her relaxed nudity captivated Connor as she stood and moved to the end of the bed. She was so comfortable with herself. That confidence had its own appeal, as did her long legs and ample breasts…

Emmy leaned down over him and ran a hand up his chest, whispering seductively. "Come on, Connor. You're ruining the moment. Isn't there something else you'd rather be doing?"

The temptation was strong, he admitted as he stared at her body, half-exposed through the gaping gown. He groaned and reached up to cup the beautiful breasts before him. With a smile, she spread the gown and straddled his lap before leaning in to kiss him. "Isn't this better than fighting?"

"I dinnae want to fight wi' ye, my love." His hands gripped her hips tightly against him as if they had a will of their own. In spite of his denial, his arousal stirred. He drew back and met her eyes seriously. "But I need an answer to my question. How many?"

Her lips twisted. "Does it really matter? You're not a virgin, neither am I. Why does the number matter?"

He cupped her cheeks and forced her to meet his eyes. "It tortures me, this image of ye wi' another man. I hate that another has had ye when I want ye to be only mine."

Emmy stared down at him at this fierce confession. "Only yours, huh?" She caressed his cheek, her expression softening. "Fine. Four."

"*Four* lovers."

Just like that they hardened again. "I will ask again, how many have you had? It's not an incredibly large number given my age. I am twenty-eight after all. Many women I know have slept with many more than that."

Connor took a deep breath and rubbed his hands over his face. Four men. Four faceless men that had had this woman who had been his wife at the time. Had she ever considered that while she was taking her lovers? Had she gone to the first without a second thought for him? Knowing that she was giving away that which should have been his and his alone? Rage and jealousy filled him against this man who had taken her innocence without any thought for her pleasure.

Still, she was right. He'd had many more lovers than she and as recently as several months before, while on business in London. Was he the hypocrite she accused him of being in holding her affairs against her?

"Was the first someone I ken? Someone here?"

She gave a short laugh. "Definitely not. The first was Andy Johnson. It was during my senior year of high school in the basement of his house during halftime of the NFC playoffs. It was brief, uncomfortable and thoroughly forgettable. I don't know that we ever even went out again after that. It was incredibly disappointing."

"Did ye no' love these men then?" His heart slowed to an aching, dreading beat.

"At the time, I would have said I did."

※◇※◇※

Emmy crawled off him and gathered the dressing gown around herself, knotting it tightly. The moment was clearly over for now. She shouldn't have said anything but the man really did know how to make a woman feel special with that declaration. It wasn't such a huge thing to answer him. She figured if she did, they might be able to get beyond it, move past it.

Apparently not.

There had been a guy the first two years of medical school on and off that she would have labeled as a 'friend with benefits', but she wasn't about to explain that concept to him. He would never understand it even if he had had more casual sex than she ever dreamed of. She went to the fireplace and took the poker, jabbing at the coals to stir them to life in the cold room. She wondered if this would be the end of it for them if he could not accept her lack of innocence.

"Four." He said it aloud more calmly as if tasting the word.

"Willingly, yes," she responded and then winced, clapping a hand over her mouth. Well, she hadn't meant *that* to come out.

"What do you mean *willingly*?" He rose and turned her to face him, gripping her upper arms. The poker clattered to the floor.

She hedged in hesitant embarrassment. She'd never told anyone about that before. She shouldn't be ashamed, but she was. She didn't know why she had admitted it to Connor of all people, but there was just something about him that made her want to talk to him. To let him know her…all of her. "Well, there was an incident my sophomore year of college."

She lowered her eyes away from him but, with a finger on her chin, he compelled her gaze to return to his. "Ye were ravished? Against your will?"

"'Date rape' they call it these days. Guy slipped me a Mickey and took advantage of me while I was passed out." She closed her eyes against the humiliating memory. "I woke up half way through to find him on top of me and tried to fight him off, but I was out of it. I was so bruised after and he joked to all his friends about it. It was awful. Worst part was that I knew him. We had several classes together. He'd asked me out a couple times but I never did like him and he knew it."

"I'll kill him." Fury raged in his voice. "Tell me where to find him."

Amazed, Emmy chuckled at his protectiveness. "My knight in shining armor."

He cradled her face between his hands. "My love, I am sorry yer flight from me resulted in such a painful incident for ye."

"Wow," she breathed in surprise, raising her brows. "That is so...compassionate of you. What, no recriminations? No saying that I brought it on myself? Most of the men I know would think so."

"Nae woman deserves to be so ill-treated at the hands of a man."

"Unwilling sex you forgive, but the four I chose you don't," she mused and caressed his cheek before placing a light kiss there. "I have never told anyone about that before. I don't know why I told you. I have always been afraid that people would give me that look that said it was my own fault."

"The only fault that can be laid at yer feet would be that if ye had ne'er left it would no' hae happened a'tall," he chided.

"Connor," she sighed, regretfully pulling away from him. "Enough of this. I know that some small part of you must realize that I'm not Heather. Admit it."

He shook his head and turned, searching for his pants and pulling them on. "Ye hae changed, beyond any doubt. Ye are in many ways, a completely different person from the woman I knew, but yer appearance on that day of all days? And look at ye. I cannae look at ye and believe that ye are anyone else. It might be possible for two women on this earth to look the same but three? Unlikely."

"You're going to have to accept it sooner or later. Honestly, I think you already have, but are denying it for reasons of your own." She turned back to the revived fire and stared down into the flames.

As silence reigned, she turned back to him and pressed on softly. "You haven't called me by that name since the night before last when we almost…made love. You call me 'my lady' and 'my love' but not Heather. Do you even think of me by that name anymore? Just say it one time, Connor." She reached for his hand and pressed it to her cheek looking up at him with pleading eyes. "Say Emmy. Call me by my own name. Please."

"What did ye expect when ye came here? That I'd welcome ye wi' open arms?" he said, evading her quiet plea, pulling away once again and sitting on the edge of the bed as he rubbed his face with his hands. A show of his exasperation. "Are things no' turning out the way ye thought and ye want to leave? If ye can convince me ye are no' Heather, then I hae nae hold on ye. Is that it? Is that what yer insistence is all aboot?"

Did she want to leave? It was the question that had been plaguing Emmy since she'd seen Donell that morning. It was a question that was getting harder and harder to answer easily. Her future as she had always imagined it or a life here? And was that even a choice? She'd come here suddenly, what was to stop her from being snapped back to her own time without warning? On the whim of an old wizard or whatever he was? Did she have a choice in her destiny? She wasn't even sure, so did it matter what she wanted? She didn't know. She knelt on the floor before him and urged him to look at her.

"What I want has nothing to do with your insane insistence that I am Heather," she argued, loath to think any longer about her dilemma. "You've already admitted that you've gotten a divorce. Even if I was Heather I could leave at anytime, don't you realize that? What other benefit is there for you if I am Heather?"

His mouth opened and closed several times as if he were fighting the words he wanted to say. In the end, he answered her question with one of his own. "If ye're no', why hae ye no' left already?"

She wanted to say it was because had nowhere else to go but it went deeper than that. She didn't want to leave him. She wanted to stay with him, near him—at least for the time being. If he wanted her, she wanted him to want her for herself. She wanted him to know that he wanted Emmy not Heather.

"This thing between us, Connor, this chemistry," she fumbled for the words, "it is worth exploring, isn't it? I'm staying for this, because of us. But I am not Heather, I swear to you, and if you want me to leave because of that alone, I will go. If you want me to go, tell me now."

⟨⟩⟨⟩⟨⟩⟨⟩⟨⟩

Connor looked down at her lovely face so familiar and yet so new. Heather or not, this woman aroused feelings in him that he had never felt before. Tender, protective, possessive.

Remaining adamant in his contention that she was indeed Heather gave him a chance to keep her near. That tie, however tenuous, provided reason. Justification. If not merely for him, but for Dory as well.

He wanted her for himself whatever that implied, short-term or long-term he did not know, but he needed time to figure it out. As she said, it was worth exploring. If he conceded she might not be Heather, she had every right to walk out the door if she wished, just as she said, and his hold on her already felt too fragile. How could he explain that to her? "Nay, my love, I dinnae want ye to go."

"Yet?"

"Nay, no' yet." The corner of his mouth lifted in a half smile and he leaned over to meet her lips in a tender kiss. "Ye're the most curious woman I hae e'er met."

"Thanks, I think, and you—

27

A quick tap sounded at the door and Margo burst in without waiting to be invited. "Milady!" she called and drew up short at the sight of Emmy kneeling between Connor's legs, and their mutual state of undress. "Oh! I'm sorry. I dinnae mean…" Margo blushed furiously and turned to leave.

Emmy stood and secured the dressing gown tighter, trying to suppress a blush over what Margo probably thought was happening. "It's okay, Margo. What's up?"

"Oh, milady," she cried. "I need yer help. My maw is ha'ing an awful time."

"What is it?" Emmy asked in concern. "You said she was feeling unwell?"

"'Tis the baby!" Margo exclaimed, her eyes bright with tears.

"What baby?" Emmy and Connor asked in unison.

"Maw's having another bairn, but she's ha'ing a terrible time wi' this one." Margo wrung her hands in worry. "Will ye come?"

"Of course I will," Emmy assured her, already shifting into doctor mode. "Hurry, help me dress!"

"I will get a carriage ready," Connor offered and snatched up his shirt before leaving the room.

"Why didn't you tell me earlier that your mother was in labor, Margo?" she chided as she pulled on a shift and shirt, since her own underwear was currently soaked.

"'Tis her tenth bairn, milady," Margo explained. "I dinnae think she'd need any help wi' it this time. Why, the last one came so quick she barely had time to get to lie down before it came." She drew up the petticoats and skirts around Emmy hips and tied them on.

"She figured she'd seen it all by this point, huh?" Emmy slipped her feet into her boots and grabbed the medical bag Connor sent. Margo swept up a cloak for her and they hurried down the stairs.

The carriage made the trip to Lochdon, about a mile and a half southwest of Duart, at a much faster clip than their earlier drive into Craignure, despite the continued rain and wind. Knowing Margo was so nervous she was about to pop, Emmy encouraged Margo to tell her about where she lived and about her family.

Though Emmy knew from reading a history of the area that members of the MacLean clan had populated Lochdon for centuries, Margo added that it was from here that the laird employed his household staff, as well as those maintained his livestock and worked at the home farm. Margo chatted on about how her mother had worked in the castle's kitchens for many years before devoting herself to her home and children. Her father, Aengus McAllen, was a second in command to Connor's steward overseeing the estate's business. Margo, the oldest of their children, had been working at the castle for three years, first as a chambermaid and now lady's maid. Because of the higher status of that position, she also resided at the castle with her footman husband.

All the wind went out of the maid when the carriage stopped in front of a small two-story cottage. Nodding encouragingly, Emmy motioned for the girl to proceed them.

Though the house seemed poor to Emmy's mind, Connor assured her the family was one of the village's more prestigious, because of the positions Margo and her father held at Duart. Six of Margo's younger siblings gathered in the main parlor of the house welcomed him shyly. Ranging in age from two to thirteen, they were largely silent and withdrawn, whether because of his presence or their mother's travails, she did not know.

The oldest present was a girl, Mairi, who offered Connor whisky which he accepted, but looked around as if wondering what to do with himself.

"Is the father here?" Emmy asked.

"Nay, I sent McAllen to Glasgow earlier this week on business."

Her brow arched. "Nice timing."

He shrugged helplessly and she almost felt sorry for him. But a muffled scream sounded from above and her concern shifted as she forged up the stairs in Margo's wake.

Emmy wasted little time introducing herself to Margo's mother, Cora, asking a series of questions to acquaint herself with the woman's history as she washed her hands and began her initial examination. "How old are you, Cora?"

"Forty and one, milady," she panted.

"This is your tenth pregnancy?"

"Twelfth, milady."

"God, that's just nuts," Emmy murmured to herself under her breath. Once she'd delivered the sixth child in a family but many people considered having too many kids irresponsible, unless you could afford to raise them all the way through college. Unusually large families were a novelty and ended up on TV reality shows or were taunted by the press. Absently Emmy wondered what a show about the McAllens and their brood would be called.

And all by forty-one. If she'd had to take a guess she would've thought the woman closer to fifty than forty. Of course, she wasn't at her best at that particular moment, she allowed. "Were the other two carried to term or miscarried?"

"Both suffered illness after birth, milady," Margo informed her as she laid a cool cloth over her mother's brow. "Please, milady, can ye help her?"

"I'll do my best." She shot the girl a smile of reassurance as she made her examination. "Have you had any difficulties in delivery before?"

"None, milady. They were all easy enough and the bairns big and braw."

Emmy's examination quickly discovered the problem. "The baby is breech, Cora. We're going to have to turn it but I need you to stay very still while I do it. Is there anyone else here who can help you hold your mother, Margo?"

"Just the little ones, milady, and my sisters."

"Are they old enough to be of any use?"

Margo and Cora looked at each other and shook their heads in unison. "The other girls are away."

As was the father. "No brothers?"

"My brother Cam went wi' my father to Glasgow this week," Margo explained.

"If it's okay with you then, Cora, I'd like to have

Connor…the laird come up and help us out."

"Okay?" Cora panted.

"She means if it's acceptable, maw," Margo translated, having gotten used to Emmy's phrasing over the past several days.

The woman hesitated, then nodded miserably. Emmy sent Margo to fetch Connor as she prepared the tools she would need on a nearby table and gathered towels.

Margo returned quickly to her mother's side. Alone.

"Where is the laird?"

Margo nodded to the doorway and Emmy turned to find Connor hesitating on the threshold. "Well, get in here, laird," she urged. "This is what happens when you send a man away on business when his wife is near her time. You get to do his duty."

"I dinnae think…" he started but stopped at her level stare. A jerk of her head him forward, but he looked horrified. Obviously he'd never attended a birthing before, never had any reason to. He wasn't looking like he especially wanted to start now.

"I'm nae mid…"

His words faded away with a sharp look from her. Then something in his gaze shifted as he looked at her. Something Emmy didn't have time to define but was infinitely curious about.

He nodded more decisively. "What do ye want me to do?"

"The baby is breech and I need to turn it," she explained. "I need you to keep her still for me; can you do that?"

Connor squared his shoulders at the deprecating question. "Of course."

"Let's get to it then." She waved him forward and he

took his place as she went to work. In truth, she'd never actually done this before in practice. She was working entirely on theory and hoped her nervousness didn't show on her face. Cora moaned in pain and was panting erratically. She was on the verge of hyperventilating. "Get her to breathe evenly, Connor. Talk to her."

The laird murmured encouraging words to the woman to breathe with him slowly. He asked her if she remembered bringing him sweets from the kitchen when his father had banished him to his room for a week for punching Ian. He couldn't remember why he had done it.

"He rode yer favorite pony and brought it up lame with a stone in its hoof," Cora said with a shaky laugh. "Ye would no' hae been able to ride it for a week anyway, but got whipped by yer father and sent to yer rooms for the week instead."

Connor laughed and nodded at the memory. "Aye, that's right. I'd forgotten. And ye slipped me my favorite sweets. Ye wisnae much more than a young lass yerself when ye did that."

"Still in the scullery, I was." She gasped and stifled a scream.

Emmy looked up. "Okay, Cora, push now! Come on!"

The woman bore down with another scream and Emmy viewed the results. "All right, one more."

"Aye, now," Connor's encouragement joined hers and he took Cora's hand.

"Push, Maw," Margo joined in.

Cora cried out and a moment later the baby's cry joined hers.

⋇⋇⋇⋇⋇

"Your color is looking better, I think."

"I've ne'er seen a bairn born before," Connor told her as the carriage rocked slowly back and forth when they finally set out to return to Duart several hours later. For a nearly an hour after the birth, he'd sat out in the chilly night with his whisky to combat the nausea and sweats that had overcome him as the child, a boy, had been born. It had been horrific. Cows and horses were one thing, but....

"Supposedly it's different when it is your own baby," she assured him. "You'll be fine." She gave his arm a comforting squeeze.

"She nearly broke my hand, her grip was so strong," he told her lightly, but he wasn't sure he ever wanted to witness such an ordeal again, even if it was his own child.

There was a reason men were not present for deliveries. Now he understood what it was. He eyed Heather—or Emmy or whoever she was—thoughtfully and pictured her heavy with his child, his first, his heir. Aye, he would love to see her in such a state, glowing with happiness as Dory had the previous night. He would place his hands on her belly and marvel with her over the life inside. A life they created together. In that moment, he wanted that fantasy more than anything.

Oblivious to the vein of Connor's thinking, Emmy yawned hugely and stretched. "Man, I am beat." She laid her head on his shoulder in fatigue. His coachman was taking the journey slowly in deference to her motion sickness, as she termed it. It would take much longer to return to the castle, but she seemed to find it more tolerable. You were wonderful, Connor," she said sleepily. "You were exactly what she needed. Calm and distracting and not a hint of worry."

"I was scared to death."

"So was I," she admitted.

Connor looked down at her in amazement. "Truly? I would ne'er hae thought so. Ye're incredibly competent. I was impressed." He was, too. Her cool command of the situation had even set him at ease. Her confidence became his own in those moments when he'd hovered between his duty as laird and fleeing the bedchamber.

Yet her praise had gone to Cora, for her hard work. With congratulations, she'd handed off the baby boy, and finished the rest of the matter with efficiency and an optimistic cheerfulness that had immediately transmitted itself to Cora, Margo and himself.

She might be a bit rough around the edges at times, but his lady was a true one at heart.

"I couldn't have done it without you." She hugged his arm and snuggled closer against the chill of the night. "Thank you for helping."

"She is one of my clan." He shrugged off her approval, knowing that it was her efforts that had saved Cora and her son. McAllen would come back to Duart and know the laird's lady had saved his wife's life.

"You care for these people so very much," she murmured tiredly.

But did she?

28

The rumbling of her stomach woke Emmy the next morning. Rubbing her hands over her face, she rolled over with a groan. She vaguely remembered Connor carrying her to bed the previous night. Now in a state of consciousness, she marveled at his strength. She was slight of build, but tall and muscular and weighed more than she looked. With a grin, she wondered if he'd hurt his back in the process.

Still, it'd been considerate, even chivalrous, for him to carry her up. His participation in the birth had also shown his caring for his people.

She'd never known anyone to accept and want the responsibility for the lives of so many people yet he seemed to thrive on it. She'd never met anyone like that, like him and was fairly sure that she would never meet another who impressed her so much.

His later praise over her performance had made her feel more flattered than the appreciation given by Margo and her mother. What did that mean? That his opinion mattered more than anyone else's?

Or only what she had already guessed, that she was falling for him hard and fast. She longed to know if his caring extended to her as well.

"Oh, God," she groaned again. "I should have gone to the Bahamas or better yet, Cabo."

"Where is Cabo?"

Emmy started and rolled over to find Connor lounging in the doorway to the parlor. "*Geez*, you scared me!" she scolded as she patted her pounding chest. "Didn't your mother teach you to knock?"

"The door was open," he replied as he strolled casually into the room. The door had been open, but only because he'd left it that way the previous night. She'd been as groggy as a drunken sailor when they returned the previous evening and so reluctant to rouse herself that he'd carried her up and put her to bed. He'd taken great pleasure in removing most of her clothing and tracing the colorful lines of her tattoo with his fingertip. As he stared down at her lovely face relaxed after slumber, tenderness such as he'd never before experienced clenched at his heart. She was so unique, unlike any other. Competent, beyond intelligent, and funny as well. His lips quirked; even half asleep she jested whether his mother had taught him to knock.

"I came to see if ye were planning on sleeping the day away." He took a seat on the edge of the bed as she propped herself up on her elbows and stifled a yawn.

"I just might," she teased and he laughed. "Care to join me?"

Connor leaned over and caught her lips in a tender kiss. "An appealing offer." He kissed her again and she arched up ´

to deepen the contact.

"Oh, milady! I'm sorry."

Emmy drew back and turned her head to see Margo backing out of the room balancing a large tray on her hip. "Wait, Margo. Is that food?"

"Aye, milady," the maid confirmed. "Ye missed dinner last night and I thought ye might be hungry since it is almost noontime." She nudged her way back into the room and put the tray on a small table by the fire. "I'll just go..."

"It's okay. I'm getting up." She shot Connor a regretful glance, which he returned with a disappointed sigh. "Oh, gimme a break, I'm starving. Aren't you?"

"I ate over an hour ago."

)O(O(O(

Emmy raised a brow at his superior tone as she slipped her dressing gown on. "Well, good for you. Either sit and keep me company or go away if you're going to be a sourpuss."

Connor seated her at the table and sat opposite of her, snatching a roll from her plate. "Hey, that's mine. I thought you already ate."

"I did," he drawled as he drizzled honey on the bread and took a bite.

"Well, just keep away from the rest or you might end up with a bloody nub for your trouble, kay?" She took a bite of eggs and closed her eyes in pure bliss. "God, that's good."

The maid hovered, drawing Emmy's attention. "What's up, Margo?"

"I finished hand washing yer smalls this morning and hung them to dry."

"Thanks, I appreciate it," Emmy responded, shoving

another forkful of food in.

"And I found this on the floor while I was picking up."

Margo held Emmy's iPhone out in one hand and the ear buds in the other. Interest was bright in her eyes. Emmy was certain the maid wanted to ask what it was, but she simply took them with a nod and tucked them in the pocket of her gown.

"Thank you. How's your mother this morning?"

"Verra well, thank ye, milady. I'll just leave ye alone to eat." She looked disappointment that her curiosity would remain just that, but bobbed a curtsey and turned to leave.

"Oh, Margo?" Emmy's eyes twinkled with mischief at Connor. "It might be best if you knocked and waited for an answer, for the time being."

"Aye, milady." The maid grinned as she departed, closing the door pointedly behind her.

"What?" Emmy drawled innocently at Connor's speculative look. They smiled at each other and she added. "Better safe than sorry, right?"

"Of course." He reached over to snatch a piece of bacon, earning a smack on his knuckles for his trouble. Rubbing his hand, he changed the subject. "I'm curious, where is this Cabo ye mentioned? I hae, naturally, heard of the Bahamas as it is a territory of the Crown, but no' the other. Is it an American colony?"

Biting into the second biscuit, she licked a drop of jam from her fingers. His eyes followed the motion and darkened. Wickedly she popped her finger into her mouth and sucked it clean. He shifted in his seat.

"No, Cabo, Cabo San Lucas is in Mexico on the Baha peninsula...south of California."

"The Cape of St. Luke?" He translated the Spanish. "I've

ne'er heard of it. Ye've been that far west? I'm astounded ye'd travel such a distance. Were ye alone? I mean, I understand many areas are still quite violent and dangerous."

Thinking of Hollywood and east L.A., Emmy admitted the west still had its dangerous elements but added, "Cabo is a resort town though; the police there try to keep it safe for the tourists."

"So ye traveled there on another holiday, then?"

"Oh, yeah, the ocean, the beaches, a little snorkeling. It's a party."

She raised her eye-brows and waited for him to say something, anything that would give her leave to approach the whole 'I'm from the future' topic, but he disappointed by merely responding with a thoughtful hum. She wondered what pictures were floating through his mind.

"What did Margo gi' ye?"

Here it was. If there were ever a perfect opening for a futuristic show and tell, this was it. She could show him the iPhone, explain how it worked and, when he said in amazement how such a thing was impossible...boom, she would drop the bomb. She opened her mouth, looked into those deep, dark eyes and deflated.

"Just something I dropped in the bathroom yesterday afternoon," she ended up responding vaguely.

Chicken.

"So what are your plans today?" she carried on instead.

"I thought to offer my company and carriage to drive ye everywhere ye need to go today." He cocked his head, his expression filled with curiosity. "Can I see what she gave ye?"

"Not right now." He knew she'd been about to say something else and was disappointed in her, though perhaps not as much as she was in herself. "Where am I going today?"

"News of yer special skills seems to hae spread overnight. Chilton told me that several women from as far as Craignure are seeking yer services. Assuming, of course, that ye'd care to provide them." He eyed her bacon once more and, with a sigh of defeat, she handed over a piece. "Why no'?"

Accepting the change of topic without batting a lash, Emmy shrugged. "It's mine and not yours and I am allowed my privacy. House calls, huh?"

She nibbled on the last of the bacon thoughtfully. Seemingly her vocation was highly sought after in this time. Could there really be so many women pregnant at the same time in such a sparsely populated place? Granted there was no real birth control around. No TV and long nights, and those nights were getting rather cold. A warm bed occupied by a warm partner had a broad appeal and the activities that could get you even warmer resulted in…well, a high percentage of pregnant women. Women who had no one to care for them on Mull except for the old doctor that Dory refused to allow near her.

"I could take it from ye."

"You'll only get to see it when you ask nicely and I decide to let you have it," she responded pleasantly, amused over their banter. "Well, house calls it is, then. When do we go?"

"I thought wi'in an hour or so." He looked at her speculatively. "I'm much stronger than ye. Any resistance ye might offer would be easily overcome."

"But that would be going against my wishes and you're not that kind of guy." Amused, Emmy watched through lowered lashes as his frustration grew. "I'll need time to bathe first. I still smell like seawater."

He studied her for a long moment then a new look dropped like a mask over his features. His mouth softened and his eyes grew heavy and hot. Connor reached across the table and took her hand, tracing circles in her sensitive palm.

"Are ye certain ye're not still fatigued from last night?" His voice turned low and seductive. "Perhaps ye should return to bed for some more…rest before we go."

Emmy shivered as he stood and pulled her to stand in front of him. He stared down at her with his dark, hungry eyes, his hands moving lightly up her arms to her shoulders, neck to cup her cheeks. His mouth lowered to hers in a light, teasing kiss, licking her lower lip before slanting across her mouth with devouring heat and intensity. She leaned in with a moan as his hands plunged into her hair and moved down her back. His lips nipped and sucked until she was void of logical thought.

So far gone was she that Emmy almost didn't feel his hand slipping into her robe pocket. Almost. She slapped a hand down over his and glared up at him in astonishment, stumbling back from his embrace.

"Now that was just cruel, Connor. You think you can seduce it out of me?"

"Almost had it," he murmured kissing her again, softly, but with a chuckle.

He was so good that he almost had, too. "No, no, you had your chance." She pushed him away. "Go away now."

"Now who is cruel?" he moaned, stepping back to reveal his aroused state. "Will ye leave me in need?"

"It is your own fault trying to use my attraction to you in such a way. You must respect my wishes and my property," she insisted fiercely. "I said no, not now, and I meant it."

"Ye dinnae truly mean it."

"Surprisingly, I did. You can't just take what you want."

"I'm the laird; I always get what I want." While the words were teasing, he could see that on some level he was serious. He might try to wheedle what he wanted from her but, in the end, he fully expected to get it, one way or another.

"You don't always get what you want."

"Surprisingly, I do." He mocked her words.

Lifestyles of the rich and powerful. She had known that he had some arrogance in him; it was part and parcel of the commanding presence he portrayed. Part of him. The Earl. But to such an extreme that he assumed his every wish would be granted? He probably didn't truly know the meaning of the word no. The world was his oyster and if he wanted the pearl, it was his too.

"Not this time."

"Are ye telling me *nay*?" he asked, torn between shock and amusement.

"I am telling you no." She crossed her arms over her chest and stared him down stubbornly. "It will be my choice if, and when, I let you see my personal belongings. You cannot command or seduce them out of me." In truth, it was probably that he used her affections and desire against her that irritated her the most. "It's not okay to toy with people like that. And besides," she went on, her anger rising over his deception, "you don't always get what you want."

"Now what are ye talking aboot?"

"I think you know what I am talking about. I can think of at least one other instance when someone denied you what you wanted." Emmy raised a brow and waited for him to catch on. It didn't take him long.

"So ye denied me once." His eyes narrowed. "Why

should I allow ye to do it again?"

"I would defy you if only to prove to you that you are not a god, Connor," she snapped back. "You might be the laird here, but you cannot command everyone in Duart like they are dogs. People have a right to their person, and their privacy, at least. Life, liberty and prosperity."

"I've read yer American constitution, but in my house…"

"In your house you are king," she interrupted sarcastically. "You are God, *blah, blah, blah.*" She made a hand puppet to deliver those words. "You know what? I'm almost glad heather left you. Yeah, you heard me. You obviously need to be brought down a notch." She poked him in the chest.

"Glad? Do ye have any idea the humiliations I've borne these past ten years because of that?" he ground out, angry now, his usually heavy brogue so thick now that Emmy could barely grasp his words.

"So you punish everyone around you for your pain, is that it? *Your* pride, *your* ego." She faced him, hands on hips, her own anger rising over his stubborn refusal to face the truth. "That's all that matters, isn't it? Well, they might suck it up, but I will not be treated that way. It isn't all about you. And I don't have to stay here. I can leave any time. I don't have to put up with a tyrant."

"Run away, then," he roared. "Run away like ye did before."

"Sometimes you deserve to be run from," she yelled back.

"If ye dinnae want to marry me, ye should hae said so. I wouldnae hae made ye do it, but ye just left wi'out a word. Do ye hae any idea how mortifying that was? The Prince of

Wales was there," he shouted, jabbing his finger back at her.

"Now you're getting to your real issues. It's all pride, Connor." She went toe to toe with him. "You didn't care that she was gone for anything more than the sake of your pride. You've let it rule your entire life. You already said that you didn't love her, so it wasn't like you had your heart broken."

"I dinnae, that's right. I dinnae love ye then." His anger was still running amok making him almost unaware of the words he spoke. "I only married ye because it was what my father wanted. I dinnae even meet ye until the previous day. How could I have cared aboot ye? Aye, 'twas all pride, I'll admit it."

"Then?" Emmy echoed, hearing nothing past that one word. All the hot air went out of her. Similarly deflated, Connor sliced his hand through the air to halt her but she ignored him. "You said 'then'. That you didn't love her 'then'. Do you love me now?"

He turned his back to her and faced the window, arms crossed in that same defensive posture he'd used the first day she met him. She ran her hand up his shoulder blades.

"Connor?"

Both hands slid under his arms, around the hard ripple of his ribs until she was hugging him from behind, resting her head against his back, relaxed against his tense body, her heart pounding forcefully between them.

"Do you, Connor? Do you love me now?" she whispered with longing.

His hands clasped hers tightly for a moment. He drew a breath as though he were about to speak but then exhaled heavily. "Go get dressed and we'll leave."

"But, Connor…"

"Just leave me be, Emmy."

Sighing heavily in defeat, she dropped her arms and moved soundlessly to the bathroom, closing the door behind her. It wasn't until she was washing her hair in the bath that she realized that he'd called her Emmy instead of Heather.

He'd called her Emmy.

29

What a horrid day. The long periods in the carriage had been sickening and awful, but what really made the day excruciatingly long was Connor's absence from it. When she arrived at the carriage, Ian, not Connor, had been waiting for her. Ian cheerfully explained that Connor suddenly had to leave on urgent business in Glasgow and would be gone for several days. He'd asked Ian to aid Emmy in her medical pursuits.

Ian filled their time in the carriage with pleasant chatter and anecdotes that Emmy regretted hadn't done more to distract her. Business in Glasgow? She didn't think so. There was no doubt in her mind that Connor—that big, fat chicken—had run off rather than face her. Perhaps he regretted suggesting that he loved her before he was certain of her feelings and he was avoiding her to allow her time to digest his revelation, but she doubted it. It was more likely that he hadn't meant it the way it sounded at all and he was afraid her feelings would be hurt.

That thought caused her breath to catch. God, she hoped not. She was pretty sure he liked her beyond the physical, had even had cause to think that he cared for her…maybe more than he knew or wanted to? It'd hardly been a week yet, she thought realistically. An impossibly short time in which to fall in love with someone. Things like that took time. Love at first sight wasn't something she'd ever believed possible before. Just because it happened to her didn't necessarily mean he felt the same.

Oh, Lord, she loved him. What a fool she was. Had she truly fallen in love at…well, almost at first sight with Connor? He was completely wrong for her. Truthfully, he was completely right for her but this was all wrong! She was supposed to fall in love with a man she could live the rest of her life with and she had no intention of staying here in Ye Olde Scotland. She needed technology, her career. Starbucks.

Yes, he was everything she had ever wanted. He was intelligent, caring and responsible. Funny and sexy and handsome. Her thoughts warmed. He made her feel challenged, made her think, made her feel like a goddess. Connor brought out every extreme of emotion in her. She'd never felt such anger as that he roused in her but she neither had she ever felt such passion and contentment either.

She loved him. Truly, honestly, deeply.

Now what?

Stay here? Hah! And then, did she even have a choice? She wasn't entirely certain what Donell's point had been in bringing her here. Second chances? For Connor? Most likely for Dory, if she had inferred correctly that Dory would not make it through her delivery. That was most likely the tragedy he spoke of. But second chances for herself? Why did she need a second chance? She had her life lined up and waiting for her. But whatever mystical force Donell had employed to get her here could just as easily yank her right back without warning. If that happened it would break her heart and maybe Connor's as well.

But an hour of his love was better than none at all. Take what you can get, wasn't that the old motto? Well, she was ready to embrace it completely, but that man, that aggravating man, had fled like a coward rather than face her and take it like a man.

Emmy could break down his thoughts pretty well. He was more vulnerable than he thought. He had a fear of rejection. *That* she'd been able to read from day one. His defenses were built from prideful humiliation rather than love and a broken heart, but clearly he feared that same shame happening again. So he fought it. He refused to allow the opportunity to present itself and he had taken himself off before she had a chance to reject him, probably never considering that she might return his feelings.

All she could hope was that he would soon overcome that impulse that had sent him off, and come back to share the love between them while they still had time.

Please, Connor, come back, she beseeched in her mind. *Before I'm gone.*

She only realized she'd moaned aloud when Ian kindly offered to open the window. Connor, it seemed, had warned him of her maleficent relationship with the carriage.

"Thank you."

She breathed in the cold air. October was drawing to a close now. Five days she'd been here. Emmy wondered if anyone had missed her yet in her time and concluded that, given she was still on her vacation, they'd probably not. But when that time was over, it was anyone's guess what would happen then. Missing person's report? Maybe they would think that she was dead in a ditch somewhere, taken by a serial killer and buried in the middle of nowhere. Amnesia. That would be interesting.

"Ye ha' the strangest smile on yer face." Ian's voice interrupted her morbid musings. "What are ye thinking about?"

"I was just wondering what all my friends might be thinking became of me if I don't come home soon."

"And that is amusing?" he questioned with a frown.

"My sense of humor can sometimes go terribly wrong."

"Can I ask ye a personal question?"

"Sure."

"What did ye say to my brother to make him leave like that?"

"Ha! I knew it wasn't a business trip." She felt very satisfied with herself. "What did he tell you?"

"Nothing beyond what I hae already said—that he had urgent business in Glasgow he maun attend to, but I knew that couldnae be true as no messages or telegrams arrived recently." His eyes were inquisitive as he awaited her response.

"Did he seem angry at all?"

"Nay, I wouldnae say so, that I could understand." Ian shook his head, thinking. "If I had to define it, I might say he was defeated in some way, but that is certainly unlike my brother."

Why defeated? What had run through his mind? "We did have a fight."

"I ken." He shrugged and grinned. "Everyone kens. The entire castle can hear yer arguments. It resonates. Ne'er knew it could do that but then I dinnae think anyone has ever yelled like that in the castle before."

"I'm sure that Connor has shown his temper plenty of times in his life," she said drily.

"Surprisingly, nae," Ian contradicted. "I've ne'er heard him yell. He ne'er even shown anger, always that icy demeanor. Connor's always been the sort to stew in his anger. When he's truly maddened, he's cold and fierce, and everyone stays out of his way, including myself. Like I said, I've ne'er heard him roar that way in my lifetime."

"You don't think he was angry when he bellowed right in my face then?" she asked in disbelief. "Because from where I was sitting, he looked pretty pissed."

"Pissed?"

"Pissed. Annoyed," she clarified. Ian grinned again.

"I rather like that one."

"We all do." It was hard not to smile at Ian, and Emmy didn't even try to contain the amusement they shared.

"Ye're a rare corker, Emmy." Ian, like Dory, had taken to calling her by the name she preferred. She wasn't sure if he believed her but was sure that Dory must have said something to him. Generally, he was too good-natured to make a fuss.

"And, you see, there is one I am not used to," she teased. "I gather it means I'm pretty funny?"

"Verra much so," he agreed. "I do so enjoy hearing ye speak. There is always an element of anticipation involved, waiting to see what will come next."

"Glad I don't disappoint." She twisted her lips. Nothing was more enjoyed than the spectacle of the class clown.

"Ne'er, ne'er," he replied, honestly oblivious to her self-disdain.

"So when do you think he'll be back?"

"I would think no' more than a day or two from now."

Five days later, Emmy's overactive imagination had developed dozens of scenarios for the cause of Connor's continued absence. The boat had sunk in the middle of the sound with all hands lost, he had been mugged, murdered, hit by a train...

She'd been unable to find Donell or any trace of him, and had even taken the despised carriage into Craignure to the inn to find him. Jimmy, the innkeeper, admitted that he hadn't seen the old man since the previous week. It seemed the sometime busybody had fled Mull much as her laird had. Finally, when visiting patients and reading books were no longer enough to distract her, she begged Ian to find him and bring Connor home.

Dutifully, Ian packed a bag, taken the ferry to Oban and boarded the train to Glasgow. As requested, he sent regular updates via telegraph to keep Emmy informed to his progress, but two days later he hadn't found Connor yet in any of his regular hotels or clubs. Ian located the estate manager, and Mr. McAllen however, and conveyed to Emmy the information that neither man had been aware of the laird's supposed presence in Glasgow. Defeated, Ian relayed that he was returning to Duart.

"What the hell are ye doing?" Ian stared down at his brother, his laird, in disgust.

Ian had left Glasgow unable to think of where his brother could possibly have gone. Concerned, he'd made his way back through Inverary to Oban searching for signs of his brother along the way. He was beginning to consider that one of the horrible possibilities Emmy regaled him with might be true when, while he was waiting for the ferry, he noticed his brother's sailboat docked in Oban harbor. A quick word with the crew had sent him to a place he hadn't thought to frequent in more than a decade.

Though the brick building was discreet enough from the street, it housed the largest brothel in Oban. Ian never knew his brother to come here and surely never expected to find him drunk, and wallowing in filth with a pair…aye, a pair! of Sally Loaman's best girls.

Ian reached down into the pile of sleeping bodies and pulled his brother roughly out of the tangle of female arms and legs, shaking him forcefully. "My God, ye reek of alcohol and perfume, Connor. What were ye thinking?"

Connor's head lolled to the side as a slur of unintelligible words emerged from him. Ian snorted in repugnance, draped his brother's arm across his shoulders and half led, half carried him from the room.

"Ye're utterly blootered," Ian muttered.

With some doing, he managed to get Connor into his waiting carriage and down to the docks, where the crew helped him to drag his brother below decks and deposit him on the bed. Given Connor's size and weight, it was an effort to do so, but not as much as being close to him.

"I feel as if I should be hauldin' ma breath," one of the crew grumbled as they had hauled him below.

"He's fair reekin'," another agreed.

"Ne'er seen the laird in such a state," yet another added, and they all nodded.

The crew returned above, and Ian dropped down in a chair and considered his brother's state. "Now what?" he wondered aloud.

Connor groaned loudly but offered no other input.

"Serve ye right if I dumped ye over," Ian muttered, rising to grab a bucket of water and a towel. Taking them to the side of the bed, he stripped his brother to his smalls and proceeded to wash the worse of the stink from him. His brother protested flinging his arms about feebly before passing out once more.

Ian had never seen Connor in such a state of drunkenness before. When Connor drank, he was always lucid and controlled, and Ian had to wonder how much alcohol he had consumed to get to this state of excess. What made him do it? And to go to Sally's. Ian shook his head, knowing that something had happened yet, from Emmy's recounting, it hadn't seemed anything so extreme to prompt this crude behavior from his brother. He wondered how different Connor's version would be.

"Where am I?" A gruff voice spoke from the bed more than two hours later. Ian looked up from his book to see Connor propped up on an elbow, rubbing his face thoroughly with his free hand.

"We're docked in Craignure," he offered only.

Connor scratched his growth of beard. "What time is it?"

"Should ye nae be asking what day it is?" Ian asked sarcastically.

"It should be Tuesday, I believe, unless time has gotten away from me." Connor glared at Ian. "Why are ye looking at me like that?"

Since it was Tuesday, Ian could only wonder how his brother had managed to know it. He'd been too muntit to mark the time. "How long were ye at Sally's?" he asked curiously.

"Assuming it is Tuesday, I just went there last night." Ian's brows shot up in surprise.

"Then where in bluidy hell hae ye been the six days before that? I know it wisnae Glasgow, because I already searched for ye there."

"Ye went looking for me? Why?"

"Ye went wi'out word for five days when ye'd said ye'd be gone but a day or two," Ian pointed out irritably. "Ye've ne'er done that before, and everyone was beginning to worry. Even Aunt Eleanor."

)O(O(O(

Ha, that was bloody unlikely, Connor snorted. "I am sure no one realized I was gone."

"If ye think that, then ye're a fool." Ian stiffened under his harsh glare. "Aye, ye heard me, a fool! Emmy has been out of her mind wi' worry, thinking ye've drowned, or been sold to a band of gypsies, or been gutted and turned on a spit for a tribe of hungry cannibals."

Connor grunted in acknowledgment of Ian's grin, though the flash of humor cost him dearly. "She told me she does that. She called it a worst-case scenario," he murmured and lay back, running his hands over his face again. "I feel like a horse sat on my head."

"An ass anyway," Ian said. "Hae ye spent the last six days here?"

"Nay, sailing," Connor confessed. "Dinnae look so surprised. Did ye think I'd been like this the whole time?"

"Aye, but where? Where were ye?"

"We actually went all the way to Liverpool." Connor covered his eyes against the bright sun coming through the porthole. "Thought I might get some supplies for the winter and some gifts for yer bairns. God, I need a drink."

"Ye smell like ye've already drank a keg or more," Ian scoffed, "and slept wi' every lassie at Sally's. She's going to kill ye, ye know?"

Connor didn't have to ask who Ian meant. "I may have drunk the ocean, but I dinnae bed anyone. I wanted to. I planned to even. But in the end..." Connor sighed. "*Och*, mon, gi' me a drink."

Finally obliging, Ian poured a glass of whisky and gave it to his brother, watching intently as Connor swished a large dram around his mouth before he swallowed. "*Ah*, that's better."

"What's gotten into ye, brother," Ian asked. "I've ne'er seen ye like this before."

"Her," Connor grunted as Ian chuckled.

"Finally caught by Cupid's arrow, hmm?"

"More like his cannon." He knocked back the remainder of the drink and dropped back down in fatigue, pulling the pillow over his head. "That woman will be the death of me."

"C'est l'amour," Ian sighed mockingly and laughed when Connor threw the pillow at him. "Come, brother, what has ye up in arms? Love is a beautiful thing, yet ye act as if ye hae the plague. Ye should be rejoicing to hae found such a woman to love. Emmy's an extraordinary lass."

"Emmy?" Connor raised a brow. "She's got ye believing it, too?"

"Dory has already told me that she knows Emmy is no' Heather. She willnae tell me how she knows, which has its own frustrations, but she is certain."

"And ye believe her?"

"I believe them both." Ian poured himself his own glass of whisky and sat back down. "Emmy just disnae seem the sort to take a farce to such an extreme. She's a bonny lass in and out."

"Aye, she is," Connor admitted finally. "I've ne'er met anyone like her."

"Everyone in the house has been saying that aboot her," Ian informed his brother. "There's just something aboot her that is…beyond us. For example, she knows so many things I've ne'er imagined knowing, much less a woman."

"Dinnae let her hear ye say that."

"Aye, and there's another thing!" Ian pounced. "She disnae act like a woman does, ye ken? She refuses to be told what to do. Women offer opinions and hope a man might keep it in mind when making his decisions and choices, but Emmy expects us to or tries to make us do what she wants."

"Why do ye say that? What has she done?"

"She wants to have the telephone installed at Duart *and*…" he pulled out the conjunction, "she expects to haw a 'public phone', that's what she called it, put in Lochdon, Craignure and wherever else she thinks might need one so folks might telephone in case of emergency. She said it just like that. In case of emergency. She said if ye are going to be the laird and be responsible for all these people, they shouldnae hae to wait for a messenger to get help."

"Lovely," Connor grumbled and lay back once more. Bossy, she was. But the idea was sound and, as he had told her before when they were discussing the suffrage question, he respected her for her reason and logic. It was a sensible idea. "She's probably right, too. She has a keen intelligence."

"Oh, I agree, but I dinnae want to tell her that." Ian chuckled and drank. "What a corker she is."

"Aye, she is." Connor sighed and tried to ignore the pounding in his skull. He'd fled Duart for just those reasons. Emmy, aye, Emmy, was having a greater affect on him than he imagined possible. It'd gone beyond wanting to simply try his hand at marriage again. He considered matrimony based on companionship in bed and out of it as a way of keeping her close by.

Looking back, his desire for sport and camaraderie was naïve. Connor knew he could not uphold that standard indefinitely. Each day he was with her, he wanted more, more of her, more of them. He wanted to lie beside her each night, touch her constantly, burrow his way under her skin and become one with her. He wanted the challenge and emotion of her. He wanted to possess her and, indeed, wanted to be possessed by her. There is where the problem had arisen.

He was vulnerable to her. She'd taken his defenses and beaten them to the ground, though she seemed unaware of her victory, and had yet to wield the power she now possessed. Emmy could flay his heart open easily with a single word or action. Even though he wanted her to stay with him always—he did accept that truth—she didn't seem to have the same hopes. She spoke often of 'when she left' and 'when she got home'.

From their conversation turned argument, he knew, too,

there was something more she was hiding from him. Whatever it was, he knew it was what remained wedged between them and what kept her from becoming his.

She didn't view them together the way he did, which meant that she might one day decide to go, leaving him and his heart ripped and broken. It might be the end of him. He did not want to retreat to the hole he had recently crawled from. He liked who he'd become with her, with her help.

Connor had thought long and hard on these things during the past week and then, like the fool Ian had accused him of being, determined to purge her from his mind with the body of another. He'd sat at Sally's for hours trying to drink himself into going through with it and had even taken the girls upstairs to have it done, but in the end he'd known Emmy was all he wanted. He could use other women, but he would be deceiving himself as well as her. He couldn't go through with it even as drunk as he had been.

He loved her. He wanted Emmy as his wife and mate for all his days. It was a terrifying truth that had taken him all these days to accept. If he confessed it to her, she would hold his life in her hands. She would have the power to destroy him because when she left him, it would not only mean a blow to his pride, but the devastation of his soul.

31

Sunlight pierced his eyelids and forced Connor to reluctant consciousness. Groaning, he covered his eyes with a forearm. Pain unlike any he could remember lanced through his temples and his stomach rolled unpleasantly. An inventory of other sensations reminded him that he was in his own bed at Duart after being supported by Ian through an excruciating trip from Craignure made longer by several necessary stops along the way. Chilton had aided his brother in practically carrying Connor up the stairs before depositing him unceremoniously in his bed. Their mutual disapproval was obvious from the fact that they had left him in his clothes on top of the covers.

"You're an utter imbecile, you know?"

Connor peeked out from under his arm to find Emmy in the doorway with her arms folded in disapproval. By God, she looked lovely. Her silk dressing gown clung to the curve of her hips and pulled tightly across her breasts above her folded arms. How could he ever have imagined that anyone could provide equal substitute for her? Words leaped to his lips but he swallowed them down.

)0(0(0(

That Connor was back safely brought Emmy a measure of relief, but also a rise of irritation. She wanted to pounce on him and demand to know what he had been thinking when he'd left. For a full week she had wondered and worried, tormented by images of his bloody demise. When she had been awoken the previous night to find Ian and Chilton hauling Connor into his room, she'd considered offering her aid until the stench of him had assaulted her senses.

Drunk! Totally shot. Shit-faced, her college friends would have called it and they would have been right. He had left her to go on a weeklong bender!

"What? Nothing to say?"

"I apologize?"

"For what?" She tapped her foot impatiently. An apology was worthless if it meant nothing to him. Even more so if he didn't know what she was angry about.

"I apologize for disappearing for so long wi'out sending word."

Connor kept his voice low in pitch and she imagined every word pounded in his head. Clearly, he'd rather put effort into speaking at all but Emmy would not be put off.

"Apology accepted. And?"

His expression blanked for a moment, but he offered, "I apologize for returning home in such a sorry state. I drank excessively and did go to a brothel…"

Shock tore through her and it must have shown, because he hurriedly continued, "I hidnae imagined Ian would remain discreet enough no' to mention where he found me, but I assure ye, I dinnae sleep wi' another woman."

Relief almost left her weeping until he went on, "I admit that I'd planned to, but knew wi'in moments of getting there that I could ne'er do it."

"Why not?" She fought to keep her voice tight and cool to hide the pain his confession roused. The thought of him laying a mere finger on another woman made her stomach heave unpleasantly. "You have no obligation to me."

His eyes met hers for a long moment and spoke volumes. "Aye, I do."

Her heart soared at the look in his eyes and his simple confession. But he couldn't be forgiven that easily, could he? Keeping her expression calm, she considered him before nodding. "Very well, then. Apology accepted. And?"

)O(O(O(

And? Connor grappled for the additional apology she was plainly searching for. He could not think of what she wanted from him though his mind was not functioning as efficiently as it might normally. He thought it through as thoroughly as his physical state allowed. Apology given and accepted for leaving and not sending word. Likewise for the drunken state he had arrived in. What else?

"I apologize...for...*uh*..."

"How about for all the heartache you have caused me and your family this past week?" she shot out as she crossed the room. "For the hours of worrying and wondering whether you were dead or alive?" She slapped his chest with each word that followed: "You. Scared. The. Shit. Out. Of. Me!"

Connor stared at her in astonishment. She was angry because he made her worry? Because she feared for his safety? It was humbling to realize that his actions could so affect the emotions of another person. Another implication struck him then. Emmy wouldn't have worried for him, and it never occurred to him that she would do so, unless she cared for him. To what extent he wasn't sure, but that knowledge brought a warmth to him.

He grasped her hand before she could hit him again and cradled it against his chest. "I apologize most sincerely for worrying ye. I've ne'er had anyone care when I left in the past. It ne'er occurred to me to send word or assurances to ye when no one has ever asked that of me before."

The tension left her body for a split second before she stiffened again rose, retreating to the door. "Apology accepted. Don't do it again."

"Wait." Connor called and then let out a groan as a shaft of agony lanced through his temples. He pressed his palms against his forehead as if he could physically force out the pain.

She returned to the door a moment later carrying two glasses, one of water, he thought, and the other containing a large quantity of reddish liquid.

"Here, hold out your hand."

He did so and she placed two objects in his palm. They were brownish red and small. He had no idea what they were. He looked up at her questioningly.

"Put them in your mouth, don't chew them. Just swallow them down with this. Chug it all."

With complete faith, he tossed them into his mouth and followed them with a mouthful of the liquid. Appalled by the taste, he tried to pull back but she tipped up the glass and forced him to finish it or pour it down his shirt.

"What the devil was that?" he sputtered when it was

gone.

"Hair of the dog that bit you," she told him matter-of-factly. "It's called a 'red eye' or as close as I could get with what was available here. Tomato juice, beer, and an Indian spice I found in your cupboard since you didn't have any Tabasco. Oh, and a raw egg."

"Ye're jesting," he rasped but, while he saw humor in her eyes he knew that it was truth she spoke. "Ye're no' jesting."

"Good for what ails you," she teased. "I was going to have you drink the juice from a jar of pickles, but your cook wouldn't let me have it." Noting the disbelief written clearly on his face, she laughed. "It's an old Dutch cure. I'm surprised you didn't know that one."

"Normally I just hae strong coffee."

"Oh, no!" She shook her head. "Coffee is one of the worst things for a hangover. The caffeine is a vasoconstrictor. It shrinks the blood vessels and only makes your head hurt more."

"Truth?"

She nodded. "Before you can ask, the pills were Advil. A painkiller. Should help. Now for this. Drink up."

Connor gulped the water, which felt cool and refreshing as it went down. His head spun suddenly and he sank back down weakly. Emmy took the glass into the bathroom and returned with it refilled, placing it gently on the table beside his bed.

"I recommend as much water as possible. It will help with the dehydration." She bent over and placed a kiss on his forehead and withdrew wrinkling her nose. "Get some more rest; you should be fine when you wake up. Then take a shower and eat something. Juice, like orange juice would be best."

"Aye, doctor."

A smile tilted the corner of her lips as she looked back over her shoulder at him. "You really are a complete idiot, you know?" she told him, though her voice was strangely affectionate.

"Aye," he returned as she shut the door behind her.

He lay for a moment in the silence thinking how nice it was to have a person care for you and take care of you. The last person he could remember coming to his aid so tenderly was his mother, before she had become ill and taken to her own bed. She would sit at his bedside when he was ill and comfort him with gentle words and a cool hand. He must have been only seven or eight years old the last time.

Emmy's bedside manner was more chiding, less tolerant, but comforting and loving nonetheless. God, he loved that woman.

Perhaps he should tell her.

Was it worth taking a chance?

32

The little battery symbol on her iPhone had lost another notch. Emmy stared at is miserably. Just two bars remained before her one viable link to her time would be gone...or at least nonfunctional. Not true, there was still her camera but this loss of connection...she was feeling the inevitability deeply. No more music. It was a tragedy.

Emmy MacKenzie was a fan of music without bias to genre or era. Old or new from classical to country, she loved it all. Her playlists reflected her eclectic tastes. All the greats were there, maybe some not so great but all loved for what they offered to the history of music. It was the reason she'd pursued the piano and guitar aside from her mother's motivations. When it came to her favorite pastimes, the only thing better to Emmy's mind than hearing music was making it.

She perched on what was quickly becoming her favorite rock on the pebbled beach northwest of the castle. Knees drawn to her chest, hair down and loose and rippling in the breeze. Soon it might be too cold to stay out long like this. She hugged her arms tightly around her calves as her ear buds piped a musical montage to the crashing of the waves against the beach and the cry of the gulls. The Bee Gees blended into the Black-Eyed Peas and away to the Doors. The soundtrack of life. Every song brought a feeling, a memory. What would she do when it was gone?

In the distance, a small fishing boat was making its way down the coastline. She shivered, thinking how chilly it must be out there today. It was the first of November. Ironically, the Styx song 'Boat on the River' came on and Emmy had to smile.

"Emmy."

A voice broke through the music and Emmy started, turning and pulling the white cords from her ears as she did so.

"I called yer name several times," Connor mentioned casually as he took a seat beside her. He obviously wanted to comment on the reappearance of the object that had prompted their argument a week ago but decided against it. "Ye maun hae been lost in thought. Or hae ye changed yer name again and willnae answer to the one ye said ye wanted?"

His voice was teasing so Emmy decided to assume he meant the comment in that light. "I was just thinking," she answered. "You look much better."

"I feel much better, thanks to ye. I've ne'er recovered so quickly from my excesses before. Ye're a good doctor. Ye maun be successful."

Her low husky laughter flowed through him as she threw back her head and laughed freely. Tossing her hair, she tucked it behind one ear. "Oh, Connor."

"What do ye find so amusing?"

"I didn't learn that at medical school." She assumed a professorial tone. "It is an ancient remedy long employed by millions of college students across America, usually shortly after their first frat party."

"Let me understand, ye've consumed such a tonic yourself?"

"Many times, though not recently."

XXXXX

She'd had a habit of drinking heavily? He stared at her, sure that his eyes were wide with astonishment. Ladies of his acquaintance imbibed lightly and rarely. Connor had never before met a woman who had admitted to intoxication let alone public intoxication if his interpretation of 'party' was correct. But then, he had already conceded to himself she was not a lady in the strictest definition of the word, though her professional calling was noble if not genteel.

He thought to bombard her with questions. There were dozens tearing through his mind, all begging for answers, but surely that would lead to a fight, and how could he think of fighting her when she looked so lovely? Her hair unbound and rippling in the breeze, she looked like a young lass this day.

"Well, however ye came to be familiar wi' the cure for my infirmity, I thank ye."

"No problem."

They sat in awkward silence for a moment, staring out over the water. Each wondered what the other was thinking, wondered who would be first to break the uncomfortable moment. Though he'd apologized for his actual absence, not doubt she wondered at the reason for it. From the way her shoulders tensed when he called her by the name she preferred, she most likely questioned what had happened for him to suddenly give over on the matter.

Connor could feel the force of her unspoken questions. She would want answers, aye. Emmy just wasn't the type of person to accept words or actions she would consider unjustified. She was not a docile, meek woman. She did not allow manly edict to be laid down; she demanded logical and reasonable requests if she were to follow them. As Ian had noted, she would not be told what to do. Though, in truth, it was a quality he found most attractive in her personality. He felt it was a reflection of her self-confidence and intelligence.

Given that intelligence, Connor knew that if he laid out a coherent explanation of his actions, she would analyze it in the same vein and respond based on reason and not pure emotion. Whether her conclusion would fall in his favor or not, he was uncertain. But before he tackled that matter, there was one explanation he felt he was owed.

"Emmy," he began, thinking her preferred name suited her in its comfortable informality, "is it truly possible that yer arrival here was a simple coincidence?"

She turned her head and regarded him over her crossed arms. It was a simple question but the answer was not nearly so straightforward. He could sense again that there was something she was hiding. "I came to the UK for a vacation...holiday."

"The UK?"

"United Kingdom," she clarified and he nodded, encouraging her to continue. "It was meant to be a ten-day trip from London to Edinburgh and over here to Mull. Duart is one of the best preserved examples of medieval architecture and I'm fond of the architecture of that period, so here, Edinburgh Castle, St. Paul's, Westminster...that kind of thing. That I arrived at your front door on the day I did, appearing as I did for the purpose of your personal history is, yes, a coincidence."

Connor studied her face for a long while. There was honesty there. Truth. But there was more she withheld than what she admitted. He wanted to know what it was but sensed that any attempts at coercion would be met in a similar fashion as his previous try. Besides, verbal sparring was not on his agenda for the day, not only because he did not wish to argue with her, but his head wasn't feeling that good just yet.

"Thus far then, ye seem content with remaining at Duart despite having nae true connection to its occupants."

"I wouldn't use the word content," Emmy responded lightly, "but you would be right in saying that I haven't been in a hurry to leave."

It was an evasive answer and Connor recognized it as such. "Is there any particular reason ye're in nae hurry?"

)O(O(O(O(

A soft smile curved her lips as she studied him. Fishing, she thought. God, she just loved him, insecurities and all. He just wanted her to say it, didn't want to be the one to say it first...well, again. She could just put him out of his misery, if that's what it was. But what if her thoughts that he hadn't meant it proved to be true?

"There are several reasons I am still here," she began. "The most basic would be that I truly feel that Dory will need assistance in delivering her babies and I can provide that. This past week, we've become close and I find I want to help her, not only because it is my job but because I care for her. She is becoming like a sister to me in a sense probably because it is hard to look at her and not feel an affinity toward her."

"Reasonable and logical, just I predicted." A ghost of a smile hovered on his lips. "And another?"

She bit her lower lip nervously. Anxious even in the face of his open affection. "This thing between us, Connor, it *is* real, isn't it? Despite the absurdly short amount of time we have known each other, it feels like I've known you my entire life. I know how you think. I bet I can tell you better than you could explain it why you left last week. Unless you've managed to completely fool me and I've read everything wrong, I know you. I hope I am not such a fool that I could be so thoroughly snowed."

"Snowed?"

"Duped, bamboozled, hornswoggled." She read his face and eyes, seeing only fondness and humor. Surely he was not so Machiavellian that he could dupe her so entirely. "Have I been?"

"Snowed?" He hesitated, then slowly shook his head. "Nay, my love, ye've no'." Connor caressed her cheek lightly. "It is real, this attraction between us. In truth, 'tis the verra reason for my persistent insistence that ye were Heather. Once I'd admitted to myself the possibility that yer story, however unlikely, might be true, anyway. If ye were Heather, then as Dory's sister there were grounds for yer continued presence at Duart. If ye were no', ye'd hae cause, even impetus, to leave. I dinnae want that."

"You wanted me to stay?"

"I still want ye to stay, though, I suppose we must reveal the truth to the others and assign ye other chambers for propriety's sake," he added regretfully.

"Let's not jump the gun on that just yet," Emmy was prompted to respond. "Other than Ian and Dory, no one knows yet and I don't think they need to. And if Dory can handle us being roomed next to each other knowing the truth then I think we're okay for now. Unless there is another reason to move me?"

"Such as?"

Emmy bit her lip, reluctant to put voice to her fear. "Perhaps you would rather not...encourage my affections or give me reason to think there is more between us?"

"What are ye trying to say?"

"I am trying to figure out if you just want to sleep with me or if you want more than that. That maybe a couple rounds in the sack will be enough for you." She looked away down the coast.

Tenderly, Connor grasped her chin and turned her back to face him. "Ye're trying to discern whether I believe ye're 'a piece of ass', I believe yer phrasing was or whether I care more fully for ye." It was not a question. Either she was an open book or he knew her as well as she knew him. "If ye will think back to the disagreement we had prior to my departure, I believe ye'll find that ye had the right of it then."

She didn't pretend to misunderstand him. "I thought that you might've regretted the words when you left so quickly or that you hadn't meant it at all. A slip of the tongue or something."

"Is your glass truly e'er half-empty?" He chuckled. "Let me make myself clear then, though I put myself at yer tender mercies in doing so...ye've won, my love. I am defeated. I love ye, Emily MacKenzie. Ye're a fascinating, intelligent woman." He stroked her cheek once more and looked down at her with that love shining in his eyes. "I felt so right from the moment I first saw ye and it has little to do with yer body—bonny as it is."

Her eyes closed and she turned into his palm, covering his hand with her own and savoring the moment. Other than her mother, no one had ever before told her that they loved her, well, discounting Billy Everson in the second grade. How brilliant it felt. Satisfying, intoxicating. Her chest ached with emotion. "Oh, Connor. I am so glad to hear you say that."

"Because?" he prompted softly.

She opened her eyes and met his gaze. She saw the stress and uncertainty there and knew she could not leave him hanging. "Because love is best when returned and, I love you. You're maddening and aggravating and challenging…"

"Why thank ye," he offered acerbically.

"But," she drawled, taking his hand in hers, "I love that you madden me and aggravate me and challenge me. You make me think and make me feel in ways I have never done before. You make me *feel*. I've had an ache in my chest since I met you, a heartache at the thought of losing you. I don't know what I would've done if it was completely one-sided."

"Unrequited love is said to be a most horrible state and I will admit that I had many fears that such a fate might be my own. Ha'ing been rejected once before had made me hesitant to allow any vulnerability. As much as I wanted ye, I dinnae want these feelings and had even considered that we might enjoy each other wi'out emotional attachment. Once I realized my feelings, I even thought to deny them. While I might feel as I did, I had nae intention of revealing myself to ye in fear that my feelings might no' be reciprocated," he confessed.

"It's hard to take a chance on love," she agreed in more simplified terms. "I doubt I would've ever said anything if you hadn'tt been braver than me and done it first."

"'Tis a man's burden."

"I wouldn't go that far, Connor," she teased. "Where I am from, women propose to men all the time."

He groaned. "Ne'er say so."

"Okay, I won't," she teased. "That's why you left? You didn't want to be emotionally vulnerable to me?"

"It is no' in my nature to appear weak."

"No, I suppose not." Emmy leaned into his arms and laid her head on his shoulder. "But I love you anyway."

His breath drew in deeply and exhaled in a rush. "I love ye, as well, so verra much."

"I am so very glad," she whispered into his neck before taking the flesh there between her teeth and nibbling and sucking lightly.

Connor leaned away and lowered his head, capturing those teasing lips with his own. Emmy clung to him as his hands cradled her shoulder and neck pulling her closer to him. Their bodies met at the chest and hip and she could almost feel his heat radiating through the layers of her outerwear and his, but it was not enough.

"How is your head?" she whispered.

"Much better, thank ye."

"Maybe we could take this inside then?" she offered, her eyes making heated promises.

Though he should be used to her manner, Connor was still taken aback by her bold implication. Never, he swore, would he ever meet another like her. A woman who felt free to express her desires, a woman who admitted to them. He might as well assume from this point forward that everything he knew about the fairer sex did not apply to his Emmy. She would keep him on his toes, to be sure.

Connor laughed and pulled her to her feet. It would be a wonderful way to experience life. With the unexpected.

XOXOXOX

They hurried back to the castle as quickly as Emmy's long skirts would allow and she cursed their very existence. They dashed through the courtyard and up the broad staircase. At the top, she squealed as he swung her into his arms and carried her, laughing, the remainder of the distance to his chamber.

Connor kicked the door shut and caught her lips passionately once more as he lowered her to her feet. She swayed and clung to him as he swung her around. "*Ah*, Em. My darling, my love," he murmured against her lips.

She broke away, turning her back and commanding breathlessly, "Help me with all of this."

He dealt with the long row of buttons with an efficiency that left Emmy dazed. He kissed and scraped his teeth against her shoulders as he lowered the bodice and set to work on the laces of the skirts.

"I love that ye dinnae wear the stays," he whispered huskily. "I will ne'er be able to look at ye again wi'out knowing that ye're nearly bare beneath yer clothing."

His hands slid up and caught her breasts through the thin chemise as her skirts and petticoats dropped to the ground. Turning, she threw her arms around his neck and kissed him again while his fingers found the ties of her drawers, loosened and dropped those as well before his arms came around her. His breath was as ragged as hers as their mouths met again and again. His fists clenched against her back and a moment later, she felt the material of the chemise give way as he tore the garment from her. A moan of excitement escaped her.

"Oh, Connor," she sighed. Eat your heart out Kevin Kline!

Catching one thick wool stocking with the toes of the opposite foot, she shoved the pair off one by one all the while massaging his chest and back while his hands returned to her breasts. His fingers brushed her nipples, tantalizing the tender flesh and he bent his head, capturing one between his lips. Emmy squealed and wrapped her arms around his head holding him to her as his tongue flicked across the tip, sending shocks of electricity down to her core.

Connor lifted her in his arms and carried her to his bed. He deposited her there and stared down at her for a moment, chest heaving. An instant later he was shedding his clothing in haste and it wasn't long before he was as naked as she. Emmy gazed at the heavy muscles of his chest and abdomen, the strength of his arms and legs as he lowered himself on top of her. She spread her legs to cradle his weight and savored the weight of him above her. He stared down at her tenderly.

"I love ye."

"I love you, too," she whispered and twitched her hips just enough to make his breath catch.

"Minx," he chided and lowered his mouth again to her breast.

He suckled there as she moaned and tossed her head. He skimmed a hand down her belly and hip before returning up the back of her thigh to squeeze her bottom. Her hands on his body nearly distracted him from his purpose but he recovered to continue his intended course. His finger slid into the valley between her legs using her moist heat to ease his way around and over her sensitive nub as she gasped and arched against him. A second finger joined the first. Her body quivered multiplying the pleasure he felt from the searching caress of her hands and her lips and tongue on his chest and neck.

Again and again his fingers circled and cajoled until she thought she would faint. She was light-headed, panting and burning and painfully near a climax already. Her lips tingled with arousal. Her thighs clenched about the turn of his hand, encouraging him on, begging him not to stop. Then he plunged those talented digits deep inside her and she cried out, arching her back. He gave no quarter as he thrust his fingers again and again curling them upward and wringing sensations from her that she had never known a body was capable of feeling.

"Connor. Please," she gasped, begging for release.

Obliging, he pulled back and then drove himself to the hilt into the slick heat that awaited him, nearly crying out in ecstasy himself. He pumped again and paused as she begged him to continue. He rolled suddenly to his back, pulling her along until she was astride him.

She stared down at him, bracing her hands against his chest to push herself up. She felt the length of him withdraw as she rose and dropped back down. They both moaned and his hands tightened on her hips urging her up again and pull her back down forcefully again.

Connor looked up at Emmy, her eyes closed, lips moist and parted, her long hair in tangled disarray around her face and shoulders. Gorgeous, sensual. The muscles of her stomach flexed and she rocked her hips again, grinding against him. Never again, never again would he leave her. She was his heart, soul and body. Nothing could ever compare to this feeling. He raised his hips to meet hers as she ground herself down on him again and they found a satisfying rhythm.

The tightening of the orgasm didn't slow Emmy this

time. She pursued it, savored it as it built, the fingers of tension reaching out from her core. Building, tensing, her head swam and then her body raptured and spasmed around his length, drawing him deeper. He gripped her hips, thrusting himself upward again and again as she pulsed around him, riding him. She cried out her release until he joined her at last, his shout of ecstasy combining with hers. His heat flooded inside her as she collapsed onto his sweaty chest, their breathing harsh and uneven in the quiet room.

Connor's arms came around her and held her close as she buried her face in his neck. They lay together like that for several minutes, recovering until Emmy shifted, allowing him to slide out of her as she rolled to his side and curled up next to him.

"Wow," she sighed at length.

"Aye," he agreed with a chuckle. He tightened his arms around her keeping her close. "That was even more profound than the first time."

Emmy knew why. It was more than a meeting of bodies this time; it was a meeting of souls. It was making love in the truest sense of the term. She had never realized there was a difference before between sex and lovemaking. It made her wish she could go back and erase her past so only he and this remained, but for all her wishing, she realized that her past provided her an even greater appreciation of what she felt now. The comparison allowed her to realize that this experience with Connor was unique and unparalleled.

"Shall we test a theory?" he asked. "That it will improve exponentially wi' repetition?"

"I'm ready for round two if you are," she agreed readily as he rolled over on top of her.

Clad in a dressing gown, Emmy sat on the edge of the bed the next afternoon staring down at Connor. The previous afternoon had blended into evening as they explored each other into the night.

Round two? She laughed inwardly. After bouts of sex, eating from the tray Margo left at the door last evening and again this morning, and napping, they'd ended at dawn with round five. They'd been so exhausted they both passed out into a deep sleep that she'd only just roused from. She now knew the feel and taste of every part of his body as he knew hers. It was a night beyond imagination and, she hoped, just one of many.

But the complete truth had not yet been told and Emmy knew that she could not continue as she had been. This one last issue needed to be resolved if she were to continue in this relationship with Connor. If there was to be love between them—true love—everything had to be out on the table.

First she had to persuade him that what she was telling

him was true—no easy matter in itself. But then what? What would his reaction be to that truth? Would he look at her as a freak of nature? As an abomination? Would she become an unspeakable *thing* that he would view with distrust or worse...revulsion?

She trembled, terrified that he might simply turn his back on her and order her from his house. That he might look at her with disgust? What would she do if he did?

But to never tell him...?

Could she stay here for however long was allowed to her and keep such a desperate secret from him? No, she could tell he was already aware that she was withholding something from him. Connor was not a fool. He was intelligent, perhaps intelligent enough to work through the facts and realize that she was still the same person who he loved and whom he was loved by in return.

She squeezed her hands around the iPhone in her hands. Evidence. Verbal claims and words proved nothing. A passport could be forged. But this advanced technology had a foundation in truth. Physical evidence that would be hard for him to deny.

Emmy prayed for his understanding and acceptance.

A while later, just when she thought her nerves were about to break, Connor opened his eyes sleepily and smiled up at her.

"Good morn, my love," he murmured, reaching up to caress her cheek before dropping his hand back as he stretched his long body.

"Good afternoon," she answered, though the playfulness she intended did not make it into her tone. Connor eyed her curiously.

"What troubles ye?"

"Do you remember yesterday I said there were several reasons I had not left Duart?" she asked quickly, before she had a chance to change her mind. She waited for him to nod. "Dory and you? Well, there is another."

※※※※

Ah, here it was.

He 'd known for some time there was something else she was not telling him. He was perceptive enough to know that while not a deception, as such, it was at least an omission. He studied her subdued face and knew it was an omission grave in nature. In that instant, a portion of him wanted to deny her confession, halt her from revealing whatever it was. Foreboding enveloped him.

She hesitated, nervously chewing her lips and staring down at her cupped hands where she kept some item concealed from him. "The other reason I haven't left," she cleared her throat, "is because I can't, or rather, I don't know how. I came to Duart for a vacation, but how I got *here* is something else entirely."

"Here?" he repeated. "I dinnae ken what ye mean."

"I'm going to need you to put on your Educated Man hat here, Connor," she told him, "because there are not many ways for me to cushion the truth."

"I am yer student," he replied, pushing himself up to a sitting position in the bed.

"Maybe I should let you get dressed and eat first," Emmy suggested. She started to rise but he caught her arm and pulled her back down.

"Please continue," he prompted. "What do ye mean when ye say *here* like that?"

"Here, as in this time," she said at length. When he

continued to watch her expectantly, she sighed. "I don't mean 'this time' as in this moment. I mean *in* this time. Connor, the birth date on the passport I showed you wasn't a mistake. That is my true birthday."

"But it said 1980-something or another." He shook his head, not understanding.

"1982. I know what you're going to say," Emmy said before he could speak. "It wasn't wrong. It wasn't forged. I was born on March 10, 1982. The day I came here, it was October 18, 2010."

Connor's first reaction was to throw back his head and laugh in amusement at her farce and await her to join him, admitting that her words were in jest. As he stared at her solemn eyes, however, he knew she was serious.

My God, she's mad, he thought, and rubbed his hands over his face in disbelief.

"I'm not crazy." Her words denied his thought. "I am perfectly sane. Contrary to what I said before when we were at lunch in Oban, there is no frequent time traveling in the future, at least that I know about. I'm not certain how it all happened but when I came here to visit the castle, it was Donell who brought me."

"Auld Donell?"

"Yes, the man from the inn. He drove me here in 2010 and somehow sent me back to this time. To you. I don't know why, he mentioned something about second chances but I haven't been able to find him again. You said he was a wizard or something?"

"Emmy," he shook his head in denial, "those are just absurd rumors…"

She cut him off. "All I know is that I got off the shuttle with a ticket to see this castle and the next I knew, I was here in 1895 and there you were riding up on your horse. Just like that." She snapped her fingers. "And Donell is the one who did it. He admitted it to me."

"Emmy," he started shaking his head. Something sad and mournful tightened his throat.

She cut him off, eyes pleading for understanding. "I know it sounds nuts, I do! I've thought and thought trying to figure out the *whys* and *hows* of this whole thing and I truthfully don't have one logical sounding reason or explanation to give you. He did it. Donell did it. Magic or whatever. I tried to send for him, to talk to him, but he's just disappeared. No one can find him."

She rubbed her own face in frustration and gazed at himexpectantly, hopefully even. Was she thinking a few moments for consideration would make him believe her? To even do so would make him question his own sanity.

Pulling away from her, he climbed out of the bed searching for a pair of trousers and slipping them on.

"There's coffee on the table." There was defeat in her voice. Sadness. "It should still be warm if not hot."

)O(O(O(O(

Emmy toyed with the phone in her hands, flipping it over and over again. She'd hoped, prayed he would simply believe her without the need for proof. He loved her after all and love required a measure of faith. But maybe she should've anticipated that the concept was too fantastical to be taken without a measure of doubt.

She could not fault him for reacting this way. A little self-analysis told her she would doubt such a revelation as well and probably more vocally than he.

Time and evidence were required.

She stood and moved to join him at the little table where he was adding sugar to his coffee. She took a seat across from him, watching him as he sipped. His dark eyes were grave.

"What ye're saying is insane," he commented at length.

"It is."

"Unbelievable."

"Absolutely," she agreed, wanting to reach across the table and hold his hands in hers. He must have realized her purpose since he wrapped both hands around the cup and propped his elbows on the table. Withdrawal. "Yes, it is that and more, but, Connor, it is also the truth. I'm not a nutcase from Bedlam. Without Donell, I can give you no rationalization on how it happened, but I only ask that you consider that you've thought me an intelligent woman. Consider that I know you're an intelligent man and how such a claim, if it were not true, would demean both our intelligence. I don't believe in magic and witchcraft but I know that once you've time to consider all the facts, you will know that I'd never lie about something like this."

)O(O(O(O(

Connor watched the woman he loved in astonishment. She thought to rely on his intelligence to accept her claims as truth? His intellect challenged her very allegation.

Time travel? Witchcraft? He dismissed the idea. It was impossible. Inconceivable. The woman was clearly havering.

In truth the Scots were a superstitious lot. Tales of witchcraft and wizardry went back a thousand years. But even if magic did exist, one could not walk through the fabric of time regardless of what Wells and Verne had written about it and that fictitious fourth dimension. Time was absolute and tramped inexorably in one direction only. Their works were but narrative. The idea that sorcery might have been the key was even more unbelievable. Sorcery was nothing but myth and legerdemain. Nothing like this.

If Emmy thought that his logic and reason would bend to allow her point... and he could see that she did believe it...then perhaps she *was* a Bedlamite escapee.

He was just opening his mouth to convey his conviction when her hand slid across the table toward him, flattened but covering something. She sat with her arm extended for a moment, her eyes searching his. Pleading. Uncertainly, she sighed and withdrew her arm leaving what had been under it on the table in front of him.

It was the item that Margo had given her the previous week; the object which had prompted their argument almost eight days ago. He leaned in and squinted at it before reluctantly picking it up. It was small and flat, one side shiny silver with the silhouette of an apple with a bite taken from it and the word IPHONE printed in white letters beneath it. The other side, black glass, was almost mirror-like in its reflectivity. From one end a white covered wire extended, split and ended in a flattened ball of some sort on each part.

He shivered in trepidation.

He had absolutely *no* idea what it was.

Emmy spoke softly as Connor studied the object. "I think I told you my mom had me learn to play the piano and guitar when I was growing up because studies had shown that music aided in learning of math. What my mom never realized was that I did it because I just really like music. When I was in high school, I'd go to see every concert that came to town just so I could hear it live. In my time, you don't have to wait for a concert, hope someone can play the piano or play it yourself because we have radio, TV, CDs and these." She gestured to the player. "This object is a telephone, much as I described to you in Oban. My own personal one, small enough to fit in my hand. It's not only a phone but also what we call an mp3 player. There are many different kinds but this one in particular is called an iPhone." She took it from him for a moment and removed the ear buds. She held them up. "These are for just one person to use it for music, so ignore them for now." She laid it back on the table, black side up.

"What does it do?" he rasped, leaning away from it.

"It is a telephone. You talk into it here." She pointed to the tiny hole of the microphone then indicated another. "Listen there. You can have a conversation with anyone in the world. It also plays music. Well, it does a lot of other things too, but let's start with the music." Emmy leaned forward leaning her elbows on the table. "Go ahead, touch it."

"That's quite all right, I believe ye."

"No, you don't," she said, her voice intense.

He looked so terrified she almost had to laugh. She might have done so if she hadn't thought he would take it as a personal offense. Instead, she reached across and touched the screen with one fingertip.

Connor jerked back as the screen lit up. A colorful picture appeared in the black field, it was square with a picture of a young blond woman in profile. Carrie Underwood it said and 'Home Sweet Home' below that. Emmy tapped once more on the picture and piano music began to emanate from the object.

"Sweet Jesus," he whispered in horror as a woman's voice joined the piano.

Emmy noted that his skin had paled dramatically and, taking pity on him, reached across, stopped the music and pulled the iPhone away from him. For a moment, he looked like he might be ill. Giving him a moment to collect his wits, Emmy toyed with the player.

"It plays music and much more." Moving to a different menu, she quickly shuffled through the pictures she had loaded on it. She found one she liked and turned it around to show it to Connor. "My mother."

XOXOXOX

Connor saw the color image of a lovely woman with flowing blond hair that appeared to be rippling in a breeze. She looked a lot like Emmy as she had been yesterday, seated by the sound with the wind tossing her hair. The image was crisp and eerily lifelike and the woman in it was smiling merrily as if just caught in a moment rather than posing for twenty seconds while an exposure was taken.

He reached a curious finger to touch the screen but the image slid away and another took its place. This one was of Emmy though she was much younger here. She was in a cheek-to-cheek embrace with her mother and both were wearing wide grins as they stared out at him. He touched it again and another slid into place. From a distance this time, the women stood in front of a building with Emmy wearing a gold gown and hat with a flat square on the top.

"My high school graduation," she said softly. "Mom died not long afterward."

"She was a bonny lady," he offered, still trying to digest and understand what he was seeing.

"She was."

"Where did ye get this…thing?" he asked finally.

"At a store," she answered, keeping her voice low and soothing. "It is not unique by any means; millions of people own one or something similar to it. On this, I have over 2000 songs, hundreds of photos, games, some movies and some audio books. Books read out loud and recorded so you can listen to them when you cannot just sit and read."

"Thousands of songs?" he repeated in amazement, turning it over in his hand. But it was so small. Surely this was impossible. He'd never dreamed of such a thing. In Paris nine years before, he'd seen a cylindrical phonograph presented. It had been large and capable of playing but a single tune. The sound it had emitted had also been rough and uneven...nothing that could be compared to this. Was it possible that Emmy was speaking the truth? That she had somehow traveled through time to him? It was fantastic and absurd, yet she was here.

He shook his head. But...

Everyone living in his castle had commented that they'd never met another like her. All of them assumed it was because she had been in America for too long, but what if it was because she had been raised a century ahead of them all?

Their conversation in Oban could be taken in a different light now. She'd been trying to feel him out regarding her origins, testing his mind's acceptance of her truth. Again, he shook his head. It could not be.

"If I had an app to make this easier for you, I would use it." Her voice was teasing but the joke was obviously beyond him. Connor remained silent, staring at the machine. "Would you like me to leave you alone?"

Nausea tightened his gut. It could not be.

)O(O(O(O(

Perhaps she had pushed him too far for now. It might be best to give him time to digest her news, to come to terms with it. Emmy was encouraged however. Aside from his astonishment and awe, he seemed to be curious between his bouts of head shaking denial. Curiosity was good and often lent itself to positive conclusions. At least Connor was not staring at her with fear and disgust...yet.

Emmy pushed back from the table and started to stand but Connor caught her hand and she sat back down.

"'Tis extraordinary, this device," he admitted. "A part of me wants to know more aboot it. CDs? Movies? I dinnae ken

290

what those things are and I'm interested in knowing. However, connecting this fascination wi' immediately accepting yer claim…" He shook his head once again. "It defies logic and is, therefore, difficult to accept."

"It's all right," Emmy assured him. "While in a perfect world you would've just accepted my word on the whole thing, I think you're taking it all pretty well so far. I was half-afraid you might completely freak out, so all in all I'm proud of you."

"I dinnae believe I've e'er *freaked out,* as ye so elegantly phrase it," he replied, squaring his shoulders. "I *am* curious though."

"Curiosity is good."

"No' for the cat and I fear I might take its place wi' this current state of affairs," Connor admitted, letting loose a long shaky sigh. "And while I'm no' yet admitting that I accept yer entire story, I maun know, how does it work?"

He pulled the iPhone back and laid it flat on the table in front of him, and Emmy demonstrated the menu, showing him how to navigate the programs and get from one application to the next. When he questioned the music, she chose some examples of different genres of music for him.

As she might have predicted, he leaned toward show tunes or ballads, finding the rhythms to be similar to those he was used to. He did not seem to care for most of it. she could only assume the sounds were so foreign to him that he could not enjoy it. She assured him that if he grew up with it he would see it differently. Connor looked so doubtful that Emmy had to laugh.

"Here then, if you're going to appreciate rock and roll, maybe we should start at the beginning." She flipped through playlists until she found what she was looking for. "This is

Elvis Presley, the King of Rock and Roll. He was there at the beginning of the whole shebang."

Tapping the screen, the opening bars of 'Don't Be Cruel' thrummed out and she waited expectantly for him to catch on and start tapping his toe to the beat but after a long moment, Connor only looked skeptical.

"Surely no'?"

"Are you kidding me?" she gaped at him in denial. "This is Elvis for crying out loud. Everyone loves Elvis. Millions of women worldwide screamed and wailed for him. He would get up on stage and do his gyrations." She stood and demonstrated. "It drove the women crazy."

Connor looked shocked and finally laughed out loud. "Now I truly doubt yer sanity. Such music sung and danced to in such a fashion will ne'er become popular or socially acceptable."

"Oh, it will," she assured him. "It already has. Elvis is the king and I wish someday I could prove it to you and tell you 'I told you so'." Still Emmy frowned at him. "You didn't like my music?"

"There were some pieces that are nicely done, but . . ." he shrugged.

"I think I might have to hate you now," she muttered, taking the iPhone back and flipping through the menu idly.

"Perhaps wi' continued exposure, as ye suggested, I might come to appreciate it more," he said in consolation.

"Don't do me any favors.".

"Tell me more about these 'movies' ye spoke of. I've ne'er heard that word before."

He tried to pull the device back to him but she hung on tightly with a muttered, "I'll do it."

Scrolling through the movies she'd downloaded for the

plane trip over, she tried to pick one for him while giving him a little background.

"A movie or motion picture was originally made by linking a series of pictures together, printed on celluloid and projected at a theater onto the big screen, a white space about twenty feet wide. Light beamed through the film and the images would show on the screen. Just like music, there are dozens of different styles of movies. But basically you could say they are stories like books brought to life for you to watch them happen rather than use your imagination only to picture them."

Inspiration struck and she started one. She forwarded over the credits and turned it toward him. Connor leaned forward in amazement as the actors spoke and the scenery moved by. "Incredible," he whispered. "Marvelous." After watching for several minutes, he turned to her with a surprised look. "I know this story."

"I thought you might," she beamed, pleased at his excitement and enthusiasm.

"It is 'Sense and Sensibility', the Jane Austen work." He watched with excitement for a while longer. "'Tis no' precisely right, however."

"No, it's not," she said. "While books and plays are often adapted for a movie, books usually have too much detail to translate in their entirety on to the big screen. 'Gone with the Wind' for example, I've heard would have been a movie seven days long if they had filmed every word and action as it was written in the book."

"'Gone with the Wind'?"

"It's another book, a long one. You'll read it one day," she said before adding in a teasing tone, "You might even like it. It's about the American Civil War."

"So they take books and plays and make movies from them."

"Not just from books and plays, though some stories like *The Time Machine* have been made and remade several times. Some stories are written just for movies about everything from historic events to day to day life and science fiction." Emmy wondered if it would be possible to sum up the whole of what movies encompassed. "You name it, it's been done. There are movies about wars, the old west, the future, the past and things that have never, could never happen. There are no limitations." Especially with CGI technologies which allowed for characters and worlds almost beyond imagination but that was an explanation for another day.

"What of Scotland? Have they made these movies about my nation?" Connor asked,his gratifyingly expression eager and inquisitive.

"Dozens, at least," she told him. "*Braveheart* was about William Wallace, there was *Rob Roy*…hmm, let me think. *Brigadoon*. Was that Irish or Scottish? Hmm…I think Mary, Queen of Scots was in…oh! I know. *Highlander*. Now there's a classic. You might like that one. And there are a lot of Scottish actors, too. Sean Connery is a Scot and probably one of the biggest names ever," she added, shooting him a seductive look from beneath her lashes. "You talk just like him. It's so sexy."

※※※※

Connor took her drawled statement and cheeky grin with a smile, but returned his attention to the tiny images again as the Austen story unfolded.

How wondrous. Stories that one could watch, already he could see the appeal and scope of such entertainment. He would have paid any sum in that moment to see one in person at a theater. He felt he could not exclaim his awe and wonder enough to truly express what he felt about this device that allowed him to see what would be.

"Will such an event be available in my lifetime?" he hesitantly asked in a low voice. "Will I hae the opportunity to watch one in person?"

"Of course," she assured him. "They are really not that far away. In fact, I think that maybe the beginnings are already in the works. But the first ones will have no sound and be in black and white like your photographs are, but they will get better as the technology progresses just like anything else."

As the technology progresses. As time goes on.

He sighed. He could not refute the truth of her claim. A logical man weighed evidence and made conclusions based on those facts. As much as his emotions wanted to deny it, Connor knew logically if not yet in his heart that Emmy spoke true.

He needed to find auld Donell. To determine his part in this whole thing. The man had been prying into everyone's business for more years than Connor could remember. Some remarkable things had occurred over the years that had been attributed to him but nothing of this magnitude. He needed to be found, but the question remained.

"How could Donell hae performed such sorcery? 'Tis beyond understanding."

✕✕✕✕✕

Emmy sighed in relief and slumped back in the chair. Connor had been staring blankly at the screen for so long that she had begun to fear where his ruminations had taken him.

If he was questioning the hows of the whole thing, he must've begun to believe the truth of her claim. From there it was a small step to total acceptance.

She didn't realize how tense she had become until her muscles were free to relax and the blood began to flow back into her fingers where they had been clenched so tightly together.

Still, she didn't have a real explanation to offer. "I don't know how it happened or how he did it. If he did indeed do it and he isn't just some crazy old man spouting nonsense when I saw him at the inn. But he was there with me. Now he is here and so am I. He is the constant." She shrugged, aware that it was a pitiful response. "He said at the inn that it was about second chances and something about a simple life but other than that I've got nothing. I just don't know."

He raised his head and met her gaze for the first time since her revelation. "Ye said that before. Second chances?"

"He said there had been tragedy in your family and that everyone deserved a second chance." Emmy thought again of the conclusion she had drawn. "I think he meant Dory. I think in my future that she might not have made it through her delivery. I looked at my guidebook after that and it said your title had passed to a cousin after your death. Not Ian and not a nephew. That either means that Ian and Dory had only girls or Ian…." She faltered.

"Died before me childless." His voice was low and distraught.

"Yes."

"And I had nae heirs."

"Yes," she repeated softly.

XOXOXOX

The gravity of the situation weighed heavily on him. He felt as if his mind were about to explode from the excess of information presented to him this past hour. His future lay out before him. Unchangeable?

Connor thought again about Emmy's passport and the birth date it had shown. She wasn't even of his lifetime. This device, this iPhone, was beyond his lifetime. He would never live long enough to see its invention. He would be dead long before she was ever born.

He tapped the edge of the music player but stared unfocused at it, beyond it. A larger issue raised its head. If she were of the future, was it against God's plan that he love her? She couldn't have been meant for him to be born beyond his years. He pondered the natural order of God's will but could not decide whether her arrival was a gift from God to complete his life or a result of sorcery that could just as easily be taken away. One thought prompted another question. One that overrode the turbulence of his already chaotic emotions.

"Ye said ye're ignorant of the force that brought ye to this time? Ye were unaware?"

"What are you thinking?"

"Ye were brought here wi'out yer knowledge, aye?"

She nodded and a sickening sense of dread began to emerge from the turmoil within. "Then what is to stop ye from being taken back in equal fashion?"

Emmy met his eyes and for a moment he saw his personal fears, hopes and anxieties mirrored in them.

"Nothing," they said together.

Connor disappeared into his bathroom obeying her suggestion to take some time alone and shut the door firmly. Running some cold water in the sink, he splashed his face and stared at his reflection in the mirror above.

For a moment, his mind was a complete blank as he stared into the dark shock of his own eyes, rounded and weary. He needed to examine the facts at his leisure and ponder the possibilities and implications of her presence. However, beyond the truth of her origin and her incredible story, it was the other issue that flooded his mind and sent him reeling. At any moment, she could be gone.

Just like that.

Was God so pitiless as to dangle happiness before him and then snap it away like a cat with its toy? They needed to find Donell; that was a certainty. If Emmy was right and it was his magic that had done this, then the old man was the key to keeping Emmy here with him. Emmy said Donell had mentioned everyone deserved a second chance. Emmy assumed that it was only Dory who needed a second chance, but when she had also told him that he would die without an heir, it had occurred to Connor that perhaps she was his second chance as well.

His life had already changed dramatically with her presence. If she were to stay, to become his countess, it would be his second chance to live the life he had imagined years ago. Life as a husband and father, not just laird of his clan.

He just needed to have some faith that Emmy was his destiny. The chain of events that delivered her into his time was part of God's greater plan. His destiny was to be hers and hers to be his. He felt certain that was it. That she was *his* second chance if he was to have one in this life. He needed to have faith.

Faith said that for everything there was a reason. Ecclesiastes.

XXXXX

While bathing and dressing, Connor had become convinced of his deduction. He found Emmy in her room, dressed and reading a book while she waited for him.

Given the plate of sandwiches and pitcher of her iced tea before her, she clearly thought that it would take some time for him to consider what she had told him.

"Had ye considered that God has a plan for each of us? That He may hae brought ye here?" he asked, his eyebrows rising nearly to his hairline in surprise when she frowned dubiously at his conclusions.

"I told you before, Connor, I have no clue what brought me here—only who," she responded. "For all we know it could be the whim of a bored old man."

"Wi'out a reasonable explanation, I feel we maub rely on something other than empirical evidence. Hence, faith." Connor joined her, taking a sandwich as he realized it had been almost ten hours since their breakfast tray that morning. Beef, tomatoes and...vinegar? Interesting. He took two more.

"So you think that Donell's actions were a part of God's plan and that we should have faith that we are meant to be together? Do you actually think God makes every decision before you do?" she wondered aloud. "Haven't you ever read Sartre? Free will and all that?"

"Who?"

"Jean-Paul Sartre? Never mind, my point is that destiny implies an absence of choice as if we can't control what happens to us," she lectured. "I like to be in control."

"I understand what ye're saying, but, if I might be so bold, ye dinnae control it," Connor pointed out with little mercy. "It snatched ye up wi'out so much as a by yer leave. Wi'out yer cooperation, knowledge or consent." He counted these out on his fingers.

He picked up his sandwiches so he could pace the room while he ate. "It is true, nae man wants to think himself helpless in shaping the events of his own life, but I do believe that on occasion God guides our path to that which is beneficial to us."

"Donell sent me here," she replied flatly. "Nothing more, nothing less, whether we understand that power or not. What we need to do is find him and figure it out from there."

"And I agree. He is the key. But..." he arched a brow at her, "have ye so little faith, my love? Truly?"

"Wow, Connor. I would have said an hour ago that I was fairly religious, but I have nothing on you. I believe in God, I do, but that He is guiding all of this...I just don't think so."

Connor wondered at her skepticism, but he needed something to believe in. Her revelation had shaken the very foundations of his intellect so much so he wasn't sure he could rely on it. Until they found Donell and determined whether he held mysterious powers or was just simply an auld bampot, the only foundation available to him was his faith. He was embracing it wholeheartedly lest he go mad trying to figure it all out.

Emmy's ambiguity regarding her hopes for the future didn't help matters. She spoke of days together, but never a lifetime. He leaned back and stared down at her face, wondering at the mind hidden behind it. He might spend the rest of his days arguing philosophy alone with her and be happy for it. He could live a lifetime utterly engaged by her. He wanted it and had known it from almost the moment he met her, confirmed it during his hiatus of the previous week, but clearly her mind wasn't looking beyond the immediate to that lifetime he pictured.

To Emmy, their liaison was short-term still.

He wondered what she would say if he asked her to marry him, to stay with him for a lifetime. To trust that it was their destiny to be together whether by God's hand or man's.

"Tell me, how do ye perceive the time ye're granted here then?"

XOXOXOX

Emmy met his serious gaze and knew it was not the time for flippant answers. His belief was so absolute she was almost envious and terrified by his conviction. She wanted the same, that knowledge that she would be with him, here, forever.

Or she wouldn't.

Without clarification from Donell about his ramblings at the inn, what else was she to do beyond what she had already been doing? She'd had several weeks of wondering but had long since settled into the approach of 'wait and see'. She meant to take each day with Connor as a gift. Why would he not do the same?

"I guess I was just thinking that we would take it as it came, appreciate each day like it might be our last," she finally said.

"As it just might be."

"But would you rather wake up each morning dreading that it might be the last or be thankful each morning that we have another day together?" she argued, rising to stand in front of him. She embraced him around his waist, laying her head on his chest and held on tightly until he finally raised his arms to return her embrace. "I will take what I can get. If it's one day or a year…I just want to enjoy it with you. We have lost so much time already." She rubbed away the creases in his forehead. "Don't look so worried, Connor." "I don't think our time is up yet. Just enjoy it with me, please."

He hugged her to him and pressed a kiss on her brow. "I love ye, Emmy. 'Tis no' a feeling content for a day or a year."

A sizzle of apprehension shot through Emmy at his words. They were possessive and absolute. He would never let her go, she thought, simultaneously awed and frightened. She was still trying to comprehend that enormity of feeling this love incited within herself. Imagining that it might be magnified by mutual love was almost overwhelming. Emmy wasn't entirely sure that she knew how to cope with it all.

For a moment she wondered if it might be better for them both if it all just ended now.

Where was he? Emmy paced the room as she waited for Connor to put in an appearance at dinner that night. After his avowal of love, she'd turned away, excusing herself to start preparing for dinner, eager for a chance to escape the intensity of that moment. She'd taken her time bathing and grooming, hearing him doing the same in his room, wondering if she'd bitten off more than she could chew.

In her mind, romantic love had always been an abstract thing. She had no memories of her parents living together and had no idea of what a healthy relationship looked like. She'd had no serious relationships of her own and most of her friends were still single. Love had always been the stuff of movies and romance novels; an idealistic dream filled with a white wedding and happily ever after.

This was not what she had imagined at all.

She'd never thought there would be uncertainty, fear and anxiety involved. Commitment was one thing. Emmy could picture herself doing commitment. When she considered marriage, she always thought/hoped when she got around to it, would be her first and last. She'd always planned on doing it right the first time, forsaking the easy out of divorce. To her a pre-nup was an expectation of certain failure. But this! It wasn't simply a commitment to Connor in the balance here. It was a commitment to this time. An absolute acceptance that she would stay *here*, for the rest of her days.

Emmy looked around the drawing room at the ladies in their magnificent dinner gowns and the men in their formal attire. Crystal glasses clinked together above the polite murmur of conversation as the staff wove through the groups serving drinks unobtrusively.

This wasn't the way she was raised. Oh sure, it was nice to never think about working all day or figuring out what to have for supper. No laundry, no cleaning. No anything. There was giddy indulgence mixed with guilt every time Margo waited on her. It extended to every servant in the castle. Still, Emmy didn't think she'd been born to be served in such a manner.

And the idleness. Thank God she had a useful skill to keep most of her days occupied. The past week had shown her that the women in the castle did little more than needlework and gossip. Dory, at least, interacted with running the castle. In fact, it took much of her time, but the others lived lives of indulgent laxity. Emmy knew she couldn't live that way forever; she had more ambition than a life permanently on vacation.

Loving Connor was one thing, but she just wasn't certain she wanted to stay here.

"Where is Connor tonight?" Ian asked as he approached with Dory.

They were late as well. Dory admitted to being worn out

by all the activity of the babies. Another examination had shown amazing growth over the past week. The weight and movement were wearing on Dory physically. Emmy debated whether to tell her that twins usually came early, but didn't have the heart to while the woman looked so worn down.

She also worried whether her skills would be enough to save Dory's life if the whole second chance idea were the real reason she was here.

She turned her gaze from Dory to Ian only to find his eyes alight with humor. Given his expression and the similar ones so many other faces, Emmy could only assume the castle gossip had revealed to everyone just where and how she and Connor spent the last twenty-four hours. She willed away the heat of a blush and stared him down until he simply quirked his lips at her and winked.

"I'm sure he'll be here shortly. He was getting dressed when I came down." Emmy looked at the door again and sighed. "I hope."

"Did you have another fight?" Dory whispered worriedly, reaching out a comforting hand.

"Not so much a fight," she said in denial, but accepted the physical display of concern with a tight smile. "Just some adjustments now that he has recognized that I am not Heather." She whispered this last as she studied Dory. "I would have thought you might've some issues with me sharing a bedroom with Connor now that it's all out in the open, at least between us four."

Dory rolled her eyes slightly. "As long as everyone here believes you're man and wife, I'll not say anything. Besides, who am I to judge your relationship with Connor?" She added this vaguely and Emmy shared a questioning glance with Ian, who only shrugged. "However, I will continue to pester you on your deportment and posture whenever necessary." Dory added the quip with a tired smile, pressing a hand to the small of her back.

"I wouldn't expect anything less." Emmy rubbed her friend's arm sympathetically. "Maybe you should get some more rest. You look whooped."

"Whatever that is, it sounds appropriate," Dory confessed. "I do feel ill tonight."

"Hang in there, sweetie." She noticed Ian's mouth was tight with worry and stress. Fatigue and pain was starting to wear on both of them. "Why don't you take her back up and just relax tonight? I'll have Susan bring you up a tray."

He nodded and thanked her. Emmy gave Dory a comforting embrace before sending them on their way. As they made their way to the door, they stopped to have words with Connor as he came in. The laird nodded and even leaned in to give his sister-in-law a light kiss on her cheek, an act that left most everyone watching in shock. The more congenial rapport between the two had become obvious and most of the family was awed by the changes that had come over him in the past several weeks.

He wended his way through the crowd talking briefly with a few of his relatives before making his way to her side. He kissed her hand and greeted her formally before commenting, "Dory is no' looking well this evening."

"It has been a long couple weeks for her," Emmy answered, wondering at his aloof formality. "Truthfully, I don't think she has long to go. I might have to put her on bed rest just to get a little more time out of her."

"I'm sure whatever ye say will be for the best," he agreed. "I've sent men to find auld Donell but hae no' had any success as yet."

"What's wrong, Connor?" she whispered, keeping a light smile on her face for the benefit of those ever curious who were watching.

"Nothing."

They were beyond such polite veneers. Perhaps he realized it as well because with a sigh, his frame visibly relaxed.

"Better?"

"A little? What's bugging you?"

"I'm simply displeased wi' the conclusion of our conversation earlier." His honesty surprised her. "It seems that our perceptions of our relationship are nae one and the same."

"It's not that I don't love you, Connor, I do," Emmy rushed to reassure him.

Connor met her gaze intently then sighed. "Aye, I ken ye do, lass." He took her hand and gave it a gentle squeeze. "What is it then that holds ye back?"

"Fear, I suppose," she admitted hesitantly then released a deep breath, letting her shoulders drop. She sent him a pleading look, begging for his understanding. "Try to look at it from my point of view, okay? You love me and your life changes little. You still have your home, your family and your job. But if I embrace this—our love for all time, a future together—my life changes completely. I lose a whole world. And what if it doesn't work out? I feel like I have a lot more to lose."

"I feel as if we hae everything to gain, my wee pessimist." He held up a hand before she could respond. "However, I will concede the point for now. Given what I hae seen, I understand that ye feel there are sacrifices. I can only hope in time they will be outweighed by the advantages."

"Connor . . ." She started shaking her head.

"Come, let us to dinner." He held out his arm and smiled lightly as she took it. "We shall start with yer one day at a time and see where it goes from there, shall we?"

Mutely, she nodded, letting him lead her to the dining room yet inside her heart was aquiver. My God, he had such faith in her, she realized. It was as if he just knew that it would come to her eventually. It was terrifying yet at the same time, she didn't want to let him down. Only her mother had ever shown such faith in her. It was wonderful and heartbreaking.

"Tell me more about the future," he prompted in a low voice as they were served their first course.

Thank God the diversion of normal...well, almost normal, dinner conversation. "What do you want to know?" She cast him an encouraging glance as she dug into her sautéed halibut.

"I recall when I mentioned the automobile to ye previously; ye seemed unimpressed and suggested that ye've seen one before. Aye?"

She nodded. "Cars, we call them."

He continued in a horrified tone. "Have ye driven one?"

A sharp *ha* of sardonic amusement escaped her before she could stop it and she covered her mouth before she choked on the bite of fish she had just taken. "Is this one of those things that you don't think women should do? Like voting?"

He had the good grace to look a bit embarrassed as he pushed his own food from side to side. "I will admit that when the thought occurred to me, my mind responded in immediate denial."

"Well, it is a negative stereotype that will last many years, so rest assured that you are not alone in that." Emmy's lips quirked in humor as she patted his arm. "I wish I could take you there. I wish you could know my world." She looked around to make sure her words were going unnoticed. "I wish I could take you for a ride in my car."

"Ye *own* one!?"

He was incredulous at the idea. A camera and an automobile? Truly her world must be rich to allow for such a thing. And her iPhone as well!

"I have a MINI Cooper," she told him before leaning back to allow the footman to change the courses. Beef medallions in red wine next. "It's pretty small. I could try to draw you a picture later if you like. Cars are nothing like the ones you have seen anymore. They come in all shapes and sizes."

"The one I saw in London could travel nearly sixty miles in an hour, I believe," he commented, showing greater appreciation of this course than the last. "How fast can yers travel?"

"The car itself can get to about a hundred and twenty," she told him, "but limits have been set by law regulating speeds depending on where you are, like an open highway versus a residential area."

Connor gulped at the thought of reaching such speeds and took a deep pull on his wine. "How fast hae ye traveled?" he asked, dread evident in his voice.

"The fastest? Maybe a hundred on the open road," she admitted but continued, "but I am not too much of a speed freak. Still there is car racing for sport as you've seen and their cars can go into the two hundreds somewhere. I'm not exactly sure."

"I cannae imagine traveling at such speeds."

"Oh, that's nothing!" she waved it away, loving that she could shock and awe him. His mixture of dread and enjoyment was like offering a fairy-tale to a small child and she so enjoyed entertaining him. She might spend a decade just telling him about such things, taking pleasure in each moment. "There are high-speed trains and planes that can go from here to New York in hours. Some can go faster than sound." A smile curved her lips as he gaped in disbelief.

"What is a plane that it can go so fast?"

"Airplanes?" She frowned, trying to place their invention in history. "Flying machines, you know?"

"Nay!" he boomed and everyone at the table turned to stare. He lowered his voice again and leaned his head close to hers. "Unbelievable."

"I think I might be hearing that word often in the next few days," she teased. "But, yes, it is true."

Emmy ate her third course quietly while Connor digested the idea. She could see the wheels of his mind spinning. "What of travel to the moon?" he added. "Ye mentioned that previously. Has man flown to the moon yet?"

Emmy nodded, pleased to see the boyishly eager look come back to his eyes. "I remember my mom saying that she had watched it on TV as a girl. It was a big moment, everyone was thrilled by it. Mom said her father cried. Neil Armstrong, the astronaut who was the first one to step on the moon said, *That's one small step for man and one giant leap for mankind.*"

She said this in a low disjointed voice that brought a reluctant smile to his face. "Hae ye gone to the moon?"

With a giggle, she sat back briefly, twirling her wineglass and staring at him in amusement before leaning back toward him. "No, though I have given you an impression of absolute progress in the future, it still hasn't gotten to the point where more than a handful of trained astronauts have been to the moon."

XXXXX

Connor felt a sigh of relief building from deep within. He was thankful that progress hadn't gone too far for it occurred to him suddenly that she'd been right earlier…with all she could have in her own time there was little appeal his could hold for her. He now understood her reluctance to stay here. The future provided a good life for her; what more could she ask for? How much could she sacrifice? Perhaps love was not enough.

They excused themselves from the rest of his family after they had eaten and returned to their rooms where Emmy drew him pictures of cars and the space shuttle, she called it. She also told him about a proposed elevator to outer space that was mentioned in *Popular Science* magazine, a periodical he was thankfully familiar with. Since she had mentioned it twice already, she also explained the TV to him. Connor thought its function must relate much to a movie in one's home but she explained that it also told shorter stories and relayed current events much like a newspaper.

She talked to him of computers that held information beyond the iPhone, and were connected to a global network of other computers, allowing her to get information from any place on earth. The power the future allowed one to hold within their hand held him in awe. Such things advanced at an amazing rate, she told him, comparing the tiny phone as having more computing power than the roomful of computers it had taken to send the first rockets to the moon.

When they retired to bed that night, together in Connor's large bed, he could only hold her body next to his, caressing her bare hip or shoulder occasionally as she snuggled next to him. Connor could not bring himself to try to make love to her. He was overwhelmed by what he had learned from her that night.

Suddenly she was no longer simply earthy but rather otherworldly. As he had thought before, she was beyond his time. Emmy knew more, had experienced more than he could ever hope to. She had seen things that daunted him, thought commonplace that which intimidated and overwhelmed him.

Connor could not compare with that, could not fight against it and felt insignificant against the scope of her experience. Perhaps even lovemaking had become more advanced in her time and his ways were old-fashioned and outdated.

It was a belittling thought.

Again he heard her words. She had so much more to lose than he if she stayed here.

He now knew it was the truth.

What would she choose? And could he fault her if…when she chose her own time? He thought about the conversation they'd had the previous week after Emmy had discovered Dory's twins. Where she came from, they knew. Here there was nothing but hope.

He might hope that she chose him.

He might not blame her if she did not.

A heaving sigh escaped him and Emmy turned in the bed to look at him with a frown. "All right, spill it."

"What?"

"I've been laying here listening to you sigh for the past ten minutes. Plus you've hardly laid a finger on me. Something's eating at you."

Connor smoothed her hair back from her face and

looked down into her eyes, trying to imagine the moment she realized that she didn't belong here with him. A day or year, how could the time come when she came to regret her time here with him? It tore at his heart knowing that it would happen eventually.

"Let me just say that yer reluctance to show faith that ye belong in my time is understandable."

"Meaning?"

"The advantages of yer time clearly overshadow those to be found here." He shrugged, trying to appear nonchalant while his heart pounded painfully. His brogue thickened with the emotion choking him. "I cannae see how there'd be any competition. Ye would...will return if ye hae the opportunity simply because yer world is a better place. I can see that now."

"The twenty-first century isn't all sunshine and roses, Connor," Emmy told him softly. "There are real problems in my time, economic, environmental; the world suffers from war, prejudice, poverty, you name it. So many people are jaded and violent. Our priorities are way out of whack, I mean, we put a man on the moon before we figured out putting wheels on our luggage. Sometimes it is just a dreadful place to be." She wrapped her arms around his neck and pressed herself against the warmth of his chest. "Please, please, please," she begged, "do not underestimate your appeal, Connor. You offer me something that my own time never has. I am twenty-eight years old and you are the first person apart from my mother that I have ever said 'I love you' to, and the first person I have heard it from since she died."

"I do love ye," he whispered in her ear and ran his hands up her bare back.

"And I love you, Connor," she returned, arching against him and running her hands over his tight buttocks. "That alone is enough to hold me. I will put my faith in that. Don't give up on me."

"I dinnae want to gi' up on us. I'd thought I might be too provincial for ye," Connor confessed, nipping at her neck. "I dinnae ken so much as ye."

"You know about things I could never dream of," she sighed. "You can really be such an idiot sometimes, you know?"

"Ye've informed me of as much," he chuckled in a low voice and ran his tongue behind her ear, earning a little shiver from her. "I maun confess I fear lovemaking has advanced as well to a point where I might seem gauche and old-fashioned."

Emmy shivered but managed a breathy laugh. "Oh, Connor, believe me, you have nothing to worry about. I'm afraid in my time you would be so mobbed by women you would never choose me from the crowd, especially if your particular skills were known."

He laughed in turn, his relief evident. "Is that so? Be assured, my love, I would always find ye."

"I'm glad." She ran her hand down his muscled arm. "Then why don't you stop lying here wondering and worrying and apply some of those special skills?"

"As ye wish, my love."

"Tell me why I have to learn this again?"

Connor tugged his oldest and most placid mare along behind him, stifling a hoot of laughter at the look on Emmy's face. Perhaps there were some things that she was not so advanced in after all. The realization felt surprisingly good.

"Daisy is verra gentle, my love. If ye plan to continue as the local midwife," he teased, winking at her when she scowled predictably, "then horseback is a more efficient means of travel. Indeed it is the best way to get to some of the more remote areas of the island."

Emmy wrinkled her nose as the horse plodded in her direction. "You know, Connor, I just think I wasn't cut out for transportation á la animal. I'm definitely more of a bus or train kind of girl."

"Aye, but those things are no' available to ye, so we maun make do wi' what we hae." He chuckled once again as she eyed old Daisy.

"Connor," she dithered, backing away. "It's so big…and

tall…and it stinks. Can't you just buy a car?"

"Pouting willnae serve," Connor responded with mock severity. She eyed with horse with such trepidation, he would've thought Daisy was giving her the evil eye. As if the old mare had the energy to spare the effort.

"I'm a city girl, Connor!"

"Nae excuses." He bit back another chuckle. "Come now, up ye go."

"I think I'm going to be sick." Emmy gulped as she approached the horse.

"At least I dinnae give ye a side-saddle." Connor's humor was running high now in the face of her edginess. His bold, fearless Emmy brought down by the oldest horse in the stables.

"Well, thank God for small favors."

XOXOXOX

Gathering all her nerve, she shoved a booted foot into the stirrup, grabbed the pommel and heaved herself upward while Connor assisted by pushing up on her bottom. She squealed as his hands cupped and squeezed, and she dropped back to the ground glaring at him.

"Behavior like that will not get me up there, you know."

"My apologies," he said humbly, though his eyes spoke another story, twinkling with merriment. "Yer…jeans, aye? They hug yer bottom so that the temptation is too strong to ignore."

"Well, my jeans are covered by a long coat, so you have no excuses," she chided and faced the animal once more, reaching up for the pommel. Connor crowded her from behind and slid his arms around her waist, nuzzling the side of her neck.

"My excuse," he whispered huskily in her ear, "is that I cannae go a moment of my day wi'out remembering ye naked above me wi' yer hair tangled about yer body as ye scream wi' pleasure."

Emmy closed her eyes and shuddered. "You are pure evil, Connor MacLean. How do you expect me to sit up on that horse when I've got that picture in my mind now?"

"'Twas the picture that occupied my mind through my entire morning," he confessed, stepping back.

That morning they'd separated to 'go to work'. Connor tended to estate business and ridden out to his home farm while Emmy examined Dory once more, putting her on bed rest, and then visited aunt Eleanor's maid who had delivered a daughter the previous week. She reasoned that they could not spend their entire lives in bed no matter how pleasing it sounded. Otherwise, she insisted, they might be dead from exhaustion in a week.

Still, it pleased Emmy to know she occupied his mind while he was away from her since she had felt the same way all morning, counting the minutes until she saw him again. When he had returned, she had nearly leaped into his arms in relief and dragged him back to their rooms. They had spent a decidedly satisfying hour together before Connor had insisted on this whole charade.

Horses, *ugh!* Give her a nice convertible any day. She yearned for her Mini with the top down and heater cranked up. Didn't he realize it was too cold for this?

Another boost put her into the saddle and she stared down at him... and the ground, as he showed her how to hook her feet into the stirrups. It was an English saddle, she realized with a mental palm to the forehead. Where did she think she was? Texas? Of course that's what they used here, but she'd never sat on a horse like this before. It felt strange, though not as uncomfortable a seat as she remembered the western saddle with her knees drawn up rather than hanging down the horse's sides. Connor gave her a brief tutorial on the reins and general instructions regarding how to stop and go.

"But what do I do if she tries to run away?"

"She willnae. Dinnae fret."

"But…"

"Daisy will do naught beyond what is absolutely necessary, I assure ye." He grinned that magnificent smile at her and she couldn't help but relax a bit. It just made her feel all mushy inside when he did that.

"I'm pitiful, I know."

"Ye are," he agreed, "but it has its own charm." He shot her an affectionate smile that melted her insides.

"Are you sure you want to put up with me?"

"Verra sure." They shared brilliant grins.

Off they went then at a walk. Connor gave her instructions on how to use her legs to soften the stride as they moved into a trot. He had been right; Daisy did nothing beyond mimicking his big horse, Bruce, named for Robert the Bruce, he informed her. Emmy just bounced along beside him having only to hold on, since steering seemed unnecessary for the moment. They moved into a canter that she liked much more since the stride was smoother. Away to the west they rode toward the mountains in the distance and eventually dropped back into a walk.

At his questioning look, she shrugged, 'Okay, it's not so bad. I feel like I'm getting a nice workout anyway, but I'm still not going to put it on my list of favorite things to do."

"What are yer favorite things to do?" he asked,

wondering how they hadn't discussed that yet, but amended quickly, "Besides delivering babies."

"Well, I like music, of course."

They'd spent the previous night running down the remainder of her phone battery as she played her favorite songs for him. She'd been pleased that he finally seemed to appreciate many of them, but almost cried when the player eventually died, the low battery warning blinking redly at her until the screen finally went blank.

"I like to travel and see new places. I like to read and visit old buildings and museums. I like to go to the movies and go to new restaurants. I love to eat good food."

Connor remembered her telling him before about all her favorite restaurants in Baltimore. She seemed to prefer seafood and he made a mental note to talk to the cook about serving her some locally caught seafood. The lobsters and clams were especially delicious.

"That's about it," she went on. "I'm not much of a party girl since college; work sees to that mostly. I love a quiet night in front of the fireplace with a good book and a glass of wine."

※※※※※

He could give her that, Connor realized. Other than the movies, her favorite things were all easily provided in his time. They could travel together, he thought, to take in the opera and theater in London, Paris and even her New York. They could dine on the finest cuisine available and visit museums. They could spend their evenings wrapped in each other's arms before a roaring fire, perhaps reading to each other.

"I can gi' ye all those things," he said softly. "

Reaching out, she caught his hand with a smile. "I already know you can give me all the things I love you, Connor. Haven't I already told you that a hundred times?"

"Ye hae, my love."

"Then stop worrying, okay? I'm happy right where I am."

But to Connor's mind a nagging *for now* dangled at the end of her sentence. He still couldn't understand how she could be happy forever. Surely the absence of all she left behind would one day lead to her discontent. Truly, he was almost discontented just thinking about everything he was going to miss! "What do ye miss the most?"

"Why do you want to torture yourself, Connor?"

He was torturing himself, he admitted, by dwelling on these things. But perhaps if he knew, he might be able to fix some of them. "Humor me," he tossed her own words back at her.

Her lips quirked a bit. "Fine, then." She thought for a moment. "I miss my car." She laughed and he joined her.

"Continue."

"Efficient heating, I guess. The fireplace is nice but it doesn't get warm everywhere, though sleeping with you is better than the best heater. And I suppose in the summer, I'll miss air-conditioning. Or maybe not, here in Scotland." She gave him a smile but he waved her on. "Ice cream..."

"We can make ice cream."

"I'll hold you to that." She tilted her head back as the horse swayed her from side to side. "I will miss my music now the battery died."

"Perhaps we could find an electrical generator, as ye mentioned, so ye can...charge it up?" He raised a questioning brow and she nodded that the terminology was correct.

"Yeah, maybe."

"Is there anything else?" he questioned, but then pounced on the obvious answer before she could provide it. "Movies, of course. I would miss movies if I were ye."

"Of course, movies."

※○※○※

What else?

Emmy thought of her little house and life in Baltimore. What else would she miss? Surely it didn't all boil down to temperature control, ice cream and music? She'd miss all kinds of things, her friends, work, restaurants and the theater. There were tons of things she would miss. Surely there were.

"I don't know, Connor. Stop stressing about it, okay?"

Still, he shook his head and smiled ruefully at her. "I will attempt to rid myself of worry," he assured her and changed the subject. "Tell me something about our future...I mean, our as in the Scots, of course."

"Of course." She wrinkled her brow as she thought and finally confessed, "I wish I knew more to tell you, but, as I mentioned, I was always more interested in the architecture rather than history as a whole. Let me think." She pondered the required college history courses she had taken and what she had seen on the History Channel. "Queen Victoria dies a few years from now, not long after her sixtieth anniversary on the throne. Have you met her?"

"Aye, I hae, she's a woman of incredible character." Connor frowned as he considered her revelation. "It saddens me that she'll soon depart this earth but 'tis no' surprising. She's led a long, fulfilling life and out-lived children of her own. What else?"

"Let me see, there will be the Spanish-American war

soon, but that will be in Cuba." Emmy racked her brain but shook her head. "The Titanic will sink, that was a pretty big deal, but no, not anytime soon. I don't know. I can't think of anything else big for about twenty-odd years."

"What happens then?"

"War," she said softly, realizing for the first time that this was not a done deal to Connor; this was his future.

It would affect him much more than it did a student in a classroom a hundred years from now. It would impact his life and possibly his cousins or future nephews would fight in that war and lose their lives to it. She swallowed as a wave of sorrow overtook her for the pain he might experience in the years to come.

"They'll call it the Great War over here I think," she went on when she realized he was waiting for her to continue. "World War I we call it in the history books. Britain, France and Russia will fight together against Germany. The US joined in 1917, I think. I can't remember why exactly. Sorry. It'll be pretty bad though. The Russian revolution is in there somewhere, too. The Tsar's entire family will be killed by revolutionaries and that monarchy will fall."

"What of our monarchy?" he asked urgently.

"Oh, you're fine," she assured him quickly. Of course he'd worry that the foundation of his nation might change dramatically in the years to come. As a peer of the realm, he took his government seriously.

"Don't worry. The English monarchy is one of the most famous in my time. "

"Ye mean the British monarchy," Connor corrected.

She frowned. "No, English." But Connor shook his head. "Are you sure? In America, Elizabeth is the Queen of England. Not the Queen of Britain."

His brow just rose haughtily.

She rolled her eyes. "Fine! The *British* monarchy is ridiculously popular. They are treated like celebrities."

Connor's brow rose even further.

"Well, they are very famous, everyone wants to see them, take a picture, you know."

"It is much the same now," he said. "Crowds line the streets each time the Queen or one of her family venture out in public." He paused for a moment then asked, "Ye say the war will be called World War I? Are there more that will follow?"

"Yes, unfortunately, in the 1940's there will be another along the same lines. Initially I think the main players were the UK, France and Poland against Germany, Italy and Russia. Then in 1941, Japan attacked the US, and so we entered the war. Also I think Russia changed sides after Germany attacked them. I was never very good with history."

"Attacking yer own allies?"

"It will be a big one, but there are many other wars big and small. Too many others. I told you the future is a violent place, Connor." She scrunched her nose. "Even when I left we were fighting."

"It seems the future isnae all sunshine and roses," he said to lighten her mood. "Tell me something that will happen besides death and war. Something good."

Emmy thought for a long time as they rode through the sunny afternoon. Surprisingly, history classes seemed to only teach the bad stuff, she thought. She could remember her high school history tests well enough to remember they were usually filled with the dates of wars and assassinations, of disasters, both natural and man-made, of economic downturns. Why didn't they ever teach anything good? Was history really just about the bad? *Huh*, she thought, what a realization to have a hundred and fifteen years in the past. It said a lot for their society.

"Something good, something good," she murmured, thinking. "Wow, I'm stumped," she admitted and gave him a rueful smile. "Sorry, I'm not much help at all."

"*Och* lass, dinnae allow me to be optimistic about my future," he chided, "if you cannae think of one good thing that we ha' to look forward to."

"Oh, good things happen all the time," she insisted. "They just always get outweighed by misfortune. The history of the entire world has been recorded that way. You know it's true."

"It is," he confessed. "Even at Cambridge history was taught through negative connotations."

"Inventions though," she realized aloud, recalling med school classes. "Most of the good stuff I can think of is more along the lines of all the cool things that will be invented in the next century. There will be a lot of medical advances coming up and some very soon. There will be vaccines against polio, diphtheria, measles, mumps and chicken pox. There will be major drops in infant mortality. I mean smallpox will actually be eradicated almost world-wide!" She gave him a wide smile, pleased she could recall something of a positive nature.

"Truly?"

"What is it?" He looked like he'd been kicked in the stomach.

"My mother and baby sister died from the pox when I was a young lad." Faced with her open empathy, he forced a smile. "Nay, nay, I'm quite all right, my love. It lifts my heart that someday a child willnae hae to fear watching his mother or sister die before their eyes."

"Oh, Connor, I'm so sorry." She reached out for his hand.

"I ken ye understand," he returned. "Hae they no' found a cure for the cancers, as well?"

"Oh, they try." Emmy shrugged philosophically. "That one is proving a little more elusive. Someday maybe. Who knows?"

"Indeed, who knows what the future will bring." He grinned. "Yer future, of course. We now already ken what my future will bring."

"Well, not your personal history. The guidebook was a little vague on which generations their information applied to. It didn't mention you specifically beyond the reference to the next laird."

They'd pored over her guidebook together, looking for anything to indicate how his family's personal history went forward, but only generalities had been mentioned.

"Well, even yer London guidebook dinnae delve deeply into the history of the monarchy. After all, it said nothing about the Queen's death or what became of her children."

"Edward," she announced brightly, nearly startling Connor from his saddle. She stared at him, snapping her fingers over and over trying to latch on to the memory forming in her mind.

"Who?"

"Edward the VIII." She snapped her fingers again, trying to pin it down. "Oh, I saw it on Biography. He was King of England…Britain… *oh, whatever*, he was the king after Victoria or the one after that. I can't remember Edward VIII abdicated the throne so he could marry Wallis Simpson. She was an American divorcée."

Connor was taken aback and it showed on his face. "My God, ye cannae be serious. That's the most appalling thing I've e'er heard. Forsaking one's birthright and heritage for a woman?"

"Are you kidding me?" Emmy asked, unable to grasp the reason for his displeasure. "It was a big deal."

"Of course, it was a bluidy 'big deal'," he agreed with a curled lip. "No one has e'er done such a thing."

"But he loved her, Connor." She frowned, not understanding his contempt. "He gave up being a king so he could marry the woman he loved. Why is that wrong?"

"Obviously she wisnae a suitable wife for a king or they would hae been allowed to wed wi'out such a drastic repercussions," he deduced. "The responsibility of a king goes beyond personal wishes. This Edward had a duty to his nation and he abandoned it for a bonny face."

"I don't think she was really that bonny." She glowered at him but shook her head, puzzled. "And there was something about the Nazis in there, too. But, I don't get it, Connor."

"Kings find love in mistresses, lass, if they cannae find it in marriage."

Emmy blinked. "Really? So adultery beats out abdication then? Because she wasn't good enough for him?" She stuck a finger out at him, nearly stuttering in her agitation. "I'll have you know the son of the current Prince of Wales is dating a commoner he met at University and his brother is dating an international nobody and...and...the Prince of Wales married his former mistress because he loved her. And almost the entire world, outside the UK is totally good with that." she yelled at him.

"What're ye so angry aboot?"

"Because, sometimes loving a *nobody* is okay, Connor," she yelled, old Daisy shifting in circles as if feeling her rider's tension. "Next thing you're going to spout is that I'm not good enough for an Earl. I'm an American nobody, you know? My father was a mechanic. He worked on cars. My grandpa was nothing more than a soldier most of his life; he spent forty years in the army. My mom was a teacher. That's it. We couldn't even claim we had money. I'm no more special than the average American. Is that good enough for you or will you find a nice wife one day, your little Miss Guthrie maybe, and keep me as a mistress because that's what you guys do? I'm better than that."

Connor burst out laughing and Emmy nearly screeched in rage to have her tirade thrown back at her with such amusement. Daisy danced in circles while she sawed at the reins trying to get the old horse to turn back to the castle. Emmy had had just about all the fun she could take for one day. Irritating man. Laughing at her!

"Lass." Connor caught the horse's bridle and pulled the horse closer to him, laughing as she fought again him. "Stop before ye fall."

Catching her about the waist, he lifted her from her horse and settled her across his lap. His eyes still alight with laughter, he looked down into her scowling face and lowered his head catching her mouth in a hot kiss. Her lips stiffened and she tried to turn her head away from him.

"Oh, no you don't." she huffed. "I'm mad at you."

"*Och*, my love." He chuckled again, softly brushing his fingers against her cheek and resting his forehead against hers. "Ye make me so happy."

"You piss me off and it makes you happy?" Astonishment stilled her. "*Ugh*, you are the most infuriating man I have ever known."

"And ye're the most entrancing woman I've e'er known," he declared in a husky, sexy brogue, turning his head to nuzzle her ear. "Yer jealousy soothes my fears tremendously. Whilst I worry that I've nothing to offer ye, ye in turn fear that ye've naught to offer me."

"I wasn't afraid, I was angry," she corrected but did not push him away.

"Yer anger was born of insecurity from my thoughtless words," he murmured into her neck. "*Och*, my love. My darling lassie, nae other woman could e'er compare to ye. And I would fear for my own safety if I e'er tried to consign ye to the role of mistress."

Emmy tilted her head to allow him greater access to her neck where he continued to suck and nibble his way down. She sighed and shifted to clasp him tightly to her. "You're never going to let me stay mad at you again, are you?"

"I'm discovering that yer anger rouses an undeniable passion in me," Connor said in her ear. "When yer cheeks flush and yer eyes heat, I want nothing more than to direct that fire in a more productive direction."

"Well, the right direction would be back toward the castle then because it is too cold to do that out here."

They turned back and Emmy snuggled against his chest, allowing her hands to drift downward. She was rewarded with a hearty moan before Connor kicked Bruce to greater speeds.

"So, I am good enough for an Earl then?"

"Aye, my love, ye are, but that King Edward…he was entirely wrong."

"No, no. You can't do that." Emmy laughed and put a hand down on the table to stop Connor's next move. "This is Texas Hold 'Em, not Five Card Draw. You have to wait for the next two cards to be laid down before you turn your hole cards."

"Are you certain?" Ian cut in. "I dinnae believe that this is a real version of poker at all, lass. Did ye just make up the rules?"

"I will say that I never experienced such a turn of the rules at any of the card salons I've attended in Edinburgh," Dory added. "It's most unusual. But intriguing."

Emmy laughed as her three companions studied their cards once again. While poker or forms of it had been played for hundreds of years in Germany and France, once the game migrated to the U. S., it had taken on a life of its own. The MacLean men were familiar with five card draw but had never seen Texas Hold 'Em which made sense since she was fairly certain it was a recent thing even in her time. While

Emmy explained the World Poker Tour to Connor, Ian and Dory simply assumed it was just an American version of the game.

It had been four days since Emmy had been compelled to put Dory on bed rest, or at least restricting her movements to and from a chair in her room as much as possible. After days of boredom with only an occasional visitor to break the monotony of her confinement, Dory was already chomping at the bit. Emmy insisted that Ian and Connor join them in a card game to pass the afternoon away. Teaching the new game had been interesting but all were familiar with games of chance so it hadn't taken too long to get the rules established.

"The placing of bets between each round becomes rather tedious over time," Connor said, glowering at his cards. "I fail to see the necessity."

"It just gives more of a chance to bet on the possibilities of your hand," Emmy insisted. She rolled her eyes at Dory who stifled a laugh in return. "You just don't like being out bluffed by a woman, I think. I mean, who would have ever thought that Dory would have such a good poker face?"

"Well, it certainly is no' yer forte," Connor said, catching her hand and raising it to his lips. "One can always tell when ye hae a good hand."

"It's why I never go to Vegas," she told him, squeezing his hand.

"What is Vegas?" Ian asked absently as he studied the river card Emmy dealt.

"Oh, it's a big gambling Mecca in the western part of America," Emmy answered vaguely. "They're really big on that type of thing out there. They do have the Cirque du Soleil running constantly there, though. I'd like to see that."

"Circus of the Sun?" Connor asked. "Ye've no' talked

aboot that before."

"I haven't talked about several things yet."

"Father took us to see the circus in Edinburgh each year when we were young," Ian told her. "Do ye remember, Connor?"

"Somehow I doubt this circus Em is referring to is anything like that," Connor slanted her a look. "Am I right?"

"You are," she nodded as play continued. "The Cirque is a show of amazing acrobatic talent unlike anything you can imagine. I've heard so much about it but I have never seen it in person."

"Sounds interesting," Dory offered. "Perhaps if they tour our side of the pond, we could all see it together."

I might just be here long enough to see that happen, Emmy thought.

They had still been unable to find any sign of that wacky old wizard who had delivered her to Duart. Emmy was fairly certain Donell deliberately avoided her. Despite his continued absence, the past couple days brought a new contentment to Duart, at least in Emmy's mind. She and Connor spent their days learning more about each other and about the work they did, and their evenings making tender love or simply talking in the dark.

Ian and Dory seemed too to have found a new satisfaction. Impending parenthood had settled them in spite of Dory's discomfort. Connor told him he had never seen the pair so publicly affectionate with each other in their entire marriage.

"Ye're certainly well traveled, Em," Ian commented.

"Just the U. S., I haven't been around the world or anything."

"Oh drat. I fold," Dory murmured and tried to get up on

her own, only to receive prompt assistance from Ian and Connor. "Please excuse me for a moment, I have to powder my nose," she murmured as she waddled to the adjoining room.

"That's six times in the past hour she's had to 'powder her nose'," Connor muttered in a voice low enough not to be overheard by his sister-in-law. He took up his cards again and made his bet on the final round of the hand.

"Perfectly normal," Emmy added calmly, calling his bet while Ian joined in on the pot. "Let's see them."

The men laid down their cards and Ian raked in the winnings with a cheerful smile. "Seems like all I ever do is haul her to her feet and watch her walk in that direction. She hisnae eaten much yet today, though, Emmy. Perhaps ye should talk to her. The babies dinnae seem to be moving as much today and it has her worried."

"She didn't tell me that."

She frowned at Dory as she lumbered back into the room while Ian shuffled the deck and started to deal the cards. She examined the expectant mother daily now. The beginnings of effacement were evident, although there were no signs of dilation. It could happen any time now. She hadn't wanted to tell Dory or Ian that lest she frighten them. If the babies had stopped moving around, they might be settling in for labor.

"Ye in, love?" Ian called.

"Yes," Dory sighed and lowered herself back into her chair. She breathed out in relief as she got there and ran both hands down her engorged stomach. "I declare I have expanded inches in just the past week."

She was definitely about done cooking, Emmy thought, as she shared a quick glance with Connor before peeking down at her hole cards. Pair of twos. She frowned. Connor was the only one she'd shared her worries with regarding the delivery of Dory's twins. She'd given him an outline of the normal delivery procedures from her time and detailed all the equipment she was missing like an ultrasound and fetal monitor that could show her how the babies were developing. She was nervous about the delivery, though she managed to preserve her calm outwardly appearance.

"I'm in." Emmy tossed in a couple coins.

The flop was laid down giving her three of a kind. She studied the faces of the others briefly. "Check." The others fell in with that.

"Ha' ye thought aboot names at all?" Connor asked pleasantly as the game moved on.

Ian tossed down his cards in defeat and looked at his brother. "I was thinking of Jamie for a boy or Roslyn for a lassie." Connor held his gaze and finally offered a slight smile. The names of their parents.

"Those are both fine names," he approved. "But do ye no' want to name one after yer parents, Dory?"

She sniffed with disdain. "If I do it would be after my mother only."

"Didn't you get along with your dad, Dory?" Emmy asked absently as she calculated her raise.

"My father and I did not part on the best of terms," Dory confessed. "He served me a great wrong not long before he died and I never forgave him. Of course, he never begged me for it either."

"Ye ne'er told me that," Ian asked with surprise and concern in his voice following his wife's terse comments.

"I am sure I still have some mysteries about me," she replied pertly.

"Aye, ye do." He waggled his eyebrows, drawing a blush from her.

"Ian MacLean," she chided, slapping his arm. "Oh, drat!"

"Again?" Connor asked in astonishment, tossing down his cards. "But ye just sat down."

"Connor," Emmy shook her head. "Really?"

"Oh, no," Dory murmured. "Oh, dear."

"What is it, love?" Ian asked, still looking at his cards.

"Oh, no," she wailed.

Emmy leaned to the side and calmly took in the pool of liquid under Dory's chair. "*Humph*," she grunted. "That happened a little faster than I thought it might."

"Ye were waiting for this?" Ian cried out.

"Waiting…expecting." She waved a hand as she pushed back from the table. "Let's just say I'm not surprised."

"Well, I bluidy well am." Ian knelt by Dory's side. She clutched her stomach and groaned in pain and he nearly started to hyperventilate.

"Okay then." Emmy nodded calmly as both Connor and Ian stared at Dory in horror. "I guess this is going to move along pretty rapidly so if all you two are going to do is panic, then you can just leave."

"Nay," Ian protested. "I want to stay."

"Then get a grip, okay?" Emmy went to the corner and yanked on the bell pull. "No, just stay there for a minute while we get everything set up," she said, as Ian moved to lift Dory to her feet. "Believe me, as much as it appears to the contrary, the babies aren't just going to drop out in the next thirty seconds."

Susan arrived moments later and Emmy rattled off a series of instructions and sent her on her way. Making her way to Dory's side, she lifted her wrist and took her pulse.

"Try to relax, breathe deeply like we practiced this week."

She'd given Dory a crash course in Lamaze breathing a few days before, thinking that it might be helpful since there were no drugs to be had.

"In. Out," she droned as she drafted Connor to help her move the furnishings away from the window as two footmen arrived carrying the table Emmy had ordered to be constructed a week or so before.

It was a homemade version of a birthing table, complete with stirrups. She had given it a try with Eleanor's maid and it had done its job well. Someone had added some upholstery to it since then. It would be more comfortable if not more functional.

Susan and Margo arrived, carrying towels, scissors and buckets to fill with water and heat by the fire. Margo also brought Emmy's new medical bag.

"All right, boys, out you go while Dory gets changed."

"But, but," Ian stuttered.

"You can come back in when she's settled," she assured him and pushed all the men from the room, giving Connor a strained smile as he left. "Show time."

He smoothed back her hair and kissed her cheek. "Dinnae worry," he whispered with assurance. "Ye'll do fine, I know it."

"I hope you're right," she whispered back though she was trembling with apprehension inside. Putting on her most professional face, she turned to her patient with a confident smile. "You ready for this?"

Emmy handed Ian a glass of ice chips to feed to his wife before resuming her position at the end of the table. No need to check for anything new just yet. An examination five minutes before had shown her that nothing had changed. Dory had been in labor for many hours already, nothing outlandishly long, but painful nonetheless.

What I wouldn't give for an epidural, Emmy sighed as she watched her new friend suffer. She wasn't a fan of natural childbirth and had always been a supporter of painless childbirth. To her way of thinking, it never did a woman any good to suffer through her ordeal or for a baby to arrive in this world to the screams of its mother. A pain free labor allowed the mother to enjoy the aftermath so much more.

But there was nothing she could do for Dory. Ether or laudanum, the only drugs readily at hand, would only cloud the minds of Dory and the babies and were likely to slow the labor. Chloroform was effective. She remembered that Queen Victoria had given birth to two of her babies with the use of chloroform, but it could be fatal if handled improperly.

Emmy took up the vintage stethoscope and listened carefully again, hoping the babies weren't in any distress. She had seen labors last longer, much longer, but with Dory's water already broken and the fact that she was carrying twins, she was starting to worry.

An hour of having Dory walk the room had done little to speed things along.

"You know, Ian," she began nonchalantly. "You've been up here a long time. Nothing is going to happen soon. Why don't you go get something to eat?"

"I'm no' hungry," he replied, squeezing Dory's hand, who in turn looked up at Emmy with pleading eyes.

"Well, I am," she continued. "Maybe you could get something for me?"

"Call a maid," was his terse response.

Emmy raised her brows and mouthed 'okay' to herself. Going to the door, she opened it to find Connor in a chair he had pulled into the hallway. He was reading a paper and drinking a cup of whiskey.

"Connor?" She waggled a finger as he rose and came closer.

"Is everything all right? I've heard her crying out." On closer inspection, she noted his pallor. What a sport.

She grabbed him by the shirtfront and pulled him down to meet her face-to-face. "I need you to get your brother out of here."

"Why, is something wrong?" he said, a worried look appearing on his face.

"Yes. He is driving us crazy," she bit out. "I might just have to cosh him over the head if he doesn't stop fussing. I've never seen a father act like such a ninny before."

Connor released a breath and allowed himself a chuckle. ""Tis why men should ne'er be allowed in the birthing room."

"I always have the fathers present when possible, but he's just getting on my nerves and Dory's as well," she insisted. "Please help? Get him outside for a while or feed him. Something. Anything."

It took several minutes to get Ian to leave but Emmy was finally able to shut the door behind him with a sigh. She leaned back against it and shared a look with Dory across the room.

"Thank God." Dory panted against the pain. "I thought you'd never get him to leave."

Emmy, Susan and Margo all shared a laugh as Emmy went back over to her delivery area. She examined Dory again briefly and found no change in the dilation.

)(')(')(')(')(

"There's something wrong, isn't there?" Dory asked through gritted teeth an hour later when what seemed like Emmy's hundredth exam was followed with a frown.

"No, no," she soothed, "not wrong, it's just not going as fast as I would like. You've had no change in dilation at all and there is nothing here that I can use to make that happen quicker. Babies just like to be born quickly and sometimes a mother's body can't keep up with that."

"So what do we do?"

"We need to get them out."

"But they won't come out. Oh, God." Dory moaned as another contraction started. "It's punishment, that's what it is."

"Don't be ridiculous," Emmy scolded lightly, used to the

ravings of a woman in labor. "I'm sure you've never done a thing in your life to be punished for. It just takes time."

"Yes, I have," she wailed as the contraction peaked and started to fade away. "I don't deserve healthy babies."

Emmy watched the tears pour down Dory's face. She had been in hard labor for more than half the day and was worn out. She was obviously nearing delirium. At this rate, she'd never have the strength to push for hours if necessary when the time came. And oddly, where most women blamed a husband for getting them in such a condition by this point, Dory appeared determined to take the blame on herself. That wasn't going to help at all. The moment she felt defeated was the moment they lost the entire battle.

Making the decision, Emmy moved to the woman's side. "Dory, I'd like to perform a caesarean section. Do you know what that is?"

"You want to cut them out." Dory panted and moaned through a jerky nod. "It's all right; I don't deserve to live. Save my babies any way you can."

"Well, I don't plan on you dying," Emmy corrected calmly. "So stop thinking that way, will you please? I have never lost a mother during delivery and you won't be the first. I will deliver your babies and you will be around to see them when I'm done. Understood?"

Dory's eyes focused on her face and she frowned in confusion. "I've never heard of a woman surviving a birth that way."

"Well, we do it all this time where I come from so you'll just have to trust me. Can you do that?"

Her friend hesitated but nodded through her pain. "This is God's punishment for my sins," she rasped as another contraction convulsed her body. "I have sinned against Him and He is taking His revenge on me."

"Dory!" Emmy patted her cheeks and got her attention. "A little positive thinking wouldn't be amiss at this point. Stop thinking about yourself and focus on your babies, okay?"

She turned to Margo and Susan who hovered nearby to help her, their faces drawn with distress. "I'll be right back; I need to talk to Ian. Take this and these." She pulled a scalpel, a needle and some clamps from the medical bag. "Boil them while I'm gone and get some freshly washed bandages, too."

Emmy found Connor and Ian in the study. Ian was pacing frantically in front of the fireplace, his hair standing on end. Wary of approaching such a hysterical looking father with the news that she was about to cut his wife open, she caught Connor's eye and indicated that he should come outside.

"Are the bairns delivered?" he asked but frowned when she shook her head and told Connor what she planned to do. He nodded gravely. She'd spoken about the possibility before and he promised to keep Ian away. "This is it then? What ye think Donell was speaking of?"

"I was afraid it was going to happen this way."

"How is Dory?"

"She's a trouper but she's losing it, I think. Keeps trying to beat herself up about something she thinks she's done." Emmy embraced Connor and turned to go back to her patient.

XOXOXOX

"I wish I could give you something for the pain, Dory," Emmy said, her voice muffled by the cloth she had tied across her mouth. There was some chloroform available that the doctor had left behind at some point, she'd been told. But in all honesty, Emmy wasn't sure how to use it. It wasn't something they taught anymore and she didn't want to end up killing Dory with too much. There was just no time to wait for the doctor. Susan and Margo pulled their cloths over their faces as well though they did not understand why and Emmy had little time for explanations. "It's going to hurt."

"It already hurts," Dory moaned weakly.

"I know," Emmy patted her hand and looked about her, making sure she had everything she needed. She was nervous and sweating herself. She didn't want to have to do this but knew there was no choice. "Ready?"

"I need a priest," Dory gasped, bracing herself.

"You don't need a priest." Emmy nodded to Margo and Susan, who took Dory by the shoulders and legs to keep her still, and cut.

Mercifully, Dory fainted.

※※※※

Emmy looked down at the two infant boys, unable to stifle a smile. One was bright red all over from screaming while the other stared up at her with as much fascination as she gazed back at him. Two wonderful, healthy—and fully developed, if small—babies were a fair trade for any amount of pain suffered, she thought. She reached and caressed a downy cheek. Perfect, each one, with heads of thick dark hair. Emmy was certain that Dory had been a bit off in her calculations. These boys were no premmies.

If Donell's hints about second chances were the true reasons for her time travel and her interpretation was right, her work here was done. There was little doubt in her mind that Dory would have died without the surgery, her sons with her. If she had been brought here to save them, then she was finished and could return home.

Since nothing had happened yet, Emmy was left wondering. Damn. Where had Donell disappeared to?

Ian came into the room and rushed to his sons with a joyful shout. He stroked their cheeks and hands but looked terrified when Emmy suggested he pick one up, although the two nursemaids Dory hired encouraged him to do so. Instead he just looked down at them with awe and wonder.

Turning, Emmy went back to her main patient and checked Dory's pulse as she slept the sleep of the exhausted. She'd roused herself not long after her faint and had gone on and on as though she were in a confessional, begging forgiveness for her sins and such. It had gotten to the point that Emmy could barely make out her words, so incomprehensible were they. She'd concentrated on delivering the babies, handing them off in turn to Susan and Margo to bathe and wrap. As she had been stitching the incisions though, she thought Dory had said something in her semi-conscious delirium that stopped Emmy in her tracks.

Now she stared down at Dory in confusion as she had in that moment before she recalled herself and continued her work. Could she have possibly meant what she said or had she been hallucinating? Emmy studied Dory's face, its similarities to her own and wondered if she had heard correctly and, if she had, what it meant to everyone in this house.

"Will she be all right?" Connor whispered, coming to stand by her side.

"I think so," Emmy sighed and leaned back against him. "She'll need to take it easy for a while and hope there is no infection. I have a few Tylenol in my bag I can give her for a fever, but there's not much I can do for the pain. Did you see the boys?"

He grunted noncommittally. "They're nae much to look at."

She gaped at him. "How can you say such a thing? They are beautiful!"

"Ye're beautiful." He dropped a kiss on her forehead. "I am so proud of ye. Ye look worn out, though. Should ye get some rest? Ye've been in here for almost a whole day."

"I am beat," she admitted, "and hungry. Maybe we could raid the kitchens before we go to bed?"

"I'll hae Chilton send someone up with a tray."

"Dory needs someone to sit with her as well," she told him. "I sent Margo and Susan to bed a while ago."

"I'll hae Chilton send someone up to sit wi' her."

"What about Ian?"

"Shall I send Chilton up to see to him, as well?" Connor teased. "Our valet will see that he gets some rest. He mothers Ian excessively." McBride, the men's shared valet, had been with them since they were boys, Connor had told her, but Emmy had not seen hide nor hair of the man since she had been at Duart. She often wondered where he hid himself.

Emmy looked back at Dory and finally nodded. She turned and went over to where Ian stood by the bassinet the two babies shared. "What do you think?"

"They're amazing," he whispered, his voice thick with emotion. "Thank ye, Em. Connor told me what ye had to do. Thank ye for saving my lads and my wife."

She gave him a tired smile. "Just fulfilling my destiny," she told him, wondering again if it were true and if she would wake up in the morning back in her own bed in Baltimore. "If Dory wakes, don't allow her to move around, she might rip her stitches. The babies will probably fuss as well..."

"We've a full nursery staff ready for them," he assured her and she nodded.

"I'll be back to check on her in the morning."

He leaned over and kissed her cheek. "Thank ye," he repeated.

"You're welcome."

Emmy ate by rote when returning to her room, and bathed quickly before climbing into bed to wait for Connor. What if this was it? she thought again. What if in giving Dory and her children a chance at life, I am done here? What if Connor had absolutely nothing to do with it? But didn't he deserve a second chance too? What else was she to do?

She didn't want to wake up in the morning and have it all be gone. Connor slid into bed and she rolled into him, clinging to him desperately. "Tell me again how it is my destiny to stay here with you," she begged. "Tell me you won't let me go..."

He glanced at her in surprise and pulled her head back so he could meet her eyes, see her fear. "'Tis our destiny to be together, my love. Dinnae fear it. Hae faith."

"I'm scared," she confessed and told him of her fears.

"Ye'll save the lives of many bairns in the coming years, my love." He kissed her lightly. "Dory's are but the first."

"You sound so certain."

"I am. I maun be." He lowered his mouth to hers, capturing her lips in a kiss that promised the world and more. Connor rolled her under him and raised himself up on his elbows as she cradled him between her thighs. "Ye maun be as well."

"I'm trying," she whispered. "Give me another reason."
He did.

.

Emmy woke the next morning in Connor's arms and felt elation unlike any she had ever known. She was still here. The joy plummeted as fast as it had come and she moaned pitifully.

She was still here.

Connor rose and left their bed, urging her to get some more sleep, but she lay awake pondering the flash of desperation that followed so quickly on the heels of the jubilation she felt on awakening. She wondered where it had come from— that dejection that had flooded her so quickly. She wondered what it meant.

Added onto that, now she truly had no idea how much longer she would be here. A week or a lifetime. She was back to wallowing in the unknown but without the optimism she had faced the last week with. She couldn't get out of her head that this day might be her last. Whether that should have brought anticipation or trepidation, she couldn't decide. She wanted to go home, back to the safety of her perfectly planned future, yet Emmy wanted to stay at Duart as well with her new patients, and Connor.

The indecision tore at her.

She should be wholly, solely triumphant that she remained with Connor. She loved him and so there should be no doubts about what she wanted.

What was it that had brought them on?

And how was she to hide her reservations from Connor? Just twenty-four hours ago, she reveled in their love, happy and content. She had indeed taken each day as a gift. Should she confess her doubts or was he better off not knowing? Still he could read her so well that if Emmy tried to hide it from him and failed...

She buried her head in her pillow, trying to smother her uncertainty.

She wasn't ready to leave him. She could provide that one assurance though she wasn't sure it would be enough for Connor.

What to do?

Unable to find a solution to that problem, Emmy turned her thoughts instead to Dory.

Her friend's words from the night before echoed through Her mind. They had the markings of delirious ramblings, but there was an element of truth to them that Emmy knew she would have to confront. She wondered what Dory could offer in her defense.

XOXOXOX

An hour later, Emmy strode around to the opposite wing to her patient's room with Dory's words pounding through her mind. It didn't take a rocket scientist to figure it out, despite her musings that perhaps she'd heard Dory wrong, but what would Dory have to say for herself? After first going to the nursery to check on the babies, she moved on to Dory's room. At her knock, Ian opened the door.

"How is she?" she asked, as he moved aside to let her in.

"She had a rough night," he confessed in worried tones. "She was in a great deal of pain and had a few nightmares."

I'll bet she did, Emmy thought with a twist of her lips. "I'd like to check her incision and change her bandages, if that's all right?"

He nodded. His eyes were red and tired. "I was just going to get something to eat anyway."

"Why not try for a nap when you're finished?" she suggested. "You look done in."

He smiled and nodded as he left.

Dory was awake when Emmy examined her, enthusing tiredly about her sons and thanking Emmy for saving them all. Emmy accepted her praise as she washed and dried her hands. But then an uncomfortable silence fell between them as she took a seat next to the bed. She regarded Dory with a level stare that finally made the woman look away. "You were quite talkative last night."

God forgive me, she'd mumbled almost unintelligibly.

"I was in pain," Dory responded evasively. "People say strange things when they think they are about to die."

God forgive me for the hurt I have caused, for the lies I have told...

"Sure they do," Emmy said, leaning forward and propping her elbows on her knees. "Confession is good for the soul, right?"

...for the bigamy I have committed.

"Nothing to say?" Dory remained silent. "No? Fine, let me start. Are you out of your friggin' mind?" Emmy hissed. "What on earth were you thinking?"

"I don't know what you are talking about."

"Like hell you don't know what I'm talking about, Dorcas MacLean." She leaned in and added, "or should I say Heather MacLean?"

"I'm not…" Dory started but was halted by the look of warning of Emmy's face.

"Don't lie to me," she warned tightly. "You confessed to bigamy last night. Begged God's forgiveness for it. Are you going to lie there now and tell me you aren't Connor's wife?"

"I am. But I'm not Heather," she protested then caved into tears. "Oh, please don't tell anyone."

"Oh, I'm not going to tell anyone." Before Dory could draw a breath of relief, Emmy continued, "You are."

"No." Dory/Heather whispered in horror. "He'll kill me."

"Which one?" was Emmy's sarcastic reply. "You married Connor then turned around and then pretended to be another person and committed bigamy with his own brother. I will ask again, what were you thinking? You had to know it wouldn't end well."

"But I'm not pretending to be another person," Dory insisted. "I am Dorcas. It is my name, my real name." There was a ring of truth in her declaration.

Emmy paused and frowned. "Now I'm confused."

"My father brought me here to take Heather's place," the woman sobbed. "Heather was ill and the doctors thought she might not make it through and the wedding had been planned for so long. Rather than risk losing the settlement the Earl had paid my father by trying to negotiate a change in brides from my sister to me, he made me take her place. It was a huge settlement! He kept insisting on calling me Heather, saying no one, not even our mother could tell us apart. I think in a moment of madness, he may have truly believed I was her."

"You expect me to buy that load of crap?" Emmy sneered. "It wasn't me, it was my twin nonsense?"

"It is true. I swear." Emmy snorted but Dory—Heather?—grabbed her hand. "I swear to you on the soul of my mother and the lives of my wee bairns that I am telling you the truth. I am not Heather."

Emmy stared into her desperate blue eyes for a long moment. She was in earnest, that much was evident. Was it possible? Had her nutty dad thrown her to the wolves for money? And at eighteen, what could she have done to stop him? "Wait, but you are Connor's wife?"

Dory nodded miserably. "What I told you before was the truth. I fell in love with Ian the moment I saw him." She swallowed painfully and continued. "At first I thought he was my betrothed, but then Father led me to Connor and introduced him…not Ian… as the one I would marry. I was devastated."

"Connor isn't a bad guy, you know."

"He scared me at the time; sometimes he still does," she admitted. "But he didn't love me and before you say anything, he never would have. I knew it and, I think, he did also. If it had been Ian, I knew I would have a chance at real happiness, but, in less than two days of Connor's company, I knew I couldn't be happy with him."

"Why not say something then? 'Hey, wait, I'm not Heather!' or just 'I don't want to marry you'?" Emmy sat on the bed next to Dory and shook her head in disgust at the whole idea of arranged marriages. Had any of them ever turned out well?

"I begged my father not to make me do it," she

confessed tearfully. "I told him I would tell the truth or run away rather than marry Connor. My father beat me and locked me in my room and set his valet to guard my door and I never had a chance to run. They watched me all the way through the ceremony. Father had threatened me against denying the vows during the ceremony. Then it was done. I was his wife."

"And then they stopped guarding you thinking that you were out of choices," Emmy concluded, picturing how it all played out.

"When I was allowed to go to the countess's chambers to prepare for my wedding night," Dory explained, "I packed a small bag and ran away."

"And left Connor to face his greatest humiliation on his own, in front of his father and yours, the Prince of Wales and a hundred other people, I suppose?"

"Don't look at me that way," Dory begged. "What would you have done if your father tried to force you into marriage? I know you quite well at this point, Emmy; you would not have stood for it."

"No, I wouldn't have," she admitted, "but I would have found a way to cut it short before I was actually married."

"It was never consummated."

"And that makes it all better?" Emmy gaped in disbelief. "The least you could have done was not come back. Why did you? For Ian? To rub Connor's face in your deception?"

Dory tried to push herself up in defense but lay quickly back down with a cry of pain. Emmy tsked and rearranged her blankets. "Don't be a twit. Lay back down before you tear your stitches."

"Please don't think of me badly," Dory begged tearfully. "You've become like a sister to me. You're so much like her.

So much like Heather." Dory gripped her hand and sobbed.

Emmy felt her righteous anger ebbing as Dory carried on. What would she have done, indeed. No force on earth could make her do something she didn't want to do, so how could she really blame Dory for that? She was a product of this age and her upbringing. But to come back!

As if reading her thoughts, Dory continued. "I never meant to come back. I was determined to find a place to stay far from Duart and my father. I could not forgive him for what he had made me do. I did all right in the beginning. I even found a job waiting tables for a little while but was let go when I refused to entertain male customers. After that I ran out of what little monies I had quickly and soon was sleeping on the streets of Inverary or in barns along the road. So I went, walked, back to my father's house. I got home seven months after the wedding. Mother had perished from the influenza and Heather was dead. Father was ill as well. He suffered a failure of his heart after I fled." Dory cried genuinely now, awash in guilt and grief. "I stayed there as long as I could but when Father died I had no choice. With no other family, most of my father's property was entailed away to a distant heir. The rest went to my husband, Connor. I could have either returned in shame as his wife or come in mourning as his sister-in-law. God forgive me, I chose the latter and for that my soul shall truly burn in Hell."

"I'm sure your soul will be just fine," Emmy consoled and patted the woman's hand.

But Dory shook her head in denial. "I arrived here in my father's carriage while Connor was away…"

"Looking for you."

41

The clearing of a deep male throat gave both women a start and they turned to find Ian framed in the doorway. His eyes were nearly black with anger or pain, Emmy couldn't be certain, but his body was tense. "I would like to talk to my...Dorcas, if ye please, Emmy."

"Ian..." both women began in unison, but Ian held up a hand.

"If ye please."

Emmy reluctantly acquiesced and cast Dory an apologetic look as she slipped out the door. It shut with a soft click that was almost worse than a slamming door. Cold rage or simple devastation? She didn't know which and wondered if she should fear for Dory, uncertain whether Ian's rage might translate to violence in an era where a man still had the right to beat his wife. She'd just given birth and was in no condition for any major confrontation.

Worried, Emmy leaned back against the bedroom door wondering whether she should go back in and protect Dory or tell Connor everything. Well, Dory was right about one thing. Connor was going to kill her when he found out. Hopefully it would be a figurative slaying. Surely an explanation was necessary. He deserved to know but was it her place to break the news to him? Should she have him come to speak with Dory? Bring him to save Dory from Ian? That would not be how she wanted him to learn of Dory's deception, but if Dory were in danger from Ian, she would need Connor's help. She hoped that he wouldn't feel compelled to violence himself. She glanced down the corridor to see the man himself striding towards her.

"What are ye doing?"

She shifted from foot to foot, unsure what to say. She was glad he was there but…"Connor, we have a problem."

"Is it Dory? Has something happened to her?"

He paled as he asked the question. Strange but he had come to like the woman over the past couple of weeks.

"She's physically fine, but she was just telling me something, and Ian overheard." Her brow wrinkled with worry that was easy for Connor to read.

"What was it?"

"I don't think it is my place . . ."

Pushing past her, he rapped on the bedroom door. He waited politely but, on receiving no answer, cracked the door and looked in. Peeking around him, Emmy could see Ian staring into the fireplace while Dory lay staring at his back with haunted eyes. When the woman saw Connor enter the room, she let out an anguished sound.

"What has happened?" he asked when no one spoke.

She went to Dory's side. "What did he say?"

"He hasn't said *anything*!" she said desperately. "I think he hates me."

"Well, you'd better tell Connor now and have done with it so you can explain."

"No." Panic was clearly written on her face and the tension of her body.

Emmy tried not to feel too much pity for Dory. She would reap what was sown. Dory should never have waited ten years for the truth to be known. Still, she did feel a twinge of sympathy.

"What is it?" Connor demanded. "Ian?" His brother remained by the fire casting him only a hollow stare before directing his gaze to Dory, who shifted uncomfortably under the weight of their dual glares.

"Well," Dory cleared her throat and glanced nervously at Emmy who waved her on in encouragement. "I know we've never been on the best of terms until just recently. Perhaps what I'm about to say will destroy any chance of that changing, but there is something that I think you should know. It has weighed on my mind for many years and has perhaps been the reason that we have never gotten on well. Even though you are my brother-in-law, I have always remained aloof because I haven't wanted to say anything."

"Really?" Emmy rebuked softly at Dory's prevaricating.

"Very well then," Dory sighed. "My lord, I think you should know that Heather is dead."

Connor straightened away from the door and stared at Dory in shock before turning to Ian for confirmation. Ian, however, was staring with equal surprise at his wife. Clearly he hadn't heard the whole story.

"Way to cushion the blow," Emmy said drily.

"How long?" Connor ground out hoarsely following a long silence.

"Almost ten years."

He blinked in surprise "Then she died after she left here?"

Dory bit her lip and shook her head. "She did die shortly after the wedding, but she never left here, my lord, because she never came here." She said this last in a tiny whisper.

"But of course she did," he said in confusion. "The wedding...she was..." He trailed off and gaped at her as the reality of her confession set in. "It was ye, wasn't it?" His voice was low and menacing, demanding the truth and Dory gave it to him with a jerky nod. "Ye deceived me all this time?"

"I didn'tt want to, my lord." She looked desperately to her husband and then to Emmy for help and finally, feeling sorry for the timid woman in the face of Connor's temper, Emmy stepped in.

"Dory is not entirely at fault here." She paused briefly as his intensely forbidding gaze swung to her but pressed on. "With Heather fallen ill and maybe dying, Dory's father coerced her to pretend to be her sister. He made her falsely marry you in order to keep the marriage settlement you had already given him. She wanted to tell you, but he beat her until she agreed to do it and then ran away." She held up a conciliatory hand. "It was wrong, she's admitted it."

"And ye believe all this?" His voice was still quietly severe, controlled. "She could be working off yer sympathy and lying to ye to gain an ally."

"I don't believe so."

"I'm not telling this falsely, my lord," Dory chimed in. "I never meant to deceive you. It has weighed on me these many years and deprived me of true happiness in my life."

"And yet, ye did deceive me," he ground out as he stood, his fists balled against his sides. "And ye've committed bigamy wi' my own brother."

Ian flinched. "Why, Dory?" he whispered, his voice filled with pain and despair. "Why did ye come back here knowing ye were my brother's wife and marry me?"

"I never wanted to come back. I never meant to." Dory appealed for understanding. "But after Father died, I had nowhere else to go. I had no money. No home."

"Aye, I heard that much of what ye said," he admitted. "But why not admit who ye were? Why did ye wed me?"

"When I arrived here and saw you again, I just couldn't do it. I'd fallen in love with you when we first met and, on my arrival, I knew that I would encourage your affections and if possible I would wed with you. I chose to damn myself." She sobbed again. "And I have damned you as well. That was why God took my other babes before they had a chance to live. I was being punished for my sins and surely, if Emmy had not been here, I would have lost the ones we have now. I am so sorry. I have been miserable for years for what I have done."

"Miserable?" Connor cold voice lashed like a whip. "*Ye've* been miserable? Ye've lived in my house for ten years amid sin and lies! Aye, I can see how ye've suffered as ye've witnessed my humiliation for so long." His voice rose to a roar.

"Connor," Emmy tried to cut in but he silenced her with a slash of his hand.

"I've heard enough. Lies. Years of lies! I want ye gone, do ye ken?" He jabbed a finger at Dory. "Gone!"

The door slammed behind him as he left in his rage leaving a cowering Dory sobbing in her bed. Emmy exchanged a long look with Ian.

"That went pretty well, don't you think? I'm glad he kinda lost it there at the end. He was just too quiet before that."

"Are you jesting?" Dory gawked at her in disbelief. "He wants me to leave! He looked ready to do me physical harm!"

"Oh, that," she waved dismissively. "He didn't mean all that. He was just mad. But mad is good. Am I right, Ian? It's like you told me before. Always stoic, never really emotional? Anger he can work out."

Ian shrugged still staring down at the woman he'd lived with as husband and wife for a decade. Her plea seemed to have touched him, but his brother had made a valid point. She had made the choice that had brought his brother the greatest misery. How could he forgive her for that?

"Ye lied to me." His voice was low and pained.

"My father forced me into it, Ian. Darling." Dory reached out a pleading hand to her husband and stifled a sob when he ignored it and turned away. "I never wanted to marry Connor. I loved you the moment I met you. But he beat me, made me do it."

"But ye came back here and perpetuated a lie for ten years. Ye saw how it had affected Connor. Why did ye ne'er tell him that Heather had died?" he questioned. "Ye could have at least done that for him."

"I don't know," she whimpered.

"Damn ye for what ye ha' done to us. For what ye ha' made us."

Emmy had been feeling awkward in the face of their marital argument and considered slipping out when a tingling of a thought caught her. "Let's not go crazy here. I'm not a lawyer by any means, but I think your mutual souls are going to be just fine."

"What do you mean?" Dory sniffed.

"I mean that I'm about ninety-nine percent certain that

you are not a bigamist."

"What?" the pair chorused in unison.

"Emmy, what are ye getting at?" Ian asked.

Her mind raced. "I mean I don't know how the law works here but… Let me ask you this, Dory, when you married Connor, what name did you use?"

"Heather's."

"The minister said something like 'do you Heather…' *blah blah blah*?"

"Aye," Ian offered. "He said Emeline Heather Stuart. Why?"

"And Dory said?"

"I just said 'Yes'."

"Right." Emmy clapped her hands together. "And when you signed the marriage certificate, you signed it…how?"

Dory and Ian exchanged a long look that spoke of their decade together. A conversation without words in spite of the present state of affairs. "With Heather's name just as Father forced me to," she said. "I think he was quite mad, you know."

"Well, I think he was quite committing fraud," Emmy responded, watching as Ian caught on to her line of thinking. "What is the legal age of consent here?"

"The legal age of consent?" Dory echoed in confusion.

"What age do you have to be to make your own decisions legally?" Emmy clarified.

"Twenty-one," Ian said quietly. "And she was eighteen when they wed…or not even that, were ye? Just short?"

"I turned eighteen a month later, but Emmy I don't see how this makes any difference at all," Dory argued. "I still said 'I do' to two men without benefit of a divorce or an annulment."

"No, that might not legally be how it happened at all! Don't you see?" Dory just continued to stare at Ian in bewilderment. "Come on, Dory. I know you are brighter than this. Think."

Dory leaned her head back against the pillows in fatigue. "I am so tired. Emmy, please do the thinking for me."

"Duh, you were never legally married to Connor at all."

"What?" Dory cried out in pain again as her body tensed in shock.

"What did I tell you? Lie still." Emmy commanded. "God, I wish I had something to give you for the pain. There is no way I'm letting you take that opium either, so don't ask."

"It's laudanum," Dory whispered, "and my maid snuck some to me last night."

"Don't do it again," the doctor in Emmy urged. "The opium will go straight into your breast milk and then straight into your babies."

"I've already hired a wet nurse," Dory flushed then waved her away. "Just tell me what you said about me never marrying Connor."

"Unless I'm completely wrong and I don't think I am," she said, "it's possible you were never legally married to Connor at all."

"How?"

"'Tis fraud and coercion on yer father's part," Ian told her and for a moment a flash of relief crossed his face. "Minors cannot sign contracts, they aren't legally responsible even if they do, plus ye dinnae even use yer real name. 'Tis likely yer marriage to Connor was null and void from the beginning."

"Yes, I think so," Emmy agreed and squealed as Ian

crushed her to him and planted a firm kiss on her mouth.

"Em, bugger it, but I'm glad ye're here."

"Thanks," Emmy reeled back into a chair and blinked up at him. Glad she was here? Was this another role she had been meant to play? Bringing the truth to light? Giving them closure to the past? Dare she say it? A second chance? Was it possible that everything Donell had said was not just a huge pile of horseshit?

Dory smiled weakly at her husband. "Do you really think so?"

"Perhaps." He pondered the situation for a moment. "I dinnae ken if our marriage is legal however. Em?"

Shaking off the realizations that had stunned her to silence, Emmy shrugged, trying to remember anything she might have learned from decades of TV law shows—the sum of her legal knowledge—but came up blank. If Donell had wanted to get this one right, why hadn't he sent in a lawyer?

"You got me. All I can think is that even if the marriage to Connor was legal, it would have been with Heather not Dory. Like a proxy wedding, right?"

"Perhaps." Ian rubbed his chin. "It could be just the opposite though. Or perhaps there was ne'er a marriage at all if it wisnae consummated. I'll need to see our solicitor then. I dinnae want my sons to be considered bastards."

A cry of despair escaped Dory's lips, but Ian gave her no pity. "If ye'd come back and told the truth ye could hae saved Connor a decade of pain. It might be fair punishment for ye to have our sons be illegitimate."

"Will you forgive me, Ian?" she begged. "I was just a girl. I didn't know what to do."

"Aye, but ye became a woman who should've known better. Ye had all this time to make it right but chose no' to."

Ian's eyes flashed with anger and betrayal. "I dinnae ken, Dory. I dinnae ken if I can forgi', but I hope for the sake of our sons that our marriage is legal. I'll leave for Inverary in the morning to meet with our solicitor." He looked as if might approach Dory but turned away resolutely, turning back as he reached the door. "And it isnae just my forgiveness ye maun receive, Dory. Ye maun beg it of my brother as well. Ye hae to make it right."

"Ian!" she cried out, but he left the room. "Emmy, what am I to do?"

"Apologize and pray for a second chance, I guess." She glanced worriedly at the door. "I must see Connor, Dory. Think about it. Put yourself in his shoes and try to think about what is best for someone else this time."

42

Emmy found Connor in his study already half way through a bottle of whisky. As she watched, he guzzled another glassful and grimaced. "I would slow down there, big guy. I am all out of aspirin to cut the after-effects."

"Go away."

"Nope, I'm not going to do that." She strolled over to the desk and turned him in the desk chair until she could face him. Kneeling before him, she rested her forearms on his thighs and stared up at him. "Alcohol is not the answer, Connor. Dory was wrong to keep this from you for so long."

He snorted rudely and downed the remaining contents of the glass.

"Okay, she was *incredibly* wrong to keep it from you," she emphasized. "She was young and stupid at the beginning but ten years of nursing the lie was awful and she knows it. I think she thought she was just trying to maintain the status quo as it were." She rubbed her palms against his muscled thighs trying to comfort him. "You couldn't defy your father to stop a marriage you didn't want and she couldn't either. She didn't have it in her to be defiant in the face of punishment and pain. For that one moment, her flight from here, I can't find her completely at fault, can you?"

"She…" he faltered. He tried to remember those days but all he could recall was Heather's…Dory's haughty behavior. Was it possible that it had been fear? He shook his head in doubt.

"Young and stupid, remember?"

Connor sighed and covered her hands with his own. Looking down into her bright blue eyes, he saw her compassion and love. How thankful he was to have her here. She would never go away when he told her to; she would fight him, aggravate him but always comfort him. Her love was soothing, calming. Her intelligence and inappropriate wit softened harsh realities. Her presence made the whole situation more tolerable.

"Now coming back," Emmy went on, "was beyond stupid. I told her she should've just stayed away, but with her entire family dead, she felt she had no alternative but to come back to Duart. She should've come forward with the truth so it could've been handled properly. She really, *really* should have but she didn't and she's lived with that guilt all this time. And I'm not trying to belittle your pain. I know your happiness has suffered because of her and she knows it, too. But her regret is real."

"And ye believe her?"

Emmy softened to him, loving that he trusted her opinion and belief. "I do."

"But her bigamy." That point still nagged at him. "Ye cannae deny that sin! And she's damned my brother, too, with her adultery."

"Well, you missed the best part when you stormed out, but," she teased lightly, "I think my 'educated man' can work it out. It's simple, really. I'll start it for you...you married Heather Stuart."

He started to agree. "Aye, I marr..." He stopped short.

"There goes the light bulb," she encouraged softly. "That *aha* moment."

"I dinnae marry Heather, I married Dory," he said in amazement. The light bulb? He shook his head and concentrated on the other thought. "But I used Heather's name when I made my vows."

"Ian is going to Inverary to fetch your solicitor, but if we're right, the marriage was invalid from day one. She was underage and under coercion. Even if the marriage was valid, perhaps it was not to Dory but to Heather. Maybe it was more like a proxy marriage, and she died not a month later." She turned her palms up to grasp his hands. "I don't think you were ever a married man, Connor. If you were, you very soon became a widower. Dorcas Stuart was never your wife and was free to marry Ian."

Connor closed his eyes and envisioned the chain of events, letting the facts roll over him. If it were only true. But, what should be done about her duplicity? Ten years of deception and betrayal. How could he let that pass?

"What was Ian's response to all of this?"

"He's angry and upset, but I think he'll be fine, hopefully sooner than later." She pushed herself up and scooted into his lap before dropping her arms around his neck. She was comforted when his arms wrapped around her waist. "Maybe later than sooner. I imagine it would be difficult to discover the woman you love had lied for a decade."

"He might ne'er forgi' her."

"Would you forgive me?" she asked then added, "eventually, of course. A period of anger and resentment is, after all, justifiable."

Connor looked down into her beautiful face and knew that he could forgive her almost anything. Some things were beyond forgiveness, of course. Infidelity. But a lie, even of this magnitude, he thought, he might eventually be able to forgive, if her reasoning were sound and her regret genuine. Occasionally even the best of intentions ended in disaster.

"You're an incredible woman." He pulled her to him and kissed her softly leaving her humming in satisfaction against his lips. "If I'd discovered all of this before ye came here, 'tis verra likely that I might hae killed her wi'out a second thought."

"Well, I am glad I was here to curb your homicidal impulses then."

"I'm glad as well. Though even when she told me I was no' as angry as I should hae been. My reaction was most unusual, I think. I was angry, enraged even, but it faded quickly. Almost as if the past nae longer mattered. The past disnae matter, lass. Isnae that strange?"

"And the future?"

"Aye, the future is all that matters. And I want a future with ye. Ye've given me a peace I've no' had in many years, allowed me to live for the moment and appreciate what I hae. And no' to...what is it ye said? No' to sweat the small stuff?" He kissed her softly. "Ye've changed my life."

"And you have changed mine." Emmy wrapped her arms more firmly around him and kissed him lovingly. "It awes me, Connor, the feelings you rouse in me. I know I've said it before, but I never imagined that such a depth of feeling was possible. I love you. Such inadequate words, but I do."

"As I love ye, my darling lass," he whispered. He kissed her with all the passion of his declaration.

"Forgive her, Connor," she said in all seriousness when they came up for air. "It's your key being dropped right in your lap. Forgive her, the Heather that has haunted you all these years and let yourself face your future without all that baggage, happy and free. Think of it as a second chance to live your life. Isn't that what Donell said? That everyone deserves a second chance. I don't think that was all just about Dory. I think she needed to confess what she had done so she and you could both move on with your lives. The truth can set you free, to borrow a much-abused cliché."

"Ye think knowing the truth can change the way I look at life? That it will change the way I live my life from now on?"

"Doesn't it?"

Connor met her gaze thoughtfully for several long moments. His life had changed...dramatically in fact, but it wasn't just the truth that had done it. The truth alone would not have done it. Without weeks of Emmy's influence before, that confession from Dory might have driven him to a murderous act. It was Emmy who had brought them to this point. Emmy, whose love allowed him to move on and forgive before the confession had ever been delivered.

"I am happy and free, my love," he replied eventually in serious measure. "No' because of that truth, but because ye came into my life and freed me." He held her closely for a long while. "Well, then, let me up so I can go wi' my brother to Inverary to save his marriage."

"That's my man," she murmured in approval and kissed him gently on the cheek.

The weather had finally cleared and the sun was shining for the first time in days. Forty-eight hours of labor and confessions had left Emmy tense and she was determined to get out and enjoy the beautiful day. Connor and Ian had said they would likely have to spend at least one night in Inverary and would probably not return until late in the day.

Free to do as she wished, she dressed in the most comfortable clothes available—her own—thinking that over the rough terrain her boots were the most practical. It felt good to be back in her jeans. There was just something about their snug containment that set everything right. Her little blazer wasn't much defense against the winds but it was warmer than any of the daily-wear blouses she had and would work well under a large coat.

Stuffing her camera into her tote, she slung the bag across her chest. She hadn't gotten one picture of this gorgeous land yet. Of course, at the moment, her digital camera was useless without a computer to download the pictures on to, and what if she never returned to her own time? What was the point? She shrugged mentally. It was something to do and she wanted to capture Duart just in case…

Emmy froze. What if she did go back? What would she do when they finally found Donell or, more accurately, he decided to grace them with his presence? Should she beg him to take her away? Beg him to let her stay? What if she didn't have a choice? What if she did?

What if she did?

It tortured her, that question. What would she do if she had a choice? Take Connor back with her, of course. Then she tried to picture him in her time. He would be lost. His purpose, his passion for his land and his people, gone. At least she knew what was coming. But, she also knew what she was missing. He would never make it in her time and she just wasn't sure she wanted to be stuck in his. But without Connor, would her own time be worth going back to?

Emmy mulled over these questions as she snuck out of the castle and courtyard and headed in long strides to the southwest. The pull of her muscles felt good. She definitely needed to get out more and keep in shape! She savored the feeling as she walked rapidly down the rocky coastline. Stopping periodically, she took pictures of Duart, the sound and carried on farther to Lochdon, taking pictures of the village and its people at work. She stopped in briefly to check on Cora McAllen and her baby before spending the last of the local coins Connor had given her on a 'bridie', a meat pie at the local tavern.

The rustic fare was infinitely more satisfying than the exotic sauces and dishes Dory arranged night after night and Emmy thought she might try to convince the woman to mix some of the local dishes in. After all, eating at Spago was nice, but not every day. Besides, everyone just needed pizza or a burger every once in a while. She wondered if the analogy could be translated.

After several hours of hiking, she neared Duart again. The day and exercise had warmed her enough that she had long ago shed her coat and draped it over her tote. She felt good. Energized. And mentally invigorated after her walk. The sun was beginning to lower in the sky, gilding the western side of the castle as she approached. She raised her camera again and took another shot from this angle. Thoughts of a hot shower, well, bath anyway, insinuated into her mind as she approached.

As she was nearing the front gates, the sound of hoof beats brought her around as Connor approached from the north. Struck by the similarity to her first sight of him, Emmy raised the camera and took several shots as he approached and swung down from Bruce. One, two and a third as he walked toward her.

"Smile," she called. He did automatically and she snapped another, though she thought he smiled more because of her silly voice than her command. "Well? How did it go?"

"The marriage was indeed between myself and Heather, no' Dory," he explained. "Ian is waiting to hear an official word from the courts in Edinburgh before he returns, but it seems that I am a widower these past ten years."

"So their marriage is legal?"

"We believe so." Connor nodded and welcomed her embrace as she threw her arms around him. "Ian said to thank ye again for everything. Wi'out ye here he wouldnae hae his wife or sons. He has a marriage and family thanks to ye."

"I am glad I was here to help," she offered sincerely. Maybe that had been it all along. Her presence had changed history. She had saved a mother and two babies, making it possible for a great wrong to be made right. Connor had been given freedom from the past that had haunted and ruled his life, allowing him to move on to a richer relationship with his family. She had made all that possible.

So much for a simpler life.

What if her job here was done?

"I've missed ye," he whispered, leaning back to capture her lips in a long passionate kiss, distracting her from her musings.

"*Mmm*," Emmy hummed dreamily returning his kiss. "I'm sure I can't wait to show you how much I missed you as well. I was so cold last night!"

"Did ye miss me or just my warmth?"

"Can't I miss it all?"

※※※※

Connor chuckled and held her close to him, savoring the meeting of their bodies. He had indeed missed her loving presence by his side and in his bed. Had missed her conversation and wit. He loved her so dearly.

"I was just thinking," Emmy said.

"Aboot what?"

"You know, when I came here with Donell, I was telling him how I considered your time simpler. I think that was part of his test too. To see that it wasn't necessarily so. When I look at Dory or at Margo's home, I can see there are hard times here as well. You have worries and fears and challenges that I never did. Your life is harder close to home, whereas our worries are for our entire world. In my time, people worry about money or success but here, people worry for their very lives and those of their children. Their existence."

"I care for my country."

"I know you do, my Earl of Strathclyde. But how about your people here? What do they care about?" She glanced down at her camera. "It was such a beautiful day, I thought I'd get out for a walk and finally take some pictures. That's what I see here. People whose lives are not as simple as one would think."

"Nae one ever said they were. Yer camera? Is that what that is?" he asked curiously. "May I see it?"

"In a sec. First let me do one of us together. Come here," Emmy commanded and stood him next to her, leaned in close and, in typically twenty-first century fashion, stuck the camera out in front of them and took a picture. Checking to make sure she'd got what she wanted on the screen, she turned it to show him. "See, here are the pictures I took today." She pushed the right arrow again and again, scrolling through the day's photos.

"'Tis amazing!" he murmured in awe, taking a turn pushing the button. "Where do the photographs go?"

"The memory card stores the pictures here." She popped it out of the compartment to show him and inserted it back in.

"Remarkable. How do ye hae them developed then?"

"I can take that memory card and put it in my computer at home...remember? I explained the computer?" She had, but the concept was so far beyond Connor's experience that he still had a difficult time believing what she was possible. "I can print them on my own printer at home." She sighed. "I wish I could show you. There are so many things

I'd like to show you."

"I should like to see them wi' ye," Connor admitted. She seemed to have had a never-ending stream of experiences beyond anything he could ever imagine. While he could live forever on the stories of her time, experiencing them with her by his side would be incredible. "Still, I thank God every day that He brought ye to me." He bent and kissed her lovingly on the lips. "I love ye so dearly."

"I love you, too," she whispered. The words were still so new. She was always struck with awe when she said them. She wanted to shout them out, but they always came out softly as if they were as uncertain as her desire to remain here. She felt torn, pulled in two directions. On one hand, her life in Baltimore, safe, uncomplicated and certain. On the other, Connor, his love and what might be unimaginable contentment. If only she knew what she really wanted.

"Has anyone been able to find Donell?"

"Nay, it seems the auld man has simply disappeared since ye saw him at the inn. Jimmy says he hisnae been in for any ale a'tall and his cottage is deserted." Connor rested his chin on top of her head and held her close. "I still dinnae understand it all, how it happened." He'd become content with thinking it God's power for, as superstitious as the Scots were, sorcery still seemed too implausible, although Emmy seemed to hold Donell entirely responsible.

"I know, I don't get it either. After all he's just a man" she admitted, turning back to the castle. "How could he do it? I was just standing here, just like this. The sun was setting and I raised my camera to take a picture…" She lifted the camera in demonstration. "And I felt…"

A wave of vertigo assailed her and she stumbled to the side, holding a hand to her temple as her vision swam.

"Connor?"

"Emmy? Em!" His voice called her name, sounding hollowly as if through a long tunnel and she turned at the note of panic in his voice. "Emmy, come back. *Nooo!*"

"Lassie? Are ye ready to be going then?"

Emmy swayed dizzily. "What?" She raised a hand to her brow as the swell of nausea subsided.

"I asked if yer ready to be returning to Craignure, lassie." She turned to see Donell leaning against the fender of the shuttle, looking at her expectantly. She looked in confusion from him to the bus. "The ferry will be leaving wi'in the hour and the next isnae for several hours after," the old man went on. "I dinnae think ye'll be wanting to miss it, if yer done here?"

"O…kay," she stuttered, moving automatically to the bus and climbing numbly on board. She dropped heavily into the seat and stared at the castle, wondering what had happened. What was going on? Why was she back? Emmy shook her head hard. She looked back at Duart and noticed the aged and crumbling exterior. It was not what she had become used to seeing every day.

"Dinnae even see ye come out of the old keep, lass. I

hidnae been waiting too long, just reading my paper," Donell said cheerfully as he took his seat and closed the door.

"How long was I in there?" She formed the question numbly.

"'Boot an hour, I'd say," he answered. "Did ye hae a nice time?"

Why was he acting like he had no clue what had happened? "Donell? What have you done?"

"Lassie?" he questioned. The confusion in his voice seemed genuine but she pressed on.

"Don't pull this bullshit with me. Send me back, right now!"

"I'm sure I dinnae ken what ye mean, lassie. Ye want to go home, right?" His eyes met hers in the rearview mirror. "That is what ye want? Ye hae yer new job waiting for ye. Dinnae ye mention that before? And ye said ye dinnae need a second chance. That ye had all ye needed of life? Or perhaps, ye needed something to remind ye that life here isnae always perfect?"

It was like he had been able to hear the conflicting thoughts racing through her mind all day. The doubts, the uncertainty. She had been looking forward to her new job, but what of the new patients she had in Duart?

"Of course, ye miss yer friends…" Donell went on.

It finally occurred to Emmy that she had gone on vacation alone because she really didn't have anyone that she had wanted to share it with. Not like she wanted to share the world with Connor.

What did she really want?

She hadn't known the answer, she realized. Her mind had been filled with questions for days. On one hand, her future as she knew it. On the other, Connor.

"So what did ye think of the castle, lassie?" Donell went on in his gravelly brogue, as if taunting her with her own doubts. "The castle is a bonny place but I'm sure ye got the sense that life wisnae so simple as ye thought, dinnae ye? Hard to imagine living like that, eh? Hard life to be sure. None of them...what do ye call them...amenities that ye hae in the States, eh?"

"No, none," she replied tonelessly. "At least the toilet flushed, though."

Emmy spent the remainder of the brief trip in silence as the bus rumbled back to Craignure. She watched the power lines loop along the shore. Up, down, up down. The haze of shock was starting to lift and heartbreak was quickly taking its place.

It was over. Gone. Connor was gone. An hour? Had it even been real?

A flash of panic. What if it had been only a dream? A daydream! Fantasy.

No, no, no, she thought as she dug out her camera again and powered it on. Pushing the play button, she scrolled through the pictures in its memory. The ferry, Craignure, Donell in front of the bus.

"Come on, come on," she urged as she repeatedly hit the right arrow. And then there they were. Duart as she remembered it, Duart from the north again and again. A physical shock of relief left her trembling. She sped through them, relaxing and finally let out a sigh as she found those of Connor on his horse and then the two of them together.

"Thank God."

Emmy rubbed her temples as Donell pulled the shuttle up to the ferry terminus. "There ye go, lass," he said, opening the door. "I hope ye enjoy the rest of yer holiday."

"Send me back, Donell." She stayed in her seat and stared him down.

"Castle's closed, lassie."

"That's not what I meant and you know it," she insisted, keeping her eyes locked with his.

"A person cannae live a life filled wi' doubts, lassie," he told her, dropping all pretense of not knowing what she was talking about. "Yer filled wi' doubts."

"What about second chances?" she asked, frantically. "You said we all deserved them."

"And ye gave them theirs," he said firmly. "The younger lad and his wife will hae a future now. Ye hae given their bairns a chance at life."

"What of Connor?" she grasped at reasons. "What of his second chance?"

"He is free of his anger," Donell reasoned. "His life will go forward wi'out malice."

She looked away at last and stared out the window at the ferry. "But what about love? Will he go forward without love?"

"He needed love given wi'out regret." The old man's soft statement drew her gaze back to his.

"It was," she responded automatically.

"Was it?" he said. His eyes seemed to search her soul. When she still hesitated, he went on, "A little more time, I think."

Scowling fiercely, she dug into her tote and retrieved her return ticket for the ferry, shouldered her bag and stood up to exit the shuttle, stopping by Donell as she passed the driver's seat. "It was a cruel thing you did, Donell. I don't even care how you did it anymore, but you can't mess with people's lives like that."

"Let me know when ye figure out what ye really want, lassie."

The sun was reflecting brightly off the water as Emmy walked up the ramp, through the terminal and out onto the huge ferry which was starting to board. She headed to the glassed-in viewing area on the right side of the ferry so she could watch for Duart on the trip back to Oban. Catching sight of a familiar sign, she stopped at the refreshment kiosk and ordered a Diet Coke. She sat and sipped at the soda, savoring the burn of the carbonation as it went down. Closing her eyes, she tilted her head back against the seat. The mechanics deep within the ferry churned to life and it began to pull itself into the sound.

Her feelings on what had just happened were chaotic and confused. She was glad she was here, but she wanted to go back. She wanted Connor. Her chest tightened and ached and she absently rubbed the pain with her palm.

Connor, Connor...she would never see him again, she realized and the pain grew. God, it wasn't right. She'd never dreamed of loving someone with this depth of feeling, much less having it happen so quickly. Why him? Why had this happened? What was she going to do? The questions had no answers.

The urge to open her eyes overwhelmed Emmy. She opened them to find Duart before her. The sun was setting low behind it leaving it little more than a dark silhouette against the orange skies.

"Oh, my God," she whispered against the ache blossoming in her core. "Connor..." She was so painfully stunned, so deeply heartbroken, in that moment that she could not even cry at what she had found and so suddenly lost. It wasn't until she was lying in bed at her hotel that night that the anguish came and she could not contain her desperate tears.

"Dr. MacKenzie?"

Emmy turned away from the window of her office to find one of the practice's nurses standing in her doorway. "Yes, Joy?"

"Dr. Lane would like to see you in her office."

The look on the woman's face said immediately and Emmy nodded. "I will go right away. Thank you."

She'd been back for almost two months. Fifty-seven days to be exact. Fifty-seven days during which she realized that her life was not as perfect as she had thought. Not without someone to share it with. In the three days after leaving Duart, she'd rented a car and taken the ferry over to Mull on her own. The first day, she just sat on her rock overlooking the sound, trying to answer the question that seemed to mean so much. What did she want? Apparently her confusion had been enough to make it impossible to find Donell for, try as she might, she'd been unable to find him in the days that followed.

The current occupants of the castle hadn't yet returned to their residence, so there was no one there to let her in—not that she would have expected them to. She sat outside the keep in the car for hours…wishing, hoping. She wanted to go back. She wanted to be with Connor.

"I figured it out, Donell," she'd shouted over the sound. "I know what I want, so get your ass over here and give it to me."

But Donell was nowhere to be found.

It seemed he doubted her sincerity.

Finally, her life had invaded. Voicemail reminders from her new boss had compelled Emmy back to London and back on her scheduled flight to BWI. Two days later she had taken her position as the newest OB/GYN at the Harbor Women's Clinic in Baltimore. She'd been given a caseload of new patients and had already delivered two babies since starting, both in the shining new maternity ward at Johns Hopkins.

Her friends encouraged her to go out with them to their favorite restaurants and even up to a show in New York, but as the weeks had passed, they called less and less. Emmy was very aware that she was not the lighthearted company she'd once been and frankly she didn't blame them for giving her the cold shoulder.

Why couldn't she be happy again?

Other than Connor and his family she hadn't particularly liked it there. There were none of the luxuries she wanted…no, needed to live comfortably there. No technology, no movies, no cars. Emmy spent a whole night recently making a list of everything she had disliked about the past and it had been grievously long. Insanely long. So why did she miss it so much? She had everything here she had ever wanted. The job, the house, the friends. What else could she want? Surely all of this was better than an ancient castle with no toilet paper?

Didn't she have what she had always wanted?

Did she know what she really wanted?

"You asked to see me, Dr. Lane?" Emmy asked as she rapped on the open door frame of the chief practitioner's office.

"Cathy, remember? You can call me Cathy" she reminded without looking up from her computer.

"Sorry." She hovered in the doorway.

"Please close the door and have a seat, Emmy." The doctor turned away from her computer, pulled off her reading glasses and studied Emmy seriously across the desk for a long moment as she did as she was asked. Emmy fidgeted nervously under the woman's assessing stare. "You've been doing an excellent job since you started here," Dr. Lane began. "Surveys from your new patients and the staff are highly favorable; you're described as friendly and knowledgeable from both sides." She slipped the glasses back on briefly and picked up a piece of paper. "This one even wrote, and I quote 'Dr. MacKenzie made it almost fun to deliver my baby'."

She smiled slightly. "Maggie Ross. She was fun, too."

Cathy placed the glasses carefully onto the desk and regarded Emmy thoughtfully. "You do an excellent job here, just as I expected when I hired you. You work hard and even volunteer to be on call on the weekends. You never say 'no' to anyone who asks you to take their turn. The other doctors will take advantage of you if you keep this up."

"I don't mind," she said with a shrug. "I like to be busy."

She did. The busier she was, the less chance she had to sit alone in her house thinking of the 'could've beens' of Connor. The times she was alone were the hardest to bear, when she would bring the pictures of him up on her computer screen and just stare at them for hours.

"Still," the doctor said with authority. "You will burn out quickly if you keep it up. Don't you have a boyfriend, or some friends rattling the cage for your attention?"

Emmy just shook her head and bit her lip.

Cathy Lane stared hard at her newest doctor for several moments. She hated to get involved in her associate's personal lives. She didn't want them to feel as if she was mothering them or pestering them to death. As a general policy, she refrained from offering comments of a personal nature on their lives, but with Emmy she felt as if she didn't have a choice. Something had to be done. "What is it, Emmy, that seems to haunt you so badly?"

Emmy was startled by the question. "What do you mean? Didn't you just say that everyone thinks I've been doing a good job?"

"I'm not talking about the job." The doctor sat back in her chair and crossed her arms over her chest. "When you're talking to someone, I mean actively talking, you're involved, interested and, I would say, almost…perky."

She cringed. Who wanted to be described as perky?

"But," Cathy continued, "when no one is looking, when you're alone in your office, you seem incredibly, I don't know, sad? I used the word haunted, but it's more like something is missing, rather than lingering about you."

"How?"

"These offices do have glass walls, you know."

Emmy sat in stunned silence for a moment. Did it show so badly? She tried hard to keep her woes and pains to herself, especially since her friends had begun avoiding her and her morose behavior. She tried to be happy and, ugh, even perky. Had she failed so badly? But Dr. Lane had been more correct in her first descriptor. Emmy did feel haunted. Haunted by the memories of Duart and of Connor.

"See, there it is again," Cathy pointed out. "That look...I don't know how to describe it. So full of longing. So!" She sat forward again and crossed her arms on the desk. "This is what I want you to do. Christmas is next week and, other than those patients who are due in the next week, we have no appointments scheduled. Doctors Hamilton and Johnson will be taking the on call rotations...yes, I know you already volunteered, but that's not going to happen...and you are taking the week off. If this is a guy thing, then figure it out. If it's something else, well, figure it out. I want you to be happy here, Dr. MacKenzie, and right now you are not."

She started to protest that, of course she was happy but her boss halted her with an upheld hand.

"Take the time off. Figure out what it is you really want."

"What I really want?" She repeated as her most burning question again raised its head.

"That's right."

Emmy drove home that night with the words pounding in her head.

What I really want, what I really want...

She had always wanted to be a doctor, always. And, after a long moment of examination, yes, she still did, she knew. It was her vocation, her calling. When she had been at Duart, though, it had been even more rewarding because the women were so appreciative of her. Here, it felt like the women considered good prenatal care their due and the doctor merely a tool to achieve what they wanted.

The only other thing she really wanted…was Connor.

"I want Connor," she said aloud, straightening in her seat. "I want Connor, I want Duart and if I have to take every nineteenth century passé piece of ancient technology that goes with it to have them, then that's what I want too. I want gas lighting." She pounded her fist against the steering wheel. "I want way too much food." She pounded again. "I want nagging relatives, that stupid carriage and a sister who's not really my sister." She pounded the steering wheel again and again. "I even want my corset!" she yelled into the silence of her car.

She whispered into the darkness. "I want my love, my happiness and the person who makes me laugh and cry and fight. "His face materialized in her mind. "I want you Connor. I love you so much I would happily give up all of this for you. You are what I really want and, damn it, I'm going to come back to you. Without regrets."

46

Five days later, Emmy leaned against the rail of the *Caledonian MacBrayne*, the ferry from Oban to Craignure. The December wind was biting, but she snuggled in the depths of her warmest winter coat, scarf and gloves. It'd taken a few days to prepare herself to try again, no, succeed, in her return to Duart. Laying it all on the line, she'd even updated her will, leaving everything she had to Johns Hopkins and St Jude's.

By her side, her largest tote was stuffed tightly. Emmy considered the bag. It'd taken her a long time to figure out what she wanted to bring with her, assuming that what she carried would go with her as it had before. Should she bring twenty new bras and pairs of underwear? As much toilet paper as she could carry? A lifetime supply of tampons?

She smiled. All those things she would just have to do without, but getting what she did want had delayed her a bit since it wasn't something she could just carry on the plane and get through customs without questions. She'd had to wait in Oban for two days waiting for the package she had sent herself to arrive.

Her focus shifted to the coastline of Mull as Duart came into view. There it was, waiting. The wind was crisp and cold against her cheeks yet she hardly noticed. All her thoughts, her consciousness were focused on one man, lost to the past. Simply yearning. A quiver of uncertainty flashed through her. What if she failed? She was at the whim of a crazy old man who, it seemed, could only be found when he wanted to be. What if she could never find him again?

So lost in thought was she that she did not notice the pair of eyes which had been focused on her for so long. She could have been mugged and not even noticed or cared for that matter. Nothing mattered any longer. She had no will, no direction, and no desire beyond what lay before her. Soft footsteps approached from behind. If she'd been paying attention, Emmy would have noticed they were slow and shuffling.

"Lassie?" The low, gruff voice repeated the word several times before it penetrated her consciousness. When it finally did, she jumped as though burned. Emmy turned to see an elderly gentleman at her side. Though he must have been in his late seventies or early eighties, he wasn't bent with age but stood straight. He was broad across the shoulders and a bit heavyset. His hair was gray and he wore a neatly trimmed beard. From the looks of his clothing and the heavy cane he held in one hand, he seemed to do quite well for himself.

"Excuse me?" she questioned a bit warily, for, despite his genteel appearance, he was still a stranger approaching her on a public ferry.

The old man chuckled deeply at her obvious wariness. "Dinnae be afraid, please. I mean ye nae harm."

"I didn't think you did," she replied tartly.

He laughed again at the obvious lie. He moved to stand at the rail, a few feet away, and looked out over the sound as well. His long heavy overcoat flapped in the wind. "I remember riding the ferries that came before this with great fondness. They were smaller, of course, no' so crowded and nae cars."

"Yes, I remember," she said without thinking.

"Do ye?" he asked gently.

Emmy started, realizing her mistake. "What I meant was I can certainly imagine . . ."

He waved her into silence. "It's all right. I know what ye meant."

For some reason, part of her warmed to the man. "You do?"

"Aye," he smiled with a nod, staring out over the waters beyond. "And ye'll see it again. Everything."

He seemed so calm and reasonable that Emmy was sure he must be mad. How could he possibly know what she meant? Did he know? Could he help her? She tried to joke lightly, "Are you a fortune-teller? Can you see my future?"

He did not laugh but merely regarded her seriously for a moment before he changed the subject. "Ye know, my grandmother used to bring me on the ferry often for trips into Oban to get ice cream. She said it was our special time."

"She did?"

"She did." He chuckled again. "She was quite fond of ice cream."

"Really, this is very interesting,." She turned away from him, frustrated by his cryptic conversation. "What else did your grandmother say?"

"She said to always be a gentleman." He turned to face

her. "Please allow me to introduce myself. Connor James Lachlan MacLean the Fourth, Earl of Strathclyde."

"Connor Jam ..."

He reached out and took her suddenly limp hand, shaking it with his large rough one. "I know. Grandmother always said ye shouldn't number yer descendants."

Emmy met his eyes for the first time and could only stare in shock. Dark brown eyes warmed with gentleness and caring. "You know."

"Of course I do."

"H-h-how?"

"Ye know, I haven't gone about this well at all. Not as all as I had planned to." Connor the Fourth shook his head and tsked himself. "It was the surprise, ye see. Seeing ye here. I didn't recognize ye at first."

"You know," she stated more clearly, staring at him with owl-like eyes. She laid her hand firmly on his arm and forced him to look at her. His eyes were unnerving. "Please, do not play with me here. How do you know? Connor MacLean was your grandfather?"

He returned her gaze in all seriousness. "I do not mean to toy with ye. My apologies. Aye, he was my grandfather."

"So, who was your grandmother then?"

"Why, ye, of course," he said evenly.. "That does sound a bit strange, doesn't it? My grandmother. Ha! Strange, but true."

Emmy's head spun. "But how can that be?"

"As I said, ye'll see it all again." He patted her hand in comfort. "Ye'll return to Duart, bring yer children and grandchildren here to the ferry ..."

"Are you sure?" she interrupted, suddenly frantic, clutching at his sleeve. "I've been so worried about it. I tried before, but it didn't work." Tears started to her eyes and she dashed them away, angry at her weakness.

He put an arm around her and led her to a nearby bench. "There now, don't cry. Of course, it will work. If not, I wouldn't be here today. Ye told me stories in my youth of this day and I came to find ye just as ye said I must. To assure ye that all would be well."

She looked up at his handsomely weathered face thinking that perhaps this was what Connor might look like at that age. Hope blossomed in her. Hoping and praying that he wasn't just some mad, loony...well, psychic, or something. "I told you that?"

"Aye, of course it's not something one would bandy about outside the family." The warm chuckle was back as this new Connor patted her hand. "The shrinks would have had a field day with us, ye know."

"But, I did try to return before," she whispered hoarsely. "I couldn't find Donell..."

"But ye weren't certain yet, were you? Ye didn't know yet."

Emmy stared at him in confusion. "I told you that? I felt like I was certain."

"Ye were given a chance," he told her. "A chance for yerself and a second chance for others. Now ye have a second chance for ye if ye truly want it. With every fiber of your being. Nothing held back. No doubts. No reservations."

"But I wanted to return right away more than anything. Why wasn't Donell there then?"

"It was yer doubts that caused yer return, ye said. Ye missed the things ye had and the first thing ye did when ye got back was order a Coke." He stared off for a moment. "One moment of doubt was all it took for it all to end. If ye decide that Duart is what ye really want, if ye clear away all those doubts and return with no reservations then ye will be there forever."

A feeling of calm descended on her. To be with Connor forever. Nothing here in this century mattered any longer, simply Connor and her life with them. "Then I will be," she whispered at last.

"I know," he said. "As I said, I wouldn't be here if ye hadn't. May I also add, a more beautiful grandmother one could never hope to find?"

Emmy smiled for the first time. "Nor a finer grandson." She patted his hand. "The family…you…are doing well?"

"Of course." His handsome MacLean eyes twinkled. "Grandmother ran our family investments until her death and then made us remember two highly useful words on her deathbed."

"Oh? What were they?"

"Microsoft and Google."

They both laughed out loud until Connor the Fourth stood, using his cane as leverage. "The ferry will be docking soon. May I give you a ride home?"

She rose to stand beside him. "I would like that very much." She bent to pick up her heavy bag and hooked the strap on her shoulder. Connor laughed aloud. "What?"

"That bag!" he said with a chuckle. "My whole life, I was fascinated by it and everything it held."

"Really?"

"Aye, did I not mention that I am a doctor?"

Emmy smiled brightly. "Are you really?"

"Retired, of course, but I still deliver a baby every now and then."

He smiled as well and held out an arm for her. She took

it as the gangplank was lowered and the crowd of passengers went ashore. The pair moved with the flow through the terminus and out the other side. A limousine waited there and Connor gestured toward it. The driver remained in the car but Connor held the door open for her.

The ride was short but by the time they arrived, Emmy had grown anxious again. "Are you sure?"

The old man laughed aloud heartily. "I don't remember ye being so jumpy."

"I'm not jumpy...just anxious." She watched as Duart came into view. "Do we have a good life?" She didn't expect an answer. In every TV show she had ever seen where a man from the future came to someone, they were never allowed to tell. Or said that it wasn't good to know how your future turned out.

"Yer marriage was one of the best I've ever seen. Ye fought like cats and dogs sometimes but yer love was always evident," he told her. "And before ye ask, obviously you will have children."

"More than one?"

"Aye, more than one."

"And," she swallowed apprehensively, afraid of the answer in the face of nineteenth century medicine. "Do we have a long life together? I know I shouldn't ask but..."

"Trying to make sure it will be worth it?" he said, humor in those warm brown eyes, so like his grandfather's.

"It would be worth it for just one minute more."

"Ye'll get more time than you imagined."

Emmy sighed happily and giggled. "God, we're going to be a couple of old farts knocking around the castle someday, aren't we?"

"Not ye, ye were always ahead of your time." The car

rolled to a halt in front of the castle and he patted her hand. "We are here."

"Duart Castle," she whispered, staring up at the old castle.

"And still open from May until October just as ye always insisted it be."

"Well, good thing it was."

"Indeed. Well, I guess it is time for yoe to go."

"Thank you so much."

"Ye helped yourself. I'm only the messenger."

"Still, I thank you. I will live a long happy life knowing what a fine future is in store for me. Especially that I shall have a grandson such as you."

"Thank ye…Grandmama." He winked.

Emmy laughed with a wince. "Not quite yet, thank you." She hugged him quickly. "Take care of yourself. I guess I'll see you in a few years."

With a shared nod, for no more words were necessary, Emmy got out of the limo as the chauffeur held the door. She pulled her bag up onto her shoulder. Duart loomed before her and she closed her eyes.

⟡⟡⟡⟡

"Are ye sure ye ken now, lassie?"

She opened her eyes to find Donell in the chauffeur's uniform standing next to her. "Where have you been? I looked all over for you."

"The time wisnae right," he said simply. "Are ye ready now?"

"I am and if you give me one moment of mystical destiny crap about it, I swear I will beat you senseless where you stand," she threatened, getting nose to nose with him.

"No' even a wee bit?" he questioned with a straight face though his eyes twinkled merrily. "I told ye I'd be around when ye were ready for me."

"Don't make me hurt you, Donell," she whispered through narrowed eyes. "I will take you out, I kid you not."

"Ye're verra fierce, lassie."

"I am not giving up my chance this time, old man. This is it." Her voice was solid and assured. "You said to come back when I was ready. Well, here I am."

"No doubts? No reservations?"

"Just anticipation."

Her eyes turned back to the castle. Anticipation and joy filled her at the thought of the life that awaited her. She could feel the pull already. Her eyes closed as she turned her face to the wind and called to him with all her heart and soul.

I'm coming, Connor, my love. I am coming.

"I'm waiting, Donell," she said in an annoyed tone.

She heard a chuckle. It seemed to come from a long way away. The wind changed, blowing strongly from behind her now. There was a loud rush. Then nothing. Silence.

Epilogue

Emmy MacLean shuffled slowly across the room with a bottle of Coke in each hand. Outside the windows, the bright lights of Manhattan sparkled against the dark sky. Life, her life in particular, had seen many changes from new to old and back to almost new again. Buildings and inventions that amazed others always brought a secret smile to her lips.

You think that was something? she'd think. *Just wait and see.*

It'd been a good life, just as her grandson had promised her.

When she walked back into Duart on Christmas Eve, Connor stared at her for a long moment in disbelief before meeting her headlong rush into his arms. He swung her around as they laughed and cried. The joy on his face matched her own.

His devastation over her disappearance had been awful, Dory told her later on, but the family had banded together, determined to help him through it.

On her return, Connor told her she was never allowed to leave his side again and, for almost twenty years, she rarely did, and was never out of his sight. When she worked, he came along. When he traveled, she went with him. But they never minded.

She never tired of living in his pocket and he never tired of her being there.

As Connor the Fourth had predicted, they often fought, over differences of opinion and such, but always loved each other truly and completely.

They traveled the world together, allowing Connor's brother and cousins to take a greater part in the family businesses that benefited them all.

They had three sons and a daughter; Connor, Jamie, Cam and Meagan, after Emmy's mother. All three boys fought bravely, despite her arguments that they not, in World War I. They lost Jamie to gunfire in Germany. The others married and had families of their own. Connor, the third of his name, stayed on Mull while Cam moved on to London and Meagan went on eventually with her husband to do the same. And they had many grandchildren including Connor the Fourth whom she'd always been especially close to.

Thanks to the black notebook Emmy filled with every significant fact she could find about the early part of the twentieth-century, the family's investments and fortunes grew. She knew just when to invest and when to withdraw. There'd always been whispers about her incredible luck. Yes, they weathered the years well. Duart thrived and the MacLeans gained back nearly all the land they'd lost hundreds of years before.

Through the years, Emmy delivered almost five hundred babies on Mull and, in other areas of medicine, felt that she saved a life or two that might otherwise have been lost, especially during the influenza epidemic in 1919. In her tote when she had returned that fateful day, she'd brought her own medical bag stocked with a true stethoscope, blood pressure cuff, and other modern goodies. The rest of the bag had held hundreds of bottles of Motrin and a dozen bottles of penicillin, all that she could get away with after breaking into the medical fridge at the clinic.

The simple fever reducer saved the lives of dozens during that year, including Ian's.

Emmy also brought the picture of herself with her mother that she'd shown Connor, and a printed copy of the picture she'd taken of herself and Connor in front of Duart. Dozens more in black and white followed over the years. Her black notebook also contained sheet music for the piano from musicals of her time, favorites she wanted to share with Connor and teach her children.

They saw every movie they could. They read 'Gone With the Wind' together when it was published and gone to the movie premier in Atlanta. As for the rest, Emmy eventually learned to appreciate the oldies.

Yes, she'd had a good long life, but there was still one more thing to do. She eased herself down on the couch and passed one of the Cokes to Connor who took a long drink and sighed in a gravelly voice. "I am so glad we invested in this all those years ago, my love."

"Me, too."

She patted his knee and leaned against his side. Connor was ninety-two years old, frail and stooped with age, but to her he was still the most handsome man she'd ever known. His dark eyes still warmed with love when they took in her aged body, sagging skin and gray hair. Unbelievable.

But she felt not a moment of regret, never a millisecond of wondering what might have been. She'd just loved this man and been loved by him for sixty-one years and never missed a thing.

What more could a woman want?

She took a sip of her cold drink and snuggled against him as he wrapped an arm around her shoulders. This would be their last trip. Tomorrow they would board their last ocean liner to Scotland (Connor had refused to ever get in an airplane). They would return to Duart and never leave again, but since there was no satellite TV yet, they had had to be in America for this moment.

"Are you ready for this?"

"Ready as I'll ever be," he teased.

They watched in silence for a few minutes until Emmy finally turned her head to look at him with a twinkle in her eye. "I told you so."

And Elvis gyrated and sang his rock and roll on the *Ed Sullivan Show*.

AUTHORS NOTE

I've set this story at the real Duart Castle on the Isle of Mull, which is the ancestral home of the Clan MacLean. In 1691, the MacLean's surrendered Duart during the Jacobean rebellion and did not regain the lands until about 1910 when it was purchased by Sir Fitzroy MacLean from the widow of Murray Guthrie who then changed the name of their estate from Duart House to Torosay. It was then that the actual restoration began.

Obviously I moved up the date of the restoration to fit with my timeline and the interior descriptions I give are completely fictional, but I've tried to be as accurate as possible with the area and the history surrounding it. From the landscape around the castle to the story of the Lady's Rock to my descriptions of Torosay and the naming of it. Craignure is the main harbor town of Mull and is where the ferry docks today much as I describe it on Emmy's return to Mull.

In the present day, Torosay and Duart are open to the public. Torosay is open for tours of the house and gardens and does have a Tea Room while you can tour the castle at Duart, which is currently owned by Sir Lachlan MacLean.

Once upon a time, I did live in Virginia and near Baltimore as well and I think it is still the best place in America to get crab bisque and steamed mussels.

Incidentally, Duart is open from May until October.

Thank you for reading *A Laird for All Time* the first in its series. I hope you enjoyed reading it as much as I enjoyed writing it.

While success for me personally is measured in bringing you joy, a moment of emotion, and escape from the hectic thing that is life, it is also measured by the quality and quantity of the reviews my books receive. They don't just help other readers decide to spend their time and money on a book, they help me, too. I read each one that is posted. I take what you say to heart and use it to improve and grow.

If you would take a few minutes of your time to leave a review, I'd be forever grateful.

Angeline

ABOUT THE AUTHOR

Angeline Fortin is the author of historical and time-travel romance offering her readers a fun, sexy and often touching tales of romance.

Her 2015 time travel romance, Taken: A Laird for All Time Novel, was awarded the Virginia Romance Writers 2015 Holt Medallion Award for Paranormal Romance. She is a PAN member of the Romance Writers of America and Midwest Fiction Writers.

A Question of Love, the first of her Victorian historical romance series Questions for a Highlander, was released later that year and quickly followed by series additions *A Question of Trust* and *A Question of Lust*. The series primarily follows the siblings of the MacKintosh clan. Ten brothers and their lone sister who end up looking for love in all the right places.

While the series continues on with familiar characters well known to those who have read the entire series, each single title is also a stand-alone tale of highland romance.

With a degree in US History from UNLV and having previously worked as a historical interpreter at Colonial Williamsburg, Angeline brings her love of history and Great Britain to the forefront in settings such as Victorian London and Edinburgh.

As a former military wife, Angeline has lived from the west coast to the east, from the north and to the south and uses those experiences along with her favorite places to tie into her time travel novels as well.

Angeline is a native Minnesotan who recently relocated back to the land of her birth and braved the worst winter recorded since before she initially moved away. She lives in

Apple Valley outside the Twin Cities with her husband, two children and three dogs.

She is a wine enthusiast, DIY addict (much to her husband's chagrin) and sports fanatic who roots for the Twins and Vikings faithfully through their highs and lows.

Most of all she loves what she does every day - writing. She does it for you the reader, to bring a smile or a tear and loves to hear from her fans.

You can check out her website www.angelinefortin.com for summaries off all her books, companion information and sign up for her newsletter for news about upcoming releases. You can contact her at fortin.angeline@gmail.com.

Or you can follow her just about anywhere!

Facebook: http://on.fb.me/1fBD1qq
Twitter: https://twitter.com/AngelineFortin
Instagram: https://www.instagram.com/angelinefortin/?hl=en
Goodreads:
https://www.goodreads.com/author/show/4863193.Angeline_Fortin
Google+: http://bit.ly/1hWXSGB
Tumblr: https://www.tumblr.com/blog/angeline-fortin
Pinterest: https://www.pinterest.com/angelinefortin1/

37171088R00243

Printed in Great Britain
by Amazon